THE THORNS REMAIN

JENNIFER HARTMANN
CHELLEY ST CLAIR

In memory of Chelley's father,
the inspiration behind the story of Josie's roses.
Thank you for sparking my first dreams of writing.
Thank you for everything.

The Thorns Remain
Copyright © 2021 by Jennifer Hartmann and Chelley St Clair
All rights reserved.

No part of this publication may be reproduced, distributed, or transmitted in any form or by any means, including photocopying, recording, or other electronic or mechanical methods, without the prior written permission of the publisher, except in the case of brief quotations embodied in critical reviews and certain other noncommercial uses permitted by copyright law.

Any references to historical events, real people, or real places are used fictitiously. Names, characters, and places are products of the author's imagination. Any resemblance to actual persons, living or dead, events or localities is entirely coincidental.
"Roses fall, but the thorns remain" is a Dutch proverb and does not belong to the authors.

Book designer: Hartmann Studios
First printing edition 2021.

PROLOGUE

*V*ENGEANCE.

The instinct lurking within us all, meticulously woven into the veil that disguises our true selves. Hiding deep within the shadows of human nature, it smolders… simmers…

Waits.

We like to forget it's a part of us, leaving it lying dormant, smothered beneath the fabrication of moral propriety for months… years… decades.

Oh, but it's there. Poking us gently, whispering in our ear when wrongs are committed against us. We ignore it, dismiss it—because that's what we have been taught to do.

And so, like good little boys and girls… we pretend.

Then comes betrayal.

The trigger that lights the spark, sets the fuse, shreds that flimsy veil, and lets our base instincts come roaring into the light.

And once it's lit, we ignite. We explode.

We avenge.

Vengeance.

For me, it was no longer a hibernating beast. The day I discovered the wrongs committed against me—atrocities I would have never imagined—vengeance clawed its way right through those layers, as though they were tissue paper.

It emerged from its lair.
And now?
Now, it was my lifeline.
My closest friend. My dark lover.
It was the air that I breathed.
My. Fucking. Purpose.

It drove me like hope drives the broken and love drives the weak, carrying me through the bleak, empty moments. Promising better days ahead… if I just kept following its plan.

It burned me from the inside out.

Isn't that the point of it, though?

We need it, in a way. We *need* it to consume us, swallow us whole, make us forget the pain that set it free in the first place—the wounds that gave it life.

Sometimes, it's the only way to survive.

Revenge.

They say it's sweet in the end, and I sure as hell believed them. I could almost taste that honey on my tongue, like a balm I needed to quell the bitterness curdling my insides.

The mere thought of it had become an addiction, and I fucking *craved* it.

But it was all a lie.

I was blindsided.

What I got was anything but sweet.

And not once did I think about who I might hurt along the way. I never considered the casualties that may fall across my path of destruction, or the people who never deserved the fallout of my wrath.

Not once.

I cared only for myself—for my own shallow, splintered heart. That dead thing within me, demanding reckoning. It was all that fucking mattered.

Until it was too late.

No… revenge is not sweet. Retaliation does not end in reward.

Vengeance is not *justice*.

The promises whispered by that beast within? Those sweet words?

They're all hollow. They were nothing more than a trick.

All it ever wanted was to be set free.

In the end, I never expected things to be worse than when it all began.

I never expected the wreckage left in my wake.

I
never
expected
her.

ONE

ENJAMIN GRANT.
His name is like a swarm of mosquitoes on my skin.

The man is a disease. An infection. A cancer, rotting me from the inside out.

My goddamn nemesis.

But he doesn't even know me. To him, I equal collateral damage, no more than a blip on his radar. Only a bug to be swatted away.

Only… *the husband.*

The husband of his mistress, to be exact.

Or at least I *was*.

People say there are signs when a spouse is having an affair—the extra hours at work, the strange credit card transactions, maybe a peculiar new perfume that tickles your nose. Secretive behavior, vanishing sex life, escalating arguments…

Signs, signs, everywhere a sign.

I beg to differ. Katrina's knack for deceit was good… so good, in fact, I never saw her grand betrayal coming, and I would like to believe I am not a stupid man.

My insides clench with simmering rage.

Seventeen months.

It's been seventeen months since the blissful rug of ignorance was pulled out from under me—since I realized the truth of how fucking delusional I had been. In a span of seventeen months, my mission in life switched from devoted husband to *Seeker of Vengeance*.

It's a fancy title for a jaded objective. Anger has become my fuel, while my heart bleeds retribution, and I'm not necessarily proud of that fact.

But it is what it is.

If nothing else, it's made for some damn good writing material. Lucky for me, that happens to be my day job.

I lean back against the side of my car, arms crossed over my chest, my mind and gaze focused like lasers on the man a few feet away. He stands at the edge of the sidewalk, one pretentious loafer-clad foot scraping casually along the curb, chatting with a colleague. The men appear identical in their corporate suits, swaying briefcases, unremarkable ties, and slicked-back hair.

But they are *not* identical.

One of them tore my family apart.

I don't really give a flying fuck who the other one is, but I've watched Benjamin Grant long enough to know that it's his business partner.

My eyes narrow through dark sunglasses as my blood pressure rises, pumping bitterness like poison through my veins. My head pounds to the beat, while Vengeance whispers sweet nothings in my ear from its perch atop my shoulder. There are no shadows to hide me, so I stand here in broad daylight, caught in a sunny spotlight intent on calling me out… on bringing attention to my nefarious plan.

Here he is: the Seeker of Vengeance.

Yeah, it doesn't really matter—the asshole doesn't notice me.

He never did.

"Evan!"

Shit. Someone does, though. My head whips around at the sound of my name being bellowed through the streets of downtown Libertyville. It's partially lost amid the steady stream of traffic and children's squeals from a playground nearby, but loud enough to make me cringe. I'm almost tempted to dive onto the floorboards of my car.

Shh… can't you see I'm stalking, here?

A petite Asian woman skips over to me from the opposite side of the street, her kimono fluttering behind her. A horn blares, the skid of car tires grating down my spine like fingernails on a chalkboard, and the ever-oblivious Hana Park offers the driver a timid wave, picking up her pace.

I swear she's going to get herself killed one day, but if she could avoid doing it while I'm covertly watching my nemesis, that would be awesome.

"Hi, Evan," she greets.

Her chocolate eyes twinkle with excitement, and lucky for her, my sunglasses disguise the fact that mine are not twinkling back. "Hey. Good to see you, Hana."

Just not right now.

No, Hana Park does not make my eyes twinkle, but she hasn't caught on to this fact. So, while I'm forced by etiquette to nod and smile at the small talk, I twist around to where Benjamin Grant had been standing, only to see the heel of one haughty loafer disappearing into his storefront office.

The gold placard announcing his title is firmly attached to the burgundy door, looking just as pompous as the rest of him: *Benjamin Grant; Attorney at Law.*

The bastard.

"Are you on your lunch break?"

Oh, yeah... Hana's here.

I haven't slept with her in at least three months, so she isn't even aware that I've stopped spinning my wheels in retail management to write full time. Apparently, our time apart hasn't phased her, though; she's standing in front of me with that familiar sparkle in her eyes, and it's clear the puppy love has been rekindled.

I have a few of those around town. Lovestruck women I sowed my post-divorce wild oats with. But now that a deeper mission has claimed my focus, they are nothing but a distraction.

"Sort of," I tell her, boredom lacing my tone. "An ongoing lunch break, you could say." I force a smile, my fingers digging at the lint in the bottom recesses of my pockets. "The writing has been going well, so I'm focusing on that. Full time, now."

"Oh, wow, Evan," she beams. "That's amazing. Summer must be excited you don't have to juggle a retail schedule anymore."

The September breeze picks up, hardly disturbing a hair in her carefully pinned ebony bun. I'm really not in the mood for small talk with one of my past flings, especially regarding my daughter, and a shrug reflects my indifference. "Yeah. I mean, she's back in school, but it's nice to have the flexibility."

Hana bobs her head, clutching her satchel to her chest. "Hey, do you want to grab something to eat? I have an hour to kill..." The offer is casual, as though I hadn't seen the wheels turning behind those twinkling brown eyes all along.

Sorry, honey—project "Get Evan Back Into Bed" is a no-go.

I'm not the kind of guy to put energy into something that has no future, and I have bigger fish to fry. She's sweet, though, so I let her down easy. "I'm actually on my way to the gym. Maybe another time."

It's not a lie. I'm not *that* much of an asshole.

"Oh! XSport?"

I can't hold back the sigh. Okay, fine, maybe I am that much of an asshole. These days, at least. There's no good way out of the truth, so I nod without enthusiasm.

"I have a membership there. Maybe we can be workout buddies?"

Workout buddies. Oh, goodie. Maybe we can braid each other's hair later, too.

I bite down on my tongue, clenching my jaw so the words don't accidentally spill out. I need this conversation to end now. "Sounds great. I'll see you around, Hana." I don't wait for her reply, leaving her gaping at me from the sidewalk as I make a break for my Mustang and hop in before she can blink.

The engine roars to life, and this time my sigh is threaded with pure relief. I love this car. She's like my comfort vehicle. I named her Francis, because no one is named Francis anymore, and that's a comforting name, right? There's a saint named Francis.

The Mustang is black, just like my heart, and she was my first big purchase after the book money started rolling in.

One should have some kind of testament after reaching success, after all.

Unfortunately... I don't *feel* like a success. Not yet. There is one, final prize I need to cash in on, and today is the day I begin to execute the plan Vengeance first awakened.

Phase. Fucking. One.

I just needed one last passive stalking of Benjamin Grant to keep the motive fresh.

My wrist is propped up on the wheel as I coast down the busy street, allowing my other arm to dangle out the open window. It's especially hot for September, and my bare skin prickles beneath the afternoon sun. The gym is only a mile from the downtown area, which still counts as the city, and I cruise into the parking lot with an unnecessary amount of speed, pissing off a soccer mom. When she flips me off, I wink at her, naturally, not slowing enough to see her response.

Since I already know exactly what I'm looking for, I make a beeline for the white Lexus SUV that reminds me of pretentious loafers and golden placards. But before I move forward, I take a second to steel myself for my next move.

This will hurt a little. I'm proud of the plan I've concocted, but there are small sacrifices that must be made along the way.

Sorry about this, Francis.

Focusing on the bigger picture, I drive forward, wincing as I tap the Lexus *just enough* to leave a long, black scratch, and when I maneuver into the parking space beside it, I let out a breath, patting the wheel apologetically. I'd like to think the inanimate object I've named after an old lady will sympathize with my plight.

It's for a good cause.

Hopping out of the car, I slip the keys into my back pocket and saunter through the entrance of the gym. Today I'll be taking on the role of the remorsefully responsible man, wrapped in confident charm.

It's *partly* true.

Okay… it's not really true, but I fake the charm well enough to pass.

When I approach the desk, flashing the bored receptionist my brand new key card, she snaps her gum at me. Apparently, more than one somewhat attractive charmer attends this gym, so she's largely unaffected.

My palms slap atop the desk as I plant them in front of her. With a theatrical sigh, I tilt my head, offering a self-deprecating smile. The brunette's interest perks slightly.

Chalk one up to my flair for drama—maybe I should've been an actor instead.

"This is really embarrassing," I start with a cringe. "But I accidentally swiped a car in the parking lot. Could you page the owner of this license plate for me, please? If I left without telling them, my conscience would never let me live it down." I hand over the scrap of paper with the scribbled license plate number. She smiles back, unaware that my conscience died seventeen months ago and this is a load of bullshit.

As she grabs the pager, I peruse the maze of sweaty bodies, club music pulsating through my ears.

Frankly, I despise the gym. I prefer to get my exercise outdoors. Hiking, running, bike riding… *nature*. It's where my muse thrives, and I almost always come away with a new story idea. Smelly, overpriced gyms with some spandex-clad housewife named Debra sneaking a peek at my calorie counter make me want to heave.

It's a muse-killer, for sure—but right now, my mission overshadows my muse.

Counter Girl dutifully pages the owner of the car two more times before giving up with a shrug of "I tried." I purse my lips. Well, shit. Now that Plan A has failed miserably, it's time for Plan B, which is slightly less organic, but what can you do? Tapping my knuckles on the counter with a nod, I abandon the brunette and wind through the treadmills. I receive a come-hither look from Joan Cusack's doppelganger, clad in a leotard that should have been left in the eighties.

However, she is not my mission, and also *no*.

I glance away.

And then…

That's when I see her, amid a sea of ellipticals.

Hair like honey. Eyes like bourbon.

Josie Grant.

I'm too far away to see her eyes, but the ability to zoom on Facebook has come in handy.

Focused on her workout, she doesn't notice me watching her as I pretend to play on my cell phone. Her high ponytail swishes back and forth as she moves, the earbuds propped in both ears explaining why she was oblivious to the receptionist's pages over the intercom. Josie is a vision of tasteful plum spandex; the picture of affluent housewife with an exercise-induced glow. Her skin is lightly bronzed and shimmering with sweat, the crop-top highlighting her slim waist and athletic physique. She's a shining example of beauty and privilege, and I hate her for it.

But I suppose if I'm going to sleep with her, it's a perk that she's attractive.

Well, now's as good a time as any to make my move. Thanks to the failed attempt at paging, I'm a little more conspicuous, but whatever. Strolling up beside her machine, I stand there until I acquire her attention with a startled double take. She keeps up her pace, assuming if she ignores me, I'll move along.

I don't.

She's going to have to deal with me.

Finally, she slows down, pulling her earbuds out one by one, her annoyance evident. I've just interrupted her cardio, a cardinal sin of the gym, but I'm not sorry, and I don't pretend to be. "Can I help you?" she inquires, impatient and out of breath. A tendril of perfect honey-colored hair has slipped from her ponytail to fall in her eyes. She blows at it, her stare unamused.

Bourbon-infused eyes drift over me, stopping when she sees the tattoos etched over my left arm, and I watch her annoyance falter momentarily as something softer flickers across her expression.

Interesting. Could it be that the wealthy housewife has a thing for dark-haired, tattooed men? This will be easier than I thought.

I give her a once-over, my lips stretching into a smile I can't hold back now that I have her attention. "I hit your car in the parking lot."

Those whiskey eyes widen, then narrow, her feet coming to an abrupt stop. She's probably trying to process the offsetting combination of my cheerful smile and ominous words.

"Excuse me, you *what*?"

"Yeah. Sorry." I'm not sorry, but hopefully that's not blatantly obvious. I can't let my acting prowess falter under the bourbon and amber gaze of Josie Grant, but this is kind of *fun,* damnit. It's… satisfying. "I miscalculated my turn radius and side-swiped you. It was only right to let you know."

My smile turns humbly regretful. I hope.

And aren't I just so thoughtfully responsible, tracking you down? We can hop into bed right now, if you want.

I realize she doesn't want me yet… but she will.

Folding my arms across my chest, I monitor her reaction. I'm calm and unfazed, watching her head jiggle with a shake of disbelief and frustration.

Then she closes her eyes, letting her head fall back with a groan. "All right. Let's go take a look at the damage." Josie doesn't seem as angry as I expected. More… inconvenienced. Hopping off the elliptical, she snatches her purse, charging ahead of me towards the front doors.

Phase one: Underway.

My eyes land on her ass as she makes a swift exit out the glass doors and into the parking lot. It's a nice ass, and I'll enjoy slapping it a little while I pound into it. Eventually. Her slim hips sway with vigor, skin-tight leggings clinging to her curves. When she glances at me over her shoulder, I avert my eyes, jogging up beside her as we approach the vehicles.

I point at the long, black scratch along her bumper. "I'd feel like an ass if I didn't say anything," I say, watching as her gaze scans the damage. Then I add with a bit of ominous inflection, "Karma's a real bitch."

The irony is lost on her.

Josie's focus shifts to my Mustang on the right, then up to me as those eyes narrow with suspicion. "How did you know this was my car?"

Perhaps I expected her to be more upset than astute, but no matter. A languid smile pulls across my face, my head cocking to the side. Might as well play on my strengths, which has recently become charming the pants off women. *Literally*. It's the end goal, anyway.

"I come here on my lunch break a lot. You're sort of impossible not to notice."

Then, I wait.

I wait for the coy grin, the bashful bow of her head, the inevitable color in her cheeks, setting the game board up perfectly for my next move.

Only… she laughs.

Actually, she snorts. She *snorts* at me.

What the fuck is that about?

"That's funny," she replies, touching the back of her hand to her nose. "I've never noticed you."

Ouch.

No, wait, maybe that's good. That implies that she knows she would have noticed me… *right?*

We'll go with the positive angle here and ignore the fact that she's still laughing.

My lips purse together. It seems both Plan *A* and Plan *B* have crashed and burned at my feet like my own personal meteor shower. Josie Grant has surprised me by being intelligent enough to necessitate a Plan *C*.

Good for her.

Luckily, I'm quick on my feet. With my hands planted casually on my hips, I show little reaction to being called out on the lie. I'm realizing I may need to play on a different set of strengths to close this deal, as Josie isn't quite the desperate homemaker I was hoping she'd be. "I'm Evan," I tell her, gifting her with my most charming smile, while my brain spins around my next words. "I suppose if I'm going to hit someone's car, I got lucky that it's the most beautiful woman in the gym."

Okay, that came out a little stronger than I intended.

Abort… Abort!

The telltale arch of Josie Grant's eyebrow alerts me to my grave miscalculation. Her amber irises are almost see-through as she narrows them at me. I need to figure out how to salvage this mess fast—it was too carefully planned, and I'm not scratching Francis for nothing.

"That's nice," she says flatly. "I'm going back inside now."

I watch as Josie turns on her heels and heads back towards the gym entrance.

What just happened? That was meant to be a compliment. I'm good at this, damnit.

Now I'm ruffled, so I follow her. "You don't care about the damage?"

"Nope," she mutters without looking at me.

"You don't want to exchange insurance and shit?"

"Nope."

Damn. I watch her ponytail sway in time with her feet as white sneakers slap against the pavement. "Listen, did I piss you off in some way? That wasn't my intention."

Besides hitting your car, I mean.

Josie whirls around to face me before we reach the doors. I can tell she's about to sling a smart comeback my way, but once again, the moment her eyes glide across the tattoos on my arm, that same look returns. Softer. Contemplative. Maybe even a little... nostalgic.

She relaxes with an exhale. "I've just had a really shitty day. I was trying to take my anger out on the elliptical machine, and you kind of threw a wrench in that."

A wrench. I suppose that's a suitable word for my appearance in her life, but I'm more inclined to go with a sledgehammer. Part of me wants to ask about her shitty day, to build rapport, but it will be fruitless. She's beyond reach right now. She's put too many walls up, and a wrench won't do.

I'll come back with that sledgehammer later.

I take a step back with a sigh, lowering my head. "Sorry again about the car," I say, adding, "And for... inadvertently hitting on you back there." I nod towards the parking lot, my lips tipping into an apologetic grin.

"Inadvertently," she repeats, the flat tone softened by a quirk of her lips I don't miss. "Right. Okay."

"Uh... yeah." Running a hand through my hair, I shoot her another smile. Maybe my sheepish version of charm will chip away at some of those walls, because apparently, I need all the help I can get right now. "I hope your day gets better."

Wanting to end this on a semi-positive note, I turn away and walk back to my car, discouraged, but not defeated.

I only make it a few steps before she calls out to me.

"I'm Josie."

My smile grows, and I pause my feet, glancing over my shoulder at her. Renewed hope shoots through me as I spin around and saunter backwards, trying not to notice the way a rogue strand of hair catches between her lips. "I'll see you around, Josie."

And I will.

TWO

"BREAKFAST!"

It is, in fact, dinnertime. But it's also Thursday, and on Thursdays we eat breakfast for dinner.

Summer comes barreling down the hallway in her jean shorts and oversized anime t-shirt, her dirty blonde hair whipping around her face as she twirls on the smooth tile. Her chair legs scrape across the floor when she plops in front of the kitchen table. The only table, actually—this place is tiny, but plenty suitable for two.

"Please don't over-crisp the bacon this time, Dad."

I spare her a side-eye. "Bacon is supposed to be crispy. That's its job. Otherwise, it's basically ham."

"Except your version of crispy is… *extra.*"

Extra.

My nine-year-old sounds like a teenager when she says "extra." This also reminds me that I need to look in the air fryer, and… okay, I suppose blackened does constitute as "extra." *Whoops.* I put the lid back on, hoping she doesn't smell the charred evidence of my failure.

She does.

Her lightly freckled button nose crinkles at the smell of burnt dreams. "That pig died for nothing," she mutters. Her theatrics make it obvious whose genes she carries.

As the bacon remnants meet the trash can, I feel mildly guilty for wasting the nameless pig's sacrifice. "It's all right. He wasn't a nice pig, anyway. He bullied the other pigs." I pause to ponder this, then finish with, "He probably would have given us indigestion."

"Nice try, Dad."

Needing to win my daughter back over, I hurry plates of scrambled eggs, waffles, and fruit to the table, prompting Summer to clap and squeal with anticipation. Breakfast for dinner is her favorite, and I'm a good cook, despite my strained relationship with the air fryer. I've been the primary chef for most of my adult life. It was never Katrina's thing, and someone had to learn, otherwise we would have been ordering takeout every single night.

I bristle at the thought of my ex-wife. My high school sweetheart. My one, true love.

What a bunch of bullshit.

This triggers the spiral into dark thoughts, and my head has already started to ache by the time I take a seat. I roll my neck to release the tension.

I blame the bacon.

It's the bully pig's fault.

"You're thinking about her, aren't you?" Summer's voice snaps me back to the present as I begin scooping eggs onto her plate.

Of course she notices because she's wise beyond her years—nine going on thirty, basically. I've always been as transparent with her as possible. Gentle, but honest. She's aware that her mother made a bad choice and that's the reason why we're not together anymore. Obviously, I haven't told her details, considering she's still too young to fully grasp the reality of our situation. She doesn't know what "cheating" is—at least, I hope she doesn't. That would mean she knows what sex is, and *Jesus*, I'm not ready for that.

But she knows her mother did a bad thing. And that I am not okay sometimes.

I can't help but feel guilty for how this affects her. Even though it wasn't my doing, I often wonder if it's too much of a burden. It's just the two of us, after all, and she's only a third-grader.

Katrina moved from our hometown in northern Illinois to Tennessee to stay with her mother as soon as we separated, keeping our daughter over summer break and during the winter holiday. It was… an adjustment. She'd been a good mom to Summer, but after certain *events* unfolded, it was best for her to get out of town.

I consider myself fortunate I don't have to accidentally run into her, and well, *good riddance.*

Summer mentions her sometimes, after she stays there awhile. I force myself to listen, fighting the temptation to stick my fingers in my ears like a kindergartener. I have no desire to hear about how well Katrina is doing, but I can't tell my daughter she can never talk about her mother.

So, I'm aware that Katrina has a live-in boyfriend named Allan who often smells like cabbage, and Allan has a baby boy named Mason from a previous relationship. Not sure how I feel about a live-in boyfriend hanging around my daughter, but they sound happy enough.

Yay, Katrina.

Squeezing a concerning amount of syrup over my waffles, I remember that Summer asked me a question. "I'm thinking about how I'm going to kick your butt at Mario Kart later."

Her smile stops at her lips. It's merely a courtesy—she sees right through me. It's a nine-going-on-thirty smile. "I know you were thinking about her. It's okay."

Damnit. I hate this. I hate that Katrina fucking *did this* to us. I hate that Summer is growing up in a broken home. I hate Benjamin Grant for putting his dick where it didn't belong, and most of all, I hate that I *hate* so much.

I feel the rise of my blood pressure as Vengeance stirs again, and I hate that it's in the same room with my daughter.

Hate. Hate. Hate.

I look at my little girl and squash it down. Summer is the only thing that drives me, other than revenge. She's my light, my sunshine, my hope… some days I think I need her more than she needs me. Her mother made her daughter a casualty of her own selfish choices, and this amazing little girl did not deserve that.

"Truth bomb?" I ask.

It's our ice breaker when we need to get heavy shit off our chest.

"Always," Summer nods, setting down her fork to give me her full attention.

I finish chewing my overly-sugared waffles and lean back in the chair, teetering it on its rear legs. My fingers link behind my head with a sigh. "I *was* thinking about her. I think about her all the time," I confess. "I was thinking about how she hated to cook. Remember when she ordered pizza every day for a week when I was in Baltimore for a manager's conference? She was too scared to even boil water."

Summer giggles at the memory. It was only a few months before our world fell apart.

"And remember that one time she *did* boil water and forgot to turn the burner off?" I continue. "The house smelled like a toxic waste zone for days."

That's right. We did not even let my wife boil water.

Ex-wife, I mentally scold myself.

More giggles. "She still orders a lot of pizza," Summer notes. "Allan isn't good at cooking like you are."

I go someplace else for a brief moment and hope that Summer doesn't notice.

She does, of course. She always notices. "She seems happy… does that make it better or worse?"

Worse. Definitely worse.

"I'm glad," I tell her, forcing a smile. "Eat up, bunny. I got cookie dough ice cream for dessert."

Bun. Bunny. It's my nickname for her. When Katrina was pregnant with Summer, we called her our bun in the oven, and it just stuck.

Besides, she's cute like a bunny.

Summer shovels a huge bite of scrambled eggs into her mouth as prospects of ice cream loom on the horizon. After we're finished and the table is clean, I keep my promise and kick her butt at Mario Kart.

Finally, homework is done, despite my less than impressive attempts to help her with this modern math shit, and Summer settles in her room to play on her tablet until bedtime.

I've had a busy day, and I made progress on my mission—or, at the very least, made *some* kind of impression on Josie Grant—but I know none of it was the kind of progress that will actually make money. And we enjoy eating.

So, it's time for me to retreat into the bedroom to work on my manuscript.

I stare at the screen. My brain feels like sludge as I backspace over the few paragraphs I managed to force out. Two steps forward, five steps back. There's often more of that to writing than people probably realize, but right now, it's worse than normal.

My current work in progress is about a woman named Penny who wakes up from a twenty-year long coma with no memory of how she got there. Nobody knows how she got there. She's a blank slate and a ghost all at once.

Sometimes I wish *I* could be Penny. I wish I could go to sleep for twenty years and wake up in a brand new world. No memories. No pain.

A blank slate.

That's right—I envy my own made-up character.

Envy, Hate, Vengeance. They're my own deadly sins, but right now they keep me going. They keep me putting one foot in front of the other.

There's a noise from somewhere behind me, and turning to look through my cracked door, I see Summer across the hallway.

That little girl needs me.

She's lying on her stomach on the bed, legs swinging back and forth to a beat I can't hear as she taps away on her tablet. She's smiling, and in that smile is purity. Joy. It's the smile of a person who hasn't been wrecked by life, and *God*, something so pathetic sweeps through me, I'm ashamed to admit it. It's only for a moment, but I can't deny the pang in my chest...

More envy.

I'm envious of my nine-year-old daughter.

I wish I were able to shut out the world, shut out the darkness, and just *live*. Put the past behind me, live in that joy—in that purity that allows one to enjoy each moment for what it is. But no, I'm always in my head. Analyzing, thinking... *overthinking.*

It's handy as a writer, but it gives me little peace.

My thoughts drift to Josie Grant and how she was nothing like how I expected her to be. I've been following her Facebook profile for a month now, and I was sure I knew her. On social media, she comes across as the stereotypical, affluent, suburban housewife. Martini mixers, fundraisers, PTO board. Her page is full of sappy, inspirational memes, like: *"Start each day with a grateful heart,"* or *"I'd rather have roses on my table than diamonds on my neck."*

What-the-fuck-ever, lady. You're rich enough to have both. It doesn't count.

Oh, and then there are the "look at how wonderful my spouse is" posts. I'm not sure if she's delusional, or trying to manipulate the jackass into being nice to her so she'll brag about him on social media. Every once in a while she'll post a picture of a thoughtful gift with a drippy comment about how great she has it. One day, there was a picture of a bouquet of roses boasting the caption: *"I love my husband more than life itself."*

Makes me want to fucking vomit.

From Facebook, I knew that Josie checks herself in at the gym every weekday at noon. Recently, she posted about her new Lexus, complete with a picture. That was the day I devised my plan.

It's a stalker's paradise, really, and it's all the more amusing that the person I'm truly interested in, is her husband.

Josie is a means to an end.

Today surprised me, though—she seemed so different in person. I suppose that's the Facebook way. Post about your shiny, perfect life, so the entire world can gush, envy, and fall all over you. God forbid an acquaintance from seventh grade sees you having a bad day.

It's become our personal artificial billboard designed to impress our fake-ass society, and I loathe Facebook. I loathe it almost as much as I loathe ketchup.

But not as much as I loathe Benjamin Grant.

Pushing back in the rolling chair, my hands scrubbing down my face, I'm stopped short by my reflection in the computer screen. In seventeen short months, I feel like I've aged an entire decade. I'm only thirty-two years old, but I feel older. Jaded and worn down. Exhausted.

You'll feel better once the plan has been completed, Vengeance says in my ear, and I'm too tired to examine whether it's all a load of bullshit or not.

It better not be—it's all I have right now.

I snap the laptop shut.

This is pointless. I'm too preoccupied with my anger to get anything accomplished tonight, so instead, I traipse across the hallway of our modest ranch home and tuck Summer into bed. She still enjoys when I tuck her in, and no matter how preoccupied I am, I know these nights are fleeting. I never miss the chance to pull the covers up to her chin, tell her she's my funny bunny, and kiss her forehead.

As I turn out her light and step towards the door, she stops me.

"Truth bomb?"

I face her in the dark. Only her *Sleeping Beauty* night light shines bright, casting an ambient pink glow across the room. This is also fleeting, I know, so I nod, giving her my full attention. "Always."

Her blankets rise and fall with every breath as she looks up at the ceiling. "I worry about you."

My chest collapses in on itself.

That's what it feels like, at least. My fists clench along with my jaw as a lump rises in my throat. I don't want her to see my reaction, so I step out of the *Sleeping Beauty* glow and take cover in the shadows where I'm most comfortable. My failure to hide my bitter grudge from my daughter is a shortcoming I'll never forgive myself for.

I swallow through my thickening throat. "Don't worry about me, bunny," I tell her, hoping she doesn't notice how stiff my voice sounds. But who am I kidding? She always notices. "The only thing you need to worry about is acing your math quiz tomorrow." The smile that slips free is genuine… because it's all for her. "Actually, don't worry about that either. You're better at math than I'll ever be. Just sleep."

Pacing out of her bedroom, I gently close the door before she has the chance to call me out, letting my weight fall back against it, my eyes closed, while I clear the mist that threatens.

My baby girl worries about me. *I've* caused that.

I've made her worry.

And the truth is… I worry about me, too.

3

THREE

*I*T'S FRIDAY. FINALLY.
 Why I even tacked on the "finally," I don't know. Fridays don't actually mean shit to me, as I work from home and set my own hours. I no longer have to worry about that—Friday, Monday, Wednesday… every day is the same.

Of course, they weren't all that special when I was working retail, either. No one in retail likes Fridays.

It could just be a throwback to school days, when I'd waste the whole week dreaming about the upcoming weekend. That's probably it. But somehow, that Friday feeling never really fades, even when it makes no difference at all.

Yay, self-employment.

The only thing that makes it different from any other day is the extra quality time I get with my daughter on the weekends when she's not in school. Although, lately she's been spending some of that time at the neighbor's house playing Roblox and doing ridiculous makeup tutorials on TikTok, and what in the hell am I going to do when she's twelve? Or fifteen? Or…

Shit, she just needs to stay nine. That's all there is to it.

Growing up is overrated.

What the hell *is* a Roblox, anyway? Does it have to do with robots? Or blocks? Maybe it's slang for "road blocks"—perhaps kids these days are just really enthusiastic about transportation and traffic configuration.

I give a sardonic head shake of concern for our future generations. At least they'll have great transportation systems and snazzy makeup, I suppose.

There's something to aspire to.

My car keys arc through the air as I toss them from one hand to the other. Adding an extra bounce in my step, I breathe in the rich autumn air, and I can't help but feel the extra energy that doesn't seem to be present Monday through Thursday.

It's that Friday feeling—a certain buzz, like luck is on your side.

I stroll through the gym parking lot where the familiar Lexus greets me from the same parking spot as the other day. It's still sporting the black scratch from the run-in with Francis, and I'm mildly surprised that hasn't been fixed yet.

Black on white. Branded like an emblem of things to come. In my writers' world, we would call that symbolism... maybe even foreshadowing. I can't help but smile as I think about those things. There's a light up ahead; I have to believe that. And now that I've begun phase one of the plan—inserting myself into Josie's life—I can see it. I see a comeuppance. Closure.

Peace, goddammit.

I just want some fucking peace.

I realize it's going to take a little longer to get there than I anticipated, given that Josie wasn't the desperate housewife I'd hoped would throw herself at me after the first charming grin, but that's all right. Vengeance can be very, very patient. It's used to waiting, after all.

I breeze through the doors like I own the place, because why the fuck not? It's a beautiful Friday, the birds are singing, and I have a great feeling about the next step of my plan to ruin Benjamin Grant's miserable life.

It's hard not to feel positive.

Nodding my head in greeting at the receptionist, I flash her both my key card and my most swoon-worthy grin. I like to practice for Josie whenever I can.

Counter Girl Number Two reacts exactly as I'd hoped, and I'm feeling even better now.

Hey, look, I've still got it.

Josie might not melt into a pile of goo like the receptionist just did, but I'm up for a challenge.

I spot her immediately. She's either raging mad, or she's just really passionate about cardiovascular health, and I can't tell which, but her legs are barely keeping up with her level of enthusiasm. Josie is on the end machine like she was the day before, which means I'm forced to wait until Timmy With The Bad Toupee decides he's met his calorie commitment for the day.

Hanging back out of sight, I allow myself to daydream about those firm, sexy thighs wrapped around me. My mind is filled with visions of peeling down spandex in the back alley as I push Benjamin Grant's wife up against the wall and…

Okay, maybe I'm getting ahead of myself, but I've got to pass the time somehow as I wait for the machine beside her to open up.

Turns out luck is on my side, and Toupee Timmy hobbles off the elliptical within five minutes.

It's that Friday feeling.

I claim the machine as quickly as I can without looking too eager, which is likely unconvincing, as there are other ellipticals available, but I doubt anyone is paying attention. Josie's eyes are closed, her head down, oblivious to the fact that Toupee Timmy is no longer on her right—if she even realized he was there in the first place. She's not wearing her earbuds today, and I appreciate that. It sure makes the wooing process a hell of a lot easier.

I press a few buttons, and the machine comes to life. I really hate ellipticals.

My feet begin to move, but she still doesn't notice me.

That's okay, I can wait.

The minutes tick by like a slug. I'm moving at a lazy pace, both because of my disdain for this machine and the sore muscles from my fifteen-mile bike ride this morning. I can afford to slack without sacrificing leg definition.

Josie keeps up her brutal pace, never looking up. Since she's my sole reason for being here, it would help if I could get her attention, so what's a guy to do?

Ah… coughing attack. Brilliant idea.

So, I cough until I sound disturbingly contagious, then I grab my water bottle, downing the whole thing while giving my target the side-eye as inconspicuously as possible.

Okay… so if I did ever decide to go into acting, my fake coughing skills might need some practice because the whole thing came off a bit amateur—but hey, it works.

She glances in my direction, then does a double take, her feet slowing to a less concerning pace. I smile, noting the flash of recognition in her eyes... and also how it promptly fades to exasperation.

Not quite the reaction I was going for, but I can work with it.

"Hey," I say to her. She looks straight ahead, ignoring me, but I risk her wrath and press my luck. "Another bad day?"

This seems to trigger her in some way, and she jerks her head towards me, her bourbon eyes locking on mine. "Is this your way of trying to get to know me?"

I pull a charming grin across my lips while I have her attention, going in all-in with my cards. After all, Katrina used to tell me that my smile was what reeled her in.

It wasn't enough to keep her, though.

"Maybe," I reply. "Maybe I'm hoping you'll want to get to know me."

She laughs in a way that implies she's anything but amused. "Oh, I already know you. You're the pompous asshat with a shitty turn radius and lack of subtlety."

Jesus. I conjure up a mental image of the Genie buzzing in Aladdin's ear: *"Warning! Warning!"*

My cards aren't working. I have shit cards.

"Yikes." I force out a chuckle, picking up the pieces of my shattered ego. I'm leaving the cards where they fell—they're worthless. "That escalated quickly."

This woman is vicious, and I can appreciate that, but it's definitely making the plan more challenging.

I watch as new emotions etch across Josie's face. She pulls her lips between her teeth, blinking slowly, and letting out a long breath. "Sorry," she says. "Sorry... that was unnecessary."

I can tell that she means it, and it's comforting to know Josie Grant isn't a complete stone-cold bitch. She certainly can rise to the occasion when she wants to, though.

Not that I wouldn't sleep with her either way. A stone-cold bitch feels just as good around my dick as anyone else. Besides, this is about revenge. She can be terrible in bed for all I care.

Josie tucks her hair behind her ear, looking even more annoyed than when I hit her car. "I'm just trying to get in the zone and you're ruining it for me."

Fine. I'll give her what she wants. I throw up my hands in surrender, sighing with defeat, and it's hard as hell, but I don't say another word for the next few minutes.

Oh... but I see her. Turns out my peripheral vision is top notch, and she's definitely doing her best to covertly study the tattoos along my shoulders and arms.

I made a point to wear a sleeveless shirt today.

Score one point for me.

I pick my cards back up, back in the game, then turn to the right to catch her stare. She flinches, seemingly embarrassed to be caught gawking at my arms.

"You like my tattoos," I state.

It's not a question. It's not even a come-on. It's just a fact.

I have eyes, and I call it like I see it.

Josie chews on her lower lip, and I swear I can see the rosy stain creeping into her cheeks, mixing with her workout flush. The shrug she gives me is indifferent, but I know better. "They remind me of someone I used to know."

Someone she used to know... well, isn't that intriguing.

She's clearly not referencing her husband, as he's very much a part of her present—not to mention, Benjamin Grant is a squeaky clean pansy who would likely faint on contact with a tattoo needle. I begin to pedal faster, breaking eye contact and diverting my gaze ahead. "Ouch, I feel sorry for them, then."

"What?" She's clearly taken aback, surprised, and maybe even a bit appalled at my suggestion.

"I just figured it must be someone you hated." I take one hand off the elliptical long enough to gesture to myself and add, "You know."

Score another point for my guilt-tripping prowess.

And it works. Josie comes to almost a complete stop, her features softening. Her eyes flicker up to me, hands clamped around the handlebars of her machine. She's about to speak when her cell phone begins to vibrate.

Damn interruptions. I'm busy here—whoever that is needs to wait.

But her expression turns stormy as she reads the text message, and I don't pretend to hide my interest as I study her. I don't exactly *care*, but my curiosity is certainly piqued. I can't help but wonder if her *wonderful* husband is stepping out on her again. It would make my job even easier if she knew it.

Hey, Josie, how about a revenge fuck with a dark-haired, tattooed writer? I'll help you get back at that cheating asshole, no problem.

But first I'll go the route of casual concern. "Everything okay?"

I'm expecting a sassy retort or an icy insult, but all she mutters is, "No."

It comes out like a whisper. I almost don't hear it as the word fades into the racket of gym noise and synthesized pop music.

Shit, now I kind of feel bad. Why do I feel bad? I don't need to be feeling *bad* for Josie Grant.

Grant. Josie Grant.

Benjamin Grant.

I remind myself of this, and that's all it takes to make me feel better.

Hardly moving my legs, I'm not even pretending to be engrossed in my workout anymore. I duck my head, settling my gaze on my right sneaker. "I'm sorry to hear that." I'm not really sure what else to say. It's not like I could try to comfort this woman—she'd probably kick me in the balls if I even *considered* approaching her.

I wince at the very thought and commit to the awkward silence instead.

She's still fixated on her phone when she speaks again. "My best friend is getting a divorce, and I'm not sure how to process this."

Well... that was a surprise. Who here expected her to confide something in *me?* Not this dark-haired, tattooed writer.

Not Josie either, I'd guess by the look on her face. Our eyes meet, and she blinks, then looks away. Before I can respond, she hops off the elliptical and reaches for her purse. "I... I have to go. Sorry."

I'm not sure what she's sorry for. It could be the scathing nicknames earlier, or her unprecedented moment of vulnerability.

My money is on the latter. Or all the above. Or none of the above.

I've always hated multiple choice.

I watch as she makes her frazzled escape, not responding, because this is one of those rare moments where I'm actually at a loss for words. But it turns out I don't have to because she hesitates. When she peeks back over her shoulder to look at me, her eyes glimmer with sadness.

"I'll see you around," she says, and then she's gone.

She mimicked my words from the day before, and I could be wrong, but I decide that this was on purpose.

I smile.

Yes, you will.

It smells like impending rain.

I used to love the smell. The sticky air. The fresh, musky aroma of a beautiful storm moving in. It was invigorating. Exciting.

Now it just reminds me of the night I discovered my wife was screwing another man.

Way to ruin rain, Katrina.

The scent makes my stomach coil with bitter memories as I walk down the busy sidewalk to a local bar called Tommy's. Summer is sleeping over at her friend Rayna's house tonight, which means my Friday night is now remarkably open. Normally, I'd dive into my current manuscript, but my mind hasn't been in it lately—so, alcohol and foolish decisions it is.

Who knows? Maybe Drunk Me is a better writer?

I tell myself that, but the truth is, if I do get drunk, I'm more likely to find myself inside a woman and passed out on my face for a day, than I am in front of a computer being productive.

Tommy's is one of those local dives that's not really noticeable unless it's already *your* place, and that's what I love about it. When I poke my head inside, it seems I'm the first of our little group to arrive, so I duck back out and lean against the dark brick wall, pulling a pack of cigarettes out of my back pocket while I wait for Logan and Amber. I've known them since college; they were best friends to me and Katrina back in the day.

Now they're just best friends to me.

By the time I pause for the requisite moment to debate whether I should smoke or not, I've already absently brought the cigarette to my lips. Summer hates when I smoke, so I do my best to conceal my weakness when she's around. I've quit at least a dozen times in the last year, but I still keep a full pack in the glove compartment of my car for nights like this.

For nights that smell like rain.

"Evan, my man!"

Amber's laughter follows Logan's greeting, and I lift my eyes to see them emerge in a halo of flickering street lamps, arms linked and smiles wide. Amber lifts one fully inked arm in a wave. Josie Grant would probably get a kick out of these two—they are both covered in so many tattoos, they make me look like an amateur.

Logan and I were college roommates when I dragged him out for his first tattoo. That's where we met Amber, working at the receptionist desk. Their attraction was that of rebel spirits with kindred hearts; instant and stormy. On-and-off for a few years, they never quite got out of each other's systems. Logan was always envious of my effortless romance with Katrina.

Until he wasn't.

My lips curve into a smile around my cigarette as they reach me. These two have a way of lifting my spirits no matter how dark the mood, and I'm happy they made it this far. A decade later, and the magnetic pull between them is stronger than ever. They really are inevitable.

"Look at you! What a DILF," Amber laughs, throwing her arms around my neck. A solid foot shorter than me, she has to lift to her toes to kiss my cheek. "I feel bad for you in a few years when Summer's girlfriends only want to hang out at your house."

I can't help but chuckle. "Oh, you missed the announcement. Summer is permanently nine," I joke as I shoot her a wink.

Her sable hair catches the breeze as she lowers herself back on her sex heels. I call them sex heels because there is absolutely no other reason a woman would wear those monstrosities. The ankle abuse must be epic.

Logan punches my shoulder teasingly, tightening his grip around Amber's waist. "I've got my eye on you, asshole," he grins.

There is no animosity. It's not like that with us.

We head inside and snag an empty pool table. Logan and Amber team up because Amber can't play for shit, and they basically count as one person. I amble up to the bar to order drinks while they set up the game, and then I wait for the inevitable...

One. Two. Three. F –

"Hey, there."

There it is. Less than four seconds before a woman approaches me. The record so far is two. It's a joke between Logan and Amber, so I count for their benefit.

It's kind of funny that I didn't comprehend how easily I attract women until post-Katrina. She was always attached to my hip before, and while I got looks, I was never approached.

Now, though... it's usually less than four seconds.

I glance at the curvy redhead sipping on her cocktail. She smells like whiskey and looks like trouble. My eyes travel over her before I turn back to the bartender and place my order.

"Buy me a drink?" she asks, fluttering her eyelashes my way.

I lean my elbow against the counter and face her with a smile. "That's bold of you," I reply. "I don't even know your name."

"I'm Lizzy."

I'm not interested in Lizzy.

Don't get me wrong—I fucking love women.

I love fucking women.

The *right* women.

Lizzy is not the right woman because she's wearing Katrina's favorite perfume. It mingles with her Whiskey Sour as she closes in on me, and I flinch back on instinct. "Sorry, Lizzy. I'm meeting someone here tonight."

I don't even try to sound convincing, and it's not likely she believes me, but she takes the rejection like a champ and steps away, winking as she gulps down the last of her beverage. I collect the drinks, juggling three rather deftly if I do say so myself, and make my way back to the pool table. I don't even blink at the way Logan and Amber are dry humping each other like hormonal teenagers. This is the norm when they're in "on" mode. They're the poster children for PDA, if that's a thing—a vision of leather and piercings, quickly garnering the attention of the prissy college girls in the corner whose silent glares issue them a death sentence for their innumerable sins.

I saunter up to the pool table and set down their Jack and Cokes before chugging mine. I'm playing third wheel tonight, as I often do. Sometimes I'll bring a woman along, but I haven't had much time to meet anyone lately now that Summer is back home for the school year, and I didn't feel like bringing a virtual stranger. I considered calling Hana for half a second, but she's already teetering on the brink of *Fatal Attraction* vibes, so I decided to keep my distance.

Folding my arms across my local metal band t-shirt, I park my hip against the game table. Waiting. Amber and Logan are oblivious to the world around them. God, I miss that feeling. "I can wait. Don't worry about me," I interrupt, clearing my throat obnoxiously.

Logan pulls back with a grin, slapping Amber's ass as he reaches for a pool stick. "Sorry, Campbell. I'm ready to destroy you now." He blows a plume of chalk off the tip of the stick like it's the barrel of a gun, and it floats through the air, the tendrils of smoke wafting over to me.

I could use a cigarette. I never got a chance to smoke that first one.

"Loser pays for drinks tonight," I challenge, holding up my own stick like a weapon.

"Shit. It's on."

Amber hops onto the edge of the table, inching her legs apart as Logan gets in position to break. Her skirt is black leather and way too short for propriety. This can only work in my favor.

"Honey, you're supposed to be on my team. That means you don't distract me," Logan says.

"I'm still pulling for ya, babe, I just can't resist watching you squirm."

Her eyes glimmer as she leans over for a kiss, and he doesn't bother with subtlety as one hand leaves the stick, inching up the inside of her thigh.

Go Amber. I definitely won't be buying drinks tonight.

I swallow back the remaining contents of my glass, cursing the bartender for not making it stronger. I love these two, but getting trashed might be necessary to take the edge off the overt sexual attraction rolling off the PDA Poster Children. "Be right back," I mutter, making my way to the bar much sooner than anticipated. I order another Jack and Coke, this time with a shot on the side.

One. Tw –

"Evan?"

Hey, that's close to a record.

Wait... she said my name.

This catches me off guard, so I spin to face the familiar voice. It's Amanda From Produce. We used to work together. "Amanda, hey. Shit, it's been a while."

Amanda sidles up beside me, twirling strands of Cookie Monster blue hair around her fingers. It's actually not a terrible look for her. "How are you? How's Katrina?"

Apparently, it's been more than awhile.

But then, it's not like I was walking around with a tattoo that said "divorcee" on my forehead, even when I was still working.

My blood turns to ice. For just a moment, I feel like I still live in a world where people can ask me, "How's Katrina?", and I can answer, "She's great. *We're* great. Life is good." Then reality smacks me upside the head, and I set my jaw, forcing out the unsavory reply. "We've been divorced for a year now."

Amanda jerks back, taken off guard by the discovery. "Wow, I didn't know."

Fortunately, she spares me the requisite *"sorry"* we both know she wouldn't mean. She was shameless in her flirting during our shifts together, but I never looked at her as anything other than Amanda From Produce.

When I was with Katrina, my eyes and my heart were full of only her. Sappy, I know, but I never noticed anyone else in all that time. Basically, I was whipped, and I didn't care.

I was also delusional.

But... things are different now.

I change the subject as the bartender slides my drinks over, regarding Amanda like I'm meeting her for the first time. My gaze skates from her slender arm down her twirling fingers, twisting even further in her long hair. She bites her lip.

It's cute. *She's* cute.

Maybe blue is my color tonight.

I smile my signature smile, taking in the way her eyes spark to life at my next words. "Have a drink with me?"

FOUR

THEN
JANUARY

*P*OSITIVE.

I stare at the pregnancy test lying on the bathroom floor, crouching down to study it like I've discovered an alien artifact. A priceless treasure. It had fallen out of the trash can as I was dumping it into a larger garbage bag, or I wouldn't have known it was in there. Profound realization sinks in, and I reach for it with fingers I didn't even notice were shaking until the test begins quivering in my hand. A jagged huff of air escapes me when I fall backwards onto the cold tile floor.

There I sit, my legs sprawled in front of me, the test resting between them.

Positive.

It's fucking *positive*.

For some reason, processing this moment is like doing calculus. Maybe it's because I'm trying to make sense of the fact that my wife is pregnant—a goal we've had for *two fucking years*—while simultaneously wondering why she hasn't told me. Now that I think of it, she *has* been acting different the last few days. A little edgy. Slightly detached.

Oh, shit... she was probably planning on surprising me with the news, and now I've spoiled it.

But *Jesus Christ*—Katrina is pregnant.

It all hits me finally, and I start to laugh, almost manically, folding over onto my knees. We've been trying *so hard*. I had all but decided it wasn't meant to be.

And Summer... *God,* my little girl is going to be so excited. She's seven now. She's been asking to be a big sister ever since she knew what it meant. She's a true nurturer, having enough dolls to fill a daycare, and playing mommy to all of them.

She's going to be the best big sister, and I'm *dying* to tell her. I want to tell her right now, just to see the look on her face, that innocent, wondrous look...

And then I remember my wife hasn't even told *me.*

It hits me that I'm sitting on the floor, clutching a pregnancy test so hard I'm surprised it hasn't broken, and I have no idea what my next move should be. One minute I'm collecting trash, and the next I'm contemplating baby names and registries, and being a father twice over, and... *holy shit.*

I'm going to be a father.

Again.

I'm going to be a father *again.*

"Evan?"

I don't have much time to think it over because Katrina is home from her waitressing shift. I hear her shuffling around in the living room and open my mouth to tell her where I am, but I can't remember how to make words. How do I approach her? What do I say? Do I pretend I didn't see it and allow her to surprise me?

Shit. I can't do that. I'm terrible with secrets, and there's no fucking way I can hold this excitement in.

The bathroom door opens just as I'm pulling myself up off the floor.

I'm holding the pregnancy test in my hand, and a moment goes by where we just... stare. I watch as her eyes drift towards it, then blink back up to me. She looks like she's just seen a ghost.

"Katrina," I breathe out, stepping forward, my heart beating wildly inside my chest. I feel like I'm choking. I'm choking on words and thoughts and sheer fucking happiness, so I wait for her to speak. To say it. To confirm this moment.

But she doesn't.

So, I say it for her.

"You're pregnant?"

Her lips part to speak, but only a gasp passes through. Her eyes are wide, her skin ashen. It takes her a minute, and then the words come sputtering out. "Evan... I was going to tell you. I – I was trying to think of a fun way to let you know." She takes in a shuddering breath, frozen in the bathroom doorway. "I found out this morning."

Makes sense. She's still in shock.

I'm smiling now. I'm smiling so hard my jaw actually aches. "Holy shit, babe."

I can't hold back any longer—I pounce on her. I grab her hand and pull her towards me, scooping her up into my arms so we can twirl around in a clumsy circle. Katrina's face is pressed up against my shoulder, and I can feel her tears begin to seep into the neckline of my t-shirt. My eyes fill with water, threatening to spill. "You're fucking *pregnant*."

I have to keep saying it. I have to keep giving those words life.

"I can't believe it. We've been trying for so long," she says in a cracked voice. "It actually happened."

I loosen my grip and step back, taking in the beauty of my pregnant wife. I know it's cliché, but I swear to God she's glowing. She looks tired as well, worn down, but still... I can see it. That subtle luminance that says: *"I'm growing a new life inside me."* No matter how exhausted she may be, it shines through.

A strand of blonde hair is stuck to a tearstain on her cheek. I lean in and gently remove it, pulling her back to me for a kiss. It surprises me when she stiffens, but then it's probably the shock. She had given up hope, just like me. I was pretty sure at this point she was only trying because she didn't want to let me down, and I'm so happy we didn't let the discouragement get to us.

If we had, we wouldn't be here. Today. With our positive pregnancy test and a new life on the way. *Completing our family.*

I'm overcome by my love for this woman; the mother of my child, of my *two* children. Walking her backwards until she's flat against the wall, I deepen the kiss. She whimpers a little, almost like it pains her, so I rein in my emotions and let her breathe. My lips trail along her jaw, down her neck, my hand resting protectively over her stomach. Then I sink to my knees, move my hands, and kiss her there.

Where my child is growing.

Our child.

She exhales.

"Are you feeling well enough to… celebrate?" I lift my eyes to skim her face, my eyebrow arching suggestively. Katrina pauses, then gives me a nod and a tiny smile, and in one motion I stand and pick her up, wrapping her legs around my hips as I walk her into the bedroom.

I set her down gently, and she sprawls out on her back, her hair splaying across the bedspread like a golden crown. A halo. I take a moment to just drink her in.

I don't know what I did to deserve her—what I did to deserve this beautiful life.

But now I need to be inside her. I need it like I need air, and though excitement bubbles over inside me, and I want to talk about the baby, too, that can wait. When I climb over her, she cups my face between her palms. There's a flicker of desperation in her eyes as they fill with fresh tears. I hope she would tell me if she wasn't feeling well, and maybe I should let her rest, but God… *I need her.*

"I love you, babe," I whisper. My kiss holds nothing back; I am desperate to tell her all that she means to me, but there's a futility there in the words I say, the kisses I offer. It's never enough…

So, I show her, instead.

NOW

The weather has cooled down over the last few days, and Fall is finally beginning to tickle the air. It's a mild sixty-two degrees, which makes it a perfect Sunday to go to the park. The leaves haven't started to turn color yet, but the change of season is apparent in the tepid breeze. I can almost taste it.

Summer and I ride our bikes a little over a mile to the nearby playground, which gives me plenty of time to muse on my love of Fall. My daughter informs me that this makes me "basic"—whatever the hell that means. She says she'll disown me if I ever start ordering Pumpkin Spice Lattes.

Shit. It's best she doesn't know that I fucking love those things.

We park our bikes against a sycamore tree, and I watch as Summer makes a mad dash to the swings. There's another little girl around her age already swinging with gusto as a few toddlers play in the adjacent sand pit. I lean back against the tree, my hands in my pockets, my sunglasses perched on top of my head. My eyes scan the playground, landing on a woman sitting alone on a bench.

Well, I'll be damned.

I squint as though that might change or confirm the fact that I'm staring right at Josie Grant.

She's preoccupied and hasn't noticed me yet, but surprisingly, she's not playing on her cell phone like every other parent here—no, she's simply watching the little girl next to Summer swing back and forth. She has a whimsical look on her face that I know all too well. I often mirror that same expression when I watch Summer jump on the trampoline in the backyard, or giggle at one of her favorite shows, or rollerblade along the sidewalk. It's a proud parent smile.

Surprise. I had no idea she had a daughter. She'd left that off Facebook.

I scratch my head, making a mental note to get a haircut, while weighing my options. I hadn't planned on running into her today, but there's little chance she's going to believe that, and creep vibes won't exactly work in my favor.

Shit—this is off book. I roll my tongue along the roof of my mouth, debating my next move.

"Dad! Come push me!"

Well, I guess a decision has been made. Leave it to your kid to out you.

I push off the tree with my shoe and flip my sunglasses over my eyes. Breezing past Josie, my peripheral vision still on point, I notice the way she straightens on the bench, looking down as she fidgets with the hem of her blouse.

Yep. I've been spotted. *Creep alert.*

But this time, I'm truly *not* here for her, so I head straight for Summer, ignoring the uncomfortable blonde on the bench. I'm aware Summer is old enough to push herself as I step behind her, but I'll never say no. These moments are fleeting.

"Do the underdog!" she demands, squealing as she sails higher.

Hell, I'm getting too old for this shit. The last thing I need right now is a herniated disk. But I do it anyway because of course I'm going to do it. I do two fake-outs, then run underneath her on the third push. The little girl beside her watches with a goofy grin and hops up and down on her own swing.

"Can you do that to me?" the girl asks.

Josie clears her throat from a few feet away. "Olivia, that's rude."

"I don't mind," I say, planting my hands on my hips as I face her, trying to disguise the fact that I'm slightly winded.

I lock eyes with Josie, and when she finally gives her consent with a small nod, I flash the least-creepy smile I have. *Two herniated disks, incoming...*

Might as well make them worth it.

I turn to the little girl, Olivia, and do the exact same thing I did with Summer. Soon, both girls are flying high, their laughter filling my ears.

I saunter up to Josie, noticing the way she stiffens. I make her uncomfortable, and not in the good kind of way—if that's a thing. Obviously, this needs to be rectified. "May I?" I remove my sunglasses and point to the vacant space beside her on the bench.

She looks away from me, but nods again.

I almost feel like I'm approaching a skittish animal, so I'm cautious in my movements, settling down next to her, but not too close. It's close enough, though, that I can smell gardenias in her perfume. I'm not even sure how I know it's gardenia, but I do.

"I know what you're thinking," I tell her, keeping my eyes pointed at the girls. "But I promise this is just a coincidence."

I watch her from the corner of my eye. She doesn't look at me right away, but when she does, a little smile slips through. "That's what all the stalkers say," she replies.

I can't hold back the laugh. She makes an excellent point, actually, and that's when I turn towards her. "Well, my nine-year-old isn't much of a stalker, but she does love the park on beautiful Fall days like this. She'll vouch for me."

"She may have been coerced." Josie narrows her eyes, but her smile remains. "I know for a fact that promises of ice cream for breakfast will work wonders."

"You got me." I hold my hands up in mock surrender, my tone still teasing, then prop my foot up on one knee and lean back. She glances at the proximity of my elbow as it rests on the back of the bench.

Josie twirls her wedding ring around her finger as she watches the two girls in front of us, and I pick up on the subtle cue.

Point taken, Josie.

When Summer and Olivia dart off the swings and skip across the woodchips, giggling as they disappear to the opposite end of the park, Josie finally breaks the tension with small talk. "They seem to have hit it off pretty well. I didn't realize you were a father," she says, glancing my way.

There's no reason she would have, but I just grin. "And here you said you knew me. Pompous asshat with a shitty turn radius, right?"

Oh, that got her. I watch the mortification cross her face, bringing a blush to her cheeks. "Not my proudest moment," she cringes. "Sorry."

"I deserved it," I shrug, playing the martyr. "I knew you were married when I gave you that ridiculous pickup line. The gigantic diamond on your finger isn't exactly inconspicuous."

"It *was* kind of ridiculous…" Josie continues to fiddle with said diamond, amusement lacing her tone.

"Yeah, they just kind of fall out sometimes. I'm not always that lame, promise. Just don't ask my daughter."

She laughs, and some of the tension drops away. "I'd just had a really bad week. I didn't mean to take it out on you."

I'm enjoying this new development. Josie isn't the ice queen I'd feared. While this certainly ups my odds of sealing the deal with her, I know I still need to tread lightly. Slow and steady will win this race. "You'll be happy to know I've made a full recovery."

She lets out another laugh and looks over at me. "Evan, right?"

She remembered. I put another tic on my mental scoreboard.

"Yeah, Evan—" I'm about to tell her my last name, Campbell, but in a split second decision, I decide to give her my pen name instead. "Evan Hart." I never crossed paths with her husband, which was for the best—I probably would have killed the son-of-a-bitch—but my last name might raise red flags if Benjamin Grant ever caught wind of my existence.

"Josie Grant," she replies.

I hold out my hand to her and she hesitates, then takes it gingerly. "It's nice to meet you under less hostile circumstances," I tease her.

Josie chuckles, releasing my hand. She shifts on the bench as she tucks a golden strand of hair behind her ear. "What's your daughter's name?"

"Summer."

A softness sweeps across her face. "I love that. It's beautiful."

Josie Grant is also beautiful. It's obnoxious, really. Benjamin Grant got away with fucking *my* wife, while he had *his own* beautiful wife waiting for him at home, and I hate him for that, too. He gets to destroy my family and go back to his charmed life, while I choke on my grief day after day.

I actually feel the heat rising in my chest, so I need to redirect my thoughts before I implode.

"Say it."

Her words startle me. "What?" I have no idea what she's talking about, so I twist on the bench to face her. Josie is gazing at me with curiosity in her eyes.

"Sorry," she says, quickly diverting her gaze to her lap, a smile blooming on her lips. "You had that look… like you went somewhere else."

I wait for her to continue because my question was not at all answered.

She gets the point and continues. "I had this… friend." Her voice pinches a little on the word, and she nibbles her lip. "Any time we would get that far-off look in our eyes, we'd turn to each other and go, "Say it." That meant we had to say exactly what was on our mind. No thinking it over—we just had to say it."

I can't help my own smile from forming. I kind of like that.

I also can't help wondering about this… *friend.*

Unfortunately, I can't say what I was actually thinking about, as it would earn me a slap across the face and a restraining order, and both sound highly inconvenient. So, I put on my acting face again.

Okay, fine… it's lying. I'm a liar, but acting sounds better.

"I was thinking that they grow up so fast. You know… kids," I tell her. Josie seems to like the Dad thing, so I'm going to run with it. "I feel like Summer was playing with dolls and teddy bears just yesterday. Now it's YouTube videos, anime, and awful music."

And TikTok and Roblox. *God help me.*

Josie's eyes settle on the two girls across the park, who are sitting cross-legged in the grass. "I know what you mean. Olivia is eight, so she's kind of in between both of those things right now."

"Is she your only one?"

Josie nods. "Yep. My one and only."

She gets that far-off look in her eyes, the one she just told me about, and I'm almost tempted to have her "Say it." But it seems too personal. Too intimate.

We won't go there… *yet.*

My phone buzzes in my back pocket, startling me, and I pull it out, my eyes skimming the face.

It's Amanda From Produce.

The screen lights up with her name—and yes, it actually says "Amanda From Produce." Josie catches the caller's name and bites down on a laugh. I reject the call, not in the mood to chat with my one-night-stand while I'm sitting beside the woman I'm trying to sleep with.

"Do you have catchy nicknames for all of your friends?" Josie wonders.

I'm about to reply when Summer and Olivia charge over to us, laughing and out of breath. Olivia bounces on both feet. "Can we have a sleepover? Please?" she begs, throwing herself into Josie's lap.

Josie and I exchange a glance as Summer slips beside me on the bench.

"Please, Dad?" Summer pleads. "Olivia is super cool."

"Yeah!" Olivia adds, bobbing her head, giving her mother some epic puppy dog eyes I am all too familiar with. "*Please?*"

Josie laughs lightly, looking at me again, then turning back to her daughter. "One, it's a school night. Two, you just met her. And three… no."

"Mom!"

I intervene, trying to dodge the puppy dog eyes coming from my own daughter, while offering the girls a semblance of hope. "Maybe another time," I suggest. That's ambiguous enough. And honestly, this could work in my favor.

Another time.

"Here." Josie reaches for my cell phone that's resting on my thigh. "I'll give Summer's dad my number, and maybe we can coordinate a play date later in the week."

"Yay!" Olivia squeals.

Yay, my brain echoes.

Josie programs her number into my phone like it's the most natural thing in the world, and a grin slides across my face. She sets it down on the bench when she's finished, then rises from her seat.

This is starting to feel more like fate, than orchestration.

"We need to get going, Olivia," Josie tells her daughter. "Say goodbye to your friend."

"Bye, Summer!"

"Bye!" Summer waves.

Josie shifts her gaze to me with a thin-lipped smile. "I'm confident I'll see you around." Her smile broadens before she turns, wrapping her arm around Olivia and heading down the sidewalk.

I collapse against the back of the bench as Summer nuzzles into the crook of my shoulder. That went surprisingly well.

"Olivia was really cool," Summer murmurs, her voice muted by my arm. "I hope you text her mom so we can hang out again."

I reach for my phone, curious and intrigued. Scrolling through my list of names, I frown when I get to the *J*'s, and I can't find her. She's not in the *G*'s, either. *What did she...*

I do another once-over before my sights land on the unfamiliar contact:

"Mean Girl From the Gym"

I laugh out loud.

FIVE

*I*T'S ALWAYS THE SHOES.

It's a breezy Wednesday morning, and Summer is on the hunt for one of her shoes. Again.

I don't really get it. Why does she have one shoe but not the other? How can someone lose a singular shoe? And how does this happen *all the time?*

I take both of my shoes off in the same place, next to the door, on the mat I put down… just for shoes. It's a great strategy, because when I need to put them back on, there they are. Right where I took them off.

Together.

Imagine that.

"I'm going to miss the bus, Dad!"

Summer is frantic as she pulls apart the couch cushions and ransacks the bedrooms. Her feet are pounding against the hardwood floors, vibrating through the entire house, as she runs down the hall.

"Wear your winter boots," I suggest as I assist in the search.

Why not? They're a type of shoes. They go on feet.

However, my suggestion is clearly horrific because I receive the death glare of all death glares.

"Sure. If you want me to ruin my reputation," she mutters, lifting up the rug and peeking underneath.

"You're nine. The only reputation you have is being nine."

My ignorant Dad Logic receives an eye roll. I am well on my way to mastery. My Sensei would be proud... if I had a Sensei... that taught Dad Logic.

"Maybe it's where all the missing socks go," I offer.

"Where's that?" Summer asks from halfway beneath the couch.

"No one knows."

Summer pulls herself out from under the furniture just to give me her best deadpan look. "Helpful, Dad."

"You're welcome," I smile.

The squeal of the school bus cuts through the air, and Summer races to the window just as it pulls up in front of the house. She groans as the bus pulls away, as though she just watched her dreams drive off on wheels.

At least she likes school.

Snatching my car keys off the kitchen counter, I toss them from one hand to another a few times before slipping them into my pocket. Apparently, I'm the designated chauffer for the morning, and that's fine with me. It means I can swing through the Starbucks drive-thru on the way home and satisfy my secret craving for a Pumpkin Spice Latte.

She can never know.

"All right, bun, I'll drive you," I tell her, heading towards the door.

"I still don't have my shoe!"

Touché. I grumble to myself as I look in all of the closets and cabinets, idly wondering why I also look in the food pantry. When I catch myself zoning out while staring at the box of Fruity Pebbles, I decide I'm just hungry.

"Found it!" Summer calls out, skipping out of her bedroom, holding the rogue shoe in the air like a prize. "In my laundry hamper."

How did a shoe get in... ?

Never mind.

She grabs her backpack while I snag the box of cereal, and we pile into the car together. Summer insists on blasting something called Billie Eilish, and it's fucking terrible. I'm grateful for the fact that we're only three miles from her elementary school.

I drop Summer off, collect my shameful latte, which goes surprisingly well with handfuls of dry fruit-flavored cereal, and head back to the house to write. I've been neglecting my manuscript and it's weighing me down. Fortunately, my deadlines are whatever I make them, as I self-publish all my books, but bills are tight, so I need to get new material out there.

How do you make money from writing books? You write more books.

I've come too far to stall now. I need to get back in the zone.

Last night I watched a Zen master on YouTube, hoping it might help me center myself—okay, so I only made it through two minutes of breathing exercises before getting distracted, but I figure that's something. Taking in a deep breath on the count of eight, I blow it out slowly as I fire up the laptop. I decided to skip the gym this week. After my unexpected run-in with Josie over the weekend, I don't want to overplay my hand. Besides, absence makes the heart grow fonder or some sappy shit like that.

That's definitely one of Josie's memes. Or it should be.

Maybe she'll miss me.

All right, time to work. I'm winging this book, more or less, but I still like to have a rudimentary outline of a chapter before I begin, so I start there, and... *ah, hell,* I have no idea what I'm doing.

When I'm close to the end of a book, my editor likes to send me messages with funny little videos to keep me going. Lately, the favorite has been Rachel from the television show *Friends* dressed as a cheerleader, complete with little pompoms and a sweater with an *L* on the front. I've never seen the episode, but when I'm feeling particularly low, I imagine the *L* stands for "loser." Harsh, I know, but when I imagine her in my head, waving her pompoms, yelling, *"Go, Loser! You've got this!"*—somehow, it helps.

I outline the next three chapters. Rachel believes in me.

As I'm about to write the first sentence, the ping of my cell phone interrupts me with a notification. It's a Facebook friend request.

It's from Josie.

Rachel's pompoms swish with enthusiasm.

She sent a friend request to my author profile, Evan Hart. I made the second account so I could link it to my business page, but I hardly ever use it. The only "friends" I have are readers who follow my work.

I accept the request, not reading too much into it—she has three-thousand Facebook friends, so she likely sends requests to every person she's ever had contact with. I skim over her profile to see if I've missed anything juicy over the last couple of days. Now that we're friends, old posts are popping up that I wasn't able to see before. Posts about Olivia.

Ah, so that's why I didn't know she had a daughter. She must have made those private.

I see that she's "active," so I take her request as an opening and shoot her a message:

ME: *Hi, Mean Girl From the Gym. Should we schedule that play date?* :)

She reads it almost instantly and sends a reply.

JOSIE: *Hi. Olivia would love that. Friday after school?*

ME: *Friday works for us. Let me know where. Summer will be excited.*

JOSIE: *She can come over here and swim if it's okay with you. We'll probably have our pool open for another week.*

ME: *Sounds great. Send me your address.*

JOSIE: *12 Ashbury Lane. Can't wait to tell Olivia :)*

I know her address. I've had it memorized for seventeen goddamn months. I've driven past her house dozens of times, wondering if I'll ever have the balls to break down the door and beat the piss out of her piece-of-shit husband.

I never have. My daughter deserves better than that.

I'm about to send a "thumbs up," but as my finger is posed over the button, I remember Katrina telling me that it's the kiss of death. I didn't understand then, and I don't understand now, but it's better to be safe than sorry. I send Josie another stupid smiley face instead, saving myself at the last minute.

Rachel waves her pompoms with approval.

I go back to the laptop and stare. One sentence. I can manage one sentence.

My fingers begin typing where I left off:

A FINGERTIP JERKS ON THE SCRATCHY HOSPITAL BLANKET. THEN A HAND. SMALL MOVEMENTS, BUT MONUMENTAL WHEN ONE HAS BEEN—

Oh, my God. This is terrible.

Delete. Delete. Delete.

Poor Penny has been in the process of waking up for months now because that's how slow I'm writing. I'm starting to wonder if it'll take the entire twenty years of her fictional coma to get her there.

Oh, well… what's one more day? She'll wait. I'm way too distracted to write, anyway.

Rachel drops her pompoms and scowls at me, but I flip her the bird and snap the laptop shut, pulling out the half-pack of cigarettes hidden in my desk drawer. I light up and do my Zen master breathing through the cigarette, calmed by the nicotine almost immediately. *Fucking hell,* I need it.

We've gone off book again.

I'm not sure how I feel about going to Josie's house. To *Benjamin's* house. What if he's there? I've never met the man face-to-face, but it's possible he knows what I look like. I don't have pictures of myself on social media because *fuck that*, but maybe Katrina showed him a photo. He could have looked into me—the husband.

It's risky.

I decide I'll just drop Summer off at the door and make a break for it. The whole damn point of this is to get closer to Josie, to get under her skin, but I can't risk running into Benjamin. I'll find another way.

Maybe I'll hit the gym today, after all.

Josie Grant is a creature of habit. This works in my favor.

I throw a towel over my shoulder, making my way through the ellipticals where she takes up her usual spot on the end machine. There's a brunette woman beside her today, and they seem to be immersed in conversation.

Well, hell… there's a wrench.

Looks like I'll need to find a different machine to pretend to work out on.

I situate myself on the elliptical to the left of the brunette—a dark-haired version of Josie in black spandex pants and a too-tight tank top. Josie is turned in my direction, her eyes drifting over with recognition, a faint smile forming on her lips.

That's encouraging. A much better reception than our other gym encounters.

Her friend twists around to see what's caught Josie's attention. I feign interest in the buttons on the machine, while concealing the fact that I can absolutely see the way this mystery brunette is drooling onto her calorie counter as she gawks at me.

"Friend of Josie's?" I glance up at the woman who is shameless in her perusal of my biceps.

She flashes me a pearly white grin. "A friend of yours, I hope."

Well, shit. She's not shy.

"Delilah!" Josie snaps. Her legs pick up speed as she releases a breath of exasperation.

I chuckle, ducking my head humbly. "I'm Evan."

"And I'm newly single." Delilah's smile brightens, her eyes glimmering with flirtation. "Nice to meet you."

"Separated," Josie admonishes. "He's barely out of the house."

"Girl, he was barely in the house when he was *in* the house," Delilah retorts.

If this is the divorcee Josie spoke of last week, this woman has certainly bounced back like a champ. I begin to move my legs, watching as Josie shakes her head with embarrassment at the end of the row. The two women go back to making small talk, and when the name "Ben" wafts over to my ears, my hackles rise. I strain to hear more, but the music is loud, and Josie's voice is muffled by the vocal stylings of Bruno Mars. I hurl silent obscenities at him.

To be fair, I would do that anyway.

"… leaves on that business trip to New York tomorrow…" Josie is winded as she speaks, her momentum rising. Beads of sweat are forming on her hairline.

What's that, you say?

Delilah lets out a sigh. She's moving at a less grueling pace as she regards her friend. "At least you guys get distance from one another. Maybe if Ryan and I had spent more time apart, things would be different."

"It's not your fault, Delilah. Ryan's been different ever since that stuff happened with his sister."

"That was years ago," Delilah huffs.

"Yeah, but it was heavy."

Delilah pedals faster as if she's trying to hold back tears. "I smothered him. He needed space."

The only part of this conversation I care about is the fact that Benjamin seems to be leaving on a business trip. Which means he won't be home when I stop by for that play date on Friday.

Which means… maybe I can overstay my welcome, after all.

Josie finally comes to a stop, wiping at her forehead with an embroidered towel and swallowing back big gulps of water. She catches her breath as she waves her hands at her face like a makeshift fan, then tightens her ponytail, smoothing back a rogue strand of hair. "Ben gets off work early today," she says to Delilah. "I should head home and shower." Gathering her purse, she exchanges goodbyes with her friend, who she's apparently leaving me with. "See you at the party next weekend?"

Delilah shoots an intentional smirk my way. "Will your handsome friend be there?" she asks Josie, then winks at me as she pulls her hair up into a messy bun.

I figure that sleeping with the best friend might hinder my chances of sleeping with Josie, so I shoo the prospect from my mind. Can't say it's not tempting, though. She seems fun.

I laugh at her boldness as I slow my feet. "We actually just met. I don't think I'm party material yet. But I appreciate the backhanded invite."

Josie steps away from Delilah with a shake of her head and mouths "sorry" to me as if I might be offended by the compliment. I expect her to keep walking, but she surprises me by pausing beside my machine. Her lips pucker, her eyes darting away from my face. I don't miss the way she scratches her chest in a nervous gesture.

"Can I talk to you for a minute?" Josie asks as she swings her purse back and forth against her hip.

"And interrupt my cardio?" I tease. "Who does that?"

She looks startled for a split second before she processes my reference of our initial encounter. I can tell once she does, as her body visibly relaxes, her fingers curling around her purse strap. "Only a true monster," she concedes with a breathy laugh. The disobedient strand of hair has fallen loose again, tickling her nose. She blows it back and crosses her arms, then nods her head to the front doors.

Looks like I won't be left with Delilah, after all.

I follow her out into the parking lot and almost ram into her when she stops abruptly, turning around to face me. A whiff of gardenias breezes across my nose, mingling with post-workout sweat. Josie inches back, leaving a more comfortable distance between us.

For *her*, anyway. I was more than comfortable with the previous amount of space.

"So... yeah, this is a little awkward." Josie clears her throat as she shifts her weight between both feet. "But... I hope I didn't give you the wrong impression at the park the other day. Looking back, it was a little forward of me to give you my number. I was just excited that Olivia made a new friend."

Bored housewife intrigued by the mysterious, tattooed stranger.

It's all right, Josie, I got the right impression.

I rock back on the heels of my shoes, my hands stuffed into the pockets of my sweatpants. I cock my head to the side with a smile that exudes complete understanding. "Don't worry about it. I didn't take it that way."

I almost scare myself by how good I've gotten at lying.

I mean... "acting."

A sigh of relief escapes her as she runs a hand along her collarbone. "I'm happily married," she adds, almost as an afterthought.

Happily. Uh-huh. I can't help but wonder if she says this to inform me, or to remind herself.

Either way, I'm looking forward to putting that theory to the test.

I'm feeling particularly bold today, so I allow my eyes to travel over her, pausing on the swell of her breasts, making sure she notices my unabashed perusal. I shift my eyes back to hers, expecting to see outrage flicker across her face at my boldness, but it's not there. Our gazes hold for a moment longer than necessary, and then I take a step back. It wouldn't be wise to push my boundaries any further, so I quit while I'm ahead. "See you around, Josie Grant." I fling my gym towel over one shoulder and saunter through the parking lot towards Francis, relishing in the zing of triumph that shoots through me.

I'm back in the game.

After the car door closes and the engine purrs to life, I glance in her direction.

She's still standing right where I left her.

SIX

THEN
MARCH

I LOVE THE SMELL OF FETTUCCINE ALFREDO.

My wooden spoon scrapes against the bottom of the pan. The act of stirring alfredo sauce is strangely soothing, and my stomach grumbles as the scent of fresh garlic and oregano wafts around me. I dip a finger in the sauce, sucking it into my mouth to taste it. Summer would like to taste it as well, I'm sure, but she's in her room reading, so I decide not to disturb her. Dinner should be ready soon; I timed it for when Katrina gets home from her shift at the restaurant.

I take another finger-full and groan.

I'm a fucking alfredo genius.

There will be no crappy store-bought sauce from a jar as long as I'm around, and those lazy-ass powder packets? Those are even worse.

Nope… I go all out. I make it from scratch.

I make a goddamn roux.

French bread is baking in the oven as I throw a salad together and gather the tableware. I wonder if our future child is going to enjoy my cooking as much as my girls do. Summer has always been a good eater, even as a toddler, and from what I've witnessed, this is a rare occurrence. Our friend has a three-year-old who will only eat chicken nuggets shaped like dinosaurs. They *have* to be shaped like dinosaurs—otherwise, they're trash.

Baffling.

I decide right now that I'll never allow a dinosaur-shaped nugget into this house. The kid can't insist on something if they never know it exists.

I'm rinsing the pasta when Katrina enters through the back door off the kitchen. I toss a smile over my shoulder as she steps through the threshold, simultaneously pulling the bread out of the oven like a multitasking superhero. "Hey, babe. I'm about to knock your socks off with this alfredo." I glance down at her naked toes peeking out through her sandals. "Okay. Well, I'm about to knock something off. Hopefully, it's your underwear."

Shooting her a wink, I falter—it takes me a moment to realize my playfulness is not matched. Katrina hesitates in the entryway, wringing her hands together with swollen eyes.

She's been crying.

I turn to her, remembering to go back and switch off the burner at the last second before moving away from the stove and heading toward my increasingly concerning wife. "Katrina? What is it?"

Her palms smooth out the wrinkled fabric of her work uniform, her bottom lip trembling as I near her. The streaks of mascara on her cheekbones are clearly visible.

She bites down on her lip, looking away from me. She's shaking.

Something is wrong.

Something is very, very wrong.

Nausea curdles my insides, and I don't even know why. The sense of impending bad news makes the seconds slog as I take another step towards her.

Crash.

"Oops! Sorry!"

Summer comes sliding into the kitchen in her Frozen socks. Giggling, her energy boundless, she greets her mother with excitement for a breathless second...

Then she goes completely still, the smile fading on her lightly freckled face. "Mommy?"

Even at this young age... she knows.

"Go to your room, Summer," Katrina says flatly.

The air is steeped in silence. Summer stares at Katrina. My eyes dart from one to the other. No one moves.

I don't know what to do.

A flush creeps into Katrina's cheeks, and her fists ball until her knuckles go white. She swallows, looking like she might sob.

Then she explodes.

"I said go to your room!"

Summer's whole body flinches as the furious demand bounces off the kitchen walls. She freezes in place. Her wounded eyes drift to mine, begging for help.

But I'm speechless.

Katrina rarely raises her voice around our daughter, let alone *at* our daughter.

And for no reason.

The breath I'm holding burns my lungs. I need to do something, say something… *fix* something. My wife is breaking in the kitchen doorway, and I need to go to her, but my little girl's eyes are so lost, so confused, so I shake myself out of it and step over to Summer. Bending down to her level, my hands lift to run up and down her stiffened arms. "Go play in your room, bun. Mommy had a bad day at work." I speak softly, like I'm in a room full of spooked animals.

Summer's eyes widen, filling with moisture.

"It's all right," I tell her. "I'll call you out for dinner soon."

She nods once and takes a step back.

Then, she spins and runs.

When I hear her bedroom door close, I rise to my feet, taking a deep breath, gathering my composure before I turn back to my wife. The bottom has dropped out of me—out of everything, maybe—but I don't even know why. I don't even…

A chill sweeps through me.

Slowly, my feel pivot until I'm facing Katrina. She's leaning against the wall with her hands covering her face. Her shoulders begin to shake and quiver as a sob spills from her mouth.

That does it. Her cry snaps me right out of this ominous fog with no name.

I cover the distance in a second flat.

Pulling her against my chest, I wrap my arms around her, my lips resting atop her head as she breaks. Her cries are muffled in the crook of my armpit, her body limp. If I weren't holding her upright, she would crumble at my feet.

God… I don't know what to do.

"Talk to me," I whisper, cradling the back of her head, kissing her hair.

The moment hangs heavy around us—the moment before I have a name for whatever has done this to my wife.

Then the chill travels through me again, comprehension settling in like a veil of dread.

I think I know.

I think I know, and I don't want to be right.

I don't want her to say it.

Don't say it, Katrina.

Katrina sniffles, her breaths quick and uneven. Finally, they slow, and something comes over her. An exhausted concession.

Defeat.

Reluctant resolve.

She pulls back a few inches, her posture hunched. Her head down. Her hand resting against her mouth.

The other hand is over her stomach, fingers clutching at her shirt.

I don't want to hear it, but I need this moment to be over. I *need* her to say it. I need to know, so we can move on.

"Katrina," I whisper.

Say it.

She closes her eyes… and then, she says it.

"I lost the baby."

The instant the words leave her, she collapses, falling into me, her fingers twisting into my t-shirt. Her face is buried in my chest as more words tumble free—apologies croaking out like sandpaper and broken dreams. "I'm so sorry… I'm so sorry, Evan. I – I lost it."

Her words are an earthquake. A tsunami. They vibrate through me with the rhythm of her sobs. They're a punch in the gut. A knife in the heart.

The shattered remnants of a missing piece.

But I can't make this about me. I need to pick up the fractured pieces crumbling around my grieving wife before I'm unable to put her back together. Her knees buckle, and gravity pulls. She's falling, so I hold on tight and let her fall.

I let her take me with her.

We fall together.

Crumpled on the cold tile, I scoop her into my lap, rocking her back and forth. Back and forth. The weight of our loss spills out in sobs. Sobs and tears and unnecessary apologies.

They spill out of her and onto me, and I hold that bitterness, those tears, that heartbreak… because it's all I can do for her.

It's all I can do.

"We'll keep trying," I tell her, smoothing back her hair. "It's okay… it's okay, we'll keep trying."

We stay like that, clinging to each other on the kitchen floor, mourning for what might have been. The sun sets outside the kitchen window, darkness falling over us like a deathly shadow, and still… we sit.

We mourn.

I don't know for how long.

All I know is that I hate the smell of fettuccine alfredo.

SEVEN

NOW

*R*OSES.

I narrow my eyes at the trellises bursting with blooming vines as if the flowers themselves took my wife away from me.

Assholes.

"Wow! Olivia's house looks like a mansion," Summer exclaims, bounding up the endless driveway with her swim goggles and beach towel.

Benjamin Grant obviously hires a top notch landscaper, so I can't disagree with the assessment, but I don't bother to fake excitement. "It's nice, I guess."

"You guess?" Summer slows down to take in the sprawling brick home. "I think our entire house can fit in their garage."

She's right.

Damnit. I need to get more books out.

Summer's flip-flops slap against the pavement when she breaks into a run, and I can already feel my anger bubbling to the surface as I make my way up the property. I wonder if Katrina has ever been here. I wonder if Benjamin brought her up this same cobblestone walkway with no thought to the husband and daughter she had waiting for her on the other side of town.

I wonder if they fucked in his bed while his wife was at a PTO meeting and mine was supposedly pulling a double shift.

I think about all those *"double shifts."*

Each slap of Summer's shoes feels like a slap in my face.

Fuck. Me.

Leaning against the brick pillar on the porch, I cross my arms as Summer rings the doorbell. My teeth grind when it chimes a ridiculous song that goes on forever.

Yep… I'm pretty sure it's mocking me.

While we wait, the fall breeze ruffles through the obnoxious roses, sending their scent my way. My molars grind harder. Benjamin Grant orchestrated all of this on purpose—I'm sure of it.

"Summer!" Olivia whips the door open with a beaming smile. Her strawberry blonde hair is parted into pigtails that bounce over her shoulders as she hops up and down on the other side of the door.

Summer doesn't wear pigtails anymore. I pause for a moment to mourn this revelation.

Olivia holds the door open, and the girls race away from me while I cautiously step into the foyer, pausing mid-step to look around me.

I don't belong here.

This house *knows* I don't belong here. There's a palpable energy; a tangible force trying to spit me right back out. The eerie sensation makes me scratch my arms in a failed attempt to subdue the goosebumps.

It's such an overwhelming feeling, I have to hold my breath, half expecting to be tossed out on the lawn by an invisible force at any second. Maybe it's haunted. Maybe it's haunted by a ghost who knows my secrets. A *clairvoyant* ghost who knows I'm the ex-husband of the former mistress, come here to enact my nefarious plan. Now I must battle the evil Benjamin Grant while being thwarted at every turn by the ghost that haunts his mansion, and—

Oh… good book plot.

I might need to write that.

After Penny fucking finally wakes up.

I can hear the pompoms shaking already. Rachel approves of this new idea.

So, now I've been abandoned in the entryway of this possibly haunted Better Homes and Gardens house that clearly hates me. I don't move away from the front door because I have no idea which direction the girls darted off in, and I'm kind of afraid I'll get lost if I try to search for them.

That's where Josie finds me in all of my awkward glory.

She casually strolls down the staircase in a floral sundress with a sheer coverup trailing behind her; the epitome of boho-chic. Her hair is down, wisped and fluffed at its golden ends, and her bracelets jangle as her hand slides down the cherrywood banister.

I can't help but wonder if she always looks like this when she's at home doing nothing, or if she put extra time into getting ready for my sake. Little does she know, it wasn't necessary.

Josie Grant could be wearing a giant kangaroo onesie, and I'm still going to seduce the fuck out of her.

"Sorry," she apologizes, meeting me at the bottom of the steps. She sweeps her honey hair over to one side, then crosses her arms over her chest, tapping a burgundy-tipped finger against her forearm. "My husband is in New York. He's been so busy with client drama, this is the first time we've had a chance to talk."

Client drama. Sure, Benjamin.

Was "client drama" your code for sleeping with Katrina, too? Or did she have a fancier title?

Josie pauses to scan the foyer, glancing into the dining room, then the study. "Did the girls go outside?"

I shuffle my feet, noticeably out of my element. "Yeah, they ditched me," I laugh, hooking my thumbs into the belt loops of my jeans. "Instantly."

A smile slips across her perfectly bronzed face, then she nods toward the opposite end of the house. "Come in."

I follow her through the hallway with unnecessarily high ceilings until an expansive kitchen and living area opens in front of us. Summer and Olivia are visible through the French doors, coasting along the inground pool in unicorn-shaped inflatables. I hate it, but I can't help myself—I'm a little awed by the beauty of this house. I'd driven by so many times, imagining the inside to be sterile, stark, and unwelcoming. But it's actually pretty fucking charming… despite the fact that it's watching my every move. A woman's touch is at work here, adding undeniable warmth in bright colors, beachy knick-knacks, and playfully patterned furniture. There's a bright orange accent wall in the family room, offering a bold focal point.

I don't envision Benjamin as being a connoisseur of patterned furniture and tangerine accent walls, so I'd say that's all Josie.

When we arrive at the spacious, fully-equipped kitchen, she breaks away to rummage through the refrigerator, glancing briefly over her shoulder. "Something to drink?"

Whiskey. Scotch. Tequila.

I'll just take Benjamin's whole undoubtedly pretentious liquor cabinet and pour it down my throat. Bonus points for the big "fuck you" to good ol' Benny, and I won't be feeling any pain.

"I'm good for now," I tell her, sauntering over and leaning forward on my arms against the kitchen island. It's a white quartz countertop, and it looks more expensive than my Mustang.

Possibly even my house.

Josie pulls one of those hard seltzers out of the fridge and pops back the tab. "I hope you don't mind. It's been a week."

I'll admit, I didn't peg her as a White Claw kind of girl. I imagined she'd be sipping delicately on a full-bodied Merlot. "Another bad week?" I ask.

I don't really care, but it's something to converse about other than the weather.

She turns to face me from the opposite end of the island, resting one of her palms atop the quartz. Her fingers drum lightly as she takes a sip of her drink. "Last week just sort of carried over into this week," she finally replies, thinning her lips. "And then there was the week before that. One of those months, I guess."

I feign interest with a raised eyebrow.

She doesn't elaborate. Gliding past me, the subtle scent of gardenias trailing her, she tilts her head for me to follow her out onto the patio. The sound of giddy, girly squeals amplifies tenfold when the doors push open and we make our way to a set of lounge chairs.

"Hi, Dad!" Summer waves wildly from the edge of the pool, then tucks her legs to her chest, plugs her nose, and dives in.

Josie and I are blasted with the aftermath of her cannonball. Dripping wet, neither of us move as we process the unexpected tsunami. I half expect Josie to mutter profanities, or yell at the kids to be more careful. Something.

But she bursts out laughing.

It bubbles out of her like music as she looks over at me, not even bothering to wipe the droplets from her face. She looks like an upper class vision with her overpriced sunglasses and perfectly coiffed hair, yet she's chugging a White Claw and laughing in her chlorine-spattered sundress.

She's a contradiction. An anomaly.

How is she married to *Benjamin fucking Grant?*

We drag the lounge chairs a safe distance back from the pool. Josie shakes the water from the skirt of her dress before settling down with one knee raised on the lounger. My eyes skim over her partially exposed leg, smooth and tanned, with beads of pool water glistening beneath the late afternoon sun. I match her stance in the adjacent chair with far less sex appeal in my scuffed jeans and four-year-old sneakers, then avert my eyes to her face. Josie is still smiling as she gazes out towards the swimming pool where the girls are racing from one side to the other.

Suddenly, I'm at a loss for what to say, which, let's face it, almost never happens. I honestly expected Josie to kick me to the curb by now. But she seems almost… comfortable. Like we've been friends for years.

Friends. We're treading on Phase Two already.

My brain wants to take an early victory lap, but I tell it to calm the fuck down, we're not there yet—though, I do have to admit, my plan of attack is appearing easier by the minute. Having daughters the same age was an unexpected leg up.

I tap my hands along my thighs and follow her gaze out to the pool. "So, does your husband go away on business a lot?" I inwardly wince at my choice of question.

Christ, Evan. What the fuck is wrong with you? I was going for the small talk angle, but it came out like a veiled attempt at finding out when she's alone so I can ravish her.

Josie hesitates mid-sip, the corners of her mouth twisting into an amused smile. She takes a drink and shifts her weight on the lounge chair. "He's a hard worker," she opts for. "He's at the office a lot and does more traveling that I'd like, but it just makes our time together more special."

Uh-huh. I bite my tongue. My money's on him scheduling these so-called business trips so he can sleep with married women and tear more families apart.

Benjamin Grant: The hard worker. For a second, I imagine us in a wrestling ring.

Vengeance Seeker vs. *Hard Worker.*

I fucking win.

"What about you?" she continues, breaking through my sour thoughts. She pushes her sunglasses up and rests them on top of her head. "Is Summer's mom still in the picture?"

A dark cloud begins to descend over me, but I detach myself from the subject and shake my head, taking it for what it's worth. She's curious about my love life, and *that* is promising.

One more point for the *Vengeance Seeker.*

"We divorced last year," I say with little emotion. "She moved to Tennessee and has our daughter during the summer."

A sadness flickers across Josie's face, like she feels sorry for me.

Good. Her asshole husband is the one who did this to us.

"That must be hard," she replies. Josie brings up a hand to shield her eyes from the sun, watching the girls giggle and splash each other. "Summer looks like she's adjusted well."

"She has."

I'm the one who's still adjusting.

Josie spins the can of hard seltzer around with her fingers, her eyes glazing over as her thoughts visibly drift. I can see she's gone to that faraway place, so I blurt it before I think it through. "Say it," I tell her.

She glances up, startled by the command, as if she's forgotten she had shared it with me. Josie blinks slowly, the grip on her can tightening. "Olivia's father died when she was just an infant. I was thinking about him."

Her confession takes me off guard. I had assumed Olivia belonged to Benjamin.

I watch her swallow down the lump in her throat as she processes the fact that she's just shared an intimate part of her life with me. I suppose that's the point of the "Say It" game. When you go someplace else in your head, it's usually a dark, personal place, and not something you generally want to voice out loud. It forces you to get uncomfortable.

"I'm sorry," I say softly.

There's a fleeting moment where I actually am... but Vengeance whispers in my ear again, reminding me there is no room for *sorry* in this plan, and I shut it off.

Benjamin Grant was not *sorry.* And neither am I.

Josie still looks reflective as she tips her head back and swallows the last few sips of her drink. Silently, she pulls herself from the chair and disappears inside the house through the French doors. I don't move, assuming she'll be back... eventually.

My eyes travel over the expanse of the back yard; there are birds zipping back and forth between a feeder and the nearby treetops, chattering about their finds. I can envision Josie sitting out here alone, watching them, and my mind wanders. I wonder about Olivia's father—what he was like, and if this might have something to do with the person my tattoos remind her of. It would certainly explain some things.

I'm beginning to ponder how such an unexpected woman ended up with *Benjamin fucking Grant* when a White Claw appears in front of my face. As I look up, Josie is smiling, holding the beverage out to me. It's a warm, friendly smile, and when I reach for the drink, our fingers brush lightly. "Thanks." I feel her hair graze my shoulder as she steps back.

Settling back into her chair, she takes a swig of her second seltzer and regards me with curiosity. "I saw that you're an author. That's pretty badass."

Ah, right. My Facebook profile.

There goes my notoriety.

"Yeah," I say, running a hand along the bristles on my jaw. "Badass is a word for it. There's also a lot of pressure that goes along with it. Creativity is a fickle thing… unfortunately, mortgage payments are not."

She chuckles. "Is it your full-time job?"

I nod. "I used to be a store manager for a big box retailer. I quit six months ago."

Josie looks impressed. Also promising.

"My girlfriends and I have a book club," she tells me. "Maybe we can read one of your books."

I highly doubt Josie and her tribe of haughty housewives are my target audience, but hell, I'll never say no to more book sales. "Most of my stories are kind of dark," I warn her.

She shrugs. "Even better."

Anomaly, indeed.

Summer and Olivia sprint over to us, leaving a trail of wet footprints behind them. They're dripping all over the lounge chairs, their teeth chattering, their arms hugged tightly around themselves.

Summer sits down at my feet, soaking my pant leg. "Can I sleep over, Dad? It's not a school night. And we didn't just meet anymore."

I look over at Josie who is masking a smile. I'm okay with it because I'm okay with anything that involves extra opportunity to worm my way into Josie's good graces, and this is just getting more convenient by the minute. "That's up to Mrs. Grant," I say to Summer. It's hard not to gag on those words.

Josie waves her hand dismissively. "Call me Josie," she insists. Then she pulls her bottom lip between her teeth, biting down on it while she contemplates the proposal. "I don't see why not." She turns to me. "You're okay with it?"

Can I sleep over, too? I feel like it's in my best interest to *not* voice my internal dialogue, so I nod instead. "It's okay with me."

Olivia and Summer leap to their feet, clapping and shouting, "Yay!" in unison.

I can't help the genuine smile that overtakes me. Summer has a few friends, but I haven't seen her this excited about a friend in a long time. I worry that she gets lonely sometimes. Single parent, only child… it can be rough.

The girls race over to the pool and jump in, and the backsplash still manages to reach us.

We both take a sip of our seltzer as our eyes meet, and Josie quickly looks away. I clear my throat. "I wasn't sure how this play date thing even worked. Do parents just drop and bolt these days?"

"Typically, that's the trend," she sighs. "People are so desensitized to other people. It makes me sad." Josie throws her legs over the side of the chair and studies me, pursing her lips together. "You should come to my party next weekend."

I straighten as I swallow down a few more sips of the seltzer. I'm thrown by the sudden invitation. "Are you trying to set me up with your friend?" I tease.

She ducks her head, almost bashfully. "Sorry about Delilah. She's kind of in that phase where one minute she's sobbing into her glass of wine, and the next minute she's trying to sleep with anyone who has a heartbeat."

Relatable. I sit up and face her, dangling my drink between my legs as I lean forward on my elbows. My eyes rove over her features. In the sunlight, her eyes match the color of her hair. "Divorces are rough," I tell her. "It's an emotional rollercoaster. I definitely did some questionable things postbreakup."

One of them being my plan to fuck you to get back at your sleazeball husband.

I stiffen.

This conversation is hitting a little too close to home, and I can't risk showing her my cards yet. My mouth tends to run away with itself, so now that I've been invited back, I'll quit while I'm ahead. I get up off the lounger and stretch. "I should run home and grab Summer's overnight bag. You're sure you're okay with her staying?"

Josie also stands and slips ahead of me toward the back doors. I follow.

"It's no problem at all," she says. "They seem to be having a lot of fun together."

We're in the kitchen again, and I find myself facing a wall I hadn't seen when I came in.

It stops me short.

There's a large canvas print hanging over a loveseat—Josie, Olivia, and *Benjamin Grant,* smiling without a care in the world.

A happy, perfect fucking family.

My stomach sours. I bite down on the inside of my cheek so hard, I think I might draw blood. "Is that Benjamin?" I ask Josie, nodding my head to the picture and swallowing down my rage.

She looks at me, something flashing in her eyes. She glances at the family photo, then back to me, as she leans her hip against the kitchen island. "I never told you his name."

Ah, fuck.

The warning sirens go off in my head: *"Abort... Abort!"*

The house scowls at me; I may get tossed at any minute.

Since it might be a little obvious if I take off running, I try to look as unruffled as possible while backpedaling my way out of this fucking mess. "I heard you talking about him at the gym to your friend."

There. That wasn't a lie—although, she did call him "Ben" and not Benjamin. I hold my breath, waiting to find out whether she remembers.

Josie seems accepting of this answer and nods.

I let out the breath.

"That's him," she says. "We took that picture on Olivia's seventh birthday." She fumbles with the bracelet hanging from her wrist, then adds with a light laugh, "We need to get an updated family photo. I'm not sure what I was thinking with that haircut."

I can't help but realize this photo was taken right around the time Benjamin was screwing Katrina.

How fucking precious.

I need to get out of this goddamn house. If I don't, I'm going to say or do something I'll regret. "Thanks for the hospitality. I need to get going." I set my half-empty White Claw down on the island, my jaw set against all the other words that want to spill free.

Josie must sense the shift in my demeanor because she takes a step toward me. "Everything okay?"

"I'm good," I tell her. While my body stays tense, I somehow manage to keep my tone level. "I've been having a lot of writer's block lately. I feel like I should take advantage of this free time."

Maybe drown my sorrows in a bottle of Jack.

Her eyes skim my face as if she's trying to pull a different response out of me. My words don't ring true, but she doesn't know why.

Ahh, the blissful rug of ignorance.

"I'll stop by with the overnight bag in a bit. Tell Summer I said to behave herself." I would wink, but I fear it would come across like a nervous tic, so, with great effort, I plaster a smile on my face. It feels like cardboard, but I manage to pull it off because that's just the person I am now.

An actor. A master of disguise. A chameleon.

A big, fat liar.

My footsteps echo down the corridor—I think that's what you call the fucking hallway in this kind of house—and before Josie can reply, I'm out the door. I'm almost to my car when I hear footsteps behind me.

"Dad, wait!"

Summer is running after me, her hair dripping wet, her skin pruned. *God, she looks happy.* "Yeah, bunny?"

She hugs me tight. She's soaked to the bone and freezing, and the pool water is seeping right through my t-shirt, but I pull her closer anyway.

"Truth bomb?" She looks up at me, her chin resting against my stomach.

I cup her beaming face in my hands. "Always."

"I think I found my new best friend."

My smile matches hers. Summer gives me a final squeeze before escaping into the house, her wet hair smacking against her back as she runs.

When she disappears inside, my smile fades.

My fucking fake, cardboard smile.

A chill trickles through me, one that isn't from the house-ghost. It's an awful realization.

Oh, yes, the plan has indeed become much easier... *because of my daughter.*

Somewhere, without intent, without even fucking *realizing* it, Summer became a part of all this. Part of my chaos.

Part of my lie.

God, I'm an asshole.

I run my hands along my face, inhaling on the eight count, and the air I exhale is poisoned with guilt.

Vengeance doesn't give a shit.

EIGHT

BENJAMIN GRANT ORDERS AN AMERICANO TO-GO.

I'm sitting at a high-top table inside the busy coffee shop, munching on a blueberry muffin as my eyes stay fixed on the man who ruined my life. He adorns a shit-eating grin and a slate gray dress suit that doesn't have a wrinkle in sight. His hair is dark, but not as dark as mine, and it's slicked back with a pretty-boy hair gel. I study the man's every move with a stone cold gaze.

He doesn't notice me, of course, because he's not trying to get into my pants.

I watch the way he flirts with the barista, putting a bill into the tip jar as she watches him, giggling. When I squint, I can see it's a ten-dollar bill—I'm quite certain he's trying to get into *her* pants. While he waits for his coffee, he makes small talk with a mom carrying her newborn in a sling. He pulls his phone from his pocket. Types something. Flirts with a different barista.

Fucker.

This muffin tastes like sand.

When my nemesis is in just the right position, I casually rise from my seat. If our daughters are going to be besties, our paths are going to cross one way or another. I need to know if Benjamin Grant recognizes me. If he *knows* me. If he does, I'm going to need to pursue his wife very, *very* carefully.

Making my way over to the counter, I reach for a stack of napkins. I turn strategically, stepping a little to the right so I purposely bump into Benjamin. The napkins slip from my hands and scatter to the floor.

Whoops.

"Sorry," I mutter, reaching down to pick them up. The blood is roaring in my ears.

I exhale on the goddamn eight count.

Benjamin bends over with me and collects a few of the napkins, handing them to me when we stand. Our eyes make contact.

I blink. I wait.

There is no recognition. No hesitation. No twitch of the mouth or furrowed brow.

There is nothing.

I nod my thanks, holding back every instinct that is screaming at me to put him in a chokehold in the middle of Birdy's Coffee House, then I step around him and slip out the front door.

That's one more point for the *Vengeance Seeker*.

I'm in the clear.

I had zero intention of making an appearance at the Grant family's annual "End of Summer Bash," but here I am.

Standing on their front porch dressed like a tool.

I can feel the silent judgment of the climbing roses.

Josie mentioned the party multiple times over the past week. When I picked Summer up from the sleepover. At the gym. In a text message. If she wants me here, that can only mean one thing—she thinks about me.

I'm getting to her.

So, here I am, wearing a stupid button-down dress shirt and fancy pants I impulse bought at Express an hour ago.

I panicked. I'm not proud of it.

So… do I knock? Am I supposed to let myself in? I have no idea how this exclusive shit works. I'm not an exclusive kind of a guy. I'm a struggling writer with a chip on my shoulder who drinks cheap whiskey, wears jeans with unintentional holes, and swears like a sailor.

I read an article one time that said if you cuss a lot, you're prone to having a healthier vocabulary and a higher intelligence. I'm gonna fucking go with that.

"Is that your car?"

I'm about to knock when a female voice interrupts me. It's a familiar voice, and I already know who I'll see as I turn. "Hey, Delilah." She smiles as she makes her way up the sloped driveway, thumbing over her shoulder toward Francis. I slip my hands into my pockets and step down to meet her, relieved to have someone else to solve the dilemma of whether to knock or not. My movements give off just the right amount of swagger to make her squirm as she looks up at me through long lashes. "Yeah, that's my baby."

I'm proud of my car. It's not an Aston Martin, but it *is* a new model with a V8 engine. Sexy as hell. Plus, I splurged on all the bells and whistles. Turns out bells and whistles cost nearly as much as an entire orchestra. I'll probably be paying for them until Summer is in college.

Worth it.

Delilah throws me a flirtatious grin, fluffing hair that is teased on top and styled into loose waves. She inches down her sequined dress, deliberately exposing more of her cleavage to me, and I accept the offering, lowering my eyes to her chest in appreciation.

Far be it from me to thumb my nose at cleavage.

"She's beautiful," Delilah says, the coy smile still in place. She reaches out to me and links her arm with mine, pulling me back up to the porch. "Come on. I'm claiming you as my date for the evening."

I allow her to be my arm candy since I don't know anybody here aside from Josie Grant, and I sure as hell can't be glued to the married host all night. And also because she smells like Jolly Ranchers.

Watermelon. My favorite.

"I didn't expect you to be here tonight," Delilah says to me as we make our way through the front door.

The house does its best to repel me as I step inside. I feel a pushback, a resistance. The house is onto me, unlike its owners, but I'm a stubborn motherfucker, and it's going to take more than a creepy feeling to deter me. "Josie insisted I come," I reply. "I think she's trying to play matchmaker." I wink at Delilah, and she lowers her chin to her chest as her grip on my arm tightens.

I wonder if that's the truth, or if Josie was looking out for her own interests, but I can't say the last part, so flirting it is. That's the furthest it will go.

The music is loud, but the mingling of voices is louder. There are at least fifty people here, spread out in the kitchen, living area, and on the outside patio. I scour my surroundings in search of Josie, while also trying to figure out a way to get her alone tonight. That'll be a challenge in this sea of exclusive guests, but I'm not one to let that stand in my way.

"Drink?"

Delilah tugs me toward the kitchen where I dodge a few curious glances from guests. I'm not sure if I stick out like a sore thumb, or if the house-ghost stuck a sign on my back, advertising my ill-intent. Maybe it's just obvious I don't belong in fancy pants.

Delilah doesn't wait for my response and shoves a craft beer into my hand. "Thanks," I tell her.

Craft beer is for hipsters, but I suppose it will do for now.

We make our way out onto the patio where antique-style string lights and tiki torches illuminate the party goers. There are a few cliques and small groups dispersed across the backyard, and there's even a group of people in the pool, despite it hardly being above sixty degrees.

They must be drinking something harder than craft beer.

Josie is in the midst of one of the small groups, and my eyes are drawn to her immediately. She is smiling and animated, talking with three other women with such passion that her cocktail is spilling over the sides of her glass. It's apparent she's already intoxicated.

"Josie!"

Delilah calls out to her, garnering her attention, and both girls squeal at the sight of one another. Josie makes a tipsy beeline towards us, her eyes dancing between Delilah and me. I can't help but notice she is wearing sex heels. I wonder if she wore them for me or her husband.

"Del!" Josie greets, her beverage still sloshing over the rim with each step. The women hug as if it's been decades since they've last seen each other.

Then Josie's attention lands on me. There's a brief awkwardness where we're both wondering what to do. I'm not sure if we've reached the "hugging" stage of our relationship yet, so I just wait, pleasantly surprised to find that the alcohol is making Josie's decisions when she leans in to hug me. "Good to see you, Evan."

I wrap my unoccupied arm around her, giving her a light squeeze, enjoying the feel of her petite frame smashed against me, warm and buzzed, as I hold her for two seconds longer than I should. When she pulls away, she doesn't look me in the eye, busying herself by tinkering with the opal pendant on her necklace chain. I allow myself a moment to appreciate her; as much as it grated on me, it really is a bonus that Benjamin Grant's wife is a fucking ten. Tonight Josie is dressed to impress, and she more than succeeds. She's a vision of dark red mesh and glitter, sporting a deep V-neckline dress with long, flowing sleeves and a form-fitting middle. It cuts off mid-thigh, and I can't help my thoughts from drifting to highly obscene territories. I'm looking forward to the day when those thighs are wrapped around me and—

Shit. She's giving me that look, and she better not ask me to fucking "Say it." I'd prefer that her Cosmopolitan *not* be thrown in my face. Cranberry juice is a bitch to get out, and this shirt wasn't cheap.

Josie grabs me by the wrist instead and starts off across her lawn. I glance back at Delilah who shoots me a wink, and I try not to trip over my feet as she clumsily pulls me to a nearby gaggle of women.

"Ladies, this is my author friend I was telling you about," Josie announces as she pushes us into the circle.

I'm sure I look like a deer in headlights as the Stepford Wives assess me. I take a few sips of my crappy beer, imagining it as a finely aged scotch, and slap on my best smile. "Evan Hart," I say. "Nice to meet you."

I can't help but notice Josie is still holding onto my wrist. She must realize this at the same time because she promptly lets go and gulps down the rest of her cocktail.

"Evan, this is Angie, Colleen, and Shayna," Josie says. "They're the girls in my book club."

I'm immediately bombarded by inquiries, their swoony smiles making me extra aware of how out of place I am here.

"What kind of books do you write, Evan?"

I've already forgotten all of their names. The bleached blonde one is fluttering her fake eyelashes at me as she sips on her wine, awaiting my reply. "I write psychological thrillers. They're a bit dark and edgy."

"We just finished reading a Nicholas Sparks book. I cried for days. Do you write anything comparable?" one of them asks.

I blink at her and deadpan, "No."

They nod, and all three of them bring their wine glasses to their lips at the same time as they silently stare at me.

I chug my beer and kind of want to jump in the pool and drown myself.

"Do you have a TikTok?" the one with obviously fake tits, boosted up to her chin, asks. "All the authors have them these days. You're very handsome… TikTok would love you."

I shake my head and chug more beer. Drowning myself in the cold pool wearing my fancy pants still sounds more appealing than making TikTok videos.

What I wouldn't give for a distraction.

"Honey, did you know we're out of ice already?"

I freeze.

Anything but *that* distraction.

The hairs on my arms stand up as a familiar presence enters the circle. It makes my stomach twist in knots. It makes me want to break my beer bottle over my knee and stab him in the jugular—witnesses be damned.

Everything be damned.

Josie takes a step away from me and reaches for her husband. She places her hand against his shoulder, grazing it gently down his arm as her gaze shifts between us. "Ben, I want you to meet Evan. Remember how I told you Olivia made a new best friend named Summer? This is Summer's father."

Benjamin Grant finally looks at me, and there's a spark of recognition on his face. I suck in a breath and hold it in the back of my throat, wondering if shit is about to hit the fan, wondering if maybe he knows me, after all—if the association with my name tipped him off.

His eyes narrow, deep in thought, then he raises a finger and flicks it toward me. "You were at the coffee shop this morning."

I exhale pure relief. "That's right," I respond. "Small world."

He throws a hand out, exuding the kind of confidence that would come in handy in the courtroom. "Benjamin," he introduces. "I'm Josie's husband. Olivia has talked about your daughter non-stop all week."

I want to spit in his face. I want to strangle him. I want to announce to all of his best friends and colleagues that he's a disgusting cheat and a homewrecker. The *last* thing I want to do is shake his fucking hand. It feels like a silent betrayal to everything I believe in.

But I do it for appearance sake, stiffening as my skin crawls. His grip is firm, and although it's only a handshake, it feels like a boa constrictor wrapped around my throat. "Likewise." It's all I can do not to choke on every word. "They seem to have really hit it off."

Benjamin offers his signature shit-eating grin, then pivots to his wife, pulling her towards him with an assertive tug. "Jos, I know you love any excuse to entertain. Maybe we can have them over for dinner one night."

I'd rather die.

Josie bobs her head, her features brightening. "That's a great idea."

Benjamin pecks an overly aggressive kiss against her hair as he takes a step back. "I'm going to run out and grab more ice. Text me if you need anything." He turns to me and nods. "Nice meeting you, Evan."

The pool beckons me once more.

As he walks away, my eyes pin to his retreating form like I'm manifesting a target on his back. I don't even realize how tense and zoned out I am until I feel Josie's hand brush my elbow. I flinch at the contact.

"Come inside," she says to me. "I'll get you a real drink."

I send a departing smile to the book club women I've dubbed "The Three *B*'s"—Blondie, Boob Job, and Botox. Josie and I stroll through the yard, which takes longer than necessary, as she greets everyone she passes with enthusiasm. She is met with equal adoration, obviously made for this shit.

We enter the crowded kitchen through the back doors, and Josie slides her body between two men deep in conversation about computer algorithms. I hover at the opposite end of the kitchen island and lean forward on my elbows, watching as she mixes a Jameson and Coke, making it extra strong.

I like her even more.

Once she's made a second drink for herself, she heads back over me, signaling her head to the right like she wants me to follow. When we reach the foyer, Josie dips her hand into the purse hanging from a coat rack, pulling out her cell phone before joining me at the edge of the staircase. We're leaning back against the rail, sequestered in virtually the only unpopulated area downstairs, almost as though we're in a world of our own. "I forgot to show you this video of the girls from last weekend," she tells me. Her face is alight with authentic joy, her eyes practically twinkling.

I move in close until our heads are nearly touching, gazing down at the video she pulls up. I see her swallow as her eyes trail up to me, like she's nervous or mildly uncomfortable by my nearness. This time, I'm confident it's the good kind of uncomfortable. I'm also not immune to the slight charge that passes between us, but in all fairness, she looks good and she smells good. Being genuinely attracted to the woman I'm aiming to have sex with is sweet icing on a revenge-flavored cupcake.

Josie presses play, and I bend forward. The screen lights up with a video of Summer and Olivia dressed in ridiculous outfits, wearing more makeup than all of the Kardashians combined, dancing their hearts out to an Imagine Dragons song.

I can't help the laugh that escapes me. "Are they really singing into a hairbrush? That fad didn't die with the nineties?"

"Are you kidding? It's a tried-and-true tradition," Josie says, slightly aghast, like I've offended females all around the world. "It does not die. It only gets better with time."

I feel thoroughly put in my place. The video continues, and the girls end the show with Summer doing a cartwheel and Olivia attempting to do a cartwheel, but toppling over instead. Both of them erupt into a fit of giggles on the floor. The recording starts to shake, and I can hear Josie laughing as she films them. It's endearing. I find myself traveling back in time to when Katrina would take adorable videos of Summer rolling over for the first time, or eating mashed peas, or learning how to pedal her bike.

My daughter and her friend are laughing hysterically on a shaky recording, and all I can see are the shattered remnants of my family.

My gut twists viciously. There's an ache in my soul so deep, I have to take a step back. The walls of this goddamn house are closing in on me. "Do you have a bathroom I could use?"

Josie looks surprised by my abrupt inquiry. She shuts off her phone and shakes her head. "We wanted to be nonconformists and purchase the only house we could find without a bathroom. But there's a lovely maple tree out back."

I just kind of stare at her for a minute because I'm still thinking about Katrina, and Josie's response doesn't register right away.

Josie's smile is now tinged with concern. "Upstairs to the right."

"Sorry." I blink, then force out a laugh. "Thanks."

I make a quick break, feeling like an idiot for choking on my goddamn emotions.

Pathetic, Vengeance grumbles in my ear.

Traipsing up the stairs, I try to relax, eager to have space to breathe and collect my thoughts. Being in Benjamin's house, interacting with him, getting close to his wife—it's affecting me more than I thought it would. I was convinced I had built an unbreakable barrier. I was certain my need for revenge was more powerful than my broken heart.

But I suppose they go hand-in-hand. There is not one without the other.

As I make my way down the long hall, the bathroom appears to the right, and I halt in front of it. Only, my eyes drift straight ahead, drawn like a magnet to the master bedroom at the end of the hallway. The door is wide open, beckoning me. The bed is perfectly made with floral bed covers, the walls a cool sea-green. My jaw clenches as I keep moving forward. An invisible force is dragging me to the room.

Fucking sadistic house-ghost.

I linger in the doorway, my gaze fixed on the king-sized bed. All I can see is one thing: Benjamin fucking Grant pile-driving my wife on that bed.

My *ex*-wife.

Does Josie even know? Does she know that her husband cheats on her? For a moment, I'm mad for myself *and* for Josie.

My eyes float around the room, skimming across several artistically framed illustrations of flowers boasting inspirational quotes. I pause on the one hanging over the nightstand—it's a rose, unsurprisingly—but behind this rose is a vine of gnarly looking thorns. There's a script over it in stark white letters. I take a step forward, squinting to read:

"Roses Fall, But The Thorns Remain"

My first instinct is to roll my eyes because Facebook isn't enough—Josie even has memes on her damn *walls*. Then I pause as the words sink in...

Okay, fine, maybe I don't actually *hate* that quote. Seems a bit depressing for a bedroom wall, but it's kind of poetic, and since I'm a writer *and* a bitter asshole whose rose fell and left me with the thorns, I can appreciate the meaning behind it.

Huh.

My eyes drop lower, pausing on something unexpected just beneath the picture, my brows pinching together as I process it. It seems so... out of place here.

Propped up against the nightstand is an acoustic guitar. I didn't peg Benjamin Grant for being a musician. Music takes soul, and that motherfucker doesn't have one.

"Are you lost?"

I jolt in place.

Caught.

I spin around to discover Josie standing behind me, pointing to the bathroom on the right with an eyebrow raised in question. I can't pretend like I didn't see the room with a toilet and a sink in the exact place she told me it would be, so I prop my shoulder against the door frame and play it cool. "Sorry, I wasn't trying to snoop. I saw the guitar and got a bit nostalgic. I used to play."

Josie softens, her eyes glazing over with something that almost resembles magic. "Really?"

I nod. "Yeah. It's been a while. I actually sold my guitar when I got divorced, and I've been dragging my feet getting another one." I watch as she approaches me. "Does your husband play?"

She laughs as if that's the funniest thing she's ever heard. "The only instrument my husband knows how to play is a tambourine, and by *play*, I mean he hits it and it makes noise."

My lips curl into a smile despite myself. Then I realize what she's implying, and I stand up straight. "You play?" I'm confounded by this development. I'd created an entirely different version of Josie Grant in my head when I first concocted my revenge scheme. She was a stuck-up trophy wife with little substance and even less intelligence. An easy target.

Now she's a musician with a brain and a sense of humor and more depth than I ever would have guessed. I have no idea what to do with this information.

Josie continues to approach me, but she's cut short when someone calls her name from the main level.

"Jos! Are you upstairs?"

It's Benjamin.

I can almost swear that her shoulders deflate at the sound of his voice. But that could easily be wishful thinking.

"Be right there," she replies.

Josie spares me a final glance before she turns to the stairs, and there's a striking shift in mood when she looks at me. It's brief. Wavering.

But I notice.

There is something in her pause, in her fleeting hesitation, that makes my breath catch as I inhale. And in that moment, I know…

I know.

I have Josie Grant exactly where I want her. And I'm going to do more than seduce her. I'm going to do more than bring her into my bed and make her scream my name.

I'm going to make her fall in love with me.

NINE

BOOB JOB. She's to my right on a leather couch so ridiculously soft, it had to have cost a fortune. Delilah is smashed up against me on the left, and I'm the proverbial meat in this sandwich. I'm interested in both of them, but not overly. I'm also intoxicated, but again, not overly—sipping on alcohol is just something to do to pass the time. I'm doing my best to stay alert; my sights are fixed on Josie, despite the fact that I haven't been able to get her alone again for the past two hours. She's been glued to her husband's side all night.

The fucking nerve.

It's a little after midnight, and I'm spinning the plastic cup of watered-down Jameson between my hands. Delilah is well past intoxicated, heading straight towards hammered. She's having a spirited conversation with Boob Job about reputable Goldendoodle breeders, and I think she might cry.

"They're just so fluffy and cute and... *hypoallergenic*."

Yep. She's crying.

I'm trapped in the middle, inching myself back against the cushions as they talk around me, wondering if this is how I go... if this is how it all ends.

With fluffy, hypoallergenic Goldendoodles.

"Ryan always wanted a Goldendoodle," she sobs as her forehead drops to my shoulder. "We had a Yorkie, but it wasn't the same."

"There, there." I pat her hair, while simultaneously chugging the rest of my cocktail.

I see the French doors open out of the corner of my eye, and laugher wafts in from outside as Josie walks in with a group of friends. She stumbles on her sex heels and wobbles forward, but one of the men in her posse reaches out, catching her before she faceplants.

He doesn't let go. I keep watching.

And... Lord help me, I'm pretty sure Delilah just drooled on my shoulder.

The man's touch goes into even bolder territory as one of his hands slinks around her waist and rests over her abdomen. Josie scowls and swats at the offending hand, removing herself from his grip. A heated conversation ensues, and I can't make it out, but I keep watching as she peels away from the rest of the group, disappearing down the corridor.

The man follows her.

"Excuse me, ladies." I pull myself up from the couch. Delilah goes limp in my absence, landing face down in Boob Job's lap.

She'll be okay.

My feet carry me down the corridor.

I don't know why, but I feel compelled to see why Josie is going off in private with some guy, and why that guy is not me. I saunter towards the front of the house, pretending to play on my phone while catching bits of their conversation coming from the study.

"You need to stop, Emmett," Josie says.

I can't hear what this so-called Emmett says in return, but Josie is less than thrilled.

Is she upset or uncomfortable? Or both?

"No," Josie tells him. Then she follows with, "Don't touch me."

And that's *it*.

I have zero tolerance for assholes who think they can put their hands on a woman after she says "no." *Fuck that.* I push the door open, clearing my throat as I enter the study with no subtlety.

Emmett's hand is squeezing Josie's upper arm.

I stare at it. He drops it.

"Everything okay?" I ask. My eyes dart between the two of them, then settle on the curly-haired son-of-a-bitch who is one poor choice away from getting kicked in the balls.

Josie steps back, wrapping her arms around herself and avoiding eye contact with me. "It's fine. We were just talking."

"You don't need to put your hands on someone to talk to them." I direct the statement to Emmett.

His jaw is set firm, but he doesn't speak. He just walks away, deliberately bumping my shoulder as he moves past me and exits the study.

That's mature, Emmett.

I look back at Josie, wondering if I'm overstepping, but honestly, I don't really give a shit. That was not okay.

"Did he hurt you?"

She jerks her chin up, shaking her head. "No. It's not like that." Josie rubs her hands along her arms as if chilled, then lowers her gaze. "Like I said, everything is fine."

She shuffles past me and heads outside without further elaboration. When the front door slams shut, I debate whether I should follow her or not.

Fuck it.

I follow her. The whole point of coming tonight was to get closer to her, after all.

The evening has cooled, a brisk breeze carrying the leftover humidity away along with the first dropping leaves. It feels like everything I love about Fall. I step down onto the front walkway, pausing to gaze at the stars, drinking my favorite season into my lungs with a deep breath. It's nothing I can put my finger on, but something about the moment feels significant. Important, even. Inhaling the crisp air, I savor the few seconds of peace that wash over me.

Peace. At Benjamin Grant's house, of all the fucking places. Maybe that's the significance.

I'm pulled from the moment by the flick of a lighter.

Curiosity draws me forward, and I continue my trek down to the driveway. I find her there, leaning back against the garage door with the glow of a cigarette between her fingers. Her eyes are on me as she brings the cigarette to her mouth and takes a long drag.

"You smoke?" I move towards her, rummaging through my pockets for my own pack of cigarettes. I seem to be accumulating more and more of them lately.

"Sometimes," she replies.

I smile, pull out the pack, and pluck a cigarette from the box. "Same."

Josie holds her lighter up like an invitation. I oblige, popping the cigarette between my lips and inching my way over to her. Our eyes stay locked as she rolls her thumb over the little metal wheel until there's a spark. The embers crackle when I suck in a sharp breath.

"We used to date," she says. "Me and that guy inside." Her voice is low, hardly penetrating the sounds of boisterous laughter trickling out from inside the house.

I wait for her to continue.

"If you could call it that, I mean. We dated for, like, five minutes." She flicks the lighter a couple more times for no reason, then takes another drag. "All right, it was more like two weeks. But it was nothing. No chemistry… on my part, at least. Then I met Ben, and it was over."

I move in closer, matching her position against the garage door. Our shoulders are touching as we puff on our cigarettes and watch the smoke dissolve into the night sky. "You must be a hard one to get over." My undertones are suggestive, but I don't apologize for it. We glance at each other, and Josie quickly looks away, biting on her lower lip.

A few minutes of silence follows, and it's not uncomfortable. I stare at the stars, and they twinkle back. The encompassing sense of peace I feel now might be from the nicotine, but damnit, I'm going to enjoy it.

"What about you?" she wonders aloud.

Her feathery earrings catch the light of the garden lantern, and I mentally slap myself for noticing. "What about me?"

"Your ex. Is she a hard one to get over?"

I don't like her question. In fact, I fucking hate it. There is something wrong about Josie Grant asking about my ex—the same woman her husband betrayed her with.

She doesn't even know.

I take a deep drag on my cigarette, allowing the nicotine to fill my lungs until I almost choke. "Yeah," I reply honestly. "She is."

Josie is looking at me again, but this time, I'm the one who looks away. My thoughts turn stormy as Katrina moves in like a black cloud. And I wonder…

Is it more that I can't get over Katrina, or that I can't get over *what she did to me?*

My dismal train of thought is interrupted when Josie slides into my line of sight, twisting her back to me and pulling the sleeve of her dress down over her shoulder. I'm confused as all hell for a minute… and then I see it.

She watches for my reaction. Josie has a nautical star tattoo on her right shoulder blade that's almost identical to mine. I'm tempted to reach out and touch it—I want to—but I stop myself.

I swallow hard and lift my eyes to meet hers.

"Olivia's father and I both got matching tattoos," she explains, studying me. She pushes her sleeve back where it belongs, and the tattoo is hidden once again. Leaning back in her original place next to me, Josie takes another drag on her cigarette before she proceeds. "I'm not sure what your situation is, but I know what it's like to grieve for someone. I understand that loss. Some people leave a giant hole in your heart, and they're just… hard to get over."

I'm frazzled by the intimacy of this moment, but I choose to go with it. "What happened to him?" I wonder if she'll answer me, or if I even deserve an answer, but she doesn't hesitate.

"Motorcycle accident."

A solemn silence settles between us. There is not an appropriate response to something like that—a "sorry" just won't do. Josie knows this, and I know this, so we simply stand there with our cigarettes and our sadness, and we allow the moment to be exactly what it's meant to be.

The moment is severed when I look up and Benjamin Grant is standing there, staring at us. Josie and I straighten and step away from the garage as Benjamin's hard gaze sets on his wife.

"What are you doing?" he demands, advancing on Josie.

Fuck. I have too much whiskey in my blood to be fully prepared for this.

Neither of us say anything as Benjamin continues to move forward, never looking at me, only focused on Josie. He stops in front of her. She's returning his gaze with equal vigor.

I'm tense with cautious anticipation, holding onto a breath, my muscles wound and ready to go. I have no idea what I'm going to say, but maybe I can just knock him out and think on it later.

Benjamin regards Josie, shaking his head, then reaches down and plucks the cigarette from between her fingertips. He lets out a sigh of disappointment. "I thought you quit, Jos."

I blink.

The cigarette? *The fucking cigarette?*

I let that breath out hard, relaxing when I know my secret is still safe.

Josie seems unfazed by the events unfolding, maintaining a rigid stance on the driveway, flipping her hair over her shoulder almost defiantly. "Maybe if you didn't invite your pig-headed business partner who can't keep his hands off me, I wouldn't have been compelled to smoke," she says. Her tone is sharp, her eyes glowing with indignation.

The muscles in Benjamin's jaw flicker with a quiet anger. I'm not entirely sure if that anger is geared towards his pig-headed business partner or his wife.

Josie doesn't grant either of us another look and sweeps past us, her sex heels clicking against the cement as she heads back into the house.

I'm left standing alone in the driveway with Benjamin fucking Grant, who was moments away from being introduced to my lead fist.

It still seems like a valid option.

Benjamin tosses the cigarette butt to the pavement and snuffs it out with his shoe. Planting his hands on his waist, his fingers curl around his hips as he expels his frustration out through gritted teeth. For a moment, I wonder if he even remembers I'm standing here.

"Are you married, Evan?"

I startle at both the sound of his voice and the weight of his words.

Well, I was *married. Right up until you put your dick in my wife. Thanks for asking.*

"Divorced," I reply, my tone flat.

A groan rumbles in his throat, and it sounds like pity. His head shakes from side to side as he kicks at a piece of gravel on the driveway. "That's a bitch."

I can't help the way the air leaves my lungs, or how my fingernails dig into my thighs, or the furious beats of my wrathful heart. My gaze settles on a rock resting at the edge of the lawn. It's a decent sized rock. Its edges are jagged, and it looks solid and heavy. It could easily put a dent in someone's skull.

Vengeance wouldn't mind this route either.

Goddammit. I shake away the morbid thoughts, telling myself that's not the kind of man I am. That's not the kind of *father* I am. I'm bigger than my rage. I'm better than my grudge.

I close my eyes, desperate for another cigarette. "Yeah. It certainly is," I manage to spit out, forcing my hands into my pockets to keep them from doing something regrettable.

Benjamin finally glances at me as if he's seeing me for the first time. "Do you still love her?"

What the fuck?

I pause, hoping I didn't actually say that out loud.

"She cheated on me," I tell him. I don't answer his question directly. I don't even know the answer, and if I did, it wouldn't be any of his fucking business. And *also*—fuck him. "I'll get over her. But I'm not sure I'll ever get over that feeling of betrayal. That's the real bitch."

And that answers that question.

I swear there's a flicker of guilt in his eyes, but he recovers quickly. It hits me then, with the sting of acid in my throat, that we do share one striking thing in common…

We're both damn good liars.

"I'm sorry to hear that," Benjamin says, his eyes still trained on me. I have the sense that he's trying to discern whether there's anything more under my words, but that might be paranoia.

No, you're not, you motherfucker.

I can't let this conversation go any further. We're in dangerous territory as it is, and if he says anything else…

We're not going off book now. I have a mission, damnit, and it's to destroy him from the inside out. Not stand here and tell him he was a bad boy.

I take a breath, swallowing my pride with a fake smile I can only hope looks more convincing than it feels. "I'm going to head out, but I appreciate the invitation tonight. It was a great party."

I nod my thanks as I move past him, feeling him watching me as I go.

I hope you suffer.

"We'll have to set up that dinner," Benjamin calls out before I reach the sidewalk.

I bite down on my tongue, closing my eyes, then twist around to face him. "Looking forward to it." I grin with all my teeth. I either look like a happy psycho, or a rabid bear.

What I *want* to do is charge at him. Tackle him. Throw the truth in his face and beat him to a bloody pulp.

But I turn back around and walk to my car.

As I approach the Mustang, I remember that I've been drinking and shouldn't drive.

Fucking hell.

I kick the tire as if she force-fed me the alcohol and is solely responsible for my current predicament. Then, I apologize.

Sorry, Francis. Please don't hate me. I'm a little drunk.

And pissed.

I exhale loudly into the night, which is much too calm for my mood, and set out to walk the two miles back to my house. I'll have to get my car in the morning before I pick up Summer from her sleepover.

I'm no more than a few feet down the sidewalk when I feel eyes on me.

I turn.

Josie stands on her front porch, her arms draped over the rail. She sees me, but she doesn't call out. Even after a long night and a dubious amount of alcohol, she is still a vision, looking like she belongs there, among the roses. The red mesh from her puffy sleeves catches the draft as her hair floats over her shoulder. Our eyes hold for a moment, and I wonder if I should say goodbye… say *anything*… but I don't.

Neither does she.

I offer her a smile, and she returns it. The seconds tick by.

One… Two… Three… Four…

And then I break away, disappearing into the night.

10

TEN

THEN
MARCH

I FEEL LIKE I'M LOSING HER.

It's been two weeks since the miscarriage, and I know this cycle of grieving is not abnormal, but I'm worried. Katrina has been depressed, easily triggered, agitated, and just… sad. I'm not sure how to fix it. I'm not sure how to fix *her*.

I feel fucking helpless.

I've done my best to pick up the slack around the house, so she can rest. She's been spending a lot of time in our room under the covers, curtains drawn against the sunlight. I check on her often, finding her sleeping, or buried in her phone, texting. She mentioned telling a close girlfriend about the miscarriage, so at least she has some outside support.

It's on the tip of my tongue to suggest she talk to a professional, but I'm still waiting to see if she'll come out on the other side of this soon.

Summer has been glued to my hip whenever I'm not at work, asking questions, wondering why Mommy is always crying. We didn't tell her about the baby—it was too soon. So, I keep things simple and tell her that Katrina isn't feeling good, and I'm sure she'll be better in no time.

I'm cautiously optimistic, or at least that's what I'm telling myself, but there's a formidable weight in my chest that's getting heavier every day.

Katrina is not okay.

Summer is playing in her room while I finish prepping chicken tetrazzini for dinner. I'm prepared to bring a plate of food to the bedroom for Katrina when she shuffles into the kitchen wearing an extra baggy sweater and messy bun. Her eyes are sunken in, her skin pasty, but it's a pleasant surprise to see her.

"Hey," she says. Her voice sounds hoarse, like she's either been yelling or crying.

I know it's the latter.

"Hey, babe. Hungry?"

Katrina shakes her head, a rogue strand of hair sweeping over her temple. "I just needed a change of scenery. Maybe something to drink."

She takes a seat and rests her elbow on the table, propping her chin in her hand. Her eyes are on me as I pour a glass of white wine… only, when I place it in front of her, she pushes it away.

"No, thanks."

Katrina never says no to wine. I can't help the sag of my shoulders, the feeling that there's nothing I can do to help. So, I settle for keeping her company, pulling out the adjacent chair to sit beside her. I cover her hand with mine, but she flinches, drawing back. Her shoulders are stiff as she stares down at the scratches on our humble kitchen table.

The breath I release comes out shaky. My chest is in a vise.

She looks up at me through sandy brown eyelashes, her eyes clouding over with something that looks like remorse, then she threads her fingers through her hair with a sigh. "Sorry. I'm just not feeling myself lately."

I've tried not to read into this too much, but I can't help but feel like there is something happening that goes even deeper than the miscarriage. I was gravely affected by the loss of our baby, and I know this is traumatic for her—she was the one carrying our child, after all. She's suffering both the physical and the emotional loss. But… I *know* Katrina. I know her better than anyone. I can't put my finger on it, but there's more going on inside her head.

There's just… something else.

We haven't been intimate since it happened, and I'm not just referring to sex. She told me her doctor said no intercourse until her body heals, and I understand that. But there has been nothing. No soft touches, no hugs, no lingering kisses. No kisses at all.

I can't get near her.

"Katrina, we should talk about this," I tell her, trying to keep my tone level despite my desperation to reach her. I *need* to break through the walls she's built between us. They're palpable, getting thicker every day, and I'm afraid that if we don't start chipping away now, it will soon be too late. "I've been trying to give you space, to let you heal, but I feel…"

She closes her eyes.

Swallows.

I continue, unable to keep my voice from cracking. "I feel like you're slipping away from me."

My words hang there in the air, splintered and raw. Unacknowledged for a moment. Then her eyes slowly trail from the tabletop to meet mine. There is something haunted in them, the ghost of more than our unborn child.

Something I can't even begin to dissect.

I sense that she's about to open up to me. I hold my breath, like if I breathe or blink, or even move, I'll miss it. Her lips part as she leans slightly forward against the table, her reply creeping up the back of her throat. But whatever those words might have been dissolve on her tongue.

I exhale. "We can keep trying, Katrina." I say it to give her some kind of hope, to raise her spirits. It's not meant to be pressure, just… a promise of better days ahead.

But I don't get the reply I'm expecting.

"I don't want to."

It's barely a whisper. A hopelessness carried on the release of a breath.

A naked truth.

I'm breaking on the inside. I'm crumbling, and I can't show her because I have to figure out how to put us back together. I have to—

"I think I need to get out of here for a few hours," she says. Her eye contact drops; she deflates before my eyes.

Katrina's chair scrapes through the silence, and she stands before I can even respond.

I don't say anything. I don't ask where she's going, or when she'll be back. She doesn't give me a chance to, honestly, and I don't know… I don't know what to say to her anymore.

I don't know how to help her.

She slips on her shoes and disappears out the back door. The rattling of the hinges echoes through me like a somber hymn. A funeral march.

But no, that's not happening on my watch. I can't let it happen.

I won't.

My eyes stay fixed on that door for a long time, wondering where I went wrong. Did she feel pressured? Does she think she's disappointing me?

I shift my gaze to the full glass of wine, promptly chugging it.

"Daddy?" Summer skips into the kitchen, her yellow Belle costume skimming along her knobby knees.

I swallow. Recover.

I have to.

"Hey, bun. Hungry for dinner?"

She nods, then jumps into my lap. I shove the dark thoughts away and enjoy the feel of my daughter's arms entangling around my neck, the warmth of her body, the clean smell of her hair. I breathe in deep, savoring every piece of her. Every precious heartbeat.

She is my world. My treasure. And right now, she feels like my anchor.

"Where did Mom go?"

Summer pulls back, watching my face. She waits for an answer that will ease her mind. She waits for an answer that I don't have.

For half a second, I consider making something up.

She got a last minute call to work.

She's getting her hair done.

She's helping her friend find their lost hamster.

But what I say is only truth.

"I don't know."

The truth is all I have. I don't *know* where my wife went.

All I know is it feels like I'm losing her.

It feels like I've lost her.

NOW

"Can you make your world famous spaghetti?"

I laugh at the term "world famous," but I don't correct her. I realize there's a time coming when my daughter won't want to be seen with me, so for now, I'll continue to let her believe that I'm a thousand times cooler than I actually am.

"Spaghetti, eh? Can't go wrong, I guess."

Summer is busy obsessively cleaning the house. She does this sometimes when she's overly excited or stressed. Today she's excited because it's Friday again and Olivia is sleeping over.

The cleaning thing is a little weird, considering she's only nine and cleaning is way up there on the list of awful, joyless ways to spend your time—right along with golf. But I sure as shit don't complain.

Her Swiffer game is strong as she pokes her head into the kitchen where I'm gathering ingredients for my world famous spaghetti that only three people have tried.

"Can you turn some music on? It keeps me motivated," Summer calls out to me.

I swear this kid aged a decade over the past year.

"Sure, bunny. Any requests?"

She slows her pace. "Hmm. Taylor Swift?"

"No."

"Justin Bieber?"

I glare at her from across the room. "Is there a word more effective than *no*?"

"Yes?"

Oh, it's on. I reach for my phone and start up a playlist I've lovingly titled, "Fucking Noise." It's an assortment of metal songs that are amazingly therapeutic for a guy chock full of anger issues... like me. But for a nine-year-old girl, it's torture.

I blame Justin Bieber.

Screechy voices grate through the room, and Summer drops the Swiffer to cover her ears, which entices me to turn the volume up louder, of course.

What's a dad to do?

"*Seriously?*" Summer yells over the music. "Olivia will be here any minute! You're going to embarrass me!"

I start head banging as I bust out an impressive air guitar solo.

Unfortunately, Summer looks the complete opposite of impressed. Her arms are crossed, her eyes are narrowed, and she may very well be wishing death upon me. There's only one clear solution.

I charge at her. Summer shrieks in resistance, knowing full well she's about to be swept up and pranced around the room like a defiant dance partner.

"Dad!" she protests. "You can't dance to music like this. It's not even music!"

"It's definitely music." I scoop her up. "There is rhythm." I dip her. "There is soul." I twirl her in a circle. "There's... guitars."

Summer is squealing, her giggles betraying her, as we dance through the living room. Her laughter is the best music I could ask for.

I halt my steps when I hear somebody clear their throat. I turn to the front door, which I forgot was wide open, and see Josie and Olivia standing behind the screen. Josie looks mildly concerned, but mostly amused. Olivia looks... bewildered. I've just been caught dancing like a fool in my living room to a band called Maggot Twat. I guess I should be ashamed or embarrassed, but it's kind of hilarious, so I grin at them instead.

Summer races to the door. She is most definitely ashamed and embarrassed.

Honestly, if you're not humiliating your kid in front of their friends, you're not doing this parenting thing right.

I amble into the kitchen and turn the music off, then go back in the living room to say hello. My crimson-faced daughter is hanging Olivia's jacket.

"Two seconds in, and she's already mortified." I brush my hands together in victory. "My work here is done."

Josie has a smirk on her face as she flips her hair over to one side. "That was... entertaining," she says, eyeing me as I approach.

"You're not hating on my exceptional dance moves, are you?" I wink at her, shoving my hands into my pockets and tilting my head to the side. "I was *oozing* skill and finesse."

She laughs, and it's a genuine laugh that makes her nose crinkle. "The dance moves were on point, but the taste in music is questionable."

My smile stretches as I maintain her gaze for as long as possible until she looks away.

Josie shuffles in place, twisting her hair. She looks at Olivia, who is hoisting her overnight bag further up her shoulder, using her for a distraction. "You'll be on your best behavior for Mr. Hart, right?"

I glance at Summer, seeing her mouth open to correct Josie on the last name—and I panic.

"Bunny, can you get the water boiling for the spaghetti?"

Summer looks up at me, then back at Josie, closes her mouth, and motions for Olivia to follow her to the kitchen.

Dodged that bullet.

Josie watches her fondly as she goes. She shifts her eyes to me, her expression charmed. "Bunny?"

"Nickname. It just kind of stuck."

"Cute… it fits her." Josie browses the room and then asks, "Do I get the grand tour?"

A grand tour of our eleven-hundred square foot ranch with only one bathroom, creaky floors, and shitty water pressure. Cool. I'm sure she'll be falling head over heels in love with me by dusk. "There's not much to see. I'm sure you've stayed in hotel rooms bigger than this."

Josie gets a look in her eyes that almost makes me wonder if I've insulted her.

"I'm not like that, you know."

I study her. Her stare is sharp, like she *needs* me to know. "Not like what?"

"I don't know…" Josie shrugs her shoulders, pursing her lips, as if trying to find the right word. "Uppity, I guess. Yes, our family has a nice house… but I really don't care about appearances or social status. My life hasn't always been like that."

Interesting.

For some reason, I believe her.

Summer joins us back in the living room with Olivia in tow, pulling her down the short hallway to her bedroom. "My room isn't as cool as yours, but I have a ton of makeup we can play with…" Her voice trails off as the girls disappear into the room and shut the door.

Josie and I look at each other at the same time; there's a bit of an awkwardness, like we don't know what to say or do now that we've been ditched. She fiddles with the hem of her pink blouse, sending me a smile that borders on shy, then ducks her head to break away from my gaze.

I'm having some sort of effect on her, but I don't want to get too sure of myself yet. It may only be the remnants of our last interaction together— when she opened up to me in her driveway, sharing a part of her heart. An old wound. When she showed me her tattoo that mirrors that of an old love…

And me.

I take a hesitant step forward, pushing my luck. "How are you?"

She snaps her head up, startled, almost like I asked her to strip naked. I suppose I did, in a way. But not in the fun kind of way.

Not in the way I'm now thinking about in great detail.

I like women, okay? My brain doesn't need much of a nudge to go there.

"Oh, um… I'm good. Things are good," she replies, wringing her hands together. She understands what I'm referencing and continues. "Sorry about all that. The party drama."

"No need to apologize," I assure her. "I didn't mind."

Josie nods, her eyes flickering toward me, then shifting to her hands. "I never thanked you for intervening in the study."

I take another step forward, inching my way into her personal bubble, wondering if she's going to retreat—wondering if my proximity is too much. Too bold.

She remains where she stands.

"Again… no need," I say. She smiles up at me, and while I have her where I want her, I press onward. "Stay for dinner."

Another look of surprise washes over her. "Oh, I can't. I appreciate the offer, but Ben will be home in a couple of hours, and I don't want him to worry."

"A couple of hours is plenty of time to enjoy the privilege of trying my world famous spaghetti."

"World famous, huh?" Josie's smile widens with amusement. I don't think she's as easily fooled as a nine-year-old.

I cross my arms, puffing out my chest with dramatic flair. "Oh, yeah. It's *renowned*. I'm just waiting for The Food Network to contact me at this point."

"Sounds fancy," Josie laughs.

I find myself liking the way she laughs, which irritates the fuck out of me, so I inwardly scold myself and gesture her towards the kitchen. "Come on, the girls will be thrilled if you stay."

Her expression wavers, and I can see the conflict running through her head, so I turn and exit into the kitchen, somehow knowing she'll follow.

She does.

"I suppose I *have* to try this now. When you're on the Food Network, I can brag that I tasted it first." Josie trails behind me, pulling out a chair from the kitchen table. She rests her elbow down, then props her chin in her hand as she watches me pull ingredients out of the pantry.

I falter when I look at her, flashing back to eighteen months ago when Katrina sat in that exact same seat, in that exact same position. I remember the moment like it was yesterday—mainly because it was the moment my world started coming undone. I take in a deep breath as I gather my bearings and hope Josie doesn't notice.

She looks perplexed when I start pulling fresh vegetables from the fridge. "You're making it from scratch?" Josie asks as if the very thought is comparable to me having just discovered life on Mars.

"What, I don't strike you as the culinary type?" I raise an eyebrow at her, but my smile is playful.

Josie drums her fingers along her cheek and hesitates, debating what she's about to say. She chews on her lip for a second, and I throw her a smile, turning back to the onions. I pause when I hear her words, so soft she could be talking to herself.

"You're not what I expected."

I stop mid-onion, my chest tightening.

Her words hit me somewhere deep.

I've been building armor around myself for the last year-and-a-half, and a mere five words just poked holes in it. Nothing huge—more like pinholes than a fissure—but it's something. I look back and see Josie gazing at me with a wistful smile, her lips the same blush color as her blouse, and I swallow back the peculiar feelings.

It makes me fucking uncomfortable.

I need to recover fast, so I attempt to return to our light-hearted banter. "You mean, you expected a pompous asshat with a shitty turn radius who sucks at cooking?" I tease. "I really need to work on my first impressions."

Josie chuckles again, burying her face into her palm. "You're never going to let me live that down, are you?" she wonders, her voice muffled by her hand.

I pour the spaghetti into the boiling water and glance at her over my shoulder. "Nope."

She glares at me; though, her expression is good-natured. "I mean, you *were* hitting on a married woman," she reminds me.

I don't need the reminder. I'm well aware of my intentions. And part of me wants to say, *"It worked. You're sitting in my kitchen while I make you spaghetti"*, but that would likely be a bad move that would end in her walking out the door. Instead, I throw her a wink as I start to chop an onion. "I don't discriminate." My tone is a little flirtatious, a little suggestive, and I look at her again to gauge her reaction. Her expression wavers again, the conflict obvious —*I'm getting under her skin.* She is not immune to my subtle advances.

And yet, she is married.

There's a fucking piece of paper that legally binds her to a cheating sack of shit.

My impression of Josie Grant is that of someone with integrity. Unlike

Katrina, I've no doubt she is committed to that fucking piece of paper, so it's going to take more than flirtatious banter to get her in bed with me. It's going to take more than damn good spaghetti.

I need to up my game. Open up.

Let her in…

I need to get uncomfortable.

11

ELEVEN

Benjamin Grant works late on Friday nights. Spaghetti dinner dates have now become somewhat of a tradition. I mean, we've only had two of them so far, but it's close enough to be called a pattern, and oddly, I'm finding myself looking forward to them. I think it's because of Summer and Olivia—the way they engage and giggle, whispering secrets into each other's ears. Their connection is undeniable, and it's endearing.

Tonight we sat around the small wooden table in my eat-in kitchen, watching the girls come to life with jokes and stories as spaghetti sauce dripped into their laps and they laughed until they cried. There was something magical about it. There was an innate joy that crept into my heart and burrowed deep while I drank in this blossoming friendship, so pure it filled the hollow parts of me. I would glance over at Josie from time to time, who delicately sucked strings of spaghetti noodles into her mouth before dabbing at her lips, equally enraptured by the girls' interaction. At one point, I zoned out, staring at Josie as she belly laughed with our daughters. She turned to me, catching my gaze. Catching me off guard.

"What?" she asked.

Her tone was both inquisitive and charmed, and it was a combination that unsettled me. I shook my head with a pathetic chuckle, not even having an answer to give, and instead, focused on how many times I could twirl the noodles around my fork.

Three times.

The girls run off to Summer's bedroom after the table is cleared, and Josie begins to wash my dishes as I pour the remaining spaghetti sauce into a Tupperware container. I'm studying her, marginally perplexed when she rolls up the sleeves to her designer sweater and begins to scrub the plates. She glances at me, then down at the sauce that dribbles over the side of the rim because I'm distracted. I look down at the pool of tomato puree quickly forming on my countertop and groan.

Josie giggles. "That sauce is too good to be wasted," she notes, multitasking far better than me. "It's probably even illegal in at least three-and-a-half countries."

I can't help the sharp laugh that escapes me as I swipe up the mess with a paper towel. Then I watch as she squeezes a soap-soaked sponge onto a dinner plate. "You don't need to do my dishes," I tell her. "In fact, Summer might get mad at you. She loves doing them."

Surprise dances across her face as she flips her hair over her shoulder with a jerk of her head. "Really? Where do I get one of those?"

I seal the lid on the container, popping it up to release the air, and sweep past her to the refrigerator, catching a whiff of gardenias as I pass. "Etsy, maybe," I joke, closing the refrigerator door. I perch my shoulder against it with my hands in my pockets, watching the smile tug at the corners of her mouth. I take in the way she's cleaning my dishes like it's nothing out of the ordinary. It unnerves me. I think it's because I'm keenly aware of Katrina's absence, and our old traditions, and the companionship of another woman in my home.

I think I miss that.

Twenty minutes later, Josie is checking her phone as she strolls into the living room and toward the front door. "Shoot, it's after seven. Ben will be home soon." She looks up at me beneath thick lashes, her golden eyes glowing. "Thank you for dinner. It's been really nice spending time with the girls." Then she ducks her head with a light laugh as if what she's going to say next is preposterous. "I don't have any friends like you."

A stab of guilt pokes at me. Her words and her movements, the way she's pressing the pads of her fingertips together and biting her lip… she's vulnerable right now. And I've been anything but. I've been hardened and manipulative and the complete opposite of a friend, and she doesn't even know it.

I take a heartbeat to center my thoughts. I need to remind myself why I'm doing this. I'm not intentionally trying to hurt Josie Grant—no, I'm trying to destroy her husband. She is merely a pawn in my game, and I need to remember that. I can't let myself feel guilty, or else the intricate web I've woven will come undone. I need to focus on the bigger picture.

I blow out a breath, hating how unstable it sounds, and roll back on my heels. "Yeah. Me, too." It's true, of course. I don't have any friends like Josie—she's the only one I'm trying to fuck in order to exact revenge on her husband. "I never gave you the grand tour last week," I say before she can turn away from me. I might as well try to soak up as much time with her as possible while she's here.

Josie glances at the door, then back at me, deciding what to do. She finally concedes with a nod. "Okay."

She follows me down the stupidly short hallway, and we poke our head into the spare bedroom that used to be Katrina's craft space but is nothing but a storage room now. I show her the one tiny bathroom with turquoise walls, iridescent penny tiles, and a frog-patterned shower curtain that Summer doesn't find nearly as cute as she used to. We stop by Summer's room next, her pink walls painted over last year with a shade of royal purple, and her girly decorations replaced with posters of terrible bands. The girls are huddled over Summer's computer, playing some game I'll never understand. They don't even see us in the doorway smiling at their easy friendship, so we move onto the final room. The master bedroom.

"This is our room," I say as we step through the threshold. I have to stop and catch my breath, wishing I could take back those words. My body tenses, my teeth grinding together in a way that makes my jaw throb. "I mean... *my* room."

Fuck. Even after all this time, it's still an impossible concept to grasp. Katrina, this house, this family... we were just always an *"our."*

Josie gives me grace and pretends not to notice the slip. She walks ahead of me, boldly entering the room that doubles as my writing space, looking around. Cheerleader Rachel lifts her head, giving me a wary look when Josie wanders over to the laptop. It sits open, my manuscript lighting up the screen. Rachel's pompoms do *not* flutter in celebration. She's as cautious as I am—this is private domain.

Yet I walked her straight in here, as though she belonged.

Josie's eyes flicker towards it as she brushes a gilded strand of hair off her forehead, illuminated by the setting sun peeking through the cracked curtains and the glow from the laptop—the only light in the room. She fiddles with the long sleeves of her chocolate sweater, then glances at me, curiosity filling her eyes. "Is that your next book?" she wonders.

Now *I'm* the one feeling vulnerable… but I suppose I need to be if I want to get closer to her. It's what I've been telling myself, anyway—that I was going to need to get uncomfortable. And here we are.

Uncomfortable isn't the word for it, though… it's like an infringement on my very soul.

I don't share my stories with anyone, nor my workspace. Writing is more than a job. It's an expression, a piece of me. A naked piece, particularly when the work is still in progress. It pains me to even show my editor before it's ready to go.

I swallow back my pride and nod my head. "Yeah. I'm only halfway done with it. I've hit a bit of a slump recently." Massaging the back of my neck, I watch Josie's lips pucker together as she absorbs my response. She steps away respectfully, moving the few feet toward the bed.

"So, this is where the magic happens," she states, her smile gentle.

She's referring to my books, but she sits down on the edge of my bed as she says this, and I can't help the mischievous tickle that sweeps through me. A grin breaks free. I nod with a quick wink to where she sits on the bed. "That's *definitely* where the magic happens."

Josie catches my not-so-subtle intent and immediately rolls her eyes, popping up from the mattress. "Gross."

The ghost of a smile on her lips betrays her, as does the blush creeping up her neck.

The peachy-orange glow from the window is casting a sliver of light on Josie Grant as if she's just taken center stage in a grand performance. *Oh, the irony.* She has no idea the role she's playing right at this very moment. She has no idea that I'm the director, feeding her lines, turning her into a character in my twisted tale of revenge.

Turning her into a character.

Guilt bubbles back to the surface, and I choke it down.

"Say it."

I blink at her. I must have zoned out, gone to that *place*, and she noticed. *Damnit.*

So far, every time she's asked this, I've had to make something up on the fly—I'm honestly *really* bad at the "Say It" game.

"I was thinking about my ex-wife," I blurt. I'm not sure if that was a better alternative, but I say it anyway, and the flash of sympathy in Josie's eyes does not go unnoticed. And, well, I suppose it wasn't a complete lie— the hard truth is that I'm always thinking about Katrina.

"What happened?" Josie asks, her voice soft and lilting.

A swarm of responses buzz through my head like a plague of insects.

I don't want to tell her. And yet… I do.

For a moment, I just watch as she watches me. The pressure of ugly truths builds inside, like a geyser ready to bust free. Part of me wants to spill my guts to her, out myself, confess my sins. I want her to know the truth about the man she married. The *monster* she's in love with. But it's too soon. At best, we're only up to the middle of my mission. Maybe it would be enough for her to leave him, and there would be a small satisfaction in that, but it wouldn't be enough for me. I need to lay claim to Josie first. I need to make her mine.

I need to hit him where it hurts.

That was the plan Vengeance first whispered in my ear, the one that gave me purpose, drove me to put one foot in front of the other, and I'm following it until the bitter end.

"She cheated on me," I tell her. "She was cheating on me for months, and I had no idea." The rage is simmering as I give my feelings life. My own words affect me physically, causing my mouth to go dry as a lump forms in the back of my throat. "She fell in love with another man, and I had no fucking clue. She played the part of a doting wife while she made plans to leave me for someone else. While she—"

I swear to God I see Josie's eyes well up with tears.

Fuck.

"I'm so sorry, Evan. You didn't deserve that," she whispers.

Deserve. I dwell on that word for longer than I should as I take a few steps to where Josie is standing at the foot of my bed. Her eyes are fixed on me as I approach, glossed over, spearing me with her pity. Part of me wants her to feel bad. She *chose* the man who did this to me. She sleeps in his bed at night.

I stop short of her as my eyes skim her face, still full of sorrow—sorrow for *me*. The sun has set lower in the sky, and the room has dimmed, but she is still lightly bathed in a warm glow.

Does Josie *deserve* any of this? Does she deserve to be collateral damage?

The conflict swirls around me as she waits for my reply, but the truth is, I have no idea what to even say. Luckily, a quarry of girly giggles breaks through the haze, and Josie clears her throat, pulling out her phone again to glance at the time.

"I need to go," she says, a little flustered, either by my proximity or my silence. Josie offers me a thin-lipped smile, doing her best to squeeze by without brushing against me.

I could step to the side... but I don't.

She maneuvers her way past me, and I watch her go without saying a word.

I stand there, staring at nothing as I listen to the voices in the hall. I hear Josie tell Olivia that it's time to go. I hear the girls say their goodbyes as the front door shuts behind them. I hear Summer call through my closed door that she'll be in her room reading until bedtime.

My reply comes from somewhere outside my body as I answer her, as I tell her I'll be there to tuck her in later.

All I can think about is Josie... her compassion for me. The way she stood here, so broken for me, so vulnerable, so flustered at my nearness.

She's not the only one feeling a little flustered. I'm hot, and I'm frustrated—and I suddenly feel the need for an ice-fucking-cold shower. I don't know if it's more to cool the boiling rage brought on by my recounting of Katrina's betrayal, or the inherent sexual tension that seems to have lingered in my bedroom, long after Josie walked out. Then I think about Josie going home to that bastard husband of hers, and how he doesn't deserve his perfect world with his beautiful wife when he stole *mine* out from under me...

Yeah. I'm going to go with rage.

At first, a cold shower seems like the perfect cure. I strip naked and turn the water on, but after a couple of minutes, I'm just as pissed off as I had been... only, now it's because my teeth are chattering as my dick tries to fucking hide. My balls are shriveling, and apparently I'm a pussy because this is not helping.

At all.

Screw it. If I'm going to be mad anyway, I might as well be comfortable. Reaching for the faucet, I turn it on hot, letting it steam away the goosebumps. Finally, my muscles start to relax, my balls loosening, and thank God for that, too... *that sucked.*

At least I'm warm—but no less angry—and now I keep thinking about how blind Josie is to what her husband has done to her. I think about her vulnerability with me lately, how appealing it is when I know she has another side that takes no shit. Then I start wondering what she might be like in bed. Is she pliant and submissive, or a naughty tigress? I can see both sides in her—and I really want to find out.

I grab the soap, scrubbing under my arms, across my chest, and by the time I've reached my stomach, my dick is half hard. *Fuck,* I need to get laid, and thinking about my plans for Josie Grant isn't helping. I reach down and stroke my cock until it's fully awakened; the water is warm and I'm horny as hell, so why not? Maybe it'll help me calm the fuck down, then I can get some work done before bed.

I tighten my hand around the base, thinking of Josie Grant's ass in yoga pants. I pull my hips back, squeeze the tip, then thrust forward quickly, in and out, as I imagine Josie Grant's ass *out* of those yoga pants. My spine arches, and I allow my head to fall back, my mouth open wide as I groan into the hot water raining over my face.

Fuck yes, I needed this.

I think about a different version of how things might have gone tonight—a version where I took Summer to her house for a sleepover. I come back home, only to find that Josie surprises me by getting a babysitter and showing up on my front doorstep. I'm in my room, writing...

Wait—no, I'm right here in the shower, under the warm water, thinking of her. It all plays out as if I were writing an erotic scene in a book:

She finds the spare key, letting herself in, following the sound of running water. I'm too busy pumping my cock to hear her open the bathroom door, but from the corner of my eye, I see the shower curtain move. My hand never loses rhythm as my head pivots, finding her on the other side of the curtain. She's wearing a flowing dress with a plunging neckline and spaghetti straps, patterned with large red roses, complete with thorny stems. Her eyes are locked on what my hand is doing to my cock, and I lean into it further, my hips moving faster.

Oh... shit. I can't hold back the moan, it feels so fucking good. My muscles tense, along with my balls. Josie's jaw goes slack as she stares, as she watches my dick sliding in and out of my hand, slippery and wet. The sound of it fills my ears, and I want to replace that water with another kind of wetness. "Take it off," I rasp, nodding at her dress. Her eyes rise slowly, trailing over the rivulets of water running down my body, until she locks her gaze with mine. It's full of lust. Want. She slowly moves the straps off her shoulders, doing exactly as I tell her. My hand moves faster, but I'm not fucking coming until I'm buried deep inside her. Her dress falls away, pooling around her feet, my breath shuddering as I envision Josie Grant in all of her naked glory. I'm panting now, my heart pumping faster, *everything* pumping faster, and without losing momentum on my cock, I reach out to pull her inside.

She grabs my ass with one hand, digging her fingernails into the muscle while she cups my balls with the other. My dick jumps, and *fuck,* I'm going to come—I *need* to come, but no, no... not yet...

There's something I need more.

I need my fucking revenge, goddammit.

Josie closes her hand over mine, helping me jerk my raging hard-on as our lips find each other, frantically. I kiss her, hard and messy, our teeth nipping and tongues twisting. My eyes are closed tightly, and I can see it, I can feel it. I can hear my hand slapping against myself as I move faster...

Josie's warm, naked body rubs up against mine as she moans into my mouth. Her moan echoes my own, and I could stay like this forever—but this isn't about romance, for fuck's sake, so I break free and spin her around. Her palms slap against the wet tile, and I imagine both of my hands holding hers there as I crush our bodies together.

She pushes her hips back to allow me access, and I can almost hear her purr, *"Evan, fuck me... Fuck me, now. I need your cock inside me... I need you."*

Fuck. Yes.

My dick swells in my hand as I shove it in her tight little hole. She cries out with pleasure, and I relish the sound. I'm consumed by the feel of the tight, hot little pussy belonging to Josie Grant. *Josie fucking Grant*—the goddamn wife of the bane of my existence.

She goes through her days thinking she has a happy marriage, but she's just as duped as I was.

They betrayed us, Josie... this is our motherfucking revenge.

Vengeance swirls around my bathroom like a shadowy hurricane.

I hate you... I hate you... I fucking hate all of you.

I pump faster, slamming all the way back to my balls and out to the tip, squeezing my dick like her inner muscles will squeeze me, as Josie Grant comes... and comes... screaming my name.

"Fuck me, Evan. Fuck me harder."

Fuck. You. Benjamin. Grant.

Fuck. You.

Pressure tightens every muscle and vein in my body. *Oh... shit... fuck...* There's so much pressure. My cock swells to nearly bursting, and then it *does* burst. I groan through my teeth as my dick pulses over and over, filling Josie to overflowing.

My hips jerk as I come all over my fucking shower, opening my eyes just in time to watch it swirl down the drain.

I exhale loud and long, relief taking the place of frustration. God, I needed that...

Finally allowing the tension inside me to release, I collapse against the shower wall.

Then, my mind begins to spin. Now that my body is relaxed, I'm plagued again by the questions that nagged me in the bedroom—questions I'd rather not think on too hard because the answer to them all is "no."

No.

I *don't* think Josie deserves what I've pulled her into... I really don't.

But this isn't about what she deserves.

This is about what I deserve.

Another week whirls by as the leaves begin to change to vibrant shades of yellow and gold. The October air is crisp and filled with promises of pumpkin carving, hayrides, and apple cider.

Hell. Yes.

My favorite month is here, and it's the only thing keeping me from teetering over the edge and succumbing to my own personal demons. That, and my daughter, of course.

Oh, and Reese's Peanut Butter Cups. I'm looking forward to confiscating them from Summer's trick-or-treat bag in a few short weeks.

I canceled spaghetti night, so I guess I can throw "keeping traditions" into my little box of growing failures. But Logan texted me to hang out tonight, and honestly, I need the escape. I dropped Summer off with Josie and Olivia for their weekly sleepover, and I'll pick her up tomorrow after my inevitable hangover passes. Benjamin is out of town on business again, so maybe I can make up an excuse to linger at Josie's house longer than necessary.

Logan and I stand outside the bustling bar, sucking on our cigarettes and talking shit. The air is chilly enough that I can't tell the difference between my breath and the plume of smoke that filters out through my nostrils. I lean back against the distressed brick with an even more distressed sigh, propping the bottom of my shoe up along the wall.

"I think I'm going to ask her to marry me."

Logan's admission has me coughing on the sharp drag I just inhaled.

"Jesus. Are you for real?" I don't mean to come off as disparaging, but the news shocks me, and to be frank, I think Logan is making a mistake. Not the Amber part, of course—the marriage part.

Fuck marriage. It's overrated.

And meaningless.

Logan lets out a knowing chuckle, smashing his cigarette with the toe of his shoe. "I get it, man. I know you had a shit experience in that department, but I'm crazy about this girl, you know? I feel like I'll regret it my whole damn life if I don't ask her."

"Shit," I breathe out through clenched teeth. I glance over at my friend and can't help but notice the light in his eyes. There is love there, and I remember that feeling all too well. I push back my unwarranted opinions on the subject and regard Logan with warm approval, slapping my hand against his shoulder and giving it a solid squeeze. "Well, I'm happy for you. You know I'll support you."

"You better," Logan smiles, pushing my arm away with a good-natured punch. "You know you're going to be my best man."

"What about your brother?" I propose with a slight frown.

"My brother's an asshole. He can be an usher."

We both laugh and pull out another cigarette. A content silence settles between us as I glance back over at Logan who still has that damn look in his eyes. I'm envious for a moment. I know I'm bitter and resentful, and he doesn't deserve that.

We're both leaning against the wall, cigarettes in hand, with almost identical black leather jackets, and it might even be hard for someone to tell us apart. Dark hair with light hazel irises, stubbled jawline, lean but well-muscled. Only... there is one large, glaring difference.

Logan is a man in love, while I'm a man drowning in loneliness, and there's no disguising it.

It's in our eyes.

It wasn't long ago when Logan and Amber were in their on-again, off-again phase, that our positions were reversed. It feels strange, having become the one without someone.

The man alone.

Our silence is interrupted by the ping of my phone, alerting me of a new text message. I rummage through the pocket of my jeans and glance at the screen.

I can see Logan looking over my shoulder, being obnoxiously nosy.

"Mean Girl From the Gym?" he questions, curiosity and amusement clear in his tone.

I open the message. It's a video of Josie and the girls lip syncing to a One Direction song—and damnit, I have zero business knowing the name of that band. I'd rather snuff my cigarette out on my forehead than ever admit to knowing this song out loud.

I feel myself smiling as I watch the three of them sing into their own respective hairbrushes, overly animated, dancing around in their pajamas, half-laughing, half-singing to the catchy pop song.

Wait… not catchy.

I meant horrid. *Dreadful*, even.

It's truly an abomination.

"Damn, who's that?"

Logan is leaning over me, glued in on Josie bouncing around with the girls, her honey hair cascading over her face, her smile as wide as mine. I clear my throat and jab Logan in the ribs with my elbow as an odd possessive feeling shoots through me. "You're practically engaged. Stop drooling on my phone."

"Are you sleeping with that chick? She's way out of your league, man. I'm impressed."

I grumble and shoot him a blatant "fuck you" look. "She's the mother of Summer's new BFF. We met last month at the gym."

"Since when are you a gym rat? And since when do you say *BFF*?" Logan shakes his head with pity. "I'm losing you, aren't I?"

I swat at him because he's annoying me and step away. I resume the video, which I had to pause twice because of Logan's tiresome interrogation, and my smile resurfaces as the girls finish their dance routine. Summer's hairbrush accidentally goes flying across the room, and Olivia laughs so hard she falls over, prompting Summer to do the same. Both kids are on the floor as Josie runs at the camera, her face close and her smile mischievous, and says, "The hairbrush microphone will *never* die."

She winks and ends the video.

I find myself staring at my screen, zoned out, and apparently still smiling because Logan kicks me in the shin to wake me up.

"I didn't know you were seeing someone," he says, flicking his cigarette to the cement.

I stuff my phone back in my pocket, suddenly craving a stiff drink. Maybe a Jack and Coke.

Maybe minus the Coke.

"I'm not." I dismiss him as I put out my own cigarette and turn to head inside the bar.

I don't want to discuss Josie Grant with my friend. He wouldn't approve, and it's none of his goddamn business.

But I can hear Logan's response before I make it through the doors, and I pause for just a moment, closing my eyes, tensing my jaw, and choosing to ignore him.

"Could have fooled me."

TWELVE

THE HANGOVER IS REAL.

It's one o'clock in the afternoon, and I still feel like I was smacked upside the head with a baseball bat, then hit by a semi, then run over by a larger semi, picked up by a tornado, and dropped in the middle of a hurricane. You would think that at thirty-two years old, I would have gotten the memo about the repercussions of excessive alcohol intake.

Alas…

I'm standing on Josie's porch, looking like I came straight from the morgue. There's a fresh scratch on my arm from stumbling into the trellis while losing my balance on the porch steps. So, now I'm hungover *and* bleeding, and the asshole flowers are laughing at my expense.

I've already been here several minutes, leaning with my forehead against the front door as I work up the motivation to interact with the living. If I were writing this scene into a book, someone would whip open the door, and I would go toppling into the house, spilling into that someone's arms. Cue hilarity.

And then it actually happens.

Only… there is no hilarity—it fucking sucks.

I'm never writing this scene.

I stagger forward, partially catching myself on the doorframe and half falling onto Josie as she teeters back, her hands clasped around my shoulders.

"Evan?"

I quickly find my footing and pull myself from her embrace. "Sorry. I was… leaning. And then you… opened…" I wave my finger as if that finishes the statement for me.

"You look terrible. Are you sick?"

My hand palms the back of my neck, gaze averted. "Hungover," I admit, slightly embarrassed.

She squints at me. "So, that's why I received four blurry pictures of some random guy doing strange poses with a pool stick."

I pull my lips between my teeth, my eyes drifting closed as I contemplate just booking it. Maybe she'll forget I was even here. Maybe she'll forget I ever existed. I sigh wearily, dragging my non-punctured palm from my neck and running it over my face. "That would be why."

"Oh…" Josie touches my arm gingerly, examining my battle wound. "What happened here?"

"Your roses attacked," I tell her, motioning in their general direction. I neglect to mention that her house is onto me, and I'm likely being punished.

Her expression wavers between amusement and sympathy. She tips her head toward the opposite end of the house, encouraging me to follow. "Come on. We can patch you up, and then I'll make you a smoothie. It should take the edge off."

I lag behind her as we enter the kitchen, not really giving a fuck about the disapproval I feel radiating from the walls.

Josie seems to have had a much better night than me; she's bright-eyed, bushy-tailed, and practically emanating rainbows and sunbeams. I'm surprised she didn't come to the door riding a fucking unicorn. Her gray sweater-dress looks like it's about to swallow her up, but I think that's the point of the look, and I have to say… it's kind of sexy. I lower my eyes as she sashays in front of me, mesmerized by the enticing sway of her hips. I shake my head, wincing when the stabbing pain reminds me I'm a dumbass.

Ow. Bad move, Evan.

She ducks into a nearby half bath. "My father was a rose gardener," she says, loud enough to be heard while rummaging through the medicine cabinet. She returns with some ointment and a damp washcloth. "He loved the thorns as much as the flowers," she continues, dabbing at my arm. "Used to say the fact that they could hurt you made them more beautiful. It seemed strange at the time, but I get it now." She smiles faintly with something like nostalgia, and I suddenly realize she spoke of her father in the past tense.

I'm a little slow today.

"Hmm, maybe roses aren't my thing," I say, wincing when she presses a little too hard. "I think I prefer my beauty *without* a side of pain."

"Truly beautiful things are like that sometimes, though, aren't they?" She takes my hand and lays it on top of the washcloth, indicating I should keep it there. "They can cut you... they can make you bleed. But that's how you know you're alive."

I'm taken aback for a moment, my fuzzy brain unable to process a response. She's clearly speaking of things deeper than me being stabbed by her flowers.

"Looks like you'll live," she notes, patting my shoulder before crossing the room to the fridge, continuing on her "Nurse Josie" mission. "Now, let me get you that smoothie I promised."

I'm pretty sure even the hungover version of me can deal with a scratch, but I'm not one to say no to the attentions of an attractive woman. "Smoothie, huh? With kale and shit?"

Josie begins pulling greens out of the fridge. "Yes... with kale and shit." She gives me a humored side-eye as she rips apart the celery. "You sound like Olivia. Minus the swearing."

I'm not sure I can safely ingest kale right now, but I decide not to disappoint her. Leaning my hip against the island, I watch her float around the kitchen like some kind of hangover doctor. "It looked like you guys had fun last night." I think back to the video and the way it made me smile, warming my cold heart. "Thanks for sending that spectacular lip sync performance, by the way. You completely put me in my place about the hairbrush. I'll never question it again."

She snorts while she peels a banana. "The girls had a blast. They always do." She glances up at me mid-peel as a genuine smile spreads across her face. "Summer is an amazing kid. You're really doing a great job, Evan."

Her comment gives me pause. I'm struck for a moment by the fact that no one has ever said that to me before. I'm not looking for validation—I love my daughter more than anything, and I give her my whole heart. I do the best I can, and she *is* an amazing kid. That's more than enough for me. But hearing it... well, it sure doesn't feel terrible. I nod as Josie goes back to prepping the assortment of fruits and veggies. "Thanks."

"Being a single parent isn't easy," she continues. "I've been there. Some days, all I wanted was someone to say that to me. I'd cry myself to sleep wondering if I was ruining my daughter." She laughs, but it's not a funny laugh. It's a little self-deprecating. "It's hard doing it alone."

I find myself unable to hold back my curiosity. As I get to know her, I'm becoming increasingly confused as to how a woman like this ended up with a douchebag like Benjamin Grant, and I really want to know more about her life before him. "Did you have friends to help you? Family?"

Josie catches my gaze for a brief second, then focuses on her task. "I lost my parents when I was a teenager. My mother died of breast cancer when I was only a freshman, then my father passed away three years later from a heart attack." She smiles, but it doesn't reach her eyes. "A broken heart, I think."

Shit. Josie lost both of her parents and the father of her child in such a short amount of time. There's a wave of empathy that rushes through me, and for the first time, I allow myself to feel it. I don't brush it off. I don't dismiss it. Josie didn't deserve to go through all that—just like she doesn't deserve a cheating husband.

I take a breath, looking down as I tap my knuckles against the quartz. "My parents are still around, but they're not really... *around*, you know? They retired to Florida before Summer was born and came to visit her once when she was a baby. Now it's just the occasional birthday card or phone call."

Josie sets down the bag of kale and leans forward on her arms, giving me her full attention. "That makes me sad." Her eyes match the wistfulness of her words. "I'm sorry."

"Don't be," I say. "I'm not. I stopped being sorry a long time ago." And then I feel awkward because Josie doesn't even have a chance at a relationship with her parents... so, I blurt out the first thing that pops into my head. "So, you keep all the roses around because of your father?"

"Originally, yes. They still make me think of him—the way he designed his garden so meticulously, picking each one for a specific reason..." Her gaze begins to drift, taking on a faraway look. "They became about more than that, though."

I raise my eyebrows in interest, but she's not focusing on me anymore. "Oh? What else?"

Josie's cheeks stretch into a smile that's as distant as wherever her memory has taken her. She chews on her lip as she reminisces. "Adam," she breathes into the still air, and suddenly I feel like an intruder on something very personal. I turn my attention back to my arm, peeking under the washcloth where the bleeding has nearly stopped. "Sorry," she murmurs, coming back to the present, her eyes trailing down my arm and coming to land on my tattoo. They linger a moment before lifting to meet mine. "The roses were how I met Olivia's father. His name was Adam. He had a summer job in a garden center the year after I lost my father. My dad and I had this ritual every year. We'd go around to the local nurseries and pick out a new rose together. So, the summer after he passed away, I was driving by one and couldn't resist stopping. I thought I could handle it."

"But it was more difficult than you thought," I discern when I notice her attention drifting again.

She takes a deep breath. "I had a meltdown in the middle of the roses," she says on the exhale. "Adam was the one who found me, sitting on the ground next to a climbing rose bush, sobbing." Her expression holds a soft sentimentality, mixed with melancholy. "It was mortifying at the time. We were both just teenagers, and he wasn't really sure what to do with the crying girl blocking his way when he came through with the hose—but he took me back to the employee break room and helped me get myself together. The next time I went back to that garden center, it was to see him." There's a warmth lighting her eyes that makes me want to reach out and touch her face, so I squeeze my arm over the washcloth, letting the brief stab of pain ground me.

"That's quite a way to meet someone."

"He ended up buying me that rose bush I broke down next to. I transplanted it when I moved… always kept it with me. It's actually the same one that "attacked" you out front," she laughs.

An eerie chill creeps down my spine; I really hope it has nothing to do with the house ghost.

I shake it off while she blinks away the heaviness of the moment. "Any siblings?" she asks, suddenly changing the subject.

"Nope. You?"

"A sister," Josie pauses as if she's debating saying more. She lifts up on her palms with a sigh. "Carrie. She lives in Appleton. She's the reason I was having a bad day when you met me."

I tilt my head to the side as I study her. I always wondered about that, but never felt it was appropriate to ask. Maybe I didn't care enough.

But now I kind of do.

"You don't get along?" I wonder.

"Quite the contrary, actually. We're extremely close." Josie bites her lip, her eyes lowering to the countertop. She tucks her hair behind her ear, revealing a golden hoop earring that dances against her cheek. "She was diagnosed with breast cancer… again. She's been in remission for four years, so it was kind of a shock."

Jesus. Now is definitely not the time to fill her in on her husband's extracurricular activities. "Damn," is all I can manage.

"Yeah."

Josie continues to busy herself around the kitchen, gathering her ingredients and bringing them over to some kind of blender contraption. I don't own any fancy shit except for my car, so I have no idea what rich people call blenders these days. But it basically looks like a blender on steroids.

"I mean, if anyone can beat this, Carrie can," Josie proceeds. "She's already a mother to two heathen twin boys who make the term "terrible twos" sound like a trip to Disney World." A smile emerges on her lips as she pours organic almond milk into the device. "Another round of chemotherapy will be a cakewalk for her."

I perch myself on a nearby stool and rest my elbows on the island counter, folding my hands together, then settling my gaze on Josie. I don't know how someone can experience tragedy after tragedy like that and still persevere. It takes a certain kind of resilience and grace that I sure as fuck don't have.

We hear the girls before they materialize from around the corner. Olivia says something about anime, and just as they appear, Josie turns on the blender, the sound grating through my head. Summer slaps her hands over her ears, jogging over to me with a horrified expression.

"Dad!" Summer shouts over the shrill cacophony of pureeing hangover juice. "This sounds just like your awful music!"

I laugh at that, pulling her into my lap with a teasing growl. "Take it back, or you're grounded for three weeks," I say into her ear.

She squeals, squirming out of my grip. "I only speak the truth!"

Josie stops the blender, lifting the lid and inspecting the contents. "Shoot, it needs more liquid," she mutters, strolling over to the refrigerator.

Summer skips her way to the blender, examining the green sludge. "This is so cool," she says, her fingers trailing up to the buttons.

Josie glances over her shoulder, doing a double take, then rushes to where Summer is standing. "Oh, honey, the lid's not—"

Too late.

I drop the washcloth and leap from my chair right as the contents of the blender shoot out the top, splattering Josie and Summer in what looks like a scene from *The Exorcist.* Josie scrambles to turn it off, and there's a deafening silence for just a moment as they look down at their outfits covered in kale puke.

Then Olivia starts giggling, while laughter simultaneously bursts from me. We all stare at each other in comical horror.

Summer is first to speak, turning her wide, mortified eyes at Josie. "I am *so* sorry."

"I'll grab you a change of clothes," Olivia offers through her giggles before darting towards the staircase.

Josie finally erupts into a fit of laughter as if the current events are just now registering. Her sweater dress is dappled green with slimy chunks of banana dripping down to the floor. She bends over, her laughter intensifying, her arms clutching at her stomach. I approach the scene of the crime, my smile as bright as the neon goop, and reach for the paper towels to start wiping the counters.

Josie regains her composure and stands straight, shaking out her arms as she sighs with enthusiasm. "I'm going to go change real quick," she says.

"I'm really, *really* sorry, Mrs. Grant," Summer says again. I pick a string of celery out of her hair, noting that my daughter definitely got the brunt of the onslaught.

"It was just an accident," Josie insists, her eyes flickering to me with amusement. "Be right back."

Olivia whirls past her mother with a new outfit for Summer to adorn and tosses it onto the island. "You look like Kermit," Olivia points, her laughter ensuing. Then she turns to me and says, "Mom has some towels in the laundry room. We can help clean the kitchen."

I take that as my cue to go find towels. I have a vague recollection of where the laundry room is, so I half-jog down the corridor, around the corner, and past the study to the mud room-laundry room combo.

Fancy-ass house. All we've got is a washer and dryer that might actually be considered vintage hidden away in the creepy, unfinished basement.

I charge into the laundry room for a towel, pushing through the door without much thought, and promptly stop in my tracks when I hear a gasp.

Josie is standing there, lips parting with shock, her hair full of static as if she'd just pulled her dress over her head. She's clad in only a bra, panties, and a wide-eyed expression.

We both freeze in place.

I can't stop my gaze from drifting to her partially exposed breasts, sheathed in black lace. Her waist is slender, the arc of her hips perfectly propor— *Jesus, why am I still standing here?*

I swallow hard, my eyes trailing back up to meet hers. A flood of heat surges through me, settling in an area I *cannot allow* in the current situation.

Visions of pounding her in my shower as I stroked my cock in a lustful rage come spiraling back, rendering me both speechless and aroused. Now I have mental images burned into my brain, stored away for the next time I decide to jerk off to Jos—

Fuck. Stay down. Get it together. I direct the thought at my rapidly stirring dick.

The look on her face surely mirrors my own, and as it registers, I shake my head to clear the daze. "Shit… sorry." Finding my voice, I back away and close the door, not sure if I'm feeling more awkward or turned on, and heave in a rickety breath that sticks in the back of my throat.

Well, fuck.

It takes a moment for me to recover. I can't go into the kitchen like this, but I can't stand here by the laundry room door with Josie on the other side either. I press the heel of my palm against my hard-on, urging it to calm the fuck down. I do the eight count. I conjure up the deeply repressed memory of accidentally walking in on Granny Lynn butt naked when I was seven.

My dick says, "fuck you" and promptly deflates.

Finally, I force my feet to move, making my way back to the kitchen with no towel and a very descriptive visualization of Josie Grant in her underwear.

It only strengthens my resolve to see more.

I blow out a swift breath. I can't help but wonder why she didn't yell at me to get out, or instinctively cover herself up, or scold me for my shameless moment of scrutiny. She just stared at me with an unreadable look in her eyes.

It had to be the shock.

"Where's the towel?"

Olivia and Summer are gawking at me as I scratch at my head with one hand and pat my thigh anxiously with the other. "No towels. The towels are gone."

Olivia scrunches up her nose. "Huh?"

"Here."

I turn to see Josie glide up behind me with a fresh towel, a new outfit, and a rosy blush speckling her cheekbones. She avoids eye contact as she passes me, and I bite down on my tongue, unsure of how to tackle the alarmingly potent elephant in the room. I decide to push it aside for the time being as I help clean up the remnants of my smoothie.

Josie and I both lower to the kitchen floor as Summer wipes down the countertop and Olivia washes the blender. I glance at Josie, who happens to glance at me at that same moment, and our eyes dart away almost instantly. I don't dare look at her again as I stand and throw my paper towels into the garbage.

Whew.

The girls finish their task and disappear back up the stairs to Olivia's room, leaving Josie and I alone with our inevitable chat. I almost want to beg the girls to stay, to save me from this awkward hell, but I let them go and quickly try to figure out what I'm going to say.

"I, uh…"

"Yeah, so…"

Josie smiles when we speak at the same time, and I'm relieved for that because I feel like maybe I'm not about to get slapped or reprimanded, after all. "I'm really fucking sorry," I say, the words spilling out like an uncomfortable laugh. "I thought you went up to your room to change. Olivia told me to grab a towel from the laundry room." I decide not to even mention the staring part. I literally have no excuse for that except that I'm a man, and she was practically naked, and *fuck*—why does she look so good naked? I blink the thoughts back before I have even more explaining to do.

And now I have to try and stop picturing her naked. Again.

Down, boy.

Josie's chin is to her chest, her bottom lip caught between her teeth, her hands gripping the edge of the countertop like a security blanket. She lets out the same kind of weird, breathy laugh and looks over at me. "It's fine. Actually, it never happened." Her smile brightens, but the flush has traveled from her cheeks to her neck. "You're cool with that, right?"

My thumbs are hooked in my belt loops as I lean against the island. "I'm definitely cool with that. I don't even know what you're talking about. Hey, weren't you making me a smoothie?" I grin at her, lessening the tension between us, watching as she relaxes in front of me.

As it turns out, Josie *does* make me another smoothie, and I'm grateful for that. It doesn't taste as foul as I'd anticipated and it gives me a little zing of energy, taking the edge off my hangover, just like Josie predicted it would. I rinse the cup out when I'm finished, and that's when Josie tugs me by the shirt sleeve, stealing my attention.

She's standing so close.

I thought things would be more awkward, even after agreeing to forget about the incident… but she's standing so close.

"How's the flesh wound?" She trails her fingers lightly over the scratch, and I really hope my skin doesn't break out into goosebumps or some embarrassing shit like that.

"I already put ointment on it. You were right—I'll live, after all."

"Good news." She breaks into a tightlipped grin, removing her touch as she nods her head in the direction of the stairwell. "Well, then... since we don't have to make a trip to the emergency room, follow me."

There's a playful spark in her eye which piques my curiosity. As we ascend the staircase, I realize she's leading me to her bedroom, and I'm flooded with inappropriate thoughts. Thoughts specifically involving Josie in her underwear, then thoughts involving Josie *not* in her underwear, and then other things that are probably illegal in various parts of the world.

God help me... if this doesn't stop, I'm going to have to excuse myself to the restroom.

Apparently, I spaced while walking to her room, because when I blink myself back to reality, Josie is sitting on her bed with her guitar in her hands. She's still fully clothed, which, I'll admit, is a bit of a disappointment, but now I'm intrigued in a different way. I smile when her fingers strum over the guitar strings, puncturing me with a melodious sound that I'm all too familiar with.

A sound that I miss like hell.

Josie peers up at me beneath her long lashes, looking timid for just a fleeting second. "Adam taught me how to play," she says wistfully, her manicured fingers plucking the strings. She looks reflective as she plays, even a little lost. Melancholy. Josie shifts her weight on the bed, taking in a breath, then starts to sing. *"Josie's on a vacation far away..."*

Our eyes settle on each other, and she crinkles her nose, a smile sprouting to life. There's a playful innocence that's come over her. She's raw and exposed... but very much in her element. I'm not sure what to make of the moment, so I simply watch her, pressing my weight against the door frame. There's something in her voice, a strange magnetism, and I'm trying not to let it seep into the cracks of my stone walls. I can't let it in—whatever the fuck it is, I can't let it penetrate what I've worked so hard to build. I'm getting closer, I can feel it...

So close, Vengeance whispers.

Josie's smile slips a little, a new look gleaming in her eyes, a look that's honest and sincere. Almost *hypnotic*. I can't seem to drag my gaze away, and it's pissing me off. It's... confusing. I have an urge to run.

But I just stand there.

Josie finally closes her eyes, and that's a goddamn relief. It gives me an opportunity to listen without the weight of her stare boring into me. She finishes the song, cutting it short, smiling again as she ducks her head with a semblance of modesty. A little color rises to her cheeks.

I think maybe I should say something, but I can't think of a single word to say.

"You're welcome for that impromptu performance," she teases, breaking through the silence. *I'm glad for that, too.* "Tips are encouraged."

I chuckle softly, running my hand along the back of my neck and scratching my hairline. "Well, I seem to have forgotten my cash," I finally reply, shaking off whatever the hell that was. "So, the only tip I have, is that maybe you should think about playing in public. You're very talented."

She smiles, glancing at the guitar fondly for a moment before her gaze drifts up to the wall, pausing on the framed picture of the rose—the one with the poetically depressing proverb. She contemplates it for a moment, saying nothing. Then, she sets the guitar down beside her on the bed, lets out a breath…

And that's that.

We go downstairs, the moment passing. Things go on as normal, and I gather Summer a half-hour later, and we head home.

But the moment doesn't *actually* pass.

It lingers. It fucking haunts me.

When I climb into bed that night, I can't fall asleep. There's something tugging at me, drawing me right back up and dragging my feet to my work desk across the room. It's one A.M. and Summer is sound asleep across the hall, but my mind is restless, brimming with urgency.

I sit down in front of my laptop, powering it on, then open up the manuscript I haven't touched in weeks. A smile pulls at my lips as I place my fingers over the keys, relishing in the smooth familiarity of them.

I take a deep breath.

And then… I write.

THIRTEEN

*J*T'S A PERFECT DAY FOR THE FARMER'S MARKET.

The October afternoon is mild, pushing sixty degrees with a cloudless sky, and it's one of the final weeks in which our favorite outdoor Farmer's Market will be open for the season. It's usually just Summer and me picking up fresh ingredients for spaghetti night and munching on kettle corn, but Logan invited us out this time. He said Amber has been bugging him to take her, and the weather could not be more perfect.

I'm sitting at my laptop, waiting for Summer to get home from school, when a Facebook message pops up from Josie. It's been four days since I've seen her—four days since the hangover from hell, the smoothie debacle, and the memorable run-in in the laundry room.

But it's also been four days since I felt a spark of life for the first time in a year-and-a-half, outside of spending time with my daughter.

Finally... something other than blind rage, hate, and bitterness.

The tickle of authentic joy.

It's been four days since I could write again.

Fucking hell. I can't even begin to explain it, and I refuse to dwell on it, but it's certainly thrown me for a loop. I pull up Josie's message.

JOSIE: *Spaghetti night on Friday?*

I smile through my reply.

ME: *I'll up your spaghetti night to a Farmer's Market adventure tonight.*

JOSIE: *Ooh. Tell me more.*

ME: *There's a wine vendor. He gives free samples.*

JOSIE: *SOLD.*

ME: *Ha. You're too easy :) We're meeting my friends there at 5. I can pick you guys up since parking is a nightmare.*

JOSIE: *Sounds good. Olivia gets off the bus around 4. Would you mind if Ben came along?*

Yes. Hell yes. Absolutely fucking yes.

ME: *Not at all.*

JOSIE: *I'll ask him. It's not really his scene, but I don't want him to feel left out.*

I debate asking my next question, but I do.

ME: *He's cool with us hanging out so much, right? Just making sure he's not getting the wrong idea or anything.*

The wrong idea… *if he only knew.*

I hold my breath through a long pause, then finally, Josie begins typing. I see the little wiggling dots disappear and reappear multiple times.

JOSIE: *I appreciate you asking. Ben isn't like that and he knows we're just friends. Besides, he really wants you to come over for dinner soon. I think he's intrigued by the author thing.*

"Ben" isn't like that. *Good ol' Ben.* Stand-up fucking husband right there. I can't help but wonder how he can be perfectly okay with me sniffing around his wife—because let's face it, I'm not a bad-looking guy. I do pretty well for myself in that department. I can't imagine even the most low-key husband being unthreatened by someone like me spending so much quality time with their wife.

Must be nice to be so arrogant—you never have to worry about your wife leaving you for the less privileged, tattooed writer. Or maybe he's too busy sleeping with other men's wives to even notice.

I grit my teeth and shoot her a response.

ME: *Cool. Just checking. See you at 5 :)*

All I can do now is fucking hope to God that Benjamin Grant has better things to do tonight.

Benjamin Grant has better things to do tonight.

I try not to look too relieved when Josie tells me this, as she and Olivia pile into my Mustang.

"That's... such a shame." I almost gag on my words. "Maybe another time." When I hear the buckles click into place, I rev the engine and speed off down the quiet neighborhood street, garnering a disapproving glare from Karen in the cul-de-sac. I may have missed the speed limit sign, but I got a Mustang GT for a reason, and I'm fairly certain going twenty-five miles per hour is actually engine abuse.

I glance at Josie, whose hair is flipping around her head from the cracked window, and I can't help but notice the peculiar look on her face—a little dreamy, maybe even romantic. She rolls the window down farther and places her hand outside, letting the whirling wind move her fingers like a playful dance. I shift my gaze between Josie and the road, wondering what she's thinking. This would be a perfect time for the "Say It" game, but she's so caught up in whatever private moment she's in, whatever magical place she's gone to, I don't have the heart to pull her away.

It's a fifteen-minute drive to the nearby town of Grayslake. Josie and I don't speak much on the ride over, but it's not an uncomfortable silence— no, it's quite peaceful, actually. We're taken by the conversation coming from the backseat. There are humorous school stories, impending Halloween chatter about Summer and Olivia's costumes, and more laughter than my heart can stand. I'm not used to moments like this. My heart has been frozen solid for well over a year... *freezer-burned*. But I feel the ice melting away —slowly, merely a trickle—and it's a feeling I wouldn't mind getting used to.

I manage to find rock star parking, and we make our way onto the busy, blocked-off street. The scent of buttered popcorn taunts me as Josie flips her sunglasses up over her hair and takes in the scene.

"Wow, this is great. We've never been to this one," she says, admiring the rows of unique vendors. Her hair almost looks like a prism as the sunshine lights her up, illuminating the reds and golds and yellows I never noticed before.

Fall leaves, my mind proposes. That's what it reminds me of.

Then I kick myself for comparing Josie Grant's hair to fucking fall leaves, blaming it on the writer in me.

"Evan!"

I look to the left, spotting Amber waving madly at me from the wine stand. This doesn't surprise me. We weave our way through the masses of families, dogs, and giant baby strollers I'm grateful I don't need to schlep around anymore. Summer jogs ahead of us, clinging to Olivia's hand and dragging her the rest of the way.

"Aunt Amber!" Summer shouts. Amber does a silly hop on both feet as she sets down her wine purchase and scoops Summer up into a tight hug.

Josie and I trail behind, and I notice Logan at a nearby stand, ordering an obscene amount of apple cider donuts, which I don't blame him for. Those things are fucking amazing, and I plan to confiscate one as soon as possible. I smile at Amber when she rushes toward me, leaping into my arms and almost knocking me over. She tousles my hair aggressively with her tattooed fingers the minute her feet touch the ground.

"You're letting your hair grow out," she notes. "It's sexy. I keep telling Logan to go longer, but he doesn't listen." She turns to Josie with a sly grin, whispering harshly, "Men never listen to us."

Josie has a mix of curiosity and intrigue on her face as she tries to read the brazen brunette. I didn't really think to prepare her for Amber. "I'm Josie," she finally says, holding out a tentative hand.

"Amber. Are you two…?" Amber flicks her finger between Josie and me, silently asking if we're *together*.

"We're friends," Josie answers, smoothing out the fabric of her black romper patterned in sunflowers. She clears her throat gently, then fiddles with her wedding ring. "Our daughters hit it off at the park last month, and now they're inseparable."

Amber nods, the motion slow and deliberate, her eyes trailing to me and lingering pointedly.

Logan sneaks up behind Amber at just the right time, snaking his arms around her waist, his one hand revealing the donuts he just purchased. Amber squeals in delight, overly enthusiastic about the gift, procuring a few glances from passersby.

Amber is overly enthusiastic about everything. It's what we love about her.

"Shit, I love you!" Amber says, twirling around to kiss him hard on the mouth.

I look over at Josie, who is taking in the scene with a smile teasing her lips. Before I say anything, Logan approaches me and punches me on the shoulder, hard enough that I stumble back. I return the gesture with equal force.

He laughs, then turns his attention to Josie. "Hey, I know you. You're *One Thing*."

I let out a groan from the back of my throat, shaking my head, watching as Josie's brows crease into a frown. "The video," I intervene. "He saw the video you sent me on Friday night singing that One Direction song. You might recognize Logan from his model-worthy poses with the pool cue."

Josie chuckles when she registers the reference. "Ahh, of course," she nods. "I should have known." She holds her hand out with a grin. "I sometimes go by Josie."

"Logan," he introduces, shaking her hand while shooting me a knowing wink.

I glare at him, almost daring him to say something.

Amber crouches down in front of Summer and Olivia with an animated smile. "Do you girls want to have a dance party? I have some pretty awesome song requests I can put in."

"Yeah!" the girls both shout in unison, their ponytails bouncing in similar time.

"If you need us, we'll be dancing our booties off," Amber says to us, reaching down to take the girls' hands in her own. Then she jerks her head over to Logan. "Boyfriend! Come," she snaps good-naturedly.

Josie giggles, swishing her hair over to one side as the group heads toward the large patio with hula hoops, bubbles, and a DJ. She looks back to me like she's waiting for me to make the next move, but I'm suddenly struck with the image of seeing her naked, and I wonder if she *knows* I'm thinking about her naked, and my feet feel frozen to the sticky cement.

"Wine?"

Josie breaks through my fog with an arched brow, and I scratch my head, nodding my agreement. We pace the few steps over to the wine booth where there's an assortment of homemade sangrias and dessert wines to sample. She catches my gaze, smiling wide, looking like a kid on Christmas morning.

The man behind the table nods in greeting as we peruse the array of goodies. I point to a raspberry wine in a slender bottle, remembering the sweet and potent flavor. "Try this one," I recommend. "There's brandy in it. It's a perfect nightcap."

Josie's eyes brighten as she looks at the man, like he's some sort of wine fairy. "Can I try that one?"

The man gives us a mini essay on the wine as he pours a sample into a tiny plastic cup. Josie takes it between her fingers and tips her head back, swallowing the burgundy liquid in one gulp, then spins to me with a look of gleaming approval.

"Good?" I question through my smile, already knowing the answer.

She nods with enthusiasm, and I watch as her tongue pokes between her lips to savor any drops left behind. "God, yes," she replies, then returns her attention to the man. "I'll take three bottles, please."

Josie gathers her purchases and an idea strikes me, though, likely not a brilliant one. But I'm feeling mischievous and a little bold, so I take her by the wrist and pull her towards my Mustang. I hear her laugh as she races to catch up beside me, then I drop her arm as we walk side-by-side.

"Where are we going?" she wonders, a smile tipping at her mouth as she nibbles her bottom lip.

I don't reply until we reach my car, ushering her inside. I pull two water bottles from the backseat that I'd brought along and remove the caps, then pour the water out onto the pavement. "I don't think this is very legal, but you only live once, right?" My grin is broad, and it only stretches further when I catch the realization sparkle in her eyes.

Josie removes one of the bottles from the brown paper bag, handing it to me as she tries to suppress a giggle. "Don't you need a wine opener?"

I'm prepared for this question, of course, so I reach over her lap and into the glove compartment. My arm brushes against the fabric of her romper, and I feel her stiffen at the contact, but she doesn't inch away. I rummage around until I find it, then pull back, waving it in the air like a trophy.

Josie shakes her head at me, both playful and pathetic. "I'm not even going to ask."

Dividing the wine between the two empty water bottles, I'm careful not to spill a single drop. I hand Josie hers, and she looks impressed, so I waggle my eyebrows in a devilish manner. She glances around, scoping out the scene for possible witnesses, then relaxes, accepting the wine.

"It's really good," she says, wincing slightly at the strong flavor and tucking her hair behind her ear.

Her eyes sneak up to me as I smile around the mouth of my bottle. I decide I kind of like drinking raspberry wine in my Mustang with Josie Grant in the middle of a Farmer's Market.

I push the thought away. "Come on," I tell her, opening my door and signaling her with a nod of my head. "Let's go check out the dance party."

"What about... ?" Josie looks down at her partially drunken wine.

My smirk is firmly in place. "Chug-a-lug."

Her eyes narrow, debating the proposal, then she throws her head back and begins to chug the rest of her cocktail. I do the same, and it's not exactly easy to do, considering it's a whopping seventeen-percent alcohol content, but I do it, shaking my head and laughing through the burn. I'm still chuckling as I stand and toss my empty bottle into the adjacent trash can. Josie joins me, and I notice a rosy bush already staining the apples of her cheeks. Her eyes are twinkling, lively, and she looks like she's having fun—letting her guard down. There is a giddiness in her smile that I haven't seen before.

I push those thoughts away, too. Damn wine is going straight to my head.

We make our way to the dance patio, stopping at the cotton candy vendor before we meet up with our group. It's a tradition I have with Summer. I buy her cotton candy, and she gives me her undying love in return.

I wonder if it will work on Josie…

"You don't need to buy me cotton candy," she insists when I pull a wad of cash from my wallet.

I purchase three of them, for Josie and the girls, then accept the treats that resemble pink and blue clouds on sticks from the vendor. I wink at Josie, handing her one of them as I lick off a dab of sugar that stuck to my thumb. "It doesn't taste as good if you buy it for yourself."

She seems to accept my answer, her mouth curling up, and plucks a piece of powder blue fluff from her stick.

"Cotton candy!"

Summer spots us heading towards them, causing both Summer and Olivia to drop their hula hoops and charge at me, eager for their sugar infusion. Their hands are held out in desperation, their legs hardly able to keep up with their excitement.

"Nope," I say, holding the treats just out of their reach. "That'll be five push-ups, twenty jumping jacks, and a solid thirty seconds of hula hoop action."

Summer plants her hands on her hips, her eyes narrowed, looking anything but amused. "Dad! Come on. You're not funny."

"Ten push-ups for that ridiculous lie."

"It's true!" Summer exclaims, a betraying smile blooming on her lips.

"Twenty."

Summer hops up and snatches one of the cotton candy sticks, and I relent, handing the other to Olivia. "Fine, but no one can know what a softie I am."

"Everyone knows," Summer mutters through a smirk, then the two girls run back out to the patio where a new song is bursting to life.

Glancing around, I see Logan and Amber slow-dancing a few feet away, and a tinge of envy trickles through me as I keep watching. Amber's head is pressed against his chest, her eyes closed in contentment, while Logan's cheek rests atop her hair, his arms wound around her. They are lost to each other. I doubt they're even aware of anything else around them—the music, the conversations, the children laughing and playing and squealing with joy.

Josie and I take a seat at a nearby picnic bench as we watch Summer and Olivia fail miserably at trying to hula hoop with their cotton candy, and I glance over at Logan and Amber again. *Damn*, they look happy. They've barely moved positions, lightly swaying to whatever song is playing in their heads.

"They look happy."

Josie's observation echoes my own internal dialogue, so I turn to face her, leaning back against the table on my elbows. "They are," I respond softly. And I could blame the wine I chugged, but I don't even think about my next words before I say them. "It's fucking awesome, and I'm happy for them—but the jealous asshole in me hates them for it, too."

Then my words sink in, and I hate *myself* a little.

I've been telling myself I needed to show Josie more vulnerability, something real… and I just did. This time, though, it wasn't for personal gain. It wasn't planned.

It just came out.

I realize I'm staring into nothing while absorbing all of this, so I snap myself out of the haze. Looking up at the scene in front of me, my eyes rove around the scattered crowd. Suddenly, I'm jealous of every happy couple engaging with each other, chowing down on hot dogs, chasing their kids, holding hands… dancing. I'm even jealous of the kids, tangled in hula hoops and laughing—carefree, without the burden of heartbreak.

Without the weight of hatred.

I'm just… *jealous.*

Tension swells in my gut like a funneling cyclone. I breathe in deep as it winds up through my chest, climbing higher, and—

There's a hand on my arm. It's only a light squeeze, no more than an acknowledgement of the place I've gone to. But the second I feel it, feel *her*, my anger dissipates. I glance down at the gesture as a trickle of peace seeps in through the bitterness, my eyes slowly lifting to meet hers.

There is warmth in that smile—sympathy, and a vague understanding of my pain. There is friendship. There is camaraderie.

There is Josie.

The anger blows away with the fall breeze.

"It's her loss, you know."

I swallow hard at her words, aware that she's referring to Katrina, and somehow knowing she means it. It's not just a line to cheer me up.

Even so, I don't know what it means or how to piece together the sentiment... I'm disoriented by it. Instead, my eyes drift across her face, landing on the speckle of blue crystals caught in the corner of her mouth.

It's all I can focus on.

Instinct takes over, and I reach out to gently swipe them away, not thinking clearly, not thinking at *all*, watching her lips part as my thumb brushes over the candy pieces. A shudder sweeps through me when I graze her bottom lip.

Her breath catches.

"Sorry..." I hate the sound of my voice—it's too low, too strangely intimate. I clear my throat. "You had cotton candy stuck to..." Trailing off, I point at her mouth with my finger, letting it finish the sentence for me. I force a smile in an attempt to counteract the serious mood that has developed between us, but I feel like it's too late.

Josie is wide-eyed, maybe a little confused, but not unaffected by whatever the hell just happened. Her breathing is coming quick, her cheeks pink, eyes glassy.

This is good, I tell myself. I'm getting to her. I'm reeling her in.

But... even my own thoughts feel shaky.

The DJ begins a new song, busting through our bubble, and I'm pulled from the moment because it's not a song I would ever expect to hear at a Farmer's Market.

It's a Slipknot song.

What the hell?

My gaze travels over to where Logan and Amber are standing... and *holy shit*, I know exactly what's happening. This is "their" song. It was playing the night Logan dragged her to a college party and kissed her for the first time. It was the beginning of everything—when they first started falling in love.

Amber looks startled, dazed, her expression matching those of almost everyone around us. Kids are looking up at their parents with curious eyes as the parents shrug their shoulders, glancing at the other members of their group in utter confusion.

The DJ speaks into the microphone, his voice sounding over the song. "Ladies and gentlemen, I'd like to bring your attention over to my two friends here." He points at Logan and Amber, and Amber raises her hand to her mouth, leaning into her boyfriend. "Logan has something he wants to ask his lovely lady, Amber."

An astonished laugh bursts from my throat while I wait for Logan to make his move. Logan spares me a glance, looking a little petrified, but his smile brightens when I nod my head in encouragement. Josie is watching with interest, sitting up straight and abandoning her cotton candy on the table behind us.

Logan lowers himself to one knee, his leather duster pooling behind him on the cement. Amber is screaming into her cupped hands before he even gets a word in. Her scream turns into a giddy laugh as Logan pulls out a ring, mirroring her laughter. I can't hear what he says, but I have a pretty good idea, and Amber jumps up and down in place, squealing, sobbing, shouting *yes* at the top of her lungs. There's no need for words… we all know.

The crowd erupts with claps and cheers, and Josie and I stand from our seats. I'm whooping and hollering as Amber jumps into Logan's arms, her legs wrapping around his waist.

The look on Logan's face is pure, indescribable joy.

God… *it's perfect.*

The jealousy is gone without a trace. There is no more petty envy or bitterness. No hate.

My friends are in love, and I can't stop smiling.

I'm happy as fuck for them.

So damn happy.

The Slipknot song continues to play as Josie and I approach them, fading into the background when we all hug. The girls come bounding towards us, Summer offering exuberant high fives with sticky hands. I glance at Josie, and it almost looks like she might cry.

She swipes at her eyes, ducking her head at my silent query. "Sorry. I'm weak when it comes to stuff like this," she half-sniffles.

The magic of the moment sweeps through me, and I can't help myself from reaching for Josie, pulling her into a lighthearted dance pose. She's taken aback at first, almost tripping on her boots.

"Evan, this is barely considered music," she teases, rich laughter escaping her. "You can't dance to this."

The growly vocals sound around us. Amber is pressed against Logan, weeping into his chest as they slow dance. The girls are jumping around with their hula hoops as Olivia attempts to head bang.

And that's when I spin Josie into a circle, snuffing out her claims, letting her giggles resonate through me.

"Sure, you can," I insist, my smile roguish, my eyes gleaming. "There is rhythm." I spin her again. "There is soul." I dip her. "There is… magic."

Our eyes meet on the dip as I pull her back up to me, my hand on the small of her back, my other hand encased in hers.

Something passes between us.

I don't have a name for it, but as I hold her to me, the air feels charged… like electricity. Like *actual* magic. Our laughter fades into something else, and we're frozen in that pose for far too long, neither of us saying anything —neither of us knowing *what* to say. My breathing is heavy, my heart beating fast, right up against hers. I'm holding her too close. It's too much.

You should let go, Evan.

I don't let go. Our eyes are still locked, until Josie finally makes the first move and… pulls away.

I'm speechless.

Something just happened; there's no denying it now. We both know it, we both felt it, we both drank it in like sweet raspberry wine. Josie steps back, finally breaking eye contact—breaking our connection. She doesn't say a word.

I watch her join Summer and Olivia in their hula hoop competition like I'm viewing the world through a fog.

My fingers riffle through my hair as I close my eyes, desperate for a cigarette.

What the *fuck?*

I watch Josie slap on a smile for the girls, beginning to relax. The song changes to something more family friendly, and the three of them dance and twirl and swing their hips as the hoops spin from their waist to their feet.

I inhale a frayed breath, feeling muddled and somewhat itchy when the fog begins to clear. All I know is that I can't dwell on this… I refuse.

I refuse to think about whatever the fuck just happened between me and the woman who's at the center of my revenge scheme—who's *married* to the very man who ruined my life.

I refuse to fucking think about it.

I refuse to think about the way Josie Grant felt against my chest, warm and alive, as we danced in a sea of hula hoops with the smell of cotton candy on her skin and her hair made of autumn.

I refuse.

14

FOURTEEN

THEN
APRIL

The park is calling us.

There are still a few bits of ice and snow scattered around the playground, but it's been a week since our spring snowstorm, and the sun is peeking between the clouds, melting away the remnants of an especially brutal Illinois winter. The temperature is finally mild enough to play outside, so Summer and I have bundled up and defrosted our bicycles. The entire town seems to have had the same idea because the park is packed.

Woodchips crunch beneath my shoes as I weave through the rowdy children, following Summer to the opposite end of the playground. I pass a honey-haired woman with a daughter around Summer's age who smiles at me, and I nod a hello in her direction.

"Dad! Catch me on the slide," Summer yells out, already at the top of the play structure.

I rub my hands together as I wait for her at the bottom of the slide. Fifty degrees sounds like a tropical oasis when you've just experienced a winter full of multiple polar vortexes, but after riding my bike here, it's pretty fucking chilly.

"All right, bunny. I got you," I call up to my daughter, who is getting in position.

A smile and a puffy jacket adorn her as she makes her way down the green slide. I catch her with ease, then scoop her up and spin her around, planting a kiss against her temple. Summer scampers free of my embrace and occupies herself at the swings, so I take a seat on a nearby bench.

My thoughts drift to Katrina because they're always on her these days. She's back to work now, picking up extra shifts at the restaurant to make up for her leave of absence. I had hoped the regular schedule would help her feel normal again, but nothing has changed much in the last couple of weeks. If anything, being out of the house has made her even more distant when she's in it.

My attempts to reach my wife have been met with stony resistance and apathy. Our relationship is... strained. That's a nice way of putting it, I guess. She's emotionally absent.

I have no idea what to do for her—*for us*—but I will never give up trying.

The distance has become even harder to brush off the last few nights. Katrina has been sleeping on the couch, claiming she fell asleep while reading, but there has been no book in sight, and I don't even remember the last time I saw Katrina read. All I can guess is that she doesn't want to be in bed with *me*.

I plan to bring up the prospect of couple's counseling tonight after supper because I feel like I'm out of options at this point. She's not responding to anything else. Trying to touch her or talk to her only seems to agitate her, while giving her space feels like I'm pushing her further away.

I can't win.

Twenty minutes pass by as I aimlessly watch the children come and go. Parents chase their toddlers through the patches of dead grass, while the sun darts in and out of swiftly moving clouds. Summer runs over to me as I'm lost in thought and staring at a curious squirrel. I've always wondered how squirrels manage to sprint down a tree trunk face-first without falling.

Summer sits down beside me on the bench, and I shake the random thoughts away.

"Having fun?" I inquire, watching the distinctive emotions splay out across her innocent features. I take in the spattering of freckles on the bridge of her nose and wonder if more will bloom with every passing year.

Summer nods slowly, blinking, watching the same squirrel that caught my attention.

"Something wrong, bun?" She's always worn her emotions on her face —it's very handy as a parent because she can't get away with hiding anything from me. And now I can't shake the feeling that my daughter wants to ask me something but doesn't know how.

She shrugs. "I don't think so."

I don't think so. Yeah, try again, kiddo… that wasn't convincing at all.

Tucking my arm around her shoulders, I pull her closer. "Is something on your mind? You know you can always talk to me."

Summer bites her lip, conflict twisting on her face. "Dad… what does abortion mean?"

The question punctures me like the salient point of a knife.

I feel a burst of air leave my lungs, and it comes out like a sharp gasp, maybe even a moan. It's a breath of shock, confusion. Summer looks up at me, registering my reaction. She presses her wind-kissed lips together, instantly looking like she regrets the question. "It's bad, isn't it?"

"I…" I pull her in even tighter, hoping to assure her she asked nothing wrong, but for the moment… I'm speechless. I don't know how to explain something like that. I don't know why she's asking me this, or how she stumbled upon this word. I wonder if maybe she learned it from school, but my instincts are swirling around in my gut, screaming at me, telling me otherwise.

I think… *I think I don't want to know.*

"Where did you hear that word, Summer?"

Her eyes widen, like maybe she's in trouble.

"It's okay, bunny, I promise. Just tell the truth."

She hesitates, her voice small. "I – I heard Mommy say it. She was on the phone with someone. A man, I think. She was crying and talking about getting an abortion." Summer swallows, her eyes coating with fresh tears. "Is it why she's been so sad lately?"

No.

No, no, *no*. The words bounce around in my head, but I'm not processing. I couldn't have heard her right. She didn't just say…

The words begin to sink.

First, they sink into my brain, which still can't comprehend them. Then they move to my lungs, squeezing until I can't breathe. They settle in my heart, each word like a hammer, breaking me into pieces, pulverizing the organ until I feel it stutter.

I rub my chest. It hurts… I can't breathe… I can't…

Fuck. *Fuck.*

"Are you okay, Dad?"

My vision is swimming, my head foggy.

I am not okay.

I think—fuck, I think I might pass out, so I stand from the bench, looking around. I don't know what I'm looking for.

The words sink further.

Katrina…

I picture her in my mind, sallow and shaking, sobbing in my arms.

She had an… *abortion?*

She aborted our baby that we waited years for?

Why? Why would she… ?

Why… Why… Why?

The words drop into my gut like rocks, boulders.

Plop. Plop. Plop. Plop.

She. Had. An. Abortion.

My stomach rolls.

There's a trash can nearby. I run to it, gripping the edges with white-knuckled fingers, like it's my lifeline.

And then I start heaving.

It spills from me like poison—the sorrow, the disbelief, the confusion. It spills in waves of bile and acid, as though my body wants to expel the words… expel the truth.

It can't be true.

Oh, my God… *it can't be true.*

Summer is by my side. I can feel her there, hear her worried voice.

The honey-haired woman is there, too. She asks me if I'm okay, and I'm not. I'm not okay…

I'm not okay.

I ignore them all, stumbling over to where our bicycles are resting against a tree. My vision is blurred, but I can see Summer running toward me while the woman and a few others watch in concern as I situate myself on my bike with shaky feet. "We have to go home," I say to Summer. My voice is a strange, distant thing. It sounds like broken glass.

She bobs her head, unsure of what has happened to her father, her face pale, her eyes wide. But she does as I say, climbing onto her bike and trailing behind me out of the playground.

I don't know how I make it home. I don't remember the ride. But I'll always remember perching my bike against the wall of the garage, telling Summer to go inside and watch TV, while I collapse onto the cold pavement with my head in my hands and my heart in pieces no glue could ever put back together.

I'll remember trembling, releasing tearless sobs into my palms, wondering how the fuck I got here. My wife aborted our baby. Katrina terminated the pregnancy we dreamed about, cried about, *begged* for, month after month. She ended the life of our child.

My child.

I don't know how she could do such a thing.

I don't know why... *my God*, I don't know *why*...

But I'm going to find out.

NOW

I tried to get out of it—I really did.

Unfortunately, there are only so many colorful excuses one can come up with before sounding like they just don't want to go to your fucking dinner party.

I have food poisoning.

I have a mosquito bite that might be fatal.

I'm thinking about my goldfish that died when I was seven, and I'm not in the right mental state.

I might stab your husband with a meat thermometer.

Okay, that last one is the only legitimate excuse, but sadly, it's also the one I can't say out loud. Instead, I'm forced to put on my damn fancy pants again with a fake smile and schmooze the night away with the Grants.

With Benjamin. Fucking. Grant.

God help me.

At least Summer is excited. She got dressed up tonight in a navy blue dress with a sparkly tulle skirt. I tried to curl her hair, but she ended up looking like Medusa, and it took a solid thirty minutes to wash the copious amounts of hairspray out and start all over.

It's in a ponytail now. She wouldn't let me near her with the curling iron again.

Josie opens the door in a little black dress, and it's the first time I've laid eyes on her in a week-and-a-half. Our gazes hold for a beat, that same distinct charge rekindling in an instant, then Josie turns her attention to Summer with a wide grin.

"You look beautiful, Summer. Is that a new dress?" she asks, leaning forward with her hands on her knees.

I force my eyes away from the tease of cleavage, but I'm already picturing her half naked in the laundry room.

Summer shakes her head, her ponytail swaying side to side. "It's my only dress. I'm kind of a tomboy," she shrugs.

Josie's laugh vibrates through me. "Well, I love it. Olivia got dressed up, too. She's in her room if you want to say hi."

Don't leave me. Please don't leave me.

"Yeah!" Summer bobs up and down, then charges past Josie and up the staircase.

She left me.

Josie clears her throat, pulling the door open so I can step inside. "Hi, Evan. Ben should be home any minute. He had to run to the office to finish something." She smiles, but it's slight, and I have no idea what she's thinking or how to proceed.

I hold out my offering of cheap Aldi wine. I panicked on the way over and didn't know what else to get. I don't do dinner parties, but I felt like I shouldn't show up empty-handed. "I come bearing gifts," I say, waving the bottle at her with a grin. She smiles again, brighter this time, and my shoulders relax a little. "It's not as good as the Farmer's Market stuff, but it gets the job done."

I notice her flinch at the mention of the Farmer's Market. Her eyes flicker to me, then away. I know what she's thinking now, but I don't think I should bring it up. I don't want to dwell on it… I don't want to give it life.

Awkward tension swirls between us.

Josie rubs her palms against the fabric of her dress, then wrings her hands together, her head bowed. "Thanks for coming tonight. My husband's been dying to pick your writer's brain."

Okay, *that's* worse than awkward.

I scratch the back of my neck, stepping farther into the foyer so Josie can close the door. "Yeah, for sure. Summer was excited about it."

She blinks, taking the wine from my hand and studying me, her eyes roving over my face. "Not your scene, huh?"

It's not the scene, itself. It's your husband. It's the feeling of wanting to commit murder in the first degree whenever he's in my line of sight.

"Sorry, I didn't mean it like that. I appreciate you having us over," I cover.

Josie's mouth twitches like she might smile, but she doesn't. She steps ahead of me, leading me towards the kitchen. Whatever is cooking smells damn good, and my stomach grumbles in response to the scent of fresh rosemary and garlic. I watch as Josie opens up a bottle of the raspberry wine, her eyes softening when she looks my way, and pours two glasses. She slides a glass to me over the island as I perch myself on one of the stools.

Before I take a sip, my eyes drift to the opposite end of the countertop, and I have to do a double take.

My book.

It's sitting there with a bookmark placed about three-quarters of the way in. I glance up at Josie, who is already halfway finished with her own glass of wine. "You're reading my book?" I nod my head to the left. My question is laced with more excitement than I meant to showcase, but I can't help the faint swell of pride that consumes me.

I also can't help hoping that she likes it.

Normally, I wouldn't care—I try to stay away from reviews. I embrace my fans and readers and give little mind to anyone else. I know I won't be everyone's cup of tea.

But... for some reason, I really want Josie to like my tea.

Josie sets her glass down, a sheepish smile stretching across her face, almost like she hadn't meant for me to see that. "Oh... um, yeah. I know you have a few books out, but this one had the most reviews and the concept looked really interesting."

"It's my most popular," I tell her. "It's basically what paid for my Mustang."

There's a glimmer in her eyes. "Well, it's great so far." Josie takes another sip of wine, her skin already flushing from the alcohol. "I mean, it's *really* great. You're extremely talented, Evan."

I shouldn't care that Josie Grant likes my book, but I do, and when her eyes meet mine over the rim of her glass, I swear to fucking hell I feel something that resembles butterflies in my stomach.

Go home, butterflies. You're drunk.

I take a few giant gulps of my wine, hoping to flush the bastards out. Swallowing hard, I nod my thanks. "I appreciate that. I wasn't sure if you'd enjoy it, being such dark story. I wrote it right after my divorce, so I was in sort of a "black hole" mindset."

Her tongue pokes between her lips as she contemplates this. "I can see that. I didn't see the serial killer twist coming at all—it really shocked me. I'm actually planning on cutting this dinner short so I can lock myself in my bedroom and finish reading. I'm dying to know how it ends." She runs her fingers along the edge of the counter, crinkling her nose in jest. "Hopefully, you weren't counting on dessert."

I can't hold back a laugh, and just like that, the mood between us finally returns to the playful repartee we've become accustomed to.

That's when the front door opens, and I can hear Benjamin Grant's booming voice from the foyer. The hairs on my arms stand to attention as a prickly sensation washes over me. Tension winds through me, every muscle in my body clenching.

"Jos?"

"Kitchen," Josie answers, finishing her wine and pouring herself another glass. She steps away from the island to busy herself near the stove, and I can't help but register her reaction to her husband's arrival as... *off*. Uncomfortable.

I stand from my stool, forcing myself to be polite, *begging* my tongue to stay in line, then turn to face my nemesis as he rounds the corner. I'm grinding my teeth so hard I could probably chew through glass.

Benjamin hesitates briefly, his shoes scuffing against the wood flooring with a squeaky sound. He stares at me, almost expressionless, before a smile quirks at his lips and he reaches for my hand. "Evan," he greets. "Excellent to see you. Thanks for coming over."

He claps the other hand around it as well, using both of his hands to shake mine in an "I'm more powerful than you" gesture. I cringe inwardly at the feel of his palms around mine. "Thanks for having us." My tone is flat, so I try to make up for it by forcing my lips to curl upward.

Nodding, he lets go of my hand, making his way into the kitchen where Josie's back is to him. She's stirring something on the stove when he comes up behind her, wrapping his arms around her waist and leaning down to kiss her neck. My eyes narrow, as if by showing affection to his wife, he's committing one of the seven deadly sins. Josie seems to stiffen in his embrace, but lets a giggle slip when he peppers kisses all the way down to her shoulder.

"That tickles," she says, nudging him away.

I want to vomit.

Benjamin paces backward, loosening his tie and opening up the refrigerator. He pulls out a cold beer and pops off the cap with a bottle opener magnet from the fridge door. "Beer?" he asks me.

"Sure. Thanks." He opens it for me, sliding it down the island. I watch him carefully, his mannerisms, his movements—the way he seems to take over the room with his presence, yet still doesn't seem completely... *present*.

I wonder what Katrina saw in him, what made her fall head over heels for this man.

I wonder what made him better than me.

He's slightly taller than I am, maybe around six-foot-two. He's broad, but less fit than me—not overweight, though. He looks like he's just had one too many beers. His hair is brown with reddish undertones, and the ghost of stubble along his jawline matches his hair. Benjamin Grant is not bad looking, but I'll never understand what Katrina saw. There's a distance in his eyes, a subtle detachment. Something... aloof.

Maybe that's what pulled her in. Some women have an inexplicable attraction to arrogant assholes, after all. Maybe that distance, that sense he gives off that he's just a bit more important than everyone else in the room, was more than she could resist.

I roll my eyes inwardly, unable to understand it. I was *good* to her, damnit. I'm the fucking opposite of this asshole, and yeah, maybe my situation is humbler, but I truly believe I made up for it with attentiveness and love and—

I stop mid-swig of my beer, the last swallow turning sour on the way down. Maybe *that* was where I went wrong.

Maybe I loved her too much.

Benjamin's voice breaks through my bitter thoughts, through my impossible string of "what ifs." "I'm going to freshen up, hon. I'll be down in ten." He moves in for another kiss, his fingers twining through Josie's hair. "Dinner smells fantastic."

He shoots me a wink as he passes, whistling while he makes his way down the hall and up the stairs. I'm chewing on the inside of my cheek to keep my secrets from spilling out of my mouth, but it's starting to hurt, and once he's out of sight, I'm able to relax a bit.

But he'll be back...

I'm feeling a bit dubious about my chances of keeping this up all night —hell, for five more minutes, even. My acting skills are being stretched like cheap elastic on bargain store underwear, and I'm not sure how they'll hold up. Maybe I should cut my losses, feign sickness, run away before I say the wrong thing and fuck up the plan completely.

I set the bottle down on the counter, my head swirling with excuses. I can't be here…

Fuck, I can't be here.

Josie turns to me from her place in front of the oven, smiling softly. "You'll like him. You two probably have more in common than you think."

I go rigid as ice trickles through my veins. I can't even begin to fake a smile at this point, so I grab my beer and lift it to my frozen lips, tipping my head back to finish it off.

You have no idea, Josie Grant.

FIFTEEN

Stop staring, Evan.

I'm sitting across the table from Josie, trying not to watch the way she sucks the tines of a fork between her lips.

It's not working.

Benjamin is at the head of the table like the pretentious prick I know he is. His knife scratches against the plate as he cuts into his Cornish hen, and I wince, stabbing my own piece of meat with more force than necessary.

"You girls have really hit it off, huh?" Benjamin says to Summer and Olivia, who are shoveling mashed potatoes into their mouths like there's going to be a grand prize. Benjamin's fork glides against his teeth as he takes a bite of his food, and I swear I'm cringing every five seconds of this fucking exhausting dinner.

I hate everything about him.

Summer bounces in her chair as Olivia grins, both girls pausing their mashed potato eating contest to take a breath. Summer swings her legs under the table, kicking me as she does so. "It's almost like we're sisters," Summer proclaims. "I've never had a best friend like her before."

Olivia bobs her head in agreement. "Can we adopt Summer?"

Josie laughs around her utensil, her eyes shifting to me, creasing with amusement. "Don't you think Summer's dad would miss her?" she counters.

I shrug, swallowing down my food and winking at my daughter. "She'd miss me way more."

"No way!" Summer protests through her smile. "You drive too fast and play awful music."

Laughter floats around us as I muss her hair, and she swats at me in return.

"So, Evan," Benjamin continues, taking a healthy sip of wine and clearing his throat. "My wife has been raving about your book. I'm not the creative type myself, but I've always admired people who have that drive. What made you decide to become a writer?"

Something inside me wants to repel his question. I don't want to give him anything—I want him to have zero part of me.

He's already taken too much.

I spin my wine glass between my fingers, watching the liquid splash and whirl, hypnotizing me for just a moment. When I glance up, Josie is gazing at me, her eyes sparkling as she sips her third glass. She's clearly eager to hear my response.

I reply for her. *Only for her.* "I read a Stephen King book when I was a kid, and it stuck with me my whole life. I wanted to write something like that, something sort of haunting, something that stays with people long after the final page has been read." I'm responding to Benjamin, but staring at Josie. "I think we all have the ability to leave our mark in the world in a unique way, and mine is with words."

"Huh." Benjamin sips his wine, then runs his tongue over his teeth as he processes my answer. "I like that," he replies. Then he lets out a deep, baritone chuckle, leaning back in his chair. "I'm a defense attorney. I'm not sure my mark is as admirable as yours, Evan. I respect you."

I look down at my food with little appetite. I don't want this man's respect.

I just want his wife.

"However, my career certainly provides financial security for my family. I'm grateful that my wife and daughter are well taken care of. That counts for something, right?"

My imagination conjures up an image of myself leaning over the dinner table and strangling the life out of this man while everyone looks on unaffected. It's the only way I can get through the rest of this evening without screaming. My lips curl into the most convincing smile I can muster.

Benjamin holds out his glass like he wants to toast to the fact that he makes more money than me. Or maybe he wants to remind his wife of just how *good* she has it. Josie nods her head and tips her glass with a thin-lipped smile.

"I think it's remarkable what you do, Evan," Josie adds, her smile blossoming as she regards me from across the table. "I like the idea of leaving your mark on people. I think that's why I enjoy music and songwriting so much. It's like you're giving a piece of yourself to others—a tangible part of your soul they can carry with them for as long as they need to."

Her words course through me, trickling into all the empty holes, filling me with warmth. I can't help but hold her gaze for a heartbeat longer than appropriate, considering her husband is merely inches from us, but then I force myself to break away and distract myself by making a mashed potato volcano with my gravy. "I feel the same way," I finally say, my voice cracking slightly, almost giving me away. "It's a good feeling."

Benjamin sucks his lip between his teeth, making a hissing sound as he analyzes me. He's not studying me or looking at me with any sort of reverence. He's just analyzing. I get the feeling this is what he does. He sizes people up. Then he decides what to do with them.

Cocking his head toward Josie, Benjamin's tone borders on patronizing as he says, "It's a great hobby, Jos."

Hobby.

He says it like it doesn't mean anything—like it's simply something to pass the time. I only just met this woman, but even I can see that music lights her soul on fire in the same way writing lights up mine. Her husband is holding her back, making her feel small, making her feel silly for her dreams and aspirations. I'm overcome with the sudden need to defend that.

"I think you should turn it into more than a hobby," I blurt, echoing my sentiment from the first time I heard her play. "You should perform somewhere. Let people hear you." My focus is on Josie, on the way her eyes spark at the very prospect.

"Well, I used t—" she starts. But then she glances over to Benjamin who has an eyebrow raised, as if I just suggested his wife resurrect Beethoven from the dead and go on tour. She closes her lips, and I watch her deflate before my eyes, that spark going dim, the smile fading on her face.

"I mean, that's a little extreme, don't you think?" Benjamin counters, running his fingers along his lightly stubbled jawline. "It's just something she tinkers around with for fun."

My voice is firm, unwavering. "I think we're all capable of great things. I think what we truly want out of life is always there, always waiting for us… waiting for us to be brave enough to take it."

Josie's eyes seem to glaze over, either from the wine or my words, maybe both, and she tries to hide her smile as she brings her wine glass to her lips.

"Interesting perspective," Benjamin says, popping a forkful of food into his mouth. "I can see why my wife likes you so much."

He winks at me as he chews, and I'm unsure if it's condescending or teasing, but an uncomfortable feeling stabs at me, causing my fingers to tense around the edge of my fork. Josie slinks back into her seat, patches of pink blush sprouting on her skin as she pushes her food around her plate.

Dinner drags on while Benjamin guzzles down his sixth glass of wine, his voice growing more intense, his stories more elaborate after each glass. The girls abandoned their half-eaten plates to retreat to Olivia's room, and Josie has begun to clear the table. So, here I sit with the jackass who ruined my life, having to play nice because the long game seems like the best way to ruin him in return.

It's one of the most painful evenings I've ever had to endure.

"Have a drink with me outside," Benjamin declares, standing from his seat, unsteady and slurred. "You like whiskey?"

I want to lie and say I despise it, but I nod instead.

"Beautiful. Blue Label it is."

A few minutes later, I'm sitting on the patio with the man I loathe. He's already solidly drunk as he twirls his whiskey between his fingers. He scratches at the rough bristles on his chin, clinking his wedding ring against the side of the glass. Both sounds make me wince and bite my tongue.

"My wife... she's a good cook, isn't she?"

God, the last thing I want to do is make conversation with this asshole, but at least focusing on Josie's cooking is one of the lesser painful subjects I can think of. "She is," I agree. "Dinner was delicious."

He takes a sip of whiskey, somehow managing to swallow obnoxiously loud as well. "She's a good woman."

Good for you, motherfucker. You have your own good woman, and yet you still had to take mine.

My mind starts whirling with thoughts of Katrina and the things she did. Her betrayal. I thought of her as a good person once... did that only change when she met Benjamin? Did he corrupt her? Or was there always another side of her I never knew?

Was I that blinded by love?

"I'm glad I found her when I did," Benjamin bursts into my thoughts. "Her situation was rough, poor girl." I'm disoriented, lost in my own head, and at first I think he's talking about Katrina. I look at him sharply, but he's not paying attention, and just before I throw the plan out the window in favor of beating him to a pulp, he keeps going. "I know I haven't been the perfect husband, but at least I was able to help her when she needed it."

What? Oh... Josie. Of course, he's talking about Josie. He swirls his drink, taking another loud gulp, when I'm struck by his words: *Poor girl... at least I was able to help her.* Well, then, isn't that just so fucking chivalrous of him. I wonder if he thought of *my* wife as a "poor girl," too. A charity case.

I'm biting the inside of my cheek so hard it's bound to be raw, and I almost, *almost*, give voice to my thoughts, managing to wash them down with another swig of alcohol. My next words border on sarcasm, but he's too involved with his whiskey to notice. "So, you were her savior, then?"

"Nah, I didn't mean it like that," he says, rubbing his ring along his damn glass again. "Has she told you about her first husband?"

Husband... ? I'm jolted for a brief moment, but I don't show him that. Josie had talked about Olivia's father briefly the day of the smoothie disaster, but hadn't mentioned being married. Truthfully, I hadn't thought much about the details. *Huh.* I take a sip of my overpriced whiskey as I choose my words. "Yeah, she told me," is what I settle on.

Benjamin looks out toward the back garden where there are multicolored rose bushes planted in a well-manicured cluster. "They were only married a month before Olivia was born... she was two months old when he had that accident." He shakes his head, ruefully. "Widowed after three months of marriage. Left on her own with a newborn at just twenty-one years old. Can you imagine?"

Well... shit. I knew it was a horrible situation, but imagining Josie, barely out of her teen years, just starting a family... then having it ripped away like that...

There's an ache in my chest; my heart is breaking for another person in a way I'm not sure I've experienced in a long time. I suddenly realize how long I've been completely wrapped up in my own pain. The next breath I take hitches—I'm at a loss for words.

It's all right, though, because Benjamin Grant always seems to have something to say. "When I met her, she and Olivia were living in a shitty one-bedroom apartment she could barely afford. Josie and her husband were still just kids, really, so there was no life insurance... no family to help her."

My throat constricts. "That's fucked up," I say, and my voice sounds just as tight.

He nods. "That girl worked her ass off trying to provide for the two of them."

He refills his glass, holding the bottle out to me in offering. Lifting my hand to decline, I glance over my shoulder at the kitchen window where Josie is cleaning up the kitchen. "You'd never know she went through all that," I say with admiration. It's only for her benefit, even though she can't hear me.

"Mmm," he grunts. "She hid it well, even then. She's stubborn like that. I learned through a friend that she could hardly pay for food, which explained why she was thin as a rail." He swirls the glass, then scratches his face again. *Holy fuck*, why is everything he does so… *loud?* "So, I found out where she lived and brought her groceries."

He leaves that sentence hanging there, like I'm supposed to fucking congratulate him or something. Like he wasn't trying to get in her pants. *Fucker.* I tip the last drops of whiskey into my mouth.

"So, you *did* come to her rescue," I manage. "I'll bet she was grateful."

Damnit, there is not enough alcohol to get me through this conversation politely, and I have to drive home.

His grating laugh makes me jump. "Hardly. She was not interested in my *charity*. Didn't want anything to do with me. Besides, she thought I was trying to get in her pants."

Smart girl. I look at him from the corner of my eye, raising an eyebrow. He notices my glass is empty and offers the bottle again, but as much as I'd like to finish the whole damn thing, I set the glass on a side table to remove the temptation.

"I mean, it's not like I would have said no if the offer were on the table," he chuckles. "But my intentions were mostly pure. She wasn't buying it, though. It took a lot of work to convince her otherwise." He pulls a rose from a vase on the side table, the thorns trimmed off, allowing him to spin the stem between his fingers. "I just couldn't get her out of my head. She was like a broken angel."

How fucking sweet. I refuse to give him a response—I'm not interested in his beautiful love story when I had one of my own, *until he came along.*

But he's not looking for a response. The guy just likes to hear himself talk. He continues spinning the rose, tapping the glass, clearing his throat. Everything he does seems specially designed to work on my last nerve. "I learned that roses were sentimental to her," he says, gesturing at the bushes with the bloom in his hand. "So, I left one outside her door every day for months. Finally, I convinced her to let me take her to dinner." He lowers his eyes to his glass, as though he's studying the contents. "There's this little Mexican cantina downtown near my office. She really liked that place."

My fists tighten around the edges of my chair as a fresh wave of rage fills my veins. *I fucking know that place…*

And now I need to decide between making a quick exit, or committing a violent felony. I clear my throat, my hands on my knees, as I begin to rise. "Well, Benjamin, I should—"

"We've changed a lot in the last few years… I guess that happens. But I'd give anything to get those early days back, before…" He exhales, leaving his confession unfinished. I pause, scrutinizing him as he gazes wistfully through the window at Josie, his eyes glazed with alcohol and melancholy. I sit back down. As much as I would love to break this whiskey bottle over his head, he's hinting at things that could benefit my cause.

Things I want to hear.

"What changed?" I try to control my tone, keeping it neutral, but to my own ears it sounds too eager.

"Oh, you know… life." He turns back around, waving off the question like it doesn't matter. "I got busy with work. She wanted more babies… that didn't work out. Maybe we didn't have that much in common in the first place. I don't know." Benjamin pours another drink, swallowing it back much too quickly, wiping his mouth with the back of his hand. "It's me, honestly… it's all me. I'm not very good at marriage. I fucked it all up."

You fucked mine up, too, you goddamn son-of-a-bitch.

I want that motherfucker to say it, I need him to fucking admit it out loud—but what, then? I lean forward, my casual pretense gone, but he's too drunk to notice. "What did you do?"

You cheated on her, you bastard. You destroyed lives.

He turns to me, his expression drunk and agonized. As his mouth opens, the glass slips from his fingers, shattering as it crashes to the pavement. He blinks at it.

The French doors open, and I'm surprised when it's not Josie's head that pokes out, but a man. I recognize him.

Emmett. That handsy bastard from the party.

Emmett squints his eyes at me, like he's trying to pinpoint me from somewhere. "Sorry to interrupt," he says, his attention darting between me and Benjamin. "I need to discuss something on this case. It's important."

Benjamin hobbles to his feet. "Yeah. Okay, yeah. I'll meet you in my study." He's hardly coherent enough to walk, let alone discuss business, but I'm grateful for his departure.

Emmett stares at me a minute longer, and I'm confident he remembers me now. His eyes narrow in my direction, flickering with distaste.

I give it right back.

When the two men disappear inside, Josie lingers in the doorway for a moment, and I stand from my seat. She looks like she may turn back inside, but she doesn't. She joins me on the patio, wrapping her arms around herself as a crisp breeze sweeps through, making her hair take flight.

"Here." I take off my leather jacket and hand it to her. She appears hesitant at first, eyeing it like it's a surprise bouquet of flowers, but as a new draft rolls in, she accepts the offering.

"Thanks," she says.

I nod, crunching in broken glass. Josie looks down as I'm opening my mouth to explain.

"Ben?" she says with the tiniest curl of her lip. When I nod again, she shrugs. "Yeah… that happens."

She wraps herself in my jacket that is much too big on her. My eyes trail over her petite frame lost inside my leather coat, and a twinge of heat jolts through me. She steps forward and takes a seat in the same chair her husband previously sat in.

I sit back down, folding my hands between my knees. "Thanks for dinner. It was great."

What I meant to say was, *"What happened between us at the Farmer's Market? What the hell was that?"*

Alas, small talk is easier, so I keep my mouth shut.

Only… Josie doesn't seem interested in small talk. She looks down at my jacket, her expression thoughtful as she rubs one hand over the leather. "You remind me of him."

Our knees are almost touching as we sit side-by-side. My eyes dance across her face, trying to read her, trying to make sense of her words. She better not say I remind her of her douchebag husband. *Fuck that*—I am nothing like him.

Josie scratches her chest, which is now flushed along her collarbone. "Olivia's father," she finishes. "Adam."

I'm not really sure what to say, so I respond with, "Oh."

"It's weird, I know," she says, ducking her head and pulling at a rogue strand of hair that caught between her lips. "Maybe it's the tattoo… and your mannerisms sometimes, and just the way you're kind of…" A heartbeat passes as she fumbles for the right word. "Free."

"Free?"

She nods. "Like you've let go of inhibitions and pretenses, I guess. You just... are who you are." Her gaze drifts, skimming over the trees as an October breeze riffles through the leaves, shaking some loose to float down around us. "He was like that."

I choose to ignore her assessment about pretenses, including the fact that she doesn't even know my real name, and instead, focus on why in the hell she's married to *Benjamin Grant*. He definitely doesn't strike me as that type.

Maybe she truly was desperate. He had money; he got her out of a bad situation. She doesn't really seem like the kind of woman who would be motivated by that... but a single parent will make a lot of exceptions when it comes to taking care of their child. And she was so young, all alone.

I flick a leaf off my pants as I contemplate their relationship for longer than I'd like. I wonder if she's happy, stuck in this house like a shiny trophy whose talents are no more than *hobbies*. I wonder if she understands what kind of man he truly is... how much she knows...

How much she *regrets*.

I can't ask that, though. I shouldn't.

When I look up, her focus has found me again. She inhales through her nose and lets it out in a rush. "I know you and I have become... closer over the last six weeks. Maybe closer than what would be considered appropriate."

Josie's eyes find mine, searching for a reaction, but I remain neutral as I wait for her to continue. "Maybe."

She blinks, then chews her bottom lip like she's nervous or anxious. "Anyway, I don't want to give you the wrong impression. I just wanted you to know that."

"That I remind you of... Adam."

She looks away from me, hugging my jacket to her, then finally whispers, "Yeah."

I'm honestly not sure how to feel about her admission. I don't want her to compare me to her dead ex-husband. I don't want her to compare me to anybody. But at the same time, there is a bit of satisfaction in the notion that I remind her of someone she loved.

That's one point for me... maybe two.

I inch towards her until our knees *do* touch, watching as her eyes drift down at the contact... but she doesn't pull away. In fact, I swear she moves in just a little closer. A whoosh of wind kisses us, and it feels decidedly less chilly in the company of Josie Grant.

Maybe it's the way the air prickles my skin, or maybe it's the liquor swimming through my blood, but I'm feeling frisky, so I throw a question at her. "If nothing was holding you back, what would you be doing right now?"

Josie faces me, her caramel eyes brimming with a certain kind of enchantment. I can see the wheels spinning as she considers her answer, her hair blowing across her face. "I think I'd be sitting on a beach somewhere with my guitar, playing music to the stars."

I can picture it. I can picture her there, her voice carrying across the waves like a siren's song while the stars twinkle and dance in reply.

"So, what's holding you back?"

Her eyebrows crease into a contemplative frown, like she's not entirely sure. "I… can't. Olivia. And Ben had too much to drink, so…" She tucks her chin to her chest and smooths her hair back, a light laugh escaping her. "What would you be doing?"

Easy: *you*.

"I'd be transported back in time to five years ago when I was madly in love with my faithful wife, and Summer was still so small and learning about the world, and I just started writing books. Life was pretty damn good then." I didn't really mean to let all of that tumble out, but it's not wrong, and I couldn't exactly say the other thing. I sigh, sliding forward a little more until my knee grazes her thigh, gentle but intentional. "But since physics seem to be holding me back there… I'm happy where I am right now."

She wrinkles her nose, questioning my response. "Sitting on my patio, freezing cold, stepping in broken glass?"

My gaze is fixed on her as I reply. "I have no complaints." I watch her lips part slowly, and my eyes slip down to her mouth, curious as to what she'd taste like. Raspberry wine? Gardenias? Something fresh and sweet like mint? There's no question I'm attracted to her, and I'm confident the feeling is mutual.

Vengeance taps me on the temple, reminding me of the fucking mission. I'm not here for *feelings*. Attraction, though—that's fine. A fun bonus. I just have to keep it in check.

Yes, that's what this is. That's all that happened at the Farmer's Market… *attraction*. She's beautiful, we have more in common than I expected, and we're spending so much time together. It's a natural development. And it's a *good* development. It's a best case scenario development.

I tell myself this as our gazes mingle, the familiar charge swirling around us. Then, because the question doesn't seem too off limits now, I ask her, "Are you happy?"

Josie blinks a few times as she absorbs my question. It's a simple question that only requires a "yes or no" answer, but we both know there is more to it than that—there are layers. It's an ambiguous question that cannot be summed up in a single word. Her eyes are on me as she thinks, processes, filters through the responses in her head. Her delay makes me wonder if *no*, maybe she's not happy. On the surface she has it all—money, security, a successful husband, a big house, a large social circle—but those are superficial things, and if I've learned anything about Josie Grant over the last six weeks, it's that she's not a superficial person. She is more than lavish cocktail parties and prestigious book clubs.

She's more than what her husband sees.

I hate that I want to dig deeper.

I never do get an answer out of her because Benjamin is staggering in the doorway, pointing at Josie with another glass wavering in his hand—a wine glass, this time. "Jos, babe, I need to run to the office. Emmett's going to drive me. I'll be home in an hour." He turns to me, offering a salute. "Great talking with you, Evan. Let's do it again some time."

A colonoscopy sounds more delightful, but I force a smile. "Will do."

Josie spares me a glance and removes my jacket, placing it over the back of the chair, then stands up and heads inside to meet her husband. The unanswered question looms in the brisk air, and maybe I'll always wonder what her reply would have been. I blow out a frosty breath and look down at the shards of glass still resting beneath my feet. I bend to pick them up, gathering up the jagged pieces and collecting them in my palm. I squeeze my fist. Not hard enough to draw blood, but hard enough to hurt. I turn my head to the glass door and glance inside, watching Benjamin kiss Josie on the cheek as he pulls his jacket on. Emmett is standing off to the side watching, *leering* at Josie while she gives a halfhearted smile to her husband and fixes the collar of his shirt.

I look back down at the glass in my hand.

Am *I* happy?

It's a question that I don't seem to have a quick answer for either. I could be happier, and maybe I will be—maybe I'll finally be exquisitely happy the moment I exact my revenge on Benjamin Grant and he and Josie are both out of my life for good.

Maybe then I'll be able to say with confidence: *Yes. Yes, I am.*

It's a little past midnight when I tuck Summer into bed, pulling the blankets up over her shoulders and gliding my hand through her hair. Her eyelids flutter as I kneel beside her, kissing her cheek. Then I whisper against her ear, "Truth bomb?"

Summer is half asleep as she blinks her eyes open to give me her full attention. "Always." Her voice is raspy and laden with sleep, but she's focused on me while I graze my thumb along her cheek.

"You're the best thing in my life, bunny. You're my whole happiness."

She smiles, snuggling deeper into the bed covers, her eyes drifting closed. "I love you, Dad."

"Love you, too."

I kiss her once more before I stand and make my way to the bedroom. As I situate myself under the blankets, I reach for my phone to put it on silent, and that's when I notice the missed message from Josie. I swipe it open to see that it's another video. I press play.

My heart leaps to my throat as I watch the scene unfold. Josie is sitting in the sand, likely at a local lake, and Olivia is beside her with her head resting against her mother's shoulder. Josie is playing her guitar, her voice interweaving with the autumn breeze like they are one. I don't recognize the song, so I assume it's something she wrote herself, which makes me even more entranced as I turn the volume up and lean back against my bed frame. Her eyes are closed most of the time as she sings, but an occasional smile catches her lips, and that's when I smile, too, lost in the moment right along with her. Olivia traces her finger in the sand as Josie looks up to the sky with a smile so wide, so poignant, I wonder if she might cry.

She is singing to the stars.

The melodies swim through me and fill me with something I can't quite explain. When her fingers strum the last chord, she lets out a noticeable sigh, her eyes still pinned upward. Then she sets her guitar down and moves toward the camera, smiling into the screen and ending the video.

I notice a final message come through, so I scroll down a bit farther and read over the words that make my breath stall in the back of my throat.

"Not holding back."

SIXTEEN

*I*T'S THE WEEKEND BEFORE HALLOWEEN.

It's always been a tradition to get dressed up with Logan and Amber and head out to the local bars. Halloween night is reserved for my daughter until she's too old to go trick-or-treating. When that day comes, I'll be the weird, lonely guy handing out candy in a ridiculous costume, probably drunk, and reminiscing about the good old days when my child was dressed like a fucking ballerina.

But the weekend *before* Halloween is reserved for fun and friends.

And hopefully females because, *fuck*... I need to get laid.

Logan and Amber clink their glasses together, toasting to something completely random like they usually do. Tonight it's Saganaki.

"To the delicious, smoky smell of burning cheese."

"To Saganaki. The best appetizer."

"The *only* appetizer."

I shake my head at them. They're dressed up as Frankenstein and his metalhead bride. A little cliché, but it works given their recent engagement. I let Summer pick out my Halloween costume this year, and she chose a chef. She even made me a nametag that says, "World Famous Spaghetti Maker." I Googled male chef costumes and haven't really recovered from the search results, so I'm literally just wearing a black apron over my everyday clothes and carrying around a wooden spoon. I wish I didn't bring it, though, because Logan keeps stealing it to smack Amber's ass, and our table is getting "looks."

I'm sipping on my Jack and Coke when Logan broaches the subject of Josie Grant. I knew it was coming. I sigh around my straw.

"So, what's the deal with you and the Farmer's Market chick?" he asks, slinking his arm around Amber's shoulders. "I was a little preoccupied that day, but you two looked cozy."

"We're just friends," I reply with little emotion.

Amber flies forward in her chair, leaning over the table, narrowing her eyes at me. "Oh, please," she says, unconvinced of my claims. "That's a married woman you couldn't stop eye-fucking. I love the hell out of you, Campbell, but you're playing with fire, and I will *not* hesitate to kick your ass if you lay so much as a finger on her." Amber jabs me pointedly with her own obsidian-tipped finger, hard enough that it kind of hurts.

Playing with fire. She has no idea.

"Jesus, babe, calm down," Logan says, pulling his fiancé back to her seat.

Amber takes a swig of her cocktail. "I am calm. You should know the difference."

I'm slightly irritated, but I know Amber well enough to know that her threats only come from a place of love. She's been protective of me ever since Katrina shattered my heart to smithereens. "It's not like that. Our daughters are friends, and so are we. We have some shit in common, so we hit it off."

"I don't buy that for a second," Amber says, swinging her head side to side and leaning back. "If anyone can read the room, it's me, and it's obvious you like her. And she's clearly infatuated with you because fucking look at you, Evan." Her finger circles around my face like it's the eighth wonder of the world. "Leave her alone, okay? You're only going to get your heart broken again."

"You say that like it's been put back together somehow."

I don't mean to be the depressing asshole in the group—in fact, I go to great lengths to avoid all talk of Katrina and her loathsome betrayal. But since we're on the subject, fuck it. I'm not okay yet, and I don't know when I will be.

Amber softens as she spins the ice cubes around her glass with a straw. "Listen, I get the appeal. She's hot. If I wasn't betrothed to this idiot, I'd probably be trying to sleep with her, too." Logan swats at her under the table, and Amber giggles in reply. "But seriously, she isn't the answer. There are plenty of unmarried women out there. Like Hana. Whatever happened to Hana?"

Logan chimes in. "Stage five clinger."

"She's a solid three," I correct him. "Headed towards four... but five seemed inevitable, so I sort of stopped returning her texts."

"That sucks," Amber says, blowing a strand of hair out of her eyes. "She was a sweetheart. You need a nice girl, Evan. A nice, *single* girl."

I collapse against the back of my seat, my shoulders sagging, my buzz fading fast. I hate that Amber's right. I hate that she can see right through my bullshit. And in this case, I hate the truth because I've been thinking about Josie Grant far more than I care to admit.

I'm not thinking about the things I *should* be thinking about, either—like how it's going to feel when her husband finds out that I fucked his wife, or the sense of victory and relief I'll have when he discovers who I really am.

I'm not even thinking about her in the way I was that night after she left my house... in the shower. Pent-up with lust and a hell of a lot of anger.

No, I'm thinking about ridiculous shit, like the sound of her voice when she's lost in a song, and the unique color of her eyes, and the smell of flowers in her hair. I think about the video she sent me, and how in the few times we've seen each other since that night, we haven't brought it up, but the memory of it is potent and palpable, connecting us in a way that makes my heart clench. I find myself writing more on the days I see her. I find myself *looking forward* to the days I see her.

I'm like a kid with a goddamn crush.

It's fucking obnoxious and unsettling, and there are moments when I want to abandon my entire plan, just so I never have to see her again. Then there are moments when I want to beat down her door, sweep inside, pick her up, and push her up against a wall. I want to fuck her until I get her the hell out of my system, and then maybe, just *maybe*, shit will go back to normal, and I'll stop thinking about her sitting on that beach, sheathed in moonlight, looking up at the stars with tears in her eyes.

Fuck. Me.

I tighten my grip around my glass, swallowing down the rest of my cocktail.

"Well, speak of the Devil. *Literally*... speak of the Devil."

I follow Amber's eyes until they land on Hana Park, who is sitting at the bar with a friend, dressed in a slutty Devil costume. Our gazes meet at the same time, and she lights up, waving and smiling at me from across the room.

Amber leans forward again, giving my shoulder a solid punch. "It's a sign from Satan, himself," she says through her grin. "Go get her, Chef."

I quirk a smile towards Hana, twirling my glass between my fingers. Maybe this is all I need—a distraction. A goddamn *cleanse*. Stage three clinger, be damned.

I don't think too much longer before I stand from my seat, approaching Hana and parking my hip against the bar. "Can I buy you a drink?"

I roll off of Hana, feeling far less satisfied than I thought I would.

Don't get me wrong—the sex is good. Hana is fun, frisky, and open-minded. She's also really nice, which is probably why I haven't cut her loose entirely. But something is missing tonight. Physically, I feel great, but mentally, emotionally… something is just *missing*.

There is a disconnect.

I'm lying on my back, my arm behind my head as I stare up at the ceiling, watching the fan spin in swift circles. I try to focus on only one blade, following it around and around until I start to get a headache and turn to glance at Hana. She's facing me, her head propped up on her palm, her dark brown eyes trying to read me.

"You seem different," she says, her voice a little timid, like she's being careful not to offend me. "I mean, it was *great*. It's always great." Hana shoots me a flirtatious smile before it slips. "You just seem… distracted, maybe."

I blink, absorbing her assessment as a tension rises inside me. Her words ring true, and I hate that she noticed. "I'm fine."

Hana pulls the blanket up to her chin, fisting the sheets between her fingers. She studies me with kindness, maybe even a trace of understanding. "Who is she?"

I grind my teeth together, looking away, then back at her again. "What?"

"It's not Katrina… she made you angry," she notes. "I enjoyed angry Evan." Hana scrunches up her nose in a teasing way, shifting slightly closer to me on the bed.

I don't move in to hold her or touch her, and she doesn't expect me to. I'm not that guy.

I mean… I *am* that guy, but only with the right woman. It's a different kind of intimacy that I reserve for someone I have more than just a physical connection with. So far, I've only experienced that with Katrina. There hasn't been a woman since that I've felt compelled to cuddle, or partake in blissful "morning afters" with.

I finally register Hana's words and run my hand over my face, focusing on the fan again. "I've been up late writing, so I'm probably just tired."

She doesn't believe me, just like Amber didn't believe me, and I wonder when I became so fucking transparent.

Hana sighs softly as she considers her response. "Can I give you a piece of advice?"

Preferably, no.

"Yeah, sure."

She rests her head down on the pillow, gazing at me through the dim-lit room. I'm almost scared to look at her, scared of what she might say, but I shift my focus in her direction and wait.

"There's a Korean proverb that says, *"At the end of hardship comes happiness."* My father would always say this to me when I was going through a tough time." Hana picks at the bed covers, nibbling on her lip. "I would wait and wait for the happiness to come. Sometimes it would come quick. Sometimes it felt like I was waiting for an eternity. But I always knew when it was coming because I'd get this feeling in my belly, this tight knot of intuition, and I knew it was a sign that I was over the hump. It was the light at the end of the dark road."

I swallow as I stare at her, my eyes skimming her face and taking her in, maybe for the very first time.

Hana continues. "I like you, Evan. I had hope that maybe *I* was that happiness for you—your light after everything you went through." There's a sadness in her smile. "I don't think I am, but that's okay. I know your happiness is out there, and it's closer than you think. You're almost there."

I'm struck by her words and feel myself drifting away, picturing Josie Grant sitting on that beach. I can hear her singing. I only stray for a moment, only for a few striking seconds, and then I'm snapped back to reality when Hana reaches out and caresses my cheek.

"Wherever you just went, whoever you thought of just now... that's your happiness," she whispers. "Don't hold back."

SEVENTEEN

"Happy Halloween!" Summer and I are standing in the driveway when Josie and Olivia pull up and join us. We decided to go trick-or-treating in our subdivision because Olivia claimed it was "creepier," which is fair. It's an older neighborhood, lined with tall, billowing trees and no sidewalks. It has a certain charm to it, especially this time of year when those trees rain down crunchy leaves that scatter throughout the quiet street.

Olivia also said her neighbors usually give out toothbrushes and pencils, so fuck that. We're getting giant chocolate bars from Lorna Gibson next door and more Reese's Peanut Butter Cups than I'll be able to successfully steal from my kid without her noticing.

Josie and Olivia approach us while I take note of their costumes. Olivia is clearly a witch with her stringy gray wig and lime green painted face. There's a black mole drawn on above her lip, and her dress is long and purple, touching the tops of her feet. Josie, on the other hand, looks like… Josie. Only, not. Her shirt is inside out, her thick hair is woven into the messiest bun I've ever seen, she has mascara smudges under her eyes, and questionable stains on her leggings. She's also carrying a Starbucks in one hand and a bottle of wine in the other.

I can't help but smile. "Rough day?" I tease, my eyes scoping her from head to toe.

Her grin is bright as she holds up her two beverages, shrugging her shoulders. "I'm a hot mess mom," she declares, taking a sip of the coffee. "Stress level: maximum." Then she covers her mouth from Olivia and whispers to me, "Shits given: zero."

I laugh, thinking she looks strangely sexy as a hot mess mom, while also impressed that she actually put effort into her costume. Katrina always dressed up as a naughty nurse.

Every. Single. Year.

Josie gives us both the once-over, grinning in approval at our costume choices. Summer is spaghetti. It seemed appropriate, considering I'm the "World Famous Spaghetti Maker," and I *did* make her, after all. She waves to Olivia and Josie, covered head to toe in white yarn that resembles noodles. We taped cutout meatballs to her, and she's carrying around a strainer as her candy collector.

Summer made me buy a chef's hat because I was too boring in just my apron, apparently. Josie steps toward me when the hat slips down my forehead, and she situates it back into place. Our eyes hold for a beat as we smile at each other, then she moves back.

"You two are adorable. I wish I could get Ben to dress up," Josie sighs wistfully.

Ben's too busy being lame and having sex with married women to care about Halloween.

"That's a bummer. He's missing out," I opt for.

"Are we ready to go?" Summer asks, bouncing up and down with eager anticipation. "This fake pasta is making me itchy."

Our first stop is the little old lady who lives next door. Her name is Lorna, and she's been widowed for a few years now. She's a kind woman—as long as she doesn't find a person morally offensive. God help you if she does, but so far, I'm in the clear. I mow her lawn once a week, and she pays me with cheek pinches, funny-smelling hugs, and homemade cookies left on the doorstep.

"Trick or treat!" the girls shout, beaming ear to ear.

Lorna answers the door in her nightgown and sweater, her reading glasses perched on her nose. She clasps her hands to her chest, delighted to see the girls, then throws handfuls of chocolate bars into their buckets. She looks up at me and Josie, tilting her head to the side with a whimsical smile on her face.

"Goodness, Evan, I'm so happy for you. I knew you'd find a nice girl again."

Oh. Well, this is awkward.

Summer and Olivia shake their heads, obviously bored now, and skip off to the next house, leaving Josie and I to fend for ourselves. I'm about to correct Lorna when I feel Josie throw her arm around my waist and pull me close.

Josie clears her throat. "He's a keeper," she states, her tone perky and overly enthusiastic. She takes the wooden spoon from my hand and holds it up for emphasis. "I just had to scoop him right up."

What. Is. Happening?

I turn my head to Josie, staring at her through a slow blink. Josie stares right back, her grin wide.

Lorna looks enamored as she watches us. "I knew Evan would find a lovely girl. He's far too handsome to be all alone. I just couldn't believe what had happened..." Lorna does the sign of the cross. "Blasphemous woman."

Jesus, we need to go. Now.

Josie shakes her head with an air of theatrics, then clicks her tongue. "Shameful. Well, I can assure you, I'm far from blasphemous. I'll take good care of him." She gives me a light squeeze.

"Do you go to church, dear?"

Josie leans in close to Lorna, her tone very serious. "Every day." She punctuates each word. "Sometimes twice a day."

Lorna gasps with joy. "Oh, Evan, she's perfect!"

We're one-thousand-percent done now. I take a step back, nodding my thanks to Lorna. "Happy Halloween, Mrs. Gibson. I need to go... find my spaghetti."

I take off down the sidewalk while Josie catches up, giggling at my side.

"You're terrible," I say to her, my own laughter slipping through.

"Blasphemous, indeed."

The next couple of hours are filled with something I haven't experienced in a long time: *peace*. I'm not plagued with bitter thoughts of Katrina, or vengeful schemes against Benjamin Grant. I'm not lost in my old life, full of remorse, and I'm not battling my army of demons. I'm perfectly present. I'm laughing more now than I've laughed in eighteen months. I'm happy and content, and life feels... *easy*.

The only thing weighing me down right now is this damn chef's hat.

The girls collect their final haul, and we head back to the house, prepared to sort and trade. I'm taking a quick peek in the overflow bag Summer has been dumping the contents of her strainer into, searching for the telltale sign of orange wrappers, when she points to a neighbor's house that had been dark when we first set out.

"Hey, they're home now… let's go!" Summer grabs Olivia's flowing sleeve, dragging her across the street and bounding up the porch stairs, just as another small group is leaving.

I look at Josie, tilting my head towards the tri-level house our daughters have taken off for. "Come on, you'll like this couple," I tell her, jogging to catch up. I pause when I get to the porch, giving Josie time to reach us, while I admire the collection of intricately carved jack-o-lanterns lining both sides of the steps.

"Wow… this is impressive," Josie says, the awe apparent on her face.

I have to agree.

"They're artists," I tell her as we climb the stairs to join the girls. Summer and Olivia are already stuffing their faces full of Rice Krispies Treats offered on a paper plate by my neighbor—a cute blonde with quirky cat-eyes glasses, clad in a superhero costume.

"Evan, I see you've brought spaghetti. It looks delicious." Sydney holds the plate out to Josie and me in offering. "You've been holding out on me. Here I thought you were just a writer, and now I find out you're a world famous spaghetti maker, too?"

"Hey, Syd," I greet, grabbing two squares off the plate and passing one to Josie. "Thanks. I do try to stay humble. Most people don't even know."

She laughs.

"Is Oliver here?" Summer asks around a sticky bite. She has a soft spot for Sydney's fiancé, who babysits her on occasion. I think it's because he treats her as though she's an equal, even though she's only nine. Oliver is that way with everyone… it would never occur to him otherwise.

Sydney twirls a yarn noodle around her finger. "He just ran upstairs to grab another stash of pencils." She pulls her lips in, holding back a laugh. "I tried to tell him that no one wants that shi— stuff," she corrects herself, aiming an apologetic grimace over the girls' heads. "But he insists that everyone appreciates everyday necessities. You know."

Summer giggles, bending to scratch the orange cat winding around their legs, while Josie side-eyes me in curiosity. Maybe someday I'll fill her in on the fascinating identity of my eccentric neighbor.

"So, do me a favor," Sydney continues, dropping her voice low like a secret as we hear footsteps on the stairs. "Just nod and smile and pretend they're the most useful thing you've ever been given."

"Evan, good to see you." Oliver lifts his bucket of pencils in greeting when he gets to the bottom of the short staircase.

Olivia squeals, spotting the creature he has cradled in his other arm. Oliver is dressed in his own superhero costume, almost identical to Sydney's. They both have capes and masks that cover their eyes, and my internal alter-ago, *Vengeance Seeker,* perks up in envy. The animal Oliver is carrying sports a mask, too—but this one is natural.

"Oh…" Josie glances my way in mild shock. "He has a raccoon."

"He does, indeed," I say as Oliver holds out the bucket of dubiously useful Halloween favors with pride. "That's Athena."

Athena takes the opportunity to jump from Oliver to Sydney, snatching a Rice Krispies Treat from the plate. She scampers down Sydney's leg and disappears into the house, heedless of Sydney's frustrated reprimands.

Everyone on the porch giggles, while Oliver merely raises a brow. "Perhaps I should have seen that coming," he states as Sydney rubs her forehead, breaking into a delayed laugh.

Oliver's attention turns toward the girls. "Good to see you, Summer. Who is your friend?"

"This is my best friend, Olivia," Summer tells him proudly, entwining their arms as she makes the introduction.

"Pleased to meet you, Olivia," he nods to the younger girl. "We are both named after a species of Mediterranean tree."

Olivia opens her mouth, then closes it, unsure of how to respond, so she just blinks. But Oliver isn't waiting for a reply. Instead, he looks up at me. "Will you be attending our wedding, Evan? We're planning for Spring."

Sydney jumps in. "Oh, yes, it's just going to be casual—more of a block party if I have my way, but you're invited, of course. I'll make sure you get the date and all those details when it's closer. I'm not much of a formal invitation kind of girl."

"Well, sure," I tell them. "Thanks. I'd love to come."

"Good," Oliver nods. "You certainly must. Lorna Gibson will be attending as well."

Sydney shrugs, laughing lightly. She takes a moment to admire the creativity of Josie's "Hot Mess Mom" costume, while Oliver good-naturedly points out that it's similar to Sydney's everyday attire. Knowing Oliver, it's a simple observation rather than an insult.

After we take another gooey marshmallow-covered square for the road and everyone receives two pencils, we thank Oliver for the most useful

Halloween favor we've ever been given, waving our goodbyes and setting off for home.

Josie leans into me on the way down the stairs. "I like them," she says. "They seem like very interesting people."

Nudging her with my shoulder, I grin. "Oh, you have *no* idea. I keep telling them their story would make a great book."

Finally, we get back to the house, tired from hours of walking the neighborhood, but too excited to let the evening wind down. It's an ideal night for a bonfire, so I grab a bag of marshmallows and disappear into the backyard to gather the wood and lighter fluid. I order a few pizzas because it's a Halloween tradition, then pull up four lawn chairs, placing them around the firepit. Josie joins me out back, her arms folded tightly around herself to ward off the crisp air, and we both take a seat beside each other. A draft sends the smoke reeling in Josie's direction, making her cough, so she inches her chair closer to mine. We share a smile. My cheeks ache from how much I've been smiling.

"You looked extra happy tonight," Josie says, crossing her legs and leaning forward on her hand.

I watch as the flames flicker across her face, bathing her in an ambient orange glow. "Yeah, I love Halloween." I downplay my true feelings because I'm not really sure how to admit them to her.

Josie's smile is still in place as she reaches over and takes my arm in her hands. I'm startled at first, confused by the gesture, and also unsure if the heat that swells inside me is from the fire or her touch. She looks down at my tattoo, somewhat dreamily.

"When did you get it?" she asks.

I follow her gaze, remembering that day like it was yesterday. "My eighteenth birthday. I did it to piss off my parents."

Josie laughs, letting go of my arm. "I was twenty. It was right before I got pregnant with Olivia." She slips away for a moment, zoning out into the dancing flames. "Adam and I decided on the nautical star with a compass. It was to symbolize the fact that if we ever got lost, we would always find our way back to each other."

The wind howls, and I watch the old memories flash in her eyes before she ducks her head.

Summer pokes her head out through the patio door, saving me from figuring out how to respond. "Dad! All my Reese's Peanut Butter Cups disappeared."

I slouch back in my seat, trying not to show my guilt. "That's so weird. Maybe they didn't give them out this year?"

Summer groans and rolls her eyes, but heads back inside without bothering to argue. I pull a handful of the candy from my pocket and hand one to Josie.

"Your secret is safe with me," she giggles, peeling back the wrapper.

"Wait. You need to make a sandwich with the marshmallows."

"Huh?" Josie crinkles her nose at me.

"You need to roast two marshmallows and stick the peanut butter cup between them. It's like an ooey-gooey sandwich from the gods."

"I'll pretend you didn't just say *ooey-gooey*," she snickers, reaching into the marshmallow bag and pulling out four. She hands me two. "How have I never heard of this before?"

"Because you haven't truly lived," I tell her. "Remember when I asked you if you were happy?"

Josie nods, her eyes twinkling.

"Well, the answer at that time was no. But I assure you—the answer is about to be *hell yes*. Just wait."

We secure our marshmallows to our sticks and toast them over the open flame. When they're perfectly crisped, we sandwich a peanut butter cup between them and watch the chocolate start to melt.

"The secret is eating it right when it starts to get melty," I explain. "That's when it's perfect."

I watch Josie take a bite with sticky fingers, laughing as she tries not to make a mess. It's impossible, though. There is no way to avoid a mess.

The mess is half the point, after all. The other half is marshmallows and peanut butter cups.

Josie is still giggling as she nods enthusiastically, holding a hand up to her mouth and saying, "It's good."

We both laugh then, because her mouth is so full, her words just come out like an obscure sound, muffled by the treat she's trying to chew.

That's when I notice it.

"I always knew when it was coming because I'd get this feeling in my belly, this tight knot of intuition, and I knew it was a sign that I was over the hump. It was the light at the end of the dark road."

I feel it. The tight knot of intuition. It's been brewing all night, coming to a peak at this very moment as I stare at Josie Grant stuffing marshmallows into her mouth, while she tries not to choke on her own laughter.

I inhale a sharp breath, partly rattled and partly mesmerized. The wind howls again, and it almost sounds like it's speaking to me, whispering words into my ear. I'm torn away from the moment when Summer and Olivia bolt outside shouting, "Pizza!"

Josie stands from her chair, tucking the candy wrappers into her pocket, hiding them away. "She'll never know," she grins.

There's a dab of chocolate stuck to her upper lip, but she turns before I can wipe it away. I watch her go, slightly dazed. I feel sucker-punched. Light-headed.

I feel… *good.*

And that fucking terrifies me.

The wind speaks to me once more as I sit there, listening to the flames crackle and pop like an eerie soundtrack to my epiphany. It outplays the low growl of Vengeance I've lived with for so long.

At the end of hardship comes happiness.

18

EIGHTEEN

A NEW GUITAR LEANS AGAINST MY COUCH.

I bought it on impulse the day after Halloween, and until now, I hadn't realized how much I'd missed it. When Katrina left, everything turned murky. It was hard to find glimmers of hope and patches of light when my world had become eclipsed. Things I used to get lost in just made me feel… *lost*. Hobbies and passions that would bring me joy were reduced to a burden—a dim reminder of my black heart. It was difficult to see through the darkness without a light. It was hard to navigate through the tumultuous tides without an anchor. It was tough to find the good in anything with no semblance of hope.

But things are different now. There's a break in the storm, a clearing. A ray of light poking through the gray clouds that have shadowed me for far too long.

I've been telling myself for weeks that it's not Josie. It's not Josie, *herself*… it's the notion that life didn't end with Katrina. I can still laugh and feel and appreciate small pleasures. Pockets of authentic happiness. *Hope*.

But… it's not Josie.

It can't be Josie.

My fingers move over the familiar strings, like I'm rediscovering an old lover. Playing the guitar is not like riding a bike, though—no, it's an art that takes continuous practice. So, I'm a little sloppy, a little rusty, but every bum note I play is a subtle reminder of how far I've fallen.

It just makes me even more desperate to climb out of this hole.

Josie is seated on my couch with her own guitar, facing me as I sit across from her on the ottoman. The smile hasn't left her face since she showed up on my doorstep after I texted her a picture of my new instrument. The girls are at school, and this is the first time we've spent time alone together without them. There was no time to feel awkward or weird about it, though, because Josie's giddiness was contagious as she sprinted through my front door and inspected my guitar. I studied her, transfixed, as she ran her fingertips along the black body, then slung the strap of her guitar over her shoulders and plopped down onto my couch like she was right at home.

She's watching me tune, her thumb lightly grazing her strings, smiling big. "I haven't played with anyone in almost eight years," Josie says with a bittersweet inflection.

I don't let myself think too hard on the significance of what she's saying, but I suppose any connection she makes between myself and the man she's remembering is good for my end goal.

I grip the neck, situating my fingers into place and glancing at her as I concentrate. "I've never played with anyone," I confess. "The closest I got was when Summer would beat her toy bongos and sing adorably off-key when I practiced."

Her grin somehow brightens even more. I don't know if I've ever seen her this... *content*. I curse my heart for the beat that it skips.

"What do you know?" Josie straightens on the couch and looks down at her instrument, her hair falling over her face like a curtain. She casually strums an *A*-minor chord before her eyes cut to me once again. "Pink Floyd? Rolling Stones? Beatles?"

I'm momentarily distracted by the way her hair matches her eyes, and I'm not sure how long I've been staring before I remember to blink and look away. "Fleetwood Mac?"

Josie looks surprised by my suggestion. "I can play the entire Rumours album in my sleep."

"Impressive." I smile as my fingers begin to caress the strings, becoming more confident with each strum. I play the first few chords to "Dreams," Josie following suit, and when we find our rhythm, it's a dynamic moment... something almost kindred. I let her sing because I'm already doing enough multitasking between trying to play and trying to keep my eyes from straying to Josie.

I fumble a few times, but she only smiles through the lyrics as if my missteps are somehow charming. There is no self-consciousness when I'm with her. There's only a little laughter, a little eye contact, a little playful tension. When the song is over, our eyes immediately land on each other, and I watch as Josie takes in a deep breath and lets it out, like she's coming down from some kind of high.

It strikes me again... this is her element.

"That was fun," she says, her voice a breathy whisper.

I swallow. It was more than fun—it felt a hell of a lot like... *healing*. An antidote to my pain. I feel the cracks in my soul being filled, almost as if there's a chance I could actually be *me* again.

Maybe one day.

But I don't know how to put my thoughts into words, and I'm not sure I want to. So, I just nod, then I launch into another song by Fleetwood Mac called "Little Lies." It's an acoustic cover version I heard one time by a male vocalist.

I think Josie is about to jump in, but she hesitates, resting her guitar on her lap instead. I'm unsure if it's because she doesn't know how to play this one, or if she just wants to watch *me* play.

I keep going.

I should probably be nervous, as I can't think of another time I've allowed myself to be this vulnerable with someone... but I'm strangely calm. Liberated, even. I sing this song on my own, and while my guitar playing is leaving little to be desired, my voice doesn't waver. I know this song well. I sang it a lot after Katrina left. It was the last song I played before selling my guitar. One day, after having played it over and over, feeling more hardened each time, I was just... done.

I cut out another piece of my soul that day. It was the day I fully committed to the plan.

Now that the light is beginning to peek through some of the cracks, I'm realizing more and more that I didn't just lose Katrina; I lost myself. And I grew comfortable with that, with the loneliness and the anger. I was complacent in my grief. I was damaged to the point where hell felt like home, and I don't think I ever really planned to leave.

But it doesn't feel like home anymore.

I want out.

So, I close my eyes and sing the song like I'm coming full circle—as if it's the last time I'll ever sing it. Maybe it is.

Maybe I'm cutting out another piece of my soul, but it's a part that had rotted. It was dark and bitter, and this time, it's a necessary break. It's a release—a *purge*. I sing with a passion that has laid dormant for too long. And as the last note fades in the air, closing the circle, I let myself soak in the moment. There's a stillness in my soul.

There is peace.

My emotions must be evident, because when I open my eyes, Josie has tears streaking down her face. The image makes my breath catch as I lower my guitar.

I'm tongue-tied.

Josie forces a laugh, wiping at the wetness with the back of her wrist. "Sorry. I'm such a sap."

I think back to what she said at the dinner table a few weeks ago: *"It's like you're giving a piece of yourself to others—a tangible part of your soul they can carry with them for as long as they need to."* I can't help but wonder if I just gave a part of myself to Josie Grant. I wonder how long she'll carry me with her...

And when she'll wish she never had.

I press my clammy palms against my denim-clad knees, feeling rattled. I'm not sure what to say or how to react right now—I'm torn between comforting her and laughing it off to lighten the mood. Part of me wants to tell her to leave, to let me be, to give me room to *breathe* since the air feels so damn scarce right now, and part of me wants to hold her in my arms and wipe the tears from her flushed cheeks.

I'm confused because I want to walk away... but I also want to kiss her.

I *want* to kiss her.

And kissing her is part of plan, yes, except...

What I feel is not out of spite. It's not for revenge.

I just want to.

Fuck.

I stand from the ottoman, abandoning my guitar on top of it, and disappear into the kitchen. I'm desperate for a reprieve. I need to breathe, get myself the fuck together. But she doesn't know I'm trying to get away from *her*, so she follows me. I can see the tearstains still reflected on her cheekbones from my kitchen light. I look away and grip the countertop, leaning forward, shutting my eyes. Shutting her out. The anger I just expelled is bubbling back to the surface, and while it's a different kind of anger, it feels familiar. *Easy.* I cling to it.

I need to hate her. This won't work if I don't hate her.

Only minutes ago, the light was flooding into the dark spaces, and I *wanted* that. But now—

Fuck, I need it back. I need the darkness. I can't do this without the goddamn darkness… so, I let it creep back in.

I embrace it.

I conjure up an image of her husband. I envision the exact moment I discovered Katrina's betrayal. I reflect on how I felt, how my heart bled out, how my future fell at my feet like ashes. I think of Benjamin Grant and how his hands looked wrapped around my wife's waist, pulling her to his chest as he kissed her in all of the places I used to kiss her.

Josie must notice that the tension between us has shifted into something heavier. She approaches me with caution, resting her hand against my arm to subdue whatever it is she thinks I'm feeling. It works for a startling moment. My body relaxes on contact, almost like it's instinct. Like it's wired that way.

Like *she* is the antidote to my pain.

But the logical part of me kicks back on, and I know that she isn't. Josie Grant is a part of my problem. She's a part of my pain. She shares his *name* for fuck's sake.

She's the way to hurt him.

I step away, ignoring the chill that sweeps through me at the loss of her touch. "You should probably get going." I don't have any good reason to tell her why she should get going. The girls will be in school for another few hours, her husband is working, and I sure as shit don't have anything spectacular going on.

Josie knows this, so the question in her eyes glimmers back at me. She clears her throat, lowering her gaze to the cream-colored tiles in my kitchen. "Did I upset you?"

Jesus, she sounds like I just kicked her puppy. Or maybe she *is* the puppy. I grit my teeth together, grinding them until they squeak. I can't throw my anger at her. I can't risk dismantling the bond I've spent the last two months assembling.

I can't reach for that sledgehammer just yet.

So, I funnel my rage into something else. I turn to Josie, pinning my eyes on her. I let my gaze travel over her so fiercely, so deliberately, there is no mistaking my intent. Her cheeks flush brighter. She's on the other side of the kitchen, but I feel her heat from across the room. I watch the way her chest expands, her breaths intensifying, her lips parting as she watches me visually undress her. Her reaction to me is a physical one—Josie is attracted to me whether she wants to be or not.

Whether it's right or wrong.

Whether she'll give in... whether she won't.

She will.

I move towards her like a hunter, evaluating her reaction.

Her eyes widen ever so slightly. She's scared. But I don't think she's scared of me... I think she's scared of *her*.

I don't think she trusts herself.

Good.

I am so in tune with her, I can almost hear her heartbeat as I close in on her, stopping when our toes touch. Josie doesn't move away, which surprises me a little. She stands firm, waiting. She's waiting for me to say something, or do something, or give her a reason to run.

The guilty part of me wants to beg her to run—to shout it, to shake her, to push her away.

Run away and never look back, Josie Grant.

Vengeance tells me to keep my mouth shut. So, I do.

This isn't over.

I'm not finished with you yet, Josie Grant.

Josie's eyes drift downward, settling on her feet. My stare is too bold, my proximity too much. She inhales a flimsy breath, still waiting... always waiting.

She still doesn't move away.

"Josie..." My voice is low, gravelly, and it sounds an awful lot like a warning. "You should probably get going," I repeat.

This time we both know why she should probably get going.

Josie swallows, then tilts her chin up to me. Our eyes lock. We're so close, I can feel her warm breath against my lips. I can smell gardenias. I can almost taste her kiss. I can envision her bent over my kitchen table, pounding into her, saying *fuck you* to Benjamin Grant with every satisfying thrust.

Then I would relish in my victory.

I fucking win.

She finally speaks. "You sing beautifully." A small smile graces her lips before she takes two steps back, her gaze lingering, then turns around and heads into the living room.

I frown, watching her collect her guitar and purse and walk out my front door.

It closes behind her, and I stand there.

I stand there, staring at it.

And then... I break.

I burst.

I *explode*.

I'm throwing dishes, pulling pictures off the walls. I'm slamming my fists against the table and kicking the chairs. I'm yelling and swearing and tugging my hair until it hurts.

It hurts.

It fucking *hurts*.

Fuck.

I storm into the living room and eye the guitar lying on the ottoman.

I reach for it...

And then I smash it.

I smash it against the floor—smash it until it splits, until it breaks, until it's no more than jagged edges and dangling strings. A splintered carcass.

Now, it's almost as damaged as I am.

I wander back into the kitchen in a daze, glancing down at the mess I've made. I threw the vase of roses Summer picked at Josie's; they're lying in the broken glass, a trace of beauty amongst the rubble. I'm numb as I bend over to pick up one of the roses, laying it in my palm to study it.

I am numb.

I close my hand around the stem, squeezing it tight, until the thorns pierce my skin and blood seeps from my fist.

That's when I feel something... but it's not the pain.

I feel *her*.

I feel her standing behind me, her eyes boring into my back, and I can almost predict the look of shock and horror on her face.

I turn.

Josie is looking at me, yes, but there is no horror.

She's not shocked or afraid.

No—what I see in her face is compassion.

I see compassion and sympathy. I see tenderness.

Fucking tenderness.

It cuts me deeper than these thorns ever could.

Time stretches between us as we stare at one another, silent and uncertain. My hand begins to throb, so I open it. I break Josie's gaze, watching the rose tumble to the floor, and I'm jolted by a flash of memory. The picture on her bedroom wall.

Roses fall.

I look at my palm. At the rivulets of blood seeping from my pierced skin. At the imprints remaining from the thorns.

"Do the thorns make the rose any less beautiful?" I ask. I don't know why I ask it. I don't know what kind of answer I'm looking for.

But Josie already knows this because she doesn't answer. She just walks toward me.

She walks toward me with tears in her eyes and tenderness on her face, and she puts her arms around me, then pulls me to her.

She holds me tight. She doesn't let me go.

I feel myself stiffen. I'm confused, I'm… *conflicted.*

I'm shredded.

Shredded from the inside out.

And then my knees are like jelly. My legs can't hold me any longer, and they give.

I am sinking.

Josie sinks along with me, and we land amongst the trampled roses, the scattered glass, and the remnants of my breakdown.

She keeps clinging to me, holding me together as if I'll shatter like the glass surrounding us, and the truth is, I already have.

We stay like this. I don't even know how long, but her arms hold me tightly, her grip unyielding.

I don't cry. I refuse to cry. But I allow my head to drop to hers as the anger drains from me. I rest against her, and I breathe, and I let the anger burn away to ash.

I've never been held like this before, I realize—not since Katrina. I went through the worst thing that's ever happened to me, and I did it all alone. Summer was there, of course, but I never allowed her to see my darkest moments. I shielded her from my demons.

There was no one there to hold my hand, to hold me together, to walk beside me through the fire.

I was all alone… until now.

Now, there is Josie.

The haze finally dissipates, and I'm embarrassed, ashamed. Anger sank its teeth into me, and *I let it.* I let it take control, I let it *consume* me. I want to explain myself, apologize, I want to say *something*, but there's nothing to say. The truth is in the fragments of glass and the broken guitar and my bleeding hand.

Josie understands, matching my silence with her own. We stand up slowly, and she bandages my hand with the first aid kit under the sink, cleaning the wound and wrapping it in gauze, her empathetic eyes occasionally straying to mine. We clean the kitchen together, sweeping the debris into dust pans, placing the roses into a new vase. We don't speak. Our conversation is in the way we look at each other, in the way we move, in the things we *don't* say.

When a sliver of normalcy returns and my house is presentable for when Summer gets home from school, Josie gathers her purse once again and heads for the door. She glances at me over her shoulder, a smile blooming. "You and Summer should join us for Thanksgiving."

It's all she says before she leaves.

She doesn't hate me. She isn't afraid of me. She doesn't think of me as a monster.

She doesn't see me for what I really am.

An hour later, Summer bounces through the front door, asking about my hand, and I tell her I cut it on the rose vase. It's not a complete lie, and she doesn't give it a second thought.

We have breakfast for dinner.

I don't burn the bacon this time.

We chat about school and life and friends, and everything is okay again.

Everything is okay… *for now.*

I'm sitting at my laptop the next day, working on my manuscript, nearing the finish line, when I hear the doorbell ring.

It's a delivery. A large, somewhat heavy box.

I bring it inside and open it, curious and a little bewildered. I didn't order anything.

When I pull apart the cardboard and discover its contents, my heart leaps into my throat and sticks there. I nearly choke.

It's a new guitar.

I reach for the attached note as I suck in a gulp of air:

Please be nicer to this one. — Josie

NINETEEN

THEN
APRIL

IT SMELLS LIKE RAIN.

The pungent musk assaults me as I stand on the busy sidewalk, hands in my pockets, eyes on high alert. It's a Saturday night in the springtime, so downtown Libertyville is alive with laughter, chatter, and possibilities. Not so long ago, I'd be right in the thick of it. Katrina and I would be having a date night on the patio of our favorite Mexican cantina with cocktails in our hands and conversation on our lips. We'd be smiling and flirting and looking forward to continuing our date at home in bed while Summer is at Rayna's house for a sleepover. We'd be tipsy on margaritas, full on enchiladas, and lost in the warmth of each other. It would be a good night.

But this is not a good night.

I'm uneasy. My stomach is in knots, and my heart is thrashing around my chest, trying to make a break for it. There's a feeling a deep-seated dread in my bones that's been there for three days now—ever since my daughter asked me why Mommy was talking about getting an abortion.

I didn't bring it up to Katrina. I wasn't ready yet.

Instead, I watched.

I watched her with new eyes as we went about our new normal routine of silence and avoidance. I studied her every move, her every blink, her every forced smile and secretive text message. She's been chewing on her nails more, which I thought was because she's been depressed and agitated, but now realize is because she's nervous. She's hiding something. And she's hiding more than just our aborted baby.

She's hiding *why* she aborted our baby.

If it was even *our* baby.

My baby.

The thought knocks the wind out of me, and I have to close my eyes, gathering my wits and blowing out a heavy breath of air.

Katrina said she was working a double shift today, but that was a lie. I called the restaurant, and she wasn't even on the schedule. She hasn't been on the schedule all fucking week.

I had to follow her. I planned a sleepover for Summer and followed my wife into town where I watched her walk right past her restaurant and enter an adjacent building: *Benjamin Grant; Attorney at Law.*

An attorney. It throws me for a moment, and I wonder if she's quietly planning a divorce… but no, I'm not going to assume anything just yet. I'm going to wait.

So, that's what I'm doing—waiting. I'm waiting across the street, watching. My stomach is in my throat. I'm jittery and nauseous and *aware*. I'm afraid a divorce is the least of my worries. I'm afraid I know what I'm about to discover… I can feel it in my gut, but I don't know how to process it. I don't know how to accept it.

I don't know how I'll ever be able to accept it.

But for now, I wait.

I look up at the storm clouds rolling in, shrouding what's left of the setting sun. It's an ominous backdrop for a night like this. It's fitting. It's the perfect scenery for the moment I'll discover my wife having an affair after so many blissful years together. After eight years of marriage, one beautiful daughter, and a future I was absolutely *certain* of.

When my eyes shift back to the building across the street, the door opens, and Katrina walks out onto the sidewalk. She's alone. I wonder for a moment if I jumped to conclusions—maybe I had it all wrong. Maybe Summer misheard the conversation, maybe there's an explanation, maybe I can salvage us, after all…

Maybe my wife still loves me.
For a moment, there is still a future. For a moment, there is hope.
And then *he* steps outside.
He turns to lock the door, then turns to *her*.
Katrina.
My wife.
He takes her hand.
The hand I took when I proposed.
He squeezes it.
The hand I squeezed as Summer was brought into the world.
He leans down and kisses her mouth.
The mouth I've kissed every single night for the last fourteen years.

He spins her around, pushing her up against the brick building, his fingers curling around her hips as he peppers more kisses along her neck. I hear Katrina's giggles float across the street—giggles that used to be for me. They land in my ears, seeping into my pores like a lethal toxin. It burns me. It stings me.

It fucking destroys me.

My legs can no longer hold me. My body isn't made to bear the weight of what I'm processing. The bench is two feet behind me, and I stumble back, collapsing onto it without breaking away from the nightmare in front of me. Someone stops to check on me, asking if I'm okay, and I realize I must look as horrified as I feel.

I don't respond. I *can't* respond. Nothing is working properly—my tongue, my brain, my heart, my lungs.

I am numb.

My vision trails them as they saunter down the bustling sidewalk, hand-in-hand, their laughter still within earshot. They enter our favorite Mexican cantina. They will soon have cocktails in their hands and conversation on their lips. They will be smiling and flirting and looking forward to continuing their date at his home, in his bed, while I am all alone in mine, wondering where I went wrong. They will be tipsy on margaritas, full on enchiladas, and lost in the warmth of each other. It will be a good night.

They will have a good night.

And I will slowly bleed out.

I watch them disappear inside the restaurant as the weight of what I've witnessed begins to sink in. I feel the anger boil my blood. I drown in it. I let it take control.

I let it *consume* me.

It's the only way. It's the only way to survive this.

Deep within me, something stirs. Awakens. It's no more tangible than a swirling shadow, seeping through the cracks of my soul—but I feel it.

I hear it whisper.

I stand from the bench just as it starts to rain.

NOW

We join The Grants for Thanksgiving dinner.

Normally, we'd spend it with Amber and Logan, but they left for Seattle yesterday to surprise Amber's parents with the news of their engagement. So, that either left spending the holiday at home, just the two of us, while Summer sulked because *it's all Olivia has talked about*—or spending it with the woman who just witnessed me at my worst *and* her husband who set it all in motion.

I debated option three: spontaneous getaway to Istanbul.

The weather is pretty nice this time of year, and they have good tea. They also have Baklava. I love Baklava. Besides, Thanksgiving dinner is overrated. Nobody likes a turkey coma, sweet potatoes are confusing—are they a side dish? A dessert? Are they good for you? Why are there marshmallows sometimes? Not to mention, the meaning behind Thanksgiving is really kind of morbid and fucked-up.

But, alas, I want my daughter to still love me, so here we are.

We're standing in the foyer as Josie gazes up at me, her hair curled and styled, her cheeks pink with a mauve blush, her lips glossy. She's wearing a long dress with a floral pattern and spaghetti straps, and the neckline is low —*so* low—and I'm trying my hardest not to look, but I'm taller than she is, and it's difficult, damnit.

I'm suddenly very aware of how close she's standing to me.

And now I can't stop thinking about the laundry room.

Shit.

Josie greets Summer, then inches up on her tiptoes to wrap her arms around my neck, pulling me in for a hug. "How are you?" she whispers into my ear.

It's a normal question. There is nothing unusual or remarkable about it. It's a standard greeting from a friend to a friend.

Only… it's not. It's personal and intimate and so much more than just a question. It's meant for me, *only me,* and I shiver at her words, along with the sensation of her body pressed fully against mine. "I'm okay."

A normal answer for a normal question.

Josie moves back, smiling at me, a silent response to all the things I did not say.

"It smells really good in here, Mrs. Grant," Summer pipes up, twirling side to side in her navy blue dress. Her only dress.

Josie returns her attention to my daughter, crouching down and fixing a piece of hair that came loose from Summer's barrette. "Thank you. Thanksgiving dinner is my favorite."

"Mine, too! Dad made corned beef and cabbage last year because he wanted to be a rebel. It was the worst."

"Save a turkey, eat a cow," I shrug, recalling my motto from last Thanksgiving.

The truth is, I couldn't handle the smell of roasting turkey and pumpkin pie—it was Katrina's favorite meal. It hurt too much.

Josie's eyes flick to mine, her smile broadening. "Come inside. I want you to meet my sister."

Carrie. I remember our conversation in her kitchen right before the smoothie disaster.

Right before I saw her naked.

In the laundry room.

Josie naked.

Scolding myself, I shake my head. *For fuck's sake, Evan, get it together.*

I'm fully immersed in the gutter when we round the corner, and I'm greeted by a shorter, lighter-haired Josie, her husband, and two twin boys playing on the living room floor with Olivia. Carrie and her husband stand from the couch upon seeing me, then approach to say hello.

"Carrie, Kyle… this is Evan," Josie says, taking her sister by the arm and pulling her farther towards me. "He's my writer friend I was telling you about. Our daughters are inseparable."

I shake both of their hands while Carrie beams up at me.

"Josie has said great things about you," she tells me.

She has? She talks to her sister about the man she's secretly attracted to who is not her husband?

Well, that's fantastic. I'll take it.

I smile and nod, glancing over at Summer who has joined Olivia and the boys on the rug. "The girls have been having a lot of fun. They really hit it off."

Carrie follows my gaze to the children. "That's Jace and Jude. Twins. They just turned two."

Kyle adds, "Twin terrors."

We laugh. My eyes stay on the boys for a beat as I envision what my child would look like now. We didn't know the gender yet, but I think he'd be a boy. I think I wanted to call him Finn.

He would be one-year-old.

Then I remember that I don't know if the baby Katrina was carrying was even mine. She wouldn't tell me. Maybe *she* didn't even know. Maybe she was too scared to find out.

Benjamin joins us then, slapping me on the back harder than necessary as he adjusts his tie. "Evan, old friend. Great to see you again."

I tense, cringing at the sting on my back from his palm, every muscle in my body freezing at his nearness. I force a pleasant expression onto my face as I turn to him, hoping it looks more convincing than it feels because I'm no longer confident in my fucking acting skills. "Thanks for having me."

Josie glides over to her husband, wrapping her fingers around his upper arm and leaning in. "Ben, can you check on the turkey?"

He frowns, grumbling to himself, and retreats into the kitchen. He shouts over his shoulder a few seconds later, after pulling open the oven, "It's definitely dead."

Carrie and Kyle chuckle as Josie sighs, making her way to the stove.

Fucking hilarious, Ben. You're a real comedic genius.

I step over to the rug and sit down beside Summer, leaning back on my hands as I watch the girls play blocks with the toddlers.

Summer looks up at me, smiling ear to ear. "They remind me of Mason," she says, placing a red block in one of the boys' chubby hands.

Mason. That's the name of Katrina's boyfriend's son. Summer talked about him a lot after she returned home from her stay in Tennessee. It filled me with a sense of deep regret that I was never able to give her a sibling.

Bitterness, too.

The taste in my mouth echoes that feeling, and I have to swallow it back before I respond. "You would be a great big sister, bunny," I tell her.

Summer nods, her smile turning as sad as her eyes, then continues to play with the two boys.

It guts me.

The adults are full on food and buzzed on wine.

The girls are upstairs playing in Olivia's room, and Jace and Jude are running in circles around the kitchen island with turkey bones they stole out of the garbage can. Carrie jumps from her chair as she notices. Jace throws his across the room when he sees his mother running towards him, while Jude shoves the bone into his mouth. I get to him first and remove the offending object, prompting the meltdown of all meltdowns.

"*My* kurkey bone!" Jude pouts, stomping his little foot and bursting into tears.

Carrie shoots me a look that reads as both a "thank you" and "save me" and plucks the screaming toddler up, carrying him out of the kitchen. Jace begins to cry when he sees his mother walk away with Jude, and I'm not really sure if I should intervene or not, so I just kind of stare at him helplessly, which only makes him cry harder. Luckily, Josie skips over to us as she shuts the dishwasher and picks up Jace, perching him on her hip and grinning wide. She twirls him around, dancing in place until his tears turn into giggles, and I can't help but watch as a peculiar feeling washes over me. It's not a bad feeling, but it pokes and tugs at me, so I force myself to look away.

"When can I borrow you?"

I jerk my head up to Josie, her expression bemused as she bounces the giddy toddler, but her eyes aim my way, holding something more poignant.

I can't fucking help myself, and my mind instantly strays back to the gutter. I imagine all the ways she can "borrow" me, and I'm confident every single one of them would make her blush. I clear my throat and go the humorous route instead. "If you need me to hang out with your husband and listen to him talk courtroom and lawyer lingo, I have somewhere to be…" I glance at my invisible watch. "Five minutes ago."

Josie's laughter pulls a smile onto my face. "Sustained," she jokes. She sets Jace down, and he scampers into the living room to where Benjamin is prattling on to Kyle about an affirmative defense case, while Carrie is changing Jude's diaper on the couch. Josie looks at me, her smile waning slightly. "I just wanted to talk. In private."

I know what she wants to talk about, but that doesn't stop the gutter thoughts from returning tenfold. I don't know what the fuck my problem is —I need to get it under control.

But as our gazes hold, I don't get it under control, and a familiar heat swells between us. Josie ducks her head to break it.

"I'll meet you out front." My tone is lower than I anticipate. It cracks a little. I step away, heading to the front of the house and reaching for my leather jacket on the coat hanger.

Josie joins me on the porch moments later, wrapped in a black peacoat, the chill in the air ebbing as soon as we're within inches of each other.

It's funny how that always seems to happen. No matter how cold it is, no matter how cold *I* am—no matter how frozen my heart feels—I always find myself melting when I'm with her. I always find warmth.

I hate it and love it all at the same fucking time.

Pulling the box of cigarettes out of my pocket, I hold them out to Josie. She considers them, biting on her lip, but eventually shakes her head with dismissal. I light up, blowing out a slow breath of smoke into the November night before I turn to her. We're both leaning forward on the porch rail, our arms dangling over the edge. "I'm sorry." It's something I should have said the moment I turned around in my kitchen and saw Josie standing behind me, my heart pounding, my hand bleeding onto the tile floor. Dripping onto the shards of glass, creating a gruesome scene that would work so well in one of my books.

But this was real. I was not a character.

I was more *me* than I've ever been in the last year-and-a-half, and I think that's what terrifies me the most.

It doesn't seem to terrify Josie, though, and I'm not sure why. She gazes at me with nothing but benevolence. "Evan, you don't need to apologize. That's not why I wanted to talk."

"Yes, I do," I insist.

"No."

Josie faces me fully, like she wants me to look at her. To *really* look at her.

So, I do.

"I've been there," she continues. "I've *had* that moment. That excruciating, blindingly painful moment of weakness and self-destruction. I walked around like a zombie for an entire year after Adam died, shut off from the world, shut off from my child, shut off from *myself*. I felt like a fraud, telling my friends and family I was fine, just because I couldn't burden them any longer... so they wouldn't pity me. I lied to myself day after day, stuffing it all down. It was exhausting, but it was easier than the inevitable breakdown I would suffer if I were to face my pain head-on."

I hold my breath... I listen... *I know.*

Josie reaches out a hand to touch my arm, much like she did in my kitchen before I broke. The instinctual calm returns.

"I was driving to work one morning when a song came on the radio. It wasn't a relevant song, it wasn't *our* song—I think it was playing one day while we drove to the movie theater, and for some reason, the memory stuck with me. That's when it happened... my trigger. My breaking point." Josie lowers her eyes to the porch rail. "I lost it," she says, picking at the paint with her fingernail. "I burst into tears. I drove my car into a tree."

Her confession stuns me. I suck in a breath, almost choking on the mouthful of smoke I inhale.

"Zero stars. Do not recommend." Josie quirks a smile, trying to lighten the mood, her eyes floating up to mine. "I walked away with a concussion and a nasty scar along my ribcage. But I also walked away knowing that I almost *didn't* walk away. I almost let my grief, and my anger, and my fear destroy me. I almost left my daughter all alone."

I want to see her scar. I want to touch it, to feel it, to graze my fingers along the physical evidence of her trauma. I look down at my hand instead, opening my palm and splaying my fingers. My cuts are healing. They won't leave a scar.

I don't know whether I'm grateful for that, or disappointed.

Josie takes my hand in hers, our eyes locking. "I'm not sure what triggered you that day. Maybe the song you played, maybe something else. But I want you to know... if you ever feel like that again, if you ever need to break apart, you don't need to break alone. I'm here, and I understand. I'll help you."

It was you, Josie Grant. You were my trigger.

I swallow down those words and squeeze her hand, looking back out at the quiet front lawn. "We were together for twelve years," I whisper. I'm overwhelmed with the desire to spill my guts to her. I want her to know what drove me to that moment. I want her to feel my pain like I feel hers. "We were the stereotypical high school sweethearts. Love at first sight. Fairytale romance." A smile wants to take over at the memories, but I set my jaw to force it back. There's nothing to smile about. Not anymore. "I never saw anyone like I saw her. I've never seen anyone *since* like I saw her… she was my world. We had that kind of relationship people envied—always touching each other, kissing, flirting." I let out a wounded sigh. "I don't know how I missed the signs, the warnings, the red flags."

"Sometimes we only see what we want to see."

I nod as my eyes sweep over Josie's face. They trail to her lips before I look away. "She was having an affair for six months before I found out. She got pregnant, and I don't know if it was my baby, or… *his* baby. I'll never know." I close my eyes as I feel the anger simmering beneath the surface. It wants to boil over. It wants to burn me. "She had an abortion."

I hear Josie gasp, so I turn to her. Her eyes are glazed over, watering with sympathy for me. "Evan, I'm so sorry."

I hate this sinking feeling in my gut.

I fucking hate it—this little voice telling me I'm just as bad as my traitorous ex-wife. I'm silently betraying the woman beside me who has only shown me kindness and compassion. I'm hurting her and she doesn't even know it. She feels *sorry* for me, and she shouldn't. She should hate me.

She will hate me.

And that fucking hurts.

And I *hate* that it fucking hurts because it means I'm starting to care about her.

Fuck.

I squeeze my eyes shut, trying to block out the battle raging on inside my head. I inhale a shuddering breath and blow it out slowly. "The guy had money. He was successful. My wife wanted more out of life than being married to a struggling writer who could hardly afford our monthly date nights. She wanted lavish gifts and tropical vacations and an extravagant, exciting life I could never give her." I glance at Josie. "And all I wanted was her. I already had everything I could ever need."

I bite my tongue against the need to spill the rest of it.

Against the desire to tell her exactly *who* Katrina betrayed me with.

A tear slips from Josie's eye, and as I watch that tear glide down her cheek, she threads our fingers together. I'm startled by the gesture. I look down at our intertwined hands, staring at them as my heart speeds up, as my head turns foggy…

This isn't something friends do.

This is something lovers do.

I turn to Josie. She's staring back at me with a look in her eyes that tells me she is questioning herself. Maybe she shouldn't have done that. Maybe she took it too far.

But she doesn't let go.

"You'll always be enough for the right person," she says softly, her gaze never diverting from mine.

I skim my thumb along her hand, and I swear she leans against me a little farther, a little closer, melting into me while I continue to melt. I glance at her mouth again, then back up to her eyes, watching as her pupils dilate.

I'm consumed with the need to kiss her.

Instead, I ask, "Do you love him?"

Josie stills, her brow creasing, her glossy lips parting with a slight intake of air. "What?"

Shit. I don't know why I asked her that, but I probably shouldn't have. Maybe I should have just kissed her.

Maybe I should go.

Maybe I should never come back.

Maybe I should kiss her.

"Josie?"

Our hands part so fast, Josie knocks her knuckles against the adjacent post and cradles her hand in the other. We discover Carrie standing behind us, poking her head out the front door with a furrowed brow of confusion.

Josie's sister saw us together, shoulder to shoulder, hands interlocked like lovers.

"We were just getting some air," Josie says shakily. She steps away, not looking back at me, and escapes into the house.

Carrie stands there for another moment, her eyes fixed on me for a beat, then lowers her gaze to the porch. There's a slight nod of her head, and I'm not sure what it means or what she's implying, but she closes the door and disappears inside.

I exhale sharply as I gather my bearings. My cigarette has burned through the paper, and it scorches my fingers. I flick it to the ground, cursing to myself, stubbing it out with my shoe. The embers extinguish, but not the fire crackling inside me. *That* burns strong. My blood is close to boiling, but this time it's not from anger.

I raise my hand in front of my face and study it. It's still tingling. I can still feel Josie's hand in mine, squeezing me, comforting me, *warming* me.

I sigh as I lean forward against the rail and look up to the stars. The same stars Josie sang to that night on the beach. As they twinkle, I wonder if they know something I don't know… if there is something they are trying to tell me.

I listen. I strain my ear. I don't even breathe.

But all I can hear is the sound of my own heart beating against my chest.

Maybe I should have kissed her.

20

TWENTY

I've never been so happy to see Delilah.

She showed up for dessert, and it's the perfect diversion from the tension enveloping the room. Well… enveloping Josie and I, at least. And then there's Carrie. Her smile has stayed pleasant, but she's been watching me.

Us.

"Sorry I'm late," Delilah says as she glides into the living room, doing a double take when she spots me. She smiles, throwing her purse over a bar stool and fluffing her hair, then turns to Josie who is setting up Pictionary. "My father went on a political tirade, and I could hardly get out of there. I didn't miss the games?"

Josie shakes her head, her focus fuzzy. "We're just getting started."

"It's so weird without Ryan this year. He's up in Wisconsin. I think he's screwing his sister's friend," Delilah sighs, plopping down on the couch beside me, closer than I anticipate. "Bastard."

"Uh-huh." Josie doesn't look up from her task. I don't think she even hears Delilah speak.

Delilah glances at me, her expression wary, then looks back to Josie. "You okay?"

Josie definitely doesn't hear her this time.

Benjamin approaches and wraps his arms around Josie from behind, leaning down to kiss her shoulder. "Pictionary, huh? You know I can't draw."

"That's why you're not on my team," Josie deadpans. She chugs down the rest of her wine and pours herself another glass.

I lean back into the couch, folding my hands between my lap. Carrie excuses herself to join Kyle in the basement where he's playing with the boys, and Summer and Olivia are still upstairs.

Delilah leans into me, tilting her head up to grab my attention. "What's up with her? Ben acting up?"

Her sister caught us holding hands and gazing into each other's eyes while her husband was only a few feet away. I almost kissed her. I still want to kiss her. I chew on my tongue and try to weave together a more appropriate reply. "Probably the turkey coma setting in."

"Alcohol is the perfect remedy for that," Delilah winks, standing from the couch and traipsing into the kitchen to pour herself a glass of wine. "Want some?"

"Sure."

Alcohol is exactly what I need when my willpower is barely hanging by a thread. My gaze shifts back to Josie, who is immersed in the game. We haven't spoken since our rendezvous on her front porch. Josie and Carrie disappeared upstairs to talk, and ever since, there has only been heavy eye contact and uncomfortable silence. I want to get her alone. I want to "borrow" her again.

I want to know what she told her sister.

I pull out my cell phone and send her a text message, watching as she reaches for her phone that just vibrated on the side table.

ME: *When can I borrow you?*

Josie looks like she reads over the question more than once, then slowly raises her eyes to me. She looks flustered, so I smile at her to ease the tension. Glancing back down at her phone, she chews her lip, considering her response, then types out a brief message.

JOSIE: *Not a good idea.*
ME: *Why?*
JOSIE: *You know why.*

Actually, I *don't* know why. I don't know if it's because she's worried her sister will see us alone together and become more suspicious, or if she's worried I'm going to kiss her.

Maybe she's worried she'll kiss me back.

I sigh, contemplating my reply, my eyes floating from my phone to Josie, then back to my phone.

ME: *What did you tell your sister?*

A glance my way. A swallow. A shaky breath.

JOSIE: *I told her the truth. We've both had a rough past and I'm helping you through yours. She caught us during a particularly heavy moment.*

We catch each other's stare after I read through her reply. Something unspoken passes between us because I think we both know that's not the whole truth, but I decide to leave it. I nod my head and slip my phone back into my pocket just as Delilah returns with a very full glass of wine.

"Don't you hate when restaurants only fill your wine glass halfway? What kind of bullshit is that?"

She giggles as I carefully accept the wine. Delilah sits close to me again, our thighs touching, and I can't help but notice Josie's gaze drift to the source of contact. She blinks and stands, sweeping a hand through her hair and joining her husband in the kitchen as he pours whiskey over ice.

We play Pictionary.

It's guys versus girls.

We lose miserably because Benjamin can't draw worth shit. Plus, he's intoxicated and kept trying to draw an elephant but was saying "meow" the whole time, and it was confusing as fuck.

Josie is quiet, reserved, distracted.

Delilah is tipsy, becoming bolder as she flirts with me. Josie's eyes stray to us every now and then, and I wonder what's going on inside her head. I can't help but feel like there's a spark of envy that flashes every time Delilah leans in to whisper in my ear, or grazes her hand along my thigh, or dips her forehead against my shoulder when she laughs at something I say. The feelings swirling around my gut are also confusing as fuck because I should be into this. Delilah is beautiful and willing and just as lonely as I am. And yet, I'm finding myself... *disinterested*.

Hell. I need a smoke.

I stand from the couch and head to the front door, pulling on my jacket and breathing in the crisp air. As I'm reaching for my cigarettes, I hear the door open behind me, so I turn, expecting to see Josie. The smile on my face slips when I discover Delilah joining me instead. She tugs her jacket tightly around her as her dark hair catches a draft.

"Do you smoke?" I offer her a cigarette before I light.

She shakes her head.

"Me neither," I shrug.

Delilah leans her back to the rail, watching me with great interest as my lighter sparks to life and the embers flare against the dusky night. "What's your story, Evan? You're kind of broody and mysterious. But also funny and charming. I'm trying to figure out why you're single, but I'm struggling."

I chuckle at the barrage of compliments and lower my head, inhaling a sharp drag.

"You're gay, aren't you?"

I laugh again. "I'm not gay. I'm…" I try to pinpoint the right word. "Recovering."

Delilah blinks as she pieces together my reply. "Alcohol? Drugs?"

"Broken heart."

There's a sadness in her eyes that I can relate to. She understands. She's recovering, too. "Even worse," she says, her voice barely above a whisper.

I nod slowly, matching her stance against the porch rail, looking down at my feet. "Yeah."

There's a comfortable silence that swims between us as we both reflect on our own pain. Our own battles. Our own path to recovery. I wonder if she's handling it better than me, and if she is, I wonder how. I wonder if there's an easier way, a *healthier* way, to navigate through the dark moments.

I glance at Delilah as I toss my cigarette to the cement and crush it beneath the toe of my shoe. She looks at me, a mischievous twinkle in her eyes.

"Do you need a rebound?"

A smile tugs at my lips as I regard her. "I'm nineteen months into my recovery. I've had my rebound. Lots of them."

She ducks her head, almost bashfully. "I haven't had one yet. They say it helps, though."

"It doesn't. Trust me."

Delilah looks back up to me, our gazes holding, and I wonder if maybe this *is* what I need. Maybe I do need a rebound… but it's no longer from Katrina.

It's from Josie.

It's from whatever the fuck is going on, whatever these goddamn *feelings* are.

I told Delilah the truth—it won't help. But it'll offer a temporary peace, a reprieve.

A distraction.

I lean in enough to see what she'll do—if she'll meet me halfway. Delilah sucks in a startled breath, her eyes fixed on my mouth. She doesn't move back. The wine has gone to my head; I feel it like a warm, comfortable haze, and I hesitate, inches away from her face. "Is this okay?"

She nods once, then closes the gap.

When her lips meet mine, I feel relief. A comfortable familiarity. There is no messiness, no complicated feelings, no internal war battling it out inside me. It's easy. It's freeing.

I can breathe.

I raise my hand to cup her cheek, deepening the kiss with my tongue, feeling her meld against me and moan softly into my mouth. I thread my fingers through her honey hair as she clings to my shirt to hold herself steady.

Wait.

Brown hair.

Delilah has brown hair.

My fingers tighten in that brown hair, and she whimpers.

Brown, brown, brown.

I jerk back and try to catch my breath, closing my eyes as visions of Josie Grant flash through my mind. I grit my teeth and swallow, feeling tainted—feeling *violated*.

Goddammit.

"Are you okay?"

Delilah is looking at me, concerned, confused, but not nearly as much as I am.

I respond by kissing her again, harder this time, as if I'm trying to cleanse myself. Wash Josie away. Expel her from the marrow of my bones.

I feel like I need a fucking exorcism.

I yank Delilah closer, and she squeaks in surprise, her hands trailing up to my shoulders. Our kiss is frenzied, desperate, as I force myself to focus.

Wash her away.

"I have a spare bedroom if you need it."

We pull apart at the sound of Josie's voice, and I turn to see her standing in the doorway. Her eyes are pinned on me, hard and pointed, and now I'm *confident* there is jealousy behind them. I swallow as I take a step back from Delilah, almost like I'm guilty of something... and I am, I am, *I am...*

But not for this.

Delilah doesn't seem to sense the tension when she giggles in reply, wiping her mouth with the back of her hand. "Sorry," she says, smiling and giddy.

Josie clears her throat, tucking a golden strand of hair behind her ear and shifting her attention to her friend. "No need to apologize, Del. You're both single. Have fun."

I'm staring at my shoes because I can't face Josie.

I can't face the fact that I wish I had been kissing *her*.

Josie steps back inside and closes the door.

The air leaves my lungs in a rush.

I'm in too deep.

It's past time for me to hit the road before anything else happens. After the kiss with the unfortunate ending, I made my excuses to Delilah, telling her we needed to get home. Now I'm searching the house for Summer, doing my best to avoid Josie on the way out.

I can't stand to see that look on her face again.

Before I have a chance to climb the stairs and check Olivia's room, a firm hand lands on my shoulder.

It definitely isn't Josie.

"Evan! I was just looking at that Johnnie Walker we cracked open a few weeks ago." Benjamin squeezes my shoulder like a touchy-feely asshole. I know he's about to coerce me into a drink, and I'm not interested. "What do you say we see if we can polish off the bottle? I have a thing about my Blue Labels—once I crack one open, I have to finish it with the same person."

Okay, that's just weird. Plus, the guy is already well-past drunk, and also… no, thank you. "I think I'm done drinking for the night, but thanks. I'm just going to collect my daughter if I can find her in your sprawling mansion…" I force a smile. "Maybe Kyle can take my place?"

"Nope. Has to be you." He ignores my protests, guiding me towards the kitchen with the hand that is *still* on my shoulder. As he trips on his own shoe, staggering a little, I wonder if I'm the only thing keeping him on his feet. Maybe if I move away quick, he'll fall on his face and pass out…

I'm still considering the option when we reach the kitchen. He steadies himself against the counter while pouring our drinks, hands me a glass, then shuffles out through the French doors leading to the patio. His drink is sloshing around in a loose fist as he carries the half empty whiskey bottle in the other.

I peruse my surroundings for Summer once more before giving up. *Fuck it—I guess I'm surviving one more round with Benjamin Grant.*

We sit in the same chairs we sat in the first time I was roped into having a drink on his patio. He seems quiet tonight, contemplative, maybe… or perhaps just outstandingly drunk. He scratches his stubbly chin, and I remember how much every little thing this guy does gets on my nerves.

He stares out over the landscaping, which still manages to look perfect, even in late November. Just when I'm beginning to appreciate the lack of conversation, he speaks.

"Thanksgiving…" he exhales heavily. "It always puts me in a reflective mood."

Oh, perfect, we're making Holiday small talk.

"I know the point is to look back on what you're grateful for," he continues. "You're supposed to save the list of things you want to change about yourself for New Year's resolutions… but I guess I'm one of those guys who can't reflect on the good stuff without thinking about what could have been better."

"And what could have been better?" I ask in a flat monotone. I don't give a fuck, of course, but I've noticed that he takes a sip of whiskey every time he speaks, and at this point, I'm hoping that if I keep him talking, he'll drink himself into a coma.

"I think…" he takes a drink, swallowing too loudly, "I think if I could go back in time, I would be a better husband."

Here we go again. Why do I feel like this fucker is trying to tell me something? I'm certain he doesn't know who I am, but I'm starting to think he's got me confused with a priest or something.

Vengeance chuckles at the very notion.

"I don't mean to treat you like a confessor, my friend," he says, unaware of the irony. "But I like you. You're a great listener, and it seems like you have your shit together. Maybe it's that writer's brain of yours." He leans over at a precarious angle, just to slap my knee. "It's no wonder my wife enjoys having you around."

I bite down on my tongue until the taste of blood mixes with the whiskey I'm barely sipping. If I open my mouth, I'm liable to tell this asshole *exactly* how much his wife enjoys having me around.

He goes silent again, studying me, and a thoughtful look crosses his face. "Have you ever done something you deeply regret, Evan? Something that haunts you forever?"

Where the fuck is this coming from?

It catches me off guard. I didn't come out here expecting deep or reflective musings from a drunken Benjamin Grant, but now that he's brought it up… I can't help but ponder it.

Regret. It's a toxic word. It can tear a person up, twist them inside out, and break them into so many scattered pieces, they may never be whole again. It's a dangerous sentiment because there's no cure for regret. No one can go back in time and change their actions, or erase their hurtful words, or alter their past into something… *better.*

Regret can eat us alive if we let it.

"No."

So what if it isn't the truth? He doesn't deserve my truths.

I'm not even sure what I do or don't regret anymore.

Fuck, I'm not even sure what's true, and what's a fabrication created by my own design…

Benjamin releases a weary sigh. "You're a lucky man. I have way too many."

I think about the things this man has ruined… and about what he still has, in spite of it. Some people do nothing wrong and still lose what they hold dear, while others take whatever they want and still get more. "You're lucky, too." The words slip out, only a whisper, and I quickly glance at Benjamin to see if he caught the unbridled emotion in my voice.

He's too drunk to notice.

"Yeah," he mutters, his breath thick with liquor, his tone matching my own. "Yeah… I fucked up, though." He rubs a hand over his chin, his mouth, his eyes. "God, I fucked up so bad," he whispers.

It's the second time he's mentioned his fuck-ups, and I know where this is heading. I stiffen in my chair, my body going tense, my senses on high alert. "You mentioned that." I'm cautious in my delivery, not asking outright, but it doesn't matter… Benjamin Grant is lost to the alcohol and his own personal demons.

Apparently, I'm the lucky man he's chosen to receive his confession.

"I wish I could take it back," he slurs. "God, I was a fucking idiot. I could have lost *everything* because I was stupid and weak. I gave into temptation, and the regret eats me up inside every day, Evan… *every fucking day.*" He turns to me, his eyes fiery and adamant. Then he leans over so far, he nearly falls out of the chair, reaching over to squeeze my leg. My entire body cringes at the physical contact, but I don't move. "You need to *fight* for her, my friend."

"What?" I'm taken aback. I don't understand what he's talking about.

"Your *wife*. You need to fight for your wife, damnit."

I almost choke on my own air. My own grief. My own goddamn rage. Benjamin Grant has *no fucking idea* how close to home he's hitting with his drunken proclamations.

"I don't have a wife," I grit out between my teeth.

"You know what I mean," he gestures with one hand, sending his whiskey sloshing over the sides of his glass, while shaking my leg back and forth vigorously with the other. "Your *ex,* then. You loved each other once. I *have* to believe that never really dies."

I jerk my leg away from him, repulsed by his pointless pep talk; my stomach is in knots, my blood is fucking boiling. "It's too late for that. My wife is gone," I snap. "Someone stole her from me, and I no longer *want* her back. I'd much rather fight for something worth fighting for."

Like destroying you.

Benjamin wags his finger in my face, slow and pointed, like he's desperate to get through to me. Desperate to fix something he doesn't even know he broke. "*Love*, Evan. Love is worth fighting for."

My voice is low, dangerous. "You don't betray the ones you love."

The words hang there, met with silence.

Benjamin's eyes flash with a specific kind of sorrow—a sorrow *he* is responsible for.

Regret.

Benjamin Grant regrets cheating on his wife. He regrets betraying her. He regrets what he did with *my* goddamn wife.

But it's too late.

It's too fucking late.

The damage is done, and he will pay.

Vengeance is roaring in my head.

He will pay, and I will have no sympathy.

No. Fucking. Sympathy.

Benjamin collapses backward into his chair, slumping, his head lulling to the side. "Shit," he murmurs, pinching the bridge of his nose. "I wish I knew you…. back then…"

My drink slips from my fingers. The glass splinters across the pavers, the whiskey oozing into the cracks, much like his words just seeped into my skin like poison.

Déjà vu washes over me as I stare blankly at the broken glass. As I watch the remnants of alcohol soak into the concrete.

You knew me, Benjamin. You knew she was married. You knew she had a husband at home waiting for her, loving her, trusting her. You knew I existed, and you didn't fucking care, you selfish son-of-a-bitch.

I look up, seething, no longer sure of what I might say or do.

But Benjamin Grant has finally passed out.

I've been pacing the room for at least a half-hour—ever since I got up from that chair, leaving Benjamin in his drunken slumber without saying a word to anyone. This time, I didn't clean up the damn glass.

Fuck it.

Fuck everything.

"Summer…" I say for the fifteenth time.

"Five more minutes, Dad."

Summer and Olivia keep asking for "five more minutes" as they finish their never-ending game of Monopoly.

You know what? Fuck Monopoly.

Who invented such a boring, drawn out, tedious game? Someone who *hates* fun, that's who. Stupid fake money, stupid railroads, stupid tiny houses. And how about that arrogant, little man with a mustache on the front of the box?

What an asshole.

Maybe he invented Monopoly.

I've been hiding up in Olivia's room with the girls, playing on my phone, counting down the minutes until we can leave. I'm hopped up on anger, frazzled and agitated. I know this because I'm hating on Monopoly far more than I normally would.

"I promise it'll just be five more minutes," Summer insists again, moving her piece around the board and collecting two-hundred-dollars.

I groan.

"Maybe you should just let me sleep over, and then you can leave now."

"Yeah!" Olivia agrees.

I stand up and stretch. "Not tonight, bunny. It's a holiday. But your bargaining skills are getting impressive." Summer gives me an air high-five, and I laugh as I step towards her. It looks like I'm just going to have to drag my daughter away from this dreadful game. "We really do need to get going, though. We'll set up another play date soon."

Summer huffs dramatically, like I'm the world's worst dad. "Fine."

She gives Olivia a hug and storms ahead of me, making me intensely fear the teenage years that lie ahead. When we make our way downstairs to say our goodbyes, Carrie gives me a friendly hug despite the circumstances, while Kyle shakes my hand, and the twins pull at my pant legs. I muss their hair as my eyes search for Josie. Benjamin is passed out on the couch now, and Delilah is outside on the patio talking with a woman I've never seen before.

"Where's Josie?" I wonder, my gaze trailing to Carrie.

Carrie clears her throat, biting her lip in a similar fashion to Josie. "She went outside to smoke, but that secret dies here." She smiles faintly. "She might be talking to Emmett. He followed her out a few minutes ago."

My hackles rise. "Emmett's here?"

"Yeah, he showed up about twenty minutes ago with his girlfriend." Carrie nods her head to the patio doors, indicating the mystery woman outside is Emmett's girlfriend.

I take Summer's hand as she waves goodbye, and I tip my head. "It was nice meeting you," I say, then lead Summer to the front door.

When we step outside, I hear her voice almost instantly. She's around the corner in front of the garage where we shared a moment together the night of her party. Then I hear that piece of shit, Emmett's, voice. I can't understand her response, but the tone is heated. I hold my arm out in front of Summer, stopping us both in our tracks, so I can listen.

"You need to let it go. I'm sick of having to hide from you every time you come over," Josie says. "I'm *married*, Emmett. To your business partner."

"That didn't stop you before."

My blood runs cold as Emmett's response sinks in.

What the fuck?

Summer looks up at me, bouncing on the toes of her shoes. "What is it, Dad? It's cold."

Josie's voice gets louder. "Get your hands off me."

I react quickly, guiding my daughter back into the house. "Go inside, bunny. We'll leave in a minute." Summer's aggravation shifts to concern, her eyes widening. "Finish Monopoly," I order gently. She obeys and runs inside.

"Jesus, Emmett. Let go of me," Josie shouts.

I pace down the walkway with white-knuckled fists at my sides. When I round the corner into the driveway, Emmett has Josie pressed up against the garage door as she struggles against him.

I see red. I see *blood* red.

I yank Emmett back by his collar, flip him around, and throw him down onto the hood of Josie's Lexus. My hand is around his throat as I hold him against the vehicle. "If you ever touch her again, I will fucking *kill* you," I seethe, my voice low, my face centimeters away from his. Emmett pushes back, but I hold firm. "Do you understand me?"

He nods, his blonde, curly hair matted to his forehead. His eyes are glazed over, and I swear I see fear. *Good.* He should be terrified.

I release my hold, straightening my stance, my eyes never leaving his smug face. Emmett's gaze trails to Josie over my shoulder, so I step to the right to block his view. "Don't even fucking look at her. Get your girl and go."

Emmett spits near my shoes, glaring daggers, then storms past me, clipping my shoulder as he retreats into the house.

I turn to face Josie. She looks stricken, but I'm not sure if it's because she's shocked by my reaction, or if Emmett truly frightened her. She's hugging herself tight, her breath escaping between her parted lips like little plumes of smoke. Her eyes are big, her amber irises glowing bright beneath the garage lantern lights. Instinct pulls me straight to her, and I move in and cup my hands around her face, inspecting her for any sign of injury. "Did he hurt you?"

She quickly shakes her head and swallows, sucking in a sharp gasp when my thumbs graze the apples of her cheeks. Maybe I'm overstepping, but I'm feeling really fucking protective right now, and I need to know that she's okay. My eyes dart over her features as her hair tickles my fingers.

Josie raises her hands and gently clutches my wrists, then inhales slowly. "I'm fine, Evan."

Her voice breaks, and I know she's lying. Her eyes are glued to the center of my shirt, no higher, like she's avoiding mine. I tilt her head up, forcing her to look at me. "Are you sure?" The words come out like a breath of air, so low, so raspy and raw, and I'm not sure why my emotions are getting the better of me. I try to swallow them down, but they refuse to recede.

Josie stares up at me with a million questions in her eyes—questions I have zero answers for because I have the same goddamn questions. She squeezes my wrists, and I feel her give, I feel her melt, and we're both melting now as she leans into me with a racing heart. I feel it beating against mine, like our hearts are dancing together, clumsy and uncertain, but unable to break away.

I think I'm going to kiss her.

I think she's going to kiss me back.

But I don't, and she doesn't, because the front door slams shut, and I hear Emmett and his girlfriend stalking towards us.

I step back from Josie, and she resumes her previous position, her arms folded, shielding herself from the ice in the air. Emmett leers at Josie as he passes, then shoots me a mighty death stare while his girlfriend hobbles on her high heels to catch up to him.

I look down at the driveway as I wait for them to disappear down the street. When the engine fades into the night, I glance back at Josie, my jaw tense and firm. I know it's none of my business, but Emmett's words are echoing all around me. "Did you sleep with that guy? While you were married?"

She lifts her head, a frown forming. I can tell by her eyes that I've just offended her, and I kind of want to take it back, but it's too late now.

"What?" she asks, her tone wounded.

I scratch the back of my neck. "I heard him… imply something."

Josie curls her fingers around her upper arms as she processes my words, her head dropping, her eyes shifting to the left. "Ben and I separated for about a month a few years back. We were having fertility issues, and it put a huge strain on our marriage, so he moved in to a hotel for four weeks." She looks uncomfortable as she scuffs her boot against the loose stones in the driveway. "I got really, *really* drunk one night, and Emmett and I kissed. I regretted it immediately, but he's obsessed over that night ever since, insisting there's still something between us."

"Is there?" The words come out before I can stop them.

Her insulted eyes are on me again. "No. God… no, Evan. Did it look like I was open to his advances?"

I swing my head back and forth, quick and certain. "No. Sorry, I didn't mean…" I don't know what I meant. It's obvious Josie has no interest in that asshole. It was nothing but a petty zing of jealousy that swept through me.

Jealousy towards a man who's interested in a woman who's married to another man.

Fucking hell. I need to go.

As soon as the thought crosses my mind, Summer pokes her head around the corner, searching for me. "Dad? Are you okay?"

"Bunny." I rush over to her, pulling her against me and cradling the back of her head. "I'm fine. I was just coming in to get you."

"Okay. I kicked Olivia's butt at Monopoly, and I thought you'd be pretty upset if we started a new game."

Chuckling softly, I run my fingers through her hair. "You know me too well."

I walk her towards the edge of the driveway, glancing at Josie with a faint smile as we pass.

Josie stops me when we reach the sidewalk. "Hey."

We turn, and before I look back to Josie, my gaze settles on the back of her Lexus. The black scratch from my Mustang is still there, still glaringly obvious. She never got it fixed. It's a brutal reminder of the chaos I've created, of my lies and my deceit. It's a knife to the heart, a punch to the gut, a searing lump in the back of my throat.

It's the physical manifestation of my guilt.

I look at Josie. She smiles.

She fucking smiles, and I almost choke on that guilt.

Her eyes drift from Summer to me, and she whispers softly, her voice kissing the chilly gust of wind that sweeps through, "Happy Thanksgiving."

TWENTY-ONE

*I*T'S THE FIRST SNOW OF THE SEASON.

To celebrate, I'm pummeling my daughter with snowballs quicker than she can recover.

"Dad! You're cheating!"

Summer keeps trying to shape her mound of snow into a sphere, but I continue chucking snowballs at her oversized winter coat, one after the other, and now she's getting pissed.

I probably shouldn't find this funny, but I do.

"There's no such thing as cheating in a snowball fight. You either have what it takes to survive, or you don't."

Summer dodges three icy blasts, and I'm sort of impressed.

Then she moves the wrong way at the wrong time and gets pelted in the side of the face.

Shit. Now I feel bad.

"You okay, bun?" I ask, approaching her as she bends over, ducking her head.

I think I hear whimpers, and my heart sinks. Is she crying?

She's crying.

My guilt carries me the rest of the way over to her, and I cradle her face in my hands. The side of her cheek is flushed red from where I clobbered her. I almost feel as guilty as the time I accidentally filled her baby bottle with eggnog during a bout of sleep deprivation, and she pooped out nutmeg for a week.

Just as I'm about to pull her into a hug, Summer's crocodile tears transform into an evil grin, and she cons me by smashing her pile of snow into my face, then sprinkles the rest of it down the collar of my jacket.

I've raised her well.

I spit out snow and shake the flurries from my hair and coat, watching as my daughter doubles over in laughter. "Gotcha," she snickers with a dramatic curtsy.

The snow melts and travels down my chest to my navel, and I wince, narrowing my eyes. "Christmas is canceled."

"No, it's not," she sighs.

"Yes, it is. Santa saw your abysmal betrayal and now you're only getting meatloaf in your stocking." I pull out my cell phone, determined to win this war. "I'm texting him right now so he's prepared to make more meatloaf than one sleigh can carry."

There is nothing Summer hates more than meatloaf.

"Santa doesn't like meatloaf. He wouldn't do that."

"Santa *loves* meatloaf."

Summer is trying to keep a straight face, but failing miserably. She plants her fists against her puffed-out waist. "Fine. I'm getting you ketchup."

I gag. There are literally only two things in this world that make me gag —boxelder bugs and ketchup.

I glance down at my phone, pretending to text, when I notice a missed message from Josie. I hate that my stomach does a pathetic little flip at the sight of her name. Well, the name she added, anyway. She will forever be known as "Mean Girl From The Gym."

We haven't seen each other in two weeks. She messaged me the morning after Thanksgiving to thank me for stepping in with Emmett. I told her not to thank me and said we should schedule a play date with the girls soon. She agreed.

That was it.

And goddammit, I fucking miss her.

I open the text, way more eager than I should feel, and read over her message.

JOSIE: *Play date? Olivia has been bugging me.*

Maybe Josie misses me, too.

ME: *Come over for dinner tonight. I'm cooking spaghetti.*

JOSIE: *I won't lie—I kind of miss your spaghetti.*
ME: *I know :)*
There's a long pause, and I'm wondering what's holding her back.
JOSIE: *I'm not sure, Evan…*
I look up at Summer who is creating an arsenal of snowballs, preparing for battle. Smart girl. I quirk a smile as I consider my reply, rolling my tongue along my teeth.
ME: *Amber and Logan will be here. Games, spaghetti, and adult beverages. Plus, we can awkwardly watch Amber and Logan make out and grope each other all night.*
Am I selling it? I'm selling it, right?
I hit send and can almost see her smile from here.
JOSIE: *It's scary how easily you convinced me. Be there at 6.*
I slip my phone into my back pocket, unable to hide my own smile. When I look up, there's a snowball careening right at my face.

"I can't believe we're having a double date with you and a married chick." Amber shovels a fistful of potato chips into her mouth as we wait for Josie and Olivia to arrive.

"It's not a date. I told you we're just friends," I bark back.

"And I told you you're a fucking liar."

She flips me off, and I roll my eyes.

That's when the doorbell rings.

Amber shoots a disapproving look to the front door, then storms away, joining Logan at the kitchen table. "Let the adultery commence."

When I pull the door open, I'm oddly nervous. My palms feel sweaty, and my heart is racing faster than I'd prefer. I keep telling myself it's just *Josie*, but in a way, it's not. It's no longer just Josie, the wife of my arch nemesis, Benjamin Grant. It's no longer just Josie, the lonely housewife I intend to seduce. It's no longer just Josie, the woman at the center of my revenge plot.

It's Josie who sings into her hairbrush and sends me silly videos. It's Josie who dances with me at the Farmer's Market and plays Fleetwood Mac with me on her guitar. It's Josie who held me on my kitchen floor during one of the lowest points of my entire life.

Now she's Josie, standing on my salt-covered stoop with fuzzy earmuffs and snowflakes in her hair. She smiles when our eyes meet, and I melt quicker than the ice chunks on my porch.

Olivia waves, causing me to blink back my fog and clear my throat, allowing them to enter.

"Hey," I greet, catching Josie's gaze as she shuffles past me and shakes the snow from her peacoat. I don't have much of a foyer—it's basically just a welcome mat and a coat hanger. The girls slip off their boots and hang their coats, and I try not to stare at Josie, while she tries not to stare at me. "It looks like it's getting bad out there."

Weather. It always comes through when you need a pointless conversation starter.

Josie nods, glancing out the window. "We're supposed to get over a foot by midnight."

You should probably just stay the night, then.

I'm tempted to offer, but I realize that Josie staying the night with me is far more dangerous than her driving home in a blizzard, and I'm sure she realizes this, too.

Summer rushes down the hallway just as Logan and Amber saunter out from the kitchen.

"Olivia!" Summer squeals. "I need to show you what I did on Roblox."

I *still* don't understand what a Roblox is.

When the girls disappear into Summer's bedroom, Amber approaches Josie, reaching for her arm and dragging her to the kitchen.

"Do a shot with me," Amber pleads. "I suck at making new friends because everyone thinks I'm a raging bitch, but I'm actually pretty awesome."

Josie spares me a look over her shoulder, her eyes sparkling with amusement. My lips pull into a smile, and I shove my hands into my pockets, trailing her until she's out of sight.

Logan lets out an effective cough, so I shift my gaze to him. "What?" I demand, already knowing what he's about to say.

He strolls toward me, scratching the top of his head. "Just friends, huh?"

"Obviously. She's married."

Logan nods, but it's not an agreeable nod. It's a nod that mimics Amber's claim of, *"You're a fucking liar."* "What?" I repeat.

"Look, man. You're my best friend, so I know you pretty damn well." He stops in front of me and lowers his voice, so the women in the adjacent room can't hear him. "You've been different the last couple of months.

Happier. More... smiley and shit." He waggles his finger around my mouth to emphasize his statement. "The only thing new in your life is her. It's not a coincidence."

"And that's a bad thing?" I cross my arms defensively. "She's cool. We have fun together."

"She's married."

"I fucking know she's married, Logan." My voice is low, a harsh whisper. "It's not like that."

"Quit lying to yourself. It's exactly like that, and you're about to put her husband in a really shitty position."

I stop short, clenching my fists.

My temper goes from zero to one-twenty at the mention of Benjamin Grant. The notion that I should have even an ounce of sympathy for the man who put *me* in the shittiest position of my life has my blood pressure rising and Vengeance whispering nasty little things into my ear. But even as the veil of red descends over my eyes, I have to tamp it down. Get it under control. Logan doesn't have any idea about the truth of Josie's identity, and I know how he would react to *that* news, so I tread with caution and switch gears. "Maybe he deserves it," I offer. "Maybe he's a terrible husband."

Logan doesn't buy it. "Maybe he is, but that's not your concern. That's *her* concern. And until her divorce papers are signed and she's a free woman, I highly suggest keeping your dick in your pants." He gives me a final, pleading glance and walks away, joining Josie and Amber in the kitchen. "You're doing shots without me?" he wonders in mock horror, slinging an arm around his fiancé.

I watch the three of them laugh together as Amber pours a second round. Josie looks down at her shot glass, grinning wide, spinning it between her fingers, and I can't help but feel like she would fit so well into my life. I find myself wishing for a brief moment, for one heart-pounding second, that she was...

Mine.

And in that moment, I despise Benjamin Grant far more than I ever thought possible.

We're playing "Taboo"—that word association game—and it's becoming intense. It's Logan and Amber versus me and Josie, and Amber is up. She's getting more aggressive with each round, so I'm holding the buzzer out in front of me, more to protect myself than anything.

"Ankle. Knee. Squawking." Logan just stares at her, shaking his head. "Feathery tibia." Amber stands from her chair, becoming more heated, waving her arms in the air. "Fucking bird limb!"

I buzz her. "You can't say bird."

"Fuck you, Evan!"

I buzz her again. "Language with children nearby."

I think she might actually hit me, but the timer goes off, and she throws the card across the table instead.

Chicken leg.

"Feathery tibia was pretty creative," I admit.

Logan throws his hands up. "How the hell would I know what a tibia is? I thought it was a place in China."

"That's Tibet, you moron." Amber glares at him as she sits back down and pours a round of shots. "I need another drink. This shit gets me so worked up."

Logan snatches one of the shot glasses and holds it up, offering his random cheers. "To every movie starring Diane Lane."

"Classy lady," Amber concedes, clinking their glasses together and downing the shots in perfect time.

I glance at Josie leaning forward on her elbows trying to stifle her laughter. Her cheeks are tinged pink from the alcohol, and her eyes are pinned on me. Her laughter ebbs when our gazes ignite with more than humor, so she pulls her lips between her teeth and averts her attention to the game.

"We're up," she says, clearing her throat. "Ready?"

I hand the buzzer to Logan, and Josie plucks a card from the pile as the timer begins.

"Shit, okay, um... world famous."

"Spaghetti."

She grins and picks a new card. "One of my beverages from my Halloween costume."

"Wine."

"The other one."

"Coffee."

Another grin.

I kind of like answering correctly for the sole purpose of seeing her face light up.

"Oh, uh…" She ponders the card, her eyes flickering to mine. "What we did at the Farmer's Market."

A million things flash through my mind, some of them not really appropriate to voice out loud… but only one thing stands out. "Dance," I say softly.

We're still dancing, Josie.

She picks another card. She hesitates, then a smile stretches across her face. "I want to know what love is. I want you to show me."

Our eyes lock, and I know the answer, but there's a ridiculous tickle climbing up my throat, rendering me momentarily speechless.

Amber kicks me under the table. Hard.

"Foreigner," I finally say.

Logan starts pressing the buzzer obnoxiously, waving it between Josie and me. "Cheaters. You're both cheaters. Game over." He tosses it down onto the table and stands from his chair.

"Our time isn't even up," I counter, leaning back with exasperation.

"Your time needs to be up." He slants his pointed eyes at me. "And I need to take a piss."

Amber slings back her shot and grimaces as she swallows. "I'm going to see if he needs help with that," she smirks, wiggling her eyebrows and escaping down the hall with Logan.

Josie scrunches up her nose as she watches them go. "They're going to do it in your bathroom, aren't they?"

"Jesus. They'd better not. The bathroom shares a wall with Summer's room." I twist around in my chair and shout over my shoulder, "Behave."

Amber winks at me as she disappears into the bathroom with Logan and slams the door.

I shake my head back and forth, facing Josie once again. She has a faint smile on her lips that turns contemplative as our eyes hold. She doesn't break away this time, and I wonder if it's because the liquor has made her bolder. "I'm going to have a smoke," I say, my tone subdued. I skim her face, reading her, absorbing her. "Join me?"

Josie nods without hesitation. "Sure."

We step out back, trudging through the eight inches of snow that has bathed my patio in white. All of the outdoor furniture is covered, so I lean back against the side of the house beneath an awning that gives a small amount of protection from the storm. Josie follows suit, standing beside me.

"It's beautiful out here," she says, pulling back her hood with a thoughtful expression. "There's something magical about the freshly fallen snow."

I follow her gaze out to where my porch lights are illuminating the fat flurries raining down from the sky. I can't deny the beauty of it. "Winter always seems so harsh and relentless," I reflect. I puff on my cigarette and exhale, glancing at Josie out of the corner of my eye. "But it feels peaceful from here."

Her smile blooms as she bobs her head. "It's so quiet. No cars, no animals, no people." Josie blows out a slow breath, and it's all we can hear in the dead of night.

We stand like that for a while, silent, listening to only the sound of our breathing, our heartbeats, and the occasional howling breeze. I toss my cigarette into the snow and watch it snuff out. When I lift my head, I feel Josie's eyes on me, so I turn to her, taking in the red wind burn on her nose. Her contemplative smile has returned, and I need to know what she's thinking. "Say it," I whisper, noting the way her eyes glaze over at my command.

She swallows, glancing down at her gloved hands. She folds them together, lacing her fingers and sighing. "It feels different between us."

I study her. I drink in her words, trying to make sense of them—trying to pinpoint what feels *different* to her, and when it all changed. Maybe it was when she saw the broken, ugly side of me as we collapsed onto a bed of splintered glass and she clung to me, keeping me from falling further apart. Maybe it was when she held my hand and it felt like the most natural thing in the world. Maybe it was when I almost kissed her. Maybe it was the second time I almost kissed her.

Regardless… I understand. I know exactly how she feels, and it's terrifying and wrong, but it's real. And I hate it. I fucking *hate* that I'm feeling this way, but at the same time, I can't seem to walk away.

I'm not sure how to respond, and I certainly can't deny her claim, so I heave in a weighted breath and let it out. "Is that bad?" I wonder, my words almost clipping on a sharp draft that sweeps through. "That it's different?"

Josie blinks, nibbling her lip between her teeth. "I'm not sure."

Me, either.

We are silent again, and it's still comfortable, but I know we're both thinking the same thoughts and feeling the same feelings.

When she eventually speaks, her voice cracks. "You asked me if I love him," she says, looking straight ahead, unable to face me. Josie pauses for a beat, then another, and I wonder if she's ever going to continue. She finally glances my way. "I'm not sure of that either."

The quiet world feels even quieter now as her words float into my ears. I wonder if noise even exists. The mute snowflakes continue to fall from the soundless sky, and even my heartbeats feel muffled. Josie is searching my face for a reaction, but I've slipped away for a moment, thrown by her words, struck by the vulnerable look in her eyes.

I realize I've zoned out, gone to that *place*, and I know what's coming. I see her lips open, and I know the words she's about to speak.

I should be more prepared.

But I'm not.

"Say it," Josie breathes out. She gasps a little at the end, hearing her words aloud—almost like she's scared, almost like she doesn't want to know.

Because she already knows.

And I don't even fucking hesitate.

I reach out, cupping her face between my palms, and pull her mouth against mine.

Her lips are cold as ice, but a tiny breath escapes, warming me, thawing me from the inside out. Her lips, her breath, her body—her very existence—it *melts* me. It sets me on fire.

She stiffens slightly, but this kiss, it's inevitable. It's always been inevitable, and the longer her lips are pressed against mine, the more they soften. The more we melt together.

And then those soft, pliable lips… they part to let me in, and I know for certain that sound does indeed exist because I will never, *never*, forget the sound she makes when my tongue touches hers. When I taste her for the first time. It's the tiniest noise, barely a whimper, but it's all that I hear, all that I know. *That* sound, and *these* lips, and my first taste of *this woman*… she melts the ice. She boils my blood. She—

Fuck… she makes me hard.

Every ounce of my heated, simmering, boiling blood is traveling downward. Straight to my groin. I'm hot and tingling and overwhelmed with the feel of her, the smell of her, the taste of her. But it's not enough. It's not fucking enough, and all I can think is more*, more…*

Fuck, I need more.

So, I take it. I dive in. Our mouths open together, and my tongue slides in deep, stroking against hers, savoring everything she gives me. Josie latches onto my wrists to steady herself, her body arching into me like an offering.

And I fucking accept that offering. I devour her.

I pour all that I'm feeling into this kiss. I kiss her hard and soft and everything in between, moaning into her mouth as she moans into mine. And as our tongues duel and dance, I feel an urgency, a potent desperation, like this moment is fleeting...

Like this won't last.

It can't last.

But it's as honest as I've ever been... and I'll take what I can get.

I push my hips against her, needing her to know what she's doing to me. To my mind, to my emotions, to my body. I need her to know what she's done.

She sucks in a gulp of air straight from my lungs, grinding into my erection on instinct and without thought.

The groan that escapes me encompasses every conflicting emotion I possess.

It can't last.

My hands slide over her jaw, coming to rest on the soft curve of her neck. I slow my movements, backing my hips away first, ignoring my pulsing cock. Then, reluctantly, I retreat from the warmth of her mouth, placing a final kiss against her lips before pulling back enough to rest my forehead against hers. Her eyes are closed, her hands clasped around my wrists like she might fall over if she lets go.

But then she opens her eyes, and they meet mine.

I watch her as reality sinks in. I watch her, knowing what comes next.

She panics.

Her eyes widen, and she pushes against my arms, stumbling back into the mounds of snow. Her chest is contracting with labored breaths, her eyes wild as she raises her fingertips to her swollen lips. I swallow, my own chest heavy, my heart heavier, and I watch as the emotions play out across her face like a film.

I'm not sure I want to know how this one ends.

The hand at her mouth trembles, her eyes still wide, horror being the final emotion that seems to stick. She stares.

All I can do is watch her.

Finally, she takes a breath that's almost a sob, lowering her eyes to the snow at her feet. Her hand leaves her lips and trails over her chin, down her throat, to her chest, until she rests it against her heart. Her fingers contract slightly, as though she could hold it, soothe it. Like it pains her. Then her arm goes limp. Her hand drops to her side.

When she finally moves, she doesn't look at me. She doesn't speak. She just shuffles past me into the house without saying a word.

The door clicks shut, and the world is silent once again.

Fuck.

I run a hand through my hair, catching wet snowflakes between my fingers as I look out at the winter wonderland around me. I watch the snow as it's falling, falling…

Falling.

I can't help but wonder when it changed.

I try to pinpoint the exact moment, the precise look, the touch, the laugh, the smile—I try to figure out when exactly this stopped being about revenge.

I try to figure out when *I* started falling.

TWENTY-TWO

THEN
MAY

SEVENTEEN DAYS.

Seventeen days have dragged on, while I silently stew in the acrid fragments of my truth. I feel like I'm rotting inside—like I'm disintegrating day by day, minute by minute. My heart has been dismantled. My perfect life has come undone.

I am lost, wandering, numb.

I am volatile, vengeful... *fucking pissed.*

I feel everything, and I feel nothing.

And right now?

Right now, I am waiting.

I'm waiting for the back door to swing open. I'm waiting for Katrina to step into the kitchen from her "long day at work" and discover the surprise of her life. I'm waiting for the moment I've been waiting for since I sat on that park bench, my soul fractured, my world unraveling with every brutal beat of my heart.

I drum my fingers along the kitchen table, my eyes fixated on the brass doorknob. Summer is at Rayna's house for a sleepover, so she won't be here for the surprise. This surprise is not meant for her.

None of this is meant for her.

I suck in a breath when the knob turns and the door pushes open, revealing a stoic-looking Katrina. She always looks like this now—unemotional and detached. It's likely her way of dealing with her lies and deceit. She simply separates herself from it. From *me*. She puts on a mask every day, hiding from me, concealing her true colors.

Little does she know, I'm wearing a mask, too.

Katrina startles when she sees me sitting in the dark kitchen, the lights off, only my shadowy outline visible. "Evan?"

I plaster a grin onto my face, but I don't think she can see it. I can see her, though—she's partially illuminated by the glow from the light outside the door. "Happy birthday, babe."

It's Katrina's birthday today. She's thirty years old. Last year, we celebrated by taking Summer up to Lake Geneva and went for a boat ride, shopped the downtown boutiques, and laughed and hugged and ate ice cream until we all got brain freezes.

This year will be a different kind of celebration.

This one is for *me*.

Katrina's features pull into a frown of confusion as she tries to find the light switch. "Why are you in the d—" She flips the light on, then audibly gasps.

"Surprise!"

Oh, and there's a room full of people behind me.

Katrina brings her hands to her chest, her eyes scanning the familiar faces. I flew her mother in from Tennessee. I invited her best friends, her casual acquaintances, a few neighborhood moms, her co-workers, and even her boss. They're all here. Everyone she cares about is here, except for our daughter.

This is not meant for her.

I watch as her gaze drifts to me, and I smile big, standing from my chair and whispering, "Surprise." I can see the conflict on her face. She swallows down a lump in her throat—a giant, hollow lump of guilt. Katrina scratches her chest, then fiddles with her hair. She's put on a little weight over the last month, probably from all those secretive dinner dates with Benjamin Grant, so she's wearing a baggy sweater that hangs loosely off her frame as she shifts from foot to foot.

"You did this for me?" Katrina forces a smile, looking at me briefly, then gazing out into the sea of loved ones.

People are clapping and blowing noise makers and singing "Happy Birthday." I nod, my smile unwavering. "Of course. You deserve this. You've been through so much lately." My steps are methodical as I approach her, planting a firm kiss against her forehead. "You deserve all this and more."

I release her to turn around to face the guests behind us. Wrapping my arm around Katrina's waist, I give her a tight squeeze, pulling her close, then clear my throat.

It's speech time.

"Before we celebrate, I want to thank you all for being here. I invited you today for a reason, and that reason is because you mean so much to Katrina."

Everyone smiles as the room goes quiet, their attention on me.

I continue. "I want to tell you a little bit about my wife. She's always been my rock. She's been the most loyal woman I've ever known." Katrina stiffens in my embrace, but I pull her even closer, smiling down at her. "We met junior year of high school in Mr. Conrad's class, as a lot of you know, and we've been crazy in love and inseparable ever since. We had this secret room in her attic where we'd hide out all day, making plans for the future, kissing and laughing, writing silly love letters."

Katrina's mother smiles warmly. The guests chuckle.

"I actually still have some of those letters that Katrina wrote," I say, pulling a piece of paper out of my back pocket.

"Evan..." Katrina's smile is strained, her eyes pleading. She shakes her head at me. "They don't need to hear about our teenage fantasies," she says, forcing a laugh.

My smile brightens. "Sure, they do." I open the letter and begin to read. "*My heart and soul, the love of my life. I see so many beautiful years ahead. I see decades of love and laughter. I see children playing in the yard while I blow bubbles and watch you in the window cooking dinner (because I can't cook).*" Everyone laughs, and I say, "Still true."

More laughter.

I carry on. "*Evan, you're my other half. My better half. I will never leave you because, how could I survive without half of my heart? I promise I will make you proud and love you forever.*"

Folding up the letter, I set it down on the counter. I read one more, and it's similar, and it's beautiful, and it used to make me smile through my happy fucking tears. I glance over at Katrina, noting the rosy blush forming on her cheeks as she looks down at her shoes. The crowd says "aww," clapping while I unfold the grand finale.

My eyes skim over the piece of paper in my hand, the printed Facebook messages, and I hesitate briefly, sharply, almost choking on the words before I read them. I inhale a deep breath.

Then I proceed.

"I need to feel you inside me, Benjamin. I can't stop thinking about you."

I watch as Katrina pales before me, her body going rigid, her eyes widening, glazed with fear. The room goes deadly quiet, and all I can hear is the sound of my heart breaking all over again.

But Vengeance is here, reminding me she deserves this.

Whispering.

I can't stop now.

"I'm going to leave him, I promise. I can't wait to start my new life with you. You're all I can think about, Benjamin. Sometimes when I'm in bed with my husband I fantasize about you, and I wish you were the one making love to me. I dream about the day you sign your divorce papers, and I sign mine, and we can finally create the life we've been talking about."

Silence.

Deafening silence.

I'm staring at Katrina, my smile long gone. Tears are streaming down her bright red cheeks. She's visibly shaking, moving her head back and forth, squeezing more tears of humiliation from her eyes.

I address the crowd, taking in the dropped jaws, the looks of horror. Katrina's mother is crying into her hands. "Benjamin couldn't make it tonight. He was too busy at home with his own wife, making plans to leave her for mine." I step over to the refrigerator and pull out a birthday cake, dropping it down hard onto the kitchen table, then grab a cutting knife from a drawer.

Katrina's eyes trail to the cake, and she begins to sob.

There is a photo of her sonogram printed onto the sheet cake. She had an eight-week ultrasound performed, alerting us of her baby's beautiful, beating heart.

I wrap my hand around the cutting knife with a death-like grip, then shove it right through the middle of the cake. "Katrina was pregnant. She told me she had a miscarriage," I announce to the guests. "Imagine my surprise when our seven-year-old daughter asked me why Mommy was talking to someone about getting an abortion."

More gasps. More cries. More sobs.

"I don't know if it was my baby or his baby. I don't know what would hurt more—the fact that my wife was carrying another man's child, or the fact that she murdered mine."

Traipsing back over to the counter, I pull a manilla envelope out from behind the microwave. I walk up to Katrina and wait for her to look at me. Her chin raises, her bloodshot eyes narrow, and her hands turn into fists by her sides.

"I hate you," she says with a quiet anger, an anger I've never seen in her before, as she stares right into my eyes.

I can't lie. Her words cut through me like a sharp knife because I know that while I hate hard, I love harder. But Katrina doesn't love me anymore. There is only hate bleeding out of every pore, every crease, every open wound.

It's over.

"Happy birthday," I bite out.

I shove the divorce papers at her and walk out of the house.

23

TWENTY-THREE

NOW

I WAS TECHNICALLY INVITED.

Josie invited me to her annual holiday party shortly before our mouths fused together and my world fell around me faster than the icy flakes of snow.

That was a week ago, and I haven't spoken to her since, but she *technically* invited me.

So, here I am.

Invitation accepted.

I'm not staying long. I'm only here for one reason, and that reason is currently standing at her kitchen island in an emerald green dress, her back to me. Her laughter swirls around me as she mixes a cocktail consisting of Rumchata and a candy cane garnish. She seems happy and social as guests mingle around her, exchanging stories, complimenting her on her hair and her dress and her impressive home. I can't see her face, but I know she is shining. Glowing. *Alive*.

And I know the moment she sees me, her brightness will dim.

Her guilt will consume her.

The thought is enough for me to turn around and leave. I can't bear to see the jaded, regretful look in her eyes. I can't fathom seeing that *horror* again.

Unfortunately, I don't get far because Benjamin rounds the corner from the staircase before I make it to the front door. "Evan, old friend," he says, and I hate that he looks genuinely *happy* to see me. "You made it. Jos said you couldn't find a babysitter."

I bristle at his words. She assumed I wasn't coming.

She didn't want me here.

I shuffle my feet and massage the back of my neck with my palm. "Someone came through," I mutter.

Benjamin slaps me on the shoulder, his drink sloshing around in his opposite hand. "Excellent. Well, make yourself at home. My wife is quite the hostess, so there's plenty of booze and food. She even made those little Rice Krispies Treats shaped like Christmas trees." Then he shoots me a knowing wink before giving my shoulder a final squeeze. "Delilah should be stopping by later."

I turn to watch him head down the corridor towards the party guests, and that's when I see her.

Josie is standing there, staring at me with wide eyes, hardly flinching when her husband presses a kiss to her hair as he passes her.

My breath is momentarily stolen from me while I gaze at her. She's fucking *beautiful*. Red lips, long, golden waves of hair, whiskey eyes sheathed in a champagne shimmer. The jade sequins on her dress are sparkling like tiny embers from the ceiling light.

When her husband is out of earshot, she cautiously approaches me, folding her arms across her chest, like she needs to protect herself. "What are you doing here, Evan?" She's trying to be strong, but the break in her voice betrays her. She pins her lips together as she waits for my response.

I link my thumbs into my belt loops as my eyes stay glued to hers. "You invited me."

"That was before…" Josie's voice trails off and she looks down, squeezing her scarlet fingernails into her upper arms. "You shouldn't be here."

"We need to talk."

Her head jerks back up. "Here? Now? In my house with my husband and all my friends around?"

"You didn't reply to my text."

"I know. Take a hint, Evan."

Josie winces at her own words. She closes her eyes, her lips parting, and I can almost see the apology pass between them.

My head nods slowly while I chew on my cheek, coming to terms with the inevitable. "Hint taken." I spin on my heel and walk back to the front door, trying not to show how fucking hurt I am.

Josie's timid voice stops me before I get too far. "Wait."

I pause, feeling her approach me from behind. Feeling her warmth. Smelling her flowery perfume.

"I'm sorry," she says softly. "I can't... I don't..." She rubs her temples, sighing in resignation before she pulls her thoughts together. "I'm just... trying to process it all. I'm not doing a very good job."

Glancing over my shoulder, I keep my back to her, my muscles locking. "It's fine. I get it."

It's not fine.

It sucks. It's fucking terrible.

But I *do* get it.

I continue my trek to the door when I feel her hand on my arm.

And just like that, I deflate.

I turn around to fully look at her, at her eyes swirling with more conflict and remorse than my heart can handle, and I release a shaky breath of air. "Josie, you're right. I shouldn't have come."

Our gazes hold as she tries to figure out what to say, what she *should* say, and why she can't seem to handle me walking out this door. She says nothing. She nods her head to the staircase and steps toward it, waiting for me to follow.

I guess we're talking, after all.

Josie guides me into her bedroom and shuts the door. I can't help but feel like this is the worst possible place to talk because all I'm going to be thinking about is how fast I can get her out of that dress and under the covers. She walks to the foot of the bed, but doesn't sit. She doesn't look at me right away as she taps a finger against her arm, jittery and full of nerves. I'm not sure if I should speak first, or what I should even say, so I just watch her with my hands in my pockets and lean my back to the door.

Josie finally raises her eyes to me, chewing on her lip. "I don't think we should see each other anymore."

Well, fuck. That was not at all what I was hoping she'd say.

I try to keep my expression unreadable as my heart plays panicked beats against my ribs. "What about Summer and Olivia?"

They matter, too. Their friendship matters.

Josie seems to have already thought that through because she doesn't falter. "That's a sacrifice I made when I chose to be selfish."

I inhale long and deep, studying her. It's obvious her resolve is hanging by a fragile thread, by the way her chin trembles and her eyes gloss over.

She shakes her head adamantly when I take a careful step forward. "Don't try to change my mind, Evan. Please."

I stop in my tracks as I exhale. "Josie, we can be mature about this. We can still allow the girls to see each other without… *this* getting in the way." I flick my finger between us, indicating what *this* is.

She doesn't stop swinging her head back and forth, and I'm wondering if she's trying to convince herself, or convince me. "No… *this* will always get in the way. *This* will escalate. *This* will eventually make me hate myself even more than I already do." She chokes on the last few words, her shoulders starting to quiver. Her face scrunches into the picture of agony. "I'm sorry, Evan. I'm sorry, but I can't."

Tears leak from her eyes, streaking through her perfect makeup. I feel her heartbreak in every word. Her desire. Her conflict. She's breaking in front of me.

Breaking.

I can't prevent my feet from moving forward. I'm overcome with desperation to comfort her, compelled to pull her into my arms and give her solace. Relief sinks into me when she doesn't stop me this time. She leans in as I reach for her, letting me cradle her head between my hands and rest my cheek on top of her halo of hair. Sobs burst from her, and I hush her as she cries against my shirt. I bring her closer, kissing the top of her head. Absorbing her tears. Her guilt. Her grief.

Fuck… I did this to her.

"God, I'm sorry," I say, and I mean it. I mean it more than I ever thought possible. "I'm sorry I let this happen. I'm *so* fucking sorry."

I broke her this way.

My arms tighten around her, and I feel her relax, the tension releasing from her body as I whisper my apologies. My regret.

This is my fault.

She has no idea how true that is. How real my apologies are. It gnaws a hole in my gut.

Josie's tears begin to ebb as she nuzzles her face against my chest with a sigh. Her breathing shifts, becoming more controlled. Heavier. I feel her fingers curling into my sides as my arms fold around her back, holding her close to me. She lifts her face, so the warmth of her cheek rests along my neck. All I can focus on is her skin against mine, the heat of her breath warming my jaw. My eyes flutter closed as the familiar charge begins to swell and surge between us. It's magnetic, electric, a force of nature... we are helpless to it.

I am helpless.

I need to fucking stop this before there's no turning back.

She doesn't want this. She doesn't want this.

I repeat it over and over. That's what she said... that she couldn't... she didn't... *but—*

The way she's pressing herself into me, inhaling my scent, squeaking out tiny gasps as I run my hands through her hair—*fuck.*

Her fingers dig into my sides like she can't get close enough. Her lips brush the skin of my neck.

She *does* want this. She just doesn't *want* to want this.

My body is responding. I can't stop it. I can't stop this runaway train we've found ourselves on. We press against each other, and it's undeniable.

We both want this so fucking much.

"What are we doing?" she asks faintly, her voice muffled by my throat—muffled by the lump of fear in hers.

Falling in love.

The thought is like a stab to my gut, and I suck in a sharp intake of air.

No, goddammit.

No, no, no... that's not it at all.

This is purely sexual. Carnal. Physical. I want her because *I can't have her*. I want her because I got carried away with the plan. I dug myself deeper than I should have, and I began to believe the lie. It's sexual, it's psychological—that's what this is. It's fucking science.

There's no way in hell I'm falling in *love* with Benjamin Grant's *wife*.

No. Mother. Fucking. Way.

I grit my teeth and let out something bordering on a growl. An illicit spark crackles between us as I thread my fingers through her hair, tugging gently, and I press her up against the foot of the bed with my hips. Josie stares up at me, half petrified, half drunk on desire.

I choose to focus on the latter. It's all I can see as I lean down to brush my lips over her forehead, then her cheek.

Her desire sings to me like a siren's call.

And then my lips connect with hers, and I kiss her.

She echoes my growl of need with her own—a mix of a mewl and a gasp and a cry and a moan.

It drives me *fucking crazy.*

I lose it. Completely. My hands are in her hair, my body pressed to hers, and I'm lost to the drive, to the need. There's no coming away from this until I have more.

More. I need more.

She opens her mouth, inviting me in, and I glide my tongue inside. I take, I consume, I stroke. I kiss her.

And I kiss her.

And I kiss her…

I kiss her like it might be the last time because it *might* be the last time.

The door is unlocked, and anyone could walk in, but I don't care. *I don't fucking care,* and there is an exquisite moment where she doesn't care, either. I know this moment is fleeting—it's as fragile as butterfly wings—but nothing else exists except for her, and us, and this moment where we'll take what we can get in case it's the very last time.

When I pull back, her eyes are glazed over with lust and audacity, her lips puffy, her cheeks stained pink.

My hands are still tangled in her honey hair as I lean in close to her ear, my balance unsteady. "Josie," I whisper, low and soft, like it's my best kept secret. "I want to be inside you… I want to fuck you."

It's an urgent plea, and I can feel her body arch into me on instinct, pressing against my hard cock, her fingernails digging into my waist so hard I wonder if they'll leave marks. I *hope* they leave marks. I would love nothing more than to wear her marks on every inch of my body.

A breathy moan escapes from the back of her throat. I know she wants me—she wants me inside her just as much as I do.

I just don't know if she has it in her to go through with it.

Slowly, I bend my knees, bringing myself lower. My lips skim from her ear, down her jawline, to the softness of her throat where I pause to place a light kiss in the hollow. Then, overcome with the need to taste her skin, I drag my tongue down to her dangerously low neckline. Josie's hands glide up over my shoulders and the back of my neck as I move down. She shudders at the feel of my tongue in the cleavage of her breasts, twining her fingers in my hair, while I reach down and fist the hem of her dress in my hands. I move back up the way I came, inching her dress up her thighs as I go, hearing her breath hitch as my hands travel behind her to grasp her backside. As I dig my fingers into her perfect flesh, she doesn't push me away—no, she's still with me, still warm and willing in my arms, clinging to me even tighter.

Jesus, I want her. I've never wanted anything more. No one exists in the world right now but Josie. And that's...

Shit. That's *everything.*

I straighten my knees, looking down at her once again. She drops her forehead to my chest, her arms wrapped around my shoulders like she might fall at my feet if she doesn't hang on for dear life. I tug her head back with one hand wrapped in her hair until she squeaks in surprise, her mouth parted, and I take it as an invitation. My lips slam down on top of hers. As our tongues collide, I'm unable to tell her groan from mine.

With her dress up around her waist, the silky skin of her thigh bared to me, I run my fingers over it, teasing her, feeling goosebumps break out beneath my touch. She squirms, pushing her hips into me, and *fuck*... she makes me hard. The evidence is pressed fully against her now, pulsing with the pounding of my heart. I'm fucking desperate for friction; *desperate* to be buried inside.

Grinding into her, I feel my balance teeter. It's all I can do to not throw her down on the bed, but I don't want to spook her—I don't want to cross a line and make her run. Without breaking our kiss, I turn us around, walking her backwards, until she's flat against the wall. My fingers graze along her inner thigh, following a path upward, reaching the junction between her legs. Emerald lace is the only thing between me and the warmth of her pussy, and I scrape my fingernails lightly over it. She pulls her mouth from mine with a gasp, her eyes glazed, her pupils blown.

She's not pushing me away.

She's not telling me to stop.

Resting my forehead against hers, I move the sliver of fabric aside. Our eyes lock on each other—we're both trembling with so much goddamn need, drowning in the thrill of it. I can't wait another second to touch her, and when I drag a finger through her wet heat, I can't help but groan out loud, knowing I've done this to her. She whimpers, and *God*, it's intoxicating. I do it again, collecting even more wetness. This time she lets out a breathy moan, arching her back, seeking more, her desperation evident.

I'm ready to combust, but I'm drunk on her moans, on those needy little sounds... and all I can think is *more*.

I need more.

I push a finger inside her tight entrance, reveling in her gasp, but it's not enough, it won't ever be enough, so I pull back and push in with two. She cries out, collapsing against me and biting down on my shoulder to silence herself.

But there are better ways to silence her, so I lift her chin and cover her mouth with mine. My fingers push deep inside her, curling slightly before pulling nearly all the way out and thrusting in again. Her muscles grip me, and I know she needs more, so I find her clit with my thumb as I keep thrusting. My cock throbs with the same rhythm, aching with my need for her.

Josie's mouth is open wide, crying out into mine, and I thrust my tongue inside, sliding along hers with the same motion as my fingers.

She pulls one of her legs up along my thigh, wrapping it around my ass to give me better access. Her breathing is quick and raspy, and I feel her inner muscles tighten. I pump my fingers faster, desperate to hear the sound she makes when I put her over the edge.

Our kiss turns messy; it's hard to concentrate my efforts on more than my thrusting fingers, my swirling thumb, and my throbbing cock. We rest our open mouths against one another's, panting as she begins to chant my name in a breathy whisper—*Evan, Evan, Evan*—like she needs to hear it out loud. Like she needs to know it's me.

And when she tightens even more, meeting my thrusts with her own, her legs shaking uncontrollably, her chants turning into something akin to a whine, I muffle the sound with my mouth once again.

Her whole body contracts sharply as she gifts me with her orgasm. She cries out into my mouth, nearly sobbing, while her muscles shake, her inner walls pulsing. I hold her up with one arm wrapped tightly around her as her weight goes slack, and she collapses into me, her forehead dropping onto my shoulder.

I need to come so fucking badly, but I'm not quite sure how she's going to react once she comes down from this high… so, I just hold her.

And I wait.

It takes a few moments for her to catch her breath, and I kiss her hair while she clings to me, gradually calming. Reluctantly, I pull my fingers from inside her, longing to replace them with my cock. I miss her warmth already.

Josie finally rolls her head on my shoulder and slowly leans back. My arms fall away as she shrugs out of them. Her posture is slumped, her eyes downcast, and I'm not sure if she's in shock, or just afraid to look up—but with a sinking in my chest, I already know what's about to happen.

I just know.

This moment was already so fragile, and now, as reality sets in, I feel it fraying... I feel it slipping away.

But I won't be the one to start it.

So, I stand there, still waiting, while a million fucking arguments run through my mind. I want take her by the shoulders and shake her, plead with her— *"Don't you dare regret this, Josie. Don't you dare be ashamed."* I want to tell her what her husband did to her, that he deserves it, and that she deserves to be with someone she could love. But she can't hear those things right now. She isn't ready, and I know this. Just like I know my arguments would fall on deaf ears, or make things worse.

So, I wait.

I watch her as she stares at the ground, inching her skirt back down. And as I wait an eternity for her to recover, I tell myself that it's okay. At least we had *this*—at least I got to touch her, I got to feel her come around my fingers. I got to make her fall apart, and I'll never fucking forget it.

She won't forget it either, and one day, I'll convince her.

This isn't the end of us. No matter what she's about to say... we don't end right at the beginning. That's not how this story works.

Her eyes are closed as she takes a deep breath in through her nose, smoothing her hands over her skirt. When she finally looks up at me, there are tears in her eyes, there is sadness and longing, and there is something that looks an awful lot like mourning.

It's over, her eyes say. *Never again.*

She opens her lips...

"Don't say it," I whisper.

She closes her mouth, holding my gaze.

Finally, she dips her chin.

Then... she walks by me and out the door, closing it behind her.

Now it's my turn to stand here for an eternity, staring at the floor. I'm doing my best not to break down—to not lose it right here in Josie's bedroom. In *Benjamin fucking Grant's* bedroom, where I just made his wife come. But it's not only the pain of Josie's confliction that I feel—I'm still fucking hard, too. My balls ache, my cock is screaming for release, and there's a deep-seated frustration weighing down my entire body. I'm not sure I can even walk down the fucking stairs like this without coming in my goddamn pants.

The door to the master bathroom catches my eye, and I don't even give myself time to think twice about it before I'm inside with the door closed behind me. There's a small nightlight illuminating the space, and I don't bother to hunt for the switch. I fumble with my button and zipper, then in one urgent movement, I have my pants undone and my hand wrapped around my pulsing, aching erection.

Fuck, fuck, *fuck*.

My cock jumps in my hand as I stroke it, one hand braced on the counter, gripping the edge as my body hunches over, immersed in finding the rhythm it craves. I imagine Josie here, that she never left the room, that this hand around me is smaller... firm, but delicate. It's warm and soft, and it's *hers*.

Josie.

My hips pump into my hand—*her* hand. "Ahh... *fuck*," I whisper into the quiet.

The hand around me tightens, moving faster. I lean into it farther, but then—no, it's not enough—I need to fuck that tight little space my fingers were just inside, and I tell her that, too. I groan it out loud in her bathroom with the scent of gardenias surrounding me— *"Fuck, I need that pussy, I need to fuck you... I need..."* But behind my closed eyes, I see her sink to her knees, I see the top of her honey head as she takes me into her warm, wet mouth. "Ahh, shit. Shit... *fuck*."

My spine arches; I throw my head back, the movements becoming faster, harder, as I pump my hips into her mouth... as my cock is enveloped by her heat.

I think I hear shuffling in the bedroom, but I don't care. I didn't lock the door, and I don't care about that either.

Let her open the door. Let her come in. Let her see me.

Let her kneel at my feet.

My rhythm turns chaotic. I grip the counter until the edge cuts into my hand. My eyes are squeezed so tightly, I see spots. My head is swimming. My ass tightens, my balls constrict... I'm going to come.

Ahh... I'm going to fucking come.

Fuck, Josie... fuck.

I grit my teeth, trying to hold the sound in my throat, but it escapes—a strangled, desperate groan. The pressure is almost unbearable.

And then I explode.

My balls contract, convulse, and release. I spill over my hand, over the floor, my movements jerky and erratic... and *fuck*, it feels so damn good.

My momentum slows with the last few pulses of my release, and I close my lips tightly around a relieved moan.

I pant into the silent room, my muscles going slack.

She never opens the door... if she was ever there at all.

A layer of sweat begins to cool on my skin as my head clears. My face is still heated, my heart still pounding, but I'm beginning to realize what I've done and where I've done it.

In Benjamin Grant's bathroom. On his tile floor. While imagining his wife. With the evidence of her orgasm still on my fingers.

I can't decide whether I feel triumphant or horrified. And it makes no sense why it would be the latter, given the plan I've held onto for so long like a lifeline. But it's different now—everything feels different—and tainting what Josie has come to mean to me with thoughts of hate and revenge seems... *wrong*.

Fuck, I need to get out of this house.

In the faint illumination of dim golden light, I find a hand towel. I wipe the floor, unsure of whether it's truly clean or not, and then I throw the towel in the corner, leaving the evidence behind. Still in a daze, I wash my hands. The walls are closing in on me. I need to get out.

I grip the knob and swing the door open.

There's a body blocking the doorway.

"Oh, Evan! You surprised me. I assumed you were my wife."

I'm face-to-face with Benjamin Grant. With Benjamin *fucking* Grant.

My nemesis. The man whose wife I just finger-fucked before leaving a cum-covered towel on his bathroom floor. I pull in a sharp breath, noting that the room smells like sex.

I wonder if he's noticed.

His smile grows as he peers around me into the darkened bathroom. "Delilah in there with you?"

Shit.

I clear my throat, unsure of what I can possibly say. "Um, the hall bathroom was occupied. All the bathrooms were occupied. Sorry."

I'm not fucking sorry.

He claps a hand on my shoulder, chuckling as I cringe. Fuck, why does he always seem so goddamn happy to see me? It's pissing me off. I look at the hand on my shoulder, then back at Benjamin. He appears a little glazed, and I notice remnants of the drink in his hand. He brings it to his lips, tips it back to get the last drop, and swallows. He's drunk... not thinking clearly.

Lucky me.

"Well, I suppose you haven't seen Josie, then. I've been looking for her."

I shake my head faintly, saying nothing.

He lifts his empty glass with an approving nod. "Well, carry on. There are a few spare bedrooms around here, you know. You're welcome to them." He shoots me a wink, turning to leave, then stops and looks over his shoulder with a grin. "Merry Christmas, my friend. I hope you enjoy the party."

I collapse against the door frame.

As he leaves, I feel my chest tighten. The familiar rise of anger simmers in my veins. I hear the low chuckle of Vengeance.

Fuck him.

Fuck.

All of this is because of that bastard. Every last bit of heartbreak. *He* started this. Benjamin Grant is the reason I'm single in the first place. He's the reason the darkness took over my life, he's the reason I've found myself falling in love with a married woman, and—fuck, *no*... scratch that last thought because *that* is not fucking allowed.

I am not in *love,* goddammit.

I'm not.

But that aside, Benjamin Grant set every bit of this in motion. He betrayed Josie. He turned *my wife* into an adulteress. He—

Oh.

Oh, fuck.

My knees give way as it hits me, and I slide to the floor, my hand over my mouth.

Josie.

Josie is good... Josie was *perfect*, and I've...

I've just turned her into the one thing I hate the most.

I've turned her into Katrina.

I recover as quickly as possible, pulling myself off the floor and staggering out of the bedroom. Now, I *really* need to get the fuck out of this house.

I race down the staircase two steps at a time, hoping I don't run into Josie before I make my escape. I can't bear to look at her right now.

Not after what I've done.

There's no one in the foyer—it looks like I'm in the clear, so I pull open the door and rush outside, inhaling giant gulps of frigid air as I stumble down the front walkway. I stop in front of the garage, leaning forward with my hands on my knees. I can't drive home like this. I need to catch my breath, need to steady myself... I'm a fucking mess right now.

I'm a fucking mess.

I'm being dragged in two different directions, torn between wanting to protect Josie's heart... or my own.

A conflict rages within me. I can't make sense of all the thoughts.

I want her... but I don't.

I need her... but I can't.

I desire her... but I shouldn't.

I'm falling, falling, *falling*... and I'm fucking terrified that the only thing that will break my fall is rock bottom.

I've been there. Hell, I've been there, and I never, *ever* want to go back.

I think back to Josie's words on Thanksgiving: *"If you ever need to break apart, you don't need to break alone. I'm here, and I understand. I'll help you."*

I'm breaking... *Christ*, I'm fucking breaking, and I don't know if I can put myself back together this time.

But Josie Grant can't help me.

No one can help me crawl out of this mess I've made.

I wanted to reap vengeance so bad, I could taste it. I didn't care about who or what stood in my way—it was all collateral damage. Nothing mattered but my lust for revenge. My hatred for Benjamin Grant.

Myself.

Now I've ripped away my daughter's best friend. I've ruined the woman who picked me up when I was down, who dusted off my battered heart and breathed life back into me. I've turned her into the very thing I spent all this time hating.

I've *ruined* her.

I can't help but wonder if I ultimately ruined Katrina, too.

I stand up straight, closing my eyes against the realization that I'm now back at square one.

Sad, bitter, and alone.

Fumbling for my cigarettes with a quivering hand, I falter when footsteps come up beside me. For the first time, I hope it's *not* Josie because I don't think I can face her right now.

I turn to my right and freeze.

I fucking wish it were Josie.

"Need a light?"

Emmett's smug face stares back at me, a smirk toying on his lips.

I don't respond.

He lights up his own cigarette, sighing into the cold night. Even his sigh sounds self-righteous.

"I just saw Josie inside," he says. "She looked upset. You wouldn't know anything about that, would you?"

I look straight ahead, pretending he isn't there.

Emmett takes a drag and scuffs his foot against the pavement, his smile never waning. "She's a real firecracker, isn't she? Looks like a fucking angel, but she's a tiger inside," he chuckles, exhaling a mouthful of smoke. "Ben's a lucky bastard. What I wouldn't give to have those thighs wrapped around me again." He bites his lip. "Damn."

I swallow. My nostrils flare, my muscles tensing. When I speak, my voice is low. Dangerous. "Careful, Emmett."

Emmett glances at me, cocking his head to the side. "Feeling a little protective, are we?" He sniggers under his breath as if the mere thought is laughable. "You honestly don't believe a woman like Josie would ever leave her husband for a guy like you, right?"

"I don't know what you're talking about."

More laughter. "Sure, you do. I see the way you look at her. You almost beat me to a bloody pulp defending her honor. You think you've got a shot with her, and it's fucking adorable."

I twist around and grab him by the collar of his ugly Christmas sweater, slamming him up against the garage door. There is no fear in his eyes this time—only a sly, sadistic smile.

Like he's in on some kind of joke that I'm not.

Like he knows something he's not telling.

Emmett purses his lips together with a knowing grin, slapping his hands against my shoulders and pushing me away. I let go because I don't have it in me to commit murder today. I'm too fucking exhausted.

He flicks his cigarette to the ground, sparing me a final, satisfied glance. "See you around, Campbell." He turns away casually with his hands in his pockets, whistling as he saunters back into the house.

I shake my head in aggravation, searching for my cigarettes again—

And then I go still.

Oh… *oh, no.*

Everything starts to spin. My vision blurs, my stomach ties in knots, and my heart rises to my throat, sticking there like a gigantic boulder of dread.

Fuck, fuck, fuck.

Campbell. He said, *Campbell.* That bastard knows my name... he knows my *real* name.

He knows my secret.

He knows who I am.

24

TWENTY-FOUR

I AM RUNNING.

I'm running hard and fast, my shoes slapping against the snowy sludge in the road. I run until it feels like my lungs might give out, then I lean over to catch my breath and give my heart a chance to normalize. Then I say, "fuck it" and keep on running because I don't really give a shit about my heart right now. It deserves to explode. It deserves to combust.

It had no business falling for her.

It's winter break, and Summer is in Tennessee. It's been three days since my ex-wife pulled into my driveway, and I had to say goodbye to my little girl for the next two-and-a-half weeks. Katrina didn't come to the door—she doesn't want to see me just as much as I don't want to see her. It almost killed me when Summer gave me a bone-crushing hug and whispered in my ear, "Truth bomb?"

I gave her my full attention. "Always."

"I wish I could spend Christmas with you."

Then she planted a kiss against my cheek and skipped out the front door to spend the holidays six-hundred-and-twenty miles away.

And I'm here alone and miserable on Christmas Eve.

Running.

Running in circles, running from my problems, running until I can't run anymore.

It's been radio silence from Josie ever since I made her hate herself even more than she already had at her holiday party. I haven't contacted her, and she hasn't contacted me. I'm telling myself it's for the best because I'm a damn good liar and it's easier than facing the reality of the situation.

She is not mine.

She never will be.

I'm not sure if Emmett revealed my true identity to her, but I'm thinking I would have heard from Josie if he had. I also realize that if he outs *me*, he outs his business partner for having an affair, and I'm banking on the fact that going there wouldn't be in his best interest.

How the fuck did he figure it out?

I run faster. My lungs ache, my chest throbs, but I keep running.

I thought about confronting her with the truth. I'd rather tell her myself than allow that sniveling weasel Emmett to confess my sins for the sake of trying to get closer to Josie. But the idea of slinging more pain and heartache at her when she's already down is too much to even consider.

It's over. There's no point.

I slow my feet when I catch sight of a familiar face running towards me from the opposite direction.

My neighbor.

Oliver.

It's not exactly a picturesque day for a run, so I wonder if he's running from something, too, just like I am. Cold sweat cases my hairline as my shoes come to a near-stop along the side of the road, my breathing trying to even itself out as Oliver jogs closer. I lift my hand in a friendly wave, then bend over, palms to my knees, collecting my bearings.

"Hello, Evan." Oliver's tone is winded when he approaches, stopping beside me. "Is everything all right? You look unwell."

My lungs squeeze in silent agreement.

Oh, you know, just trying to dig myself out of this endless hole of bad decisions, including but not limited to orchestrating a nefarious revenge plot that spiraled pathetically out of control and ruined the innocent woman at the center of it, who I'm ironically falling for.

I also finger-fucked her in her bedroom with her husband only a few feet away, then jacked-off in one of her linen bath towels, embroidered with the phrase, *"When it rains, look for rainbows."*

Choosing *not* to sound like a sociopath, I scratch the back of my neck as I straighten. "I'm trying to write this book," I opt for, and hell, it's not a complete lie. I'm making progress. "I keep getting stuck. Running usually helps."

Oliver smiles fondly, crossing his arms over his chest. "Perhaps I can assist. I do like to read."

I falter. The urge to spill my guts to this guy I hardly know stabs at me—the desire to purge, confess my sins. I want to ambush him with my dark secrets, and not for forgiveness, not for sympathy or comfort, just… to be free.

Free from the shackles of Vengeance, chained by my own hands.

My fingers tousle through my damp hair, the words teasing the tip of my tongue, but I swallow back the truth because I've gotten really good at that. "I, uh… have this character," I begin, watching as Oliver stares at me, patiently, his eyes glimmering with warm curiosity. "He's not a good guy. I mean, he was, but…" I swallow, my gaze drifting to the slush beneath my shoes. "He got hurt… really hurt. Betrayed. And instead of trying to heal and move on, he chose a darker path. A path of revenge, not really caring about who could get hurt along the way."

"That sounds compelling."

I blink. "Right… yeah, totally compelling. Only, he's in too deep now, and I can't figure out a way to pull him out of it without causing more pain."

Oliver nods, smiling with affection. He tips his head towards the end of the neighborhood street, a silent beckon to follow. We walk side-by-side for a few beats, the brisk wind kissing our skin, before Oliver replies. "Pain for your main character, or pain for the ones around him?"

I pause when his question settles in, lifting my eyes and catching his.

Oliver takes my silence as an answer and continues. "You know, I was never well-versed in the human condition. Emotions, feelings, things that make us tick. Being isolated from people for so many years affected my ability to understand those things. I was knowledgeable on the subject, yes, but truly understanding is much different." He slips his hands into his pockets, glancing my way. "However, my fiancé is quite fluent in that department, wearing her emotions on her sleeve. I've come to learn a thing or two."

A trace of guilt sweeps through me when I think about what Oliver's been through and how resilient he still is. Encouraging and kind. He's been through far worse than I have, yet he never sacrificed his goodness. His integrity.

Self-Loathing pokes at me, Vengeance's dearest companion. It whispers in my ear.

It laughs.

Clearing my throat, I look away and clench my jaw. "Emotions give us fuel," I tell him. "They keep us going."

"Certainly. It's a matter of finding the *right* emotions. The ones that will drive us forward, make us better. Give us a purpose we can be proud of." Oliver slows his feet, pivoting to face me as a car rolls by, misting us with muddy snow. "Your character… perhaps he needs a new purpose."

I massage the back of my neck, nodding as my mind races. "What's your purpose?"

Oliver smiles. He doesn't hesitate. "Love. My love for Sydney."

Love.

Of course, it's love.

"Her happiness drives me," he continues. "The desire to see her utterly fulfilled in every possible way keeps me going." Oliver's smile is soft and wistful. There is no judgment there, no righteousness. Only truth. "Love is my fuel. I'd sacrifice everything for her, and I think… I think that's where you'll find your answers. Once you discover an objective more powerful than revenge, you'll begin to find your way out of that hole."

Josie's face flashes through my mind.

I've been trying to convince myself over the last couple of weeks that my attraction to Josie Grant is purely physical. And yet, I know, I *know*, I'd give up the chance of ever sleeping with her just to have her sitting on my living room couch playing Fleetwood Mac on her guitar, smiling, singing, looking at me like she truly sees me. Like she sees *all* of me—the best parts, the vulnerable parts, the dark and frightening and broken parts. And she accepts them all. She *embraces* them all.

My lungs burn, my chest humming with revelation.

I don't think she knows this.

Josie might spend the rest of her life thinking I only wanted her for sex, that getting in her pants was more important than getting inside her heart. And I *wanted* her to believe that because *I* wanted to believe that.

But I want so much more.

I want spaghetti nights and inside jokes and sing-a-longs with our girls. I want to drink raspberry wine with her in my car. I want to hear her laugh, and watch her smile, and dry her tears. I want to make love to her, but even more than that, I want to do the things that come after. I want to hold her and feel her in my arms, and wake up to her lying beside me, entwined in my bed sheets, glowing and perfect and *mine*.

I want to do all the things I thought I'd never want to do again.

I'm breathing hard, and not because I'm tired or winded—*no*. It's because my heart can't keep up with the epiphanies spreading through me like wildfire. I know I can't have these things, but I *want* these things. I can see beyond Katrina. I can see a light and hope and a future, and it's all because of her.

Oliver's eyes are twinkling with awareness, and I blow out a long, uneven breath, trying not to fall apart. Trying not to collapse right here in the snow. "Thanks," I murmur, choking back the sentiment caught in my throat. "That was helpful."

He offers a quick nod. "I'm delighted to hear I could help," he says, then falters. "For the holidays, I thought it would be a brilliant idea to get Syd a puppy. As you know, we already have a cat and a raccoon…" He clears his throat. "Well, the three of them managed to obliterate our Christmas tree, eat through two sofas, and start a small fire in the den." His eyes glaze over, like he's reminiscing the consequences of that obvious failure. A tense chuckle escapes him. "I misjudged the dynamic. I fear I was not at all helpful in that regard and have quite a bit more research to tackle on the subject of animal behavior."

"Well, consider it a wash," I laugh, idly wondering if that's why Lorna Gibson suddenly has a puppy now.

"Take care of yourself, Evan," Oliver says.

As our eyes hold for another beat, I can't help but frown thoughtfully when his words echo through me: *"You'll begin to find your way out of that hole."*

You. He knows I'm full of shit.

Pacing backwards, I nod my head, shooting him a knowing smile and lifting my hand in a final wave. "Thanks again, Oliver."

And then… I run.

I run and run and *run*.

I run all the way to the gym.

Hair like honey. Eyes like bourbon.

Josie Grant.

She's exactly where I hoped she'd be, pedaling swift and steadfast on her usual elliptical machine at the end of the row. Her ponytail is bobbing back and forth, her eyes closed, her stance tight and focused. I watch her for a few minutes as I collect my thoughts and my breath. I'm cold and sweaty, and my muscles feel like putty, but I'm oddly… calm. I'm filled with a certainty and honesty I haven't experienced in a long goddamn time, and even though this is an end, it's also a beginning.

I approach her, stopping beside her machine. I take in the sheen of her skin, the bow of her lips, the sunny highlights in her hair. Her eyes are still closed, and I wonder where she is right now. I wonder where she's gone. She must feel my presence because her eyes flutter open, and she turns her head toward me. Her legs immediately begin to slow as her gaze locks on mine, a flurry of emotions caressing her pretty face.

Shock. Relief. Confusion.

Guilt.

I try not to focus on the last one.

"I hit your car in the parking lot."

Josie comes to a gradual stop, her breathing heavy, her eyes flickering with bewilderment.

I place my hands into the pockets of my sweatpants and dip my head with a sigh. "I hit your car in the parking lot sixteen weeks ago, and it completely changed my life." I blink slowly, then dare to look back up at her, swallowing hard.

Josie's mouth parts as she sucks in a sharp breath, closing her eyes. She absorbs my words. I can see them flowing through her, filling her up, making her fingers tighten around the handlebars of her machine.

She doesn't know how to respond, but that's okay—I just need her to listen. "I know you don't want to see me, but there's something I need to say. And then I'll leave you alone. I'll walk away for good."

Josie lowers her head, her bottom lip pressed between her teeth. "Evan…"

"You told me you thought I was free," I continue. I watch her eyes lift, landing on mine, brimming with inner turmoil. "I wasn't free, Josie. I was stuck. I was trapped. I was spinning my wheels, fueled by hate, haunted by grief. I despised what I'd become, but I didn't think there was any other way. Hate became my survival, because as long as I was hating, I was *feeling*—and if I was feeling, I was living."

I can see the tears rim her eyes as her tension eases and she shifts her weight. Josie inhales a flimsy breath, waiting for me to continue.

"Then there was you."

Her eyes close. Her tears spill.

I take a cautious step towards her, but I'm not going to reach for her. If I touch her, my resolve will break. If I touch her, I'm not sure I'll ever be able to stop touching her. "You gave me a light when my world had gone dark. And I'm so fucking sorry if I stole your light, and I pray you get it back, but I couldn't walk out of your life without you knowing the impact you had on mine."

Josie is crying quiet tears, her breath quivering, while she wipes her pain away with her fingertips.

I drop my voice, leaning in closer. "You asked me what we were doing, and I said I wanted to fuck you."

She looks away, crossing her arms.

"But I can't let you believe that's all I wanted. I said that because it was easier. It was easier to lie and pretend that what we have is only physical, only attraction." Her eyes flick back to mine as her jaw sets. "I'm sick of lying, Josie. I'm falling for you, and it's terrifying... but being stuck in my old life, living through hate and revenge and bitterness, never knowing what it's like to fall in love again—that's the most terrifying thing of all."

Josie squeezes her eyes shut and ducks her head.

God, I want to hug her. "You're the one who's free, Josie Grant." I lean in farther until her hair tickles my cheek, and I sigh deeply, imprinting her scent into my marrow. I whisper softly, but with the utmost conviction, "Never hold back. Never stop singing to the stars."

I look at her, and she looks at me, and I think we both stop breathing, and time ceases to exist, and *fuck...* I want to kiss her and hold her and never let go.

But I *need* to let go.

I need to walk away.

And I do.

TWENTY-FIVE

"I miss you."

I hold the phone up to my face as I lie in bed, leaning back against the headboard. I smile, trying to make it the brightest, happiest smile I've ever smiled... but I know I'm failing.

It's a sad fucking smile. *Really* sad.

"I miss you, too, bunny."

Summer walks as she talks, and I can see Christmas lights and commotion behind her. She takes her phone to a quieter place, possibly her bedroom, and sits down against the solid oak door. "Mom tried to cook a ham, but it didn't go well. We made spaghetti instead. It wasn't nearly as good as yours. The sauce was out of a jar." She makes an appropriately horrified face.

I smile again, and this time, it's genuine. "I'm world famous for a reason. You know this."

Summer giggles. "I got a Nintendo Switch," she tells me.

"And meatloaf, right? So much meatloaf?"

She shakes her head, her eyes rolling dramatically. "No meatloaf. Did you get ketchup?"

"Nope. I wasn't on the naughty list this year."

That's a lie. I was definitely on the naughty list this year.

Before Summer can reply, there's a loud tapping sound behind her. She scoots away from the door and turns to open it, revealing an adorable, blonde-haired little boy. He toddles into the room with a toy truck, clumsy and unsteady, like he only just figured out how to walk.

"Mason!" Summer squeals, laughter lacing her voice. "You rascal. Come say hi to my dad."

I watch as my daughter pulls the child onto her lap, lifting his hand up to wave at me. "Hey, little buddy," I say. I'm taken by how sweet Summer is with him, so affectionate and nurturing. I try not to let the "what ifs" consume me. "Nice to meet you."

Mason makes a cooing sound and flaps his arms. The truck falls from his hand, while drool dribbles down his chin.

"You're a good baby, Mason," Summer proclaims, kissing the boy on the head.

I watch them interact, noticing that Mason's eyes are blue like Summer's. I wonder if my second child would have had blue eyes. Katrina's are blue, but mine are a greenish-hazel—or pond scum, I would always joke. I was so happy when Summer got Katrina's eyes.

"I'm gonna go, Dad," Summer says, chasing after Mason who is now crawling to the other side of the room. "Can I call you tomorrow?"

"You never have to ask that, bun. You can call me any time."

She grins, then waves into the screen. "Merry Christmas."

"Merry Christmas."

Summer ends the call, and everything goes quiet.

I am alone.

So alone.

Before I toss my phone to the opposite side of the bed, I notice an unread Facebook message. It's from Josie. All it says is, *"Merry Christmas."*

I wonder how much courage it took for her to send that. I wonder if she debated sending it; I wonder if she debated sending *more* than that. There is still so much left unsaid.

Hovering my thumb over the notification, I'm about to open it, *wanting* to open it and spill my guts to her, but I choose to ignore it. I let out a slow breath and swipe the notification away, leaving the message unread.

It's for the best.

I go about my evening like it's a normal day—like I'm not entirely alone on Christmas. I write. I cook myself a steak and drink two beers too many. I watch a new show on Netflix, only to realize I zoned out seven minutes in and have no clue what's going on. I turn it off and play my guitar instead. It makes me think of Josie, so I stop playing. I call my parents to wish them happy holidays.

My call is cut short when the doorbell rings.

Who the fuck would be at my front door on Christmas night?

Maybe it's the Ghost of Christmas Present here to tell me what an asshole I am.

I trek over to the front of the house and pull the door open, flabbergasted when the person standing on my front stoop is none other than Benjamin fucking Grant. The last person I ever want to see again.

Apparently, it's the Ghost of Christmas Past.

I'm certain my look of confoundment is evident as I stare at him through the screen, silent and still. I'm not exactly sure what to say except for, *"What the fuck are you doing here?"*

I don't say that, though, because he's holding an item wrapped in tinfoil, and Jesus Christ, did he bring me a fucking pie or something?

"Evan, old friend," Benjamin beams, holding up the offering, bundled up in a heavy winter coat and Burberry hat. "Jos said you might be alone tonight. She wanted me to bring you dessert."

I swallow, words still escaping me. I don't… would she… ? And if she did, why send *Ben?*

There's a fucking pit in my stomach. This guy thinks I'm his friend, and now he's standing here at my door on Christmas—the day I feel more alone than ever—delivering dessert.

I hate this man more than I've ever hated anyone. He's guilty of stealing my wife away. He's guilty of ruining my life. Without him, everything would be different.

I wouldn't be so damn alone.

He is the guilty one.

Yet somehow, I feel like the guiltiest motherfucker who ever walked the planet.

I have no choice but to open the door and let him in. "Thanks," I mutter, unsettled by his presence.

Benjamin steps through the threshold, stomping his snowy boots against the welcome mat at my front door. He sets the dish down beside him on the entry table. "I hope you enjoy it. My wife is an excellent baker," he says.

I roll my tongue along my teeth, glancing at the tin-foiled dessert. I'm distracted for a moment, wondering what's inside, wondering why she made me something.

I'm so distracted that I don't even see it coming.

Two fists grab me by the shirt collar, slamming me up against the wall. The air rushes from my lungs, like I've been sucker-punched.

Benjamin's arm presses to my throat, hard and firm. "But she's a terrible judge of character."

He knows.

I look into his eyes, and I know that he knows.

Fuck.

It's over.

My act is up.

But somehow... I feel like it was over long before now.

The shock wears off, and I find my strength, shoving him away. He teeters back. His jaw twitches, his nostrils flaring. Disbelief is etched into every angry crease as he shakes his head. "Apparently, I'm just as big of a fool as she was."

My breath is coming heavy now, quick and fast. Adrenaline courses through my veins, and I'm prepared to fight, prepared to finish this war once and for all. "Go to Hell," I bite out. "You ruined my fucking life."

Benjamin huffs a rueful exhale and sniffs, running his hand along his clean-shaven jaw. "You're good," he says, still swinging his head back and forth, laughing... but there's no humor in it. "You're real good. You had me completely fooled—right up until Emmett enlightened me."

Of course, he did. The fucker.

My heart is beating so fast, it feels like it's ricocheting off my ribs. I study Benjamin Grant with his overpriced coat and shoes, the pompous set of his jaw. There is something else fusing with the rage in his eyes—something like *hurt*. I'm not sure what to do with it. Hurting him used to be the focal point of my entire life. He took center stage. No one else mattered.

Now he's just in the way.

"Come on, you can't be that oblivious. All that time we were spending together; the way we'd look at each other. You're a defense attorney—where are your instincts?"

His glare is volatile. "I *know* my wife. She's loyal, and I've given her everything. Everything and more. She had no reason to stray."

I can't help the pang of guilt that zips through me.

I changed her. I turned her into someone else.

"You could have just come to my office and confronted me, you know," Benjamin continues. "You didn't have to infiltrate my family. Pretend to be our friend."

My eyes narrow at the suggestion—confronting him was never the point. I wanted to him to *feel*; I wanted him to know what *I* felt.

Broken. Ruined.

And then the rest of his words hit me. They knock the wind out of me, like I've been slammed into the wall again. He said... *pretending*.

But I wasn't pretending with Josie, at least not later on.

That was real. What we feel for each other is real.

"You're a special kind of asshole, that's for sure," he says, still shaking his head self-righteously. "Using your innocent daughter to get close to us."

Whoa.

Bile rises in my throat at the suggestion. "Watch it, *Ben*. I *never* used Summer. Her friendship with Olivia is real."

And even as I say it, I remember that first play date at their house when I realized I had pulled her into my chaos... and, hell, I'm not so sure he's wrong.

God, I feel sick.

"Right," he laughs incredulously. "And what happens to their friendship now? Who gets hurt from *that?* You know... I'm not Olivia's birth father, but she's become a daughter to me, and I could *never* do what you did."

Fucking sanctimonious asshole.

"Leave the kids out of this." I'm almost yelling now, my fists clenching hard. "This isn't about them."

"Isn't it? Did you really think all of this was *only* going to hurt me?"

Fuck. I did at first, but... not anymore. Not for a while, now. I've been lying to myself this whole time, trying not to see the truth. Trying to keep moving forward with my plan of revenge until I got the end result I was so sure would be the fix to this emptiness.

But it's worse now. The emptiness.

It's worse.

I rub a hand across my face. I can't let him see the effect his words have on me.

Blowing out a sharp breath of air, I ask the only other thing I really care about at this point. "Does she know?"

Josie. My God... what this will do to her.

Benjamin pauses, pushing his tongue against his cheek and averting his eyes. "No."

I try to keep my exhale of relief slow, so he can't see. I'm safe... for now, when it comes to Josie, I'm safe. It makes sense. If Josie finds out who

I really am, then she finds out who her husband really is, and I don't think he's ready for that.

"Don't look so smug, Evan... do you really think I want to see her hurt like that?"

I laugh out loud, but it's anything but funny. "Really, Benjamin? You're worried about hurting her *now?*

His face twists into a sneer, his voice rife with disgust. "Wow. You *still* think you're better than me? I had an affair. Yes. I did that. And I hate myself for it every day. You already know that because I told you, back when I was still the fucking idiot, thinking I was confiding in a *friend.*"

I wince internally, and I don't know why... I don't know why because he *deserves* to hurt. This is what I wanted. He deserves it for what he did to me.

He deserves it, Vengeance echoes.

His voice is low and full of contempt as he continues. "I fell for another woman. I cheated on my wife. It happened, and I'm not proud of it. But only one of us went to all these lengths, all this time and energy, *just* to hurt other people."

Fuck. I have to resist the urge to cover my ears like a petulant child.

This wasn't how it was supposed to be. I need him to go. I can't hear this, I can't *do* this anymore.

"Thanks for the dessert," I seethe through gritted teeth. "Now, get out of my house."

His eyes flash, traveling over me from head to toe, oozing judgment. "I hope you didn't really think you could take her from me."

Oh... he fucking went there.

I know I can, you son-of-a-bitch.

And then I can't resist jabbing him where it hurts. "I don't think you know your wife as well as you think you do."

Benjamin whips forward, on me again, his fists curling around my t-shirt as he yanks me to him. Our faces are only inches apart when he snarls, "Fuck you. You weren't enough for Katrina, and you sure as *fuck* aren't enough for Josie."

He's wrong.

Rage takes over and I gain the upper hand, pulling free and spinning him around until he crashes against my entertainment center. Picture frames tip over, and books slide out, landing at our feet. We're both eerily quiet for a moment until Benjamin begins to chuckle. It's not a real laugh—more like something born from adrenaline and bitterness, but still, he just stands there.

Laughing at me. "Something funny?" I spit out, my teeth grinding together so hard, I think they might crack. The more he laughs, the more my rage boils until it's all I can do to keep from planting my fist in his face, just to make him stop. I let go of him and step back, holding myself together, reining it in.

I can't go to jail. Summer needs me.

"Shit…" His laugh twists to pure disdain. "You're delusional. You actually believe this egomaniacal vendetta of yours will work? That you're so irresistible just because you have tattoos and a fast car, and write edgy books?"

All I want to do is wipe that smug grin off his fucking face without treading on assault. I don't even think before I speak. "Oh, I don't know, *Ben*—it felt pretty believable when my fingers were inside her and my tongue was down her throat at your holiday party. She's so pretty when she comes, isn't she?"

Silence descends.

Oh.

Oh… fuck.

I smash the delete button in my head, only… this isn't my laptop. I can't take those words back.

The disdainful smile fades. Benjamin visibly pales in front of me, his face flooding with confusion. "What?"

I close my eyes, filling with instant regret.

"You're lying. Josie wouldn't do that," he breathes out.

I wanted to hurt Benjamin, but I'm hurting Josie in the process.

I don't want to hurt Josie.

He's shaking his head again, his features crumpling with disbelief. "No, no… she *wouldn't.*"

For a moment, I'm caught by the audacity. He thinks he can betray his wife, but that it could never happen to him?

And then he says, "That's not like Josie… what did you do to her? *What did you do?*" His face is stricken, expression wild. The last few words are barely a whisper.

I want to vomit right here on his shoes.

It's the same damn thing I've been berating myself with, ever since the reality hit me in the entryway of his master bathroom…

What did I do to her? What did I do?

Benjamin recovers from the horror, and I watch his face as anger morphs in its place. Then he storms past me towards the front door.

I'm riddled with panic. He's going to take it out on Josie.

Fuck... *fuck*.

"Wait," I say, moving in front of him to block his path.

"Get out of my way, you son-of-a-bitch," he growls.

But I can't let him go now. Not like this. "Just wait. Listen to me, will you?"

"You wanted to hurt me? Well, congratulations. Merry. Fucking. Christmas."

His hands come up, and a flash of realization hits me as I brace for the punch. Only, he shoves me instead—he shoves me hard, and I'm off my feet, flying through the air until I crash into the wall, my head knocking back with a thud. I slide to the floor, unable to keep myself upright; I sit there, dazed, as he towers over me.

"What do you think all of this has *done* to her, huh?" Benjamin's words are thorns cutting into my soul as he voices everything that's been haunting me. "You can hurt me, and maybe I had it coming, but... *Josie* is a good person. And look what you've done to her."

I can't even focus on the twisted truth of what he's saying. On the parallels to Katrina.

Desperation sinks into me, and I struggle to my feet. He's going to storm out of here and tell her what an idiot she was. He's going to tell her what I did to her, and I can't bear to even think of her heartbreak. "It's over," I insist, my balance unsteady as I move in front of him once again. *Let him hit me. I don't even care.* "You don't have to worry about me. You'll never see me again."

"You're fucking right I won't."

He tries to leave, but I thwart him once more. The last thing I ever expected to do was beg Benjamin Grant for *anything*, but here we are. I'll beg on my knees if it saves Josie from the humiliating backlash of my goddamn ego. "*Please.* Just leave it alone. You fucked up, she fucked up, and now you're even. It was *my* fault. Don't use this to hurt her even more."

It's as raw and real as I could ever be. This isn't about me anymore. I no longer give a fuck about my goddamned crusade to destroy Benjamin Grant.

His eyes narrow as he scans my face, reading me like an open book. He nods slowly as if coming to some kind of grandiose realization. "You're in love with her." Benjamin seems to ponder this for a moment when I don't deny it, and then a disbelieving bark of laughter leaves him. "Jesus, this is rich. You try to seduce my wife to satisfy your lust for revenge, but you fall for her in the process. Now you can't go through with it, can you?"

The irony is not lost on me.

"That's really sad." Benjamin's lips curl bitterly as he wags his finger in front of my face. "You should write a book about this, Evan. It'll be a goddamn bestseller... I can feel it."

When he moves around me to the door, I let him go, watching as he puts his hand on the knob. He hesitates then, turning to look at me over his shoulder. There is guilt swimming in his eyes—guilt and sorrow, and something more...

Regret.

"I didn't set out to break up your marriage," he says, pinning his lips in a thin line. "What happened with Katrina just... *happened.* I didn't plan it. It was never intentional. I fell for her, and it was wrong. And when things went too far, I ended it."

"Too little, too late," I mutter, my tone even and unemotional. I'm dazed and exhausted and so fucking heavy with this emotional burden, I just want to collapse.

"Yeah." He nods again, pivoting away, his shoulders deflating as he stands in front of my doorway. "You know, it takes a special kind of person to devise a plan like this. On the way over here, I wondered if you were a sociopath or something... but you're not, are you? You just let the anger turn you into this. You let it win. It's pathetic, really... I almost feel sorry for you." Benjamin spares me a final glance before he opens the door. "Enjoy your pie."

The door slams shut, rattling on its hinges, and I stare at it. I don't know how many minutes go by.

Vengeance swirls around me.

Untethered. Victorious.

It's finally free.

And I am empty.

I'm empty and alone, but not for long. Its companion has joined the victory party.

Self-Loathing is here to fill the gaping wounds left in the wake of my *brilliant* plan, and I am struck with the reality of the lie I stupidly bought into.

When this started, I was angry and betrayed... and now?

Now... I am so many fucking worse things.

Rage moves in next, and that rage is
all
for

me.

I seethe. I growl into my hands. I pull at my hair.

Then, alone on Christmas day, in the living room of my empty house, I yell into the silence.

I yell and scream until I'm hunched over with my hands on my knees.

I scream until I'm hoarse, and it's a miracle the neighbors aren't beating down my door.

I scream until hot tears burn my eyes, but they do nothing to soothe my splintered soul.

I curse, and I shout, and I *scream*, and I hate myself more and more with every painful, passing second.

And then…

I go quiet.

Everything is quiet.

Vengeance has abandoned me. It got exactly what it wanted, and now it's moved on, eager to infect its next victim. It left me here alone with the remnants of my shameful choices.

I

am

alone.

Inhaling a long, punishing breath, I rise to my feet.

Then I grab the pie dish and hurl it at the front door.

TWENTY-SIX

*T*HE END.

I write my two favorite words, then click "save."

Letting myself savor the moment, I lean back against my desk chair and link my fingers behind my head, twisting side to side, admiring my finished manuscript—all 97,334 words of it. This book took me eight whole months to finish, the longest time period yet.

I usually celebrate the completion of a book by taking Summer out for ice cream, but tonight she's having a sleepover with Rayna, so I'm left to celebrate on my own. Naturally, this will involve alcohol. Copious amounts of it, I hope.

I pull out my cell phone and text Logan.

ME: *Finished the book & feeling celebratory. Drinks at Tommy's?*

I linger, my eyes roving over my contacts. "Mean Girl From The Gym" stares back at me, as it's the name that sits directly under Logan's. I've considered deleting her number from my phone probably a dozen times over the last ten weeks. I should have. I should *right now*.

But I don't.

I'm not sure if I ever will.

I have no reason to keep Josie Grant's number saved into my phone since I know I won't ever be contacting her again, but I'm physically incapable of performing the simple task. It's only two swift flicks of my thumb, then—*poof*.

Gone.

Abra-fucking-cadabra.

The thought alone makes me feel sick inside.

I toss my phone onto the desk and sigh heavily. I haven't heard from Josie since Christmas. I haven't heard from her husband since he showed up on my doorstep with cherry pie and vitriol in his veins.

I've concluded that Benjamin never told her about me—about who I really am—nor about the fact that I used her just to hit her husband where I knew it would hurt.

He didn't tell her about my *betrayal*… because that's what it feels like.

God, that's exactly what it is.

At this point, though, I can only assume she's still blissfully unaware of my lies and deceit, and I'm not sure why. I'm baffled by it. I woke up every morning for weeks, wondering if that would be the day Josie barreled through my front door with tears in her eyes and *"how could you?"* on her lips.

I'm still waiting for that day to come.

Maybe I'll always be waiting.

My phone dings with a text message, so I scoop it off the dresser. It's Logan.

LOGAN: *Hell yeah, man. Meet you there at 9.*

He follows it up with the metal horns emoji, and I shoot back a quick response.

Leaning into my chair, my eyes drift to the two final words on my manuscript.

The End.

It's the end of my book. The end of this story. But somehow, it feels like an end to so much more. There's a thick sense of finality in the air as I run my hands over my stubbled face, which might actually be bordering on scruff at this point.

I close my laptop.

I don't think those are my two favorite words anymore.

The early March air is still brutally cold. A caustic wind picks up and whips me in the face, forcing my breath to catch in the back of my throat as I saunter down the city sidewalk with my hands in my coat pockets. It's a welcome reprieve when I step into the bar—warmth, friends, familiarity…

Relief.

Logan and Amber are already seated at a high-top table. Well, Logan is seated there, anyway. Amber is on his lap, her arms wrapped around his neck as they suck face.

I interrupt them. "Don't you two ever get sick of each other?"

They pull apart, and Amber squeals in delight when she spots me. "What is it now? Book number seven?" She grins wide, diving into my arms and hugging me tight. "So fucking proud of you, Evan."

I cut my eyes to Logan and fist-bump him over Amber's shoulder. "Thanks. I'm excited about this one."

Amber pulls back to bounce up and down on her pumps, feigning giddiness. "Can I get your autograph since you're about to be super famous? Will you sign my boobs?"

Logan smacks her on the ass. "If he touches your boobs, he loses a hand."

"Ooh, so territorial. I like it." She sashays back to Logan and climbs onto him.

"And… they're making out again." I sigh out loud to no one.

Time to get intoxicated.

We collect our shots and cocktails and situate around the small table, holding up our glasses in cheers. I look forward to what Logan and Amber are going to cheers to tonight—it's always random as hell.

"Cheers to Evan for slaying the hell out of the author thing," Amber proclaims with a smile. "And cheers to bearded dragons."

"Definitely cheers to bearded dragons. Fuck Evan." Logan winks at me. "But seriously, bearded dragons are crazy cool. We should get one, babe."

Amber lights up at the suggestion. "They even make cute little outfits for them—harnesses with dragon wings. I saw them on Etsy."

"Holy shit," Logan says, lowering his glass slightly as he processes this. "That's ridiculous. And oddly intriguing."

"Right? We're getting one. I'm naming her Sue."

Logan raises his glass again, nodding emphatically. "To Sue, the bearded dragon, and her wings… and to Evan, I guess."

I clink my glass with theirs, shaking my head, not even entirely sure what's happening anymore. I sling back the liquor and feel it warm my blood, filling the empty holes that have begun to duplicate over the last couple of months. Three more shots later, I make my way to the bathroom.

I stop short when I see a familiar face walking out of the women's side. "Evan?"

I stare at her, then smile in greeting. "Delilah. Good to see you." We step away from the entrance of the restrooms while she fiddles with a strand of hair, looking a little nervous. I suppose I can't really blame her—the last interaction we had was when my tongue was in her mouth on Josie's front porch. It sets the stage for a bit of awkwardness.

Especially considering I was picturing Josie the whole time.

"How are you?" she asks, smoothing out the fabric of her mustard-colored sweater dress. Her eyes sweep over my face as she continues to fidget. "It's been a while."

I cross my arms, swaying lightly on my feet. I'm feeling a little buzzed. I'm not sure how to respond to her question, despite the fact that it's a remarkably simple and to-the-point question. But I don't know Delilah well enough to be honest, and replying with a standard "fine" or "good" gives no room to further the conversation, leaving us feeling even *more* awkward than we already do... and damn, I'm definitely buzzed. I kind of just want to ask how Josie is doing.

But I shouldn't do that.

I shouldn't... *I won't.*

"I got the drinks, Del. They just ran out of grenadine, so your Rum Runner is running on straight rum. I improvised a little. What I'm saying is, I bought us shots instead, because why bother with all those extra sugar calories when—" Josie finally looks up mid-ramble, and one of the shots slips from her hand when her eyes land on me. "Oh."

Yeah. *Oh.*

Patrons glance at Josie when the sound of shattering glass spills around her feet. But my eyes don't ever leave her face, and her eyes don't leave mine, and the building could be collapsing down all around us right now, and maybe there's a bomb, and there could even be a fire, but neither of us would likely notice.

"Um, you dropped something." Delilah steps over to Josie and snaps her fingers in front of her face. "Earth to Josie Bennett. How much have you had to drink, girl?"

Bennett?

My attention leaves her wide-eyed expression, traveling down to the hand still clutching the lone shot glass that managed to survive our unexpected reunion. I can't stop staring at her fingers.

She's not wearing her wedding ring.

Josie blinks, forcing herself out of her trance. She clears her throat and hands the shot to Delilah, dipping her chin to her chest. "Hey, Evan."

She's not wearing her wedding ring.

I swallow, my mind reeling with a thousand questions, desires, and hopes…

Why aren't you wearing a ring?
Why did Delilah call you Josie Bennett?
Did you leave him?
Can we be together?
Why didn't you tell me?

"Hey," I respond.

Before we're able to continue our riveting conversation, Logan appears to my right, likely checking to see if I passed out in the bathroom or got lost somewhere along the way. He quickly spots my source of tardiness.

His eyes double to me, then back to Josie. I never told Logan or Amber about what happened between us because I couldn't handle the *"I told you so"* and *"You're a fucking idiot"* remarks that I would absolutely deserve, so he's genuinely happy to see Josie standing in front of us looking like a deer in headlights.

An incredibly sexy deer, dressed in a black camisole top with a dangerously revealing neckline and skin-tight jeans.

Fucking hell.

"Josie," he greets, rushing over to her and pulling her into a clumsy, one-armed hug. "Are you here to celebrate Evan's new book?"

Her eyes flash to me again, filling briefly with something that looks like pride. "Oh, uh, no. We just happened to run into each other. I'm here with my friend. But… congratulations, Evan."

Logan nods his head at Delilah. "Come on, join us. We'll grab a bigger table."

"Logan—" I try to interrupt, but he wraps his arms around both Josie and Delilah and guides them to the other side of the bar. I reluctantly follow.

Amber pounces on Josie the moment she sees her, like they are long lost friends. Like she's been missing her just as much as I have.

Not possible.

"Girl, you look amazing," Amber says, scoping Josie up and down, from the gold lariat necklace around her neck to the sex heels on her feet. "Did your boobs get bigger?"

Josie instinctively looks at me, and I instinctively look at Josie's chest. She releases an awkward laugh. "I don't think so."

Amber shrugs and pulls her down into the seat beside her. "Well, you look hot. Your husband is a lucky man."

"Actually..." Josie's gaze shoots to me once again. I hold her stare, daring her, begging her to finish that sentence. She swallows. "I'm... in the middle of a divorce. Well, we're separated right now, but... yeah."

A silence washes over the table, and Logan and Amber's eyes are on me —as if I had something to do with it. But I can't answer that question. Josie never bothered to fill me in on this new development, and I don't know why I feel slightly offended by this because I suppose it's none of my fucking business... but I do.

I'm offended and kind of pissed. If she's no longer with Benjamin...

I try not to finish the thought. I shouldn't go there.

Why isn't she with me?

I sigh aloud at my failure and sit down at the table across from Josie, my eyes still glued to her. She slinks back beneath my brazen perusal, biting her lip and skating her gaze away from me.

Delilah breaks the tension. "Yep, she's officially in the soon-to-be divorcee club with me. We came here tonight to get our rebounds on. I'm extremely behind schedule," she jokes, throwing a wink my way that I only partially register.

Rebound? Josie came here to fuck some random stranger?

My anger flares from a five to a solid eleven.

I watch as she closes her eyes, a blush seeping into her cheeks. Every muscle in my body tenses and my jaw hardens as I stare. I can't peel my eyes away. The alcohol is cruising through me, heating me up almost as quickly as the blaze that travels between us when Josie finally looks at me. I lean back in my chair, pretending to be indifferent. "Sorry to hear that, Josie. I had no idea."

I wonder if she's as unconvinced by my casual act as I am.

Apology is swimming all over her face. She knows what I'm thinking, I can see it her eyes. "Yeah, it was kind of sudden. We only finalized things last month. I needed time to process everything." Her eyes are pointed and fixed on me. "Olivia and I have been staying with Delilah until I get back on my feet."

I nod slowly, taking in her response.

"Mmm-hmm," I hear Delilah mutter from somewhere in the background, "I've been kicking around in a big house all by myself, so..."

I stand, desperate for air. Desperate for a cigarette.

Desperate to rid my mind of the image of Josie screwing some random guy after I basically gave her my heart on a fucking platter, then walked away to protect hers.

Jesus, it hurts like hell.

I'm also wondering why Benjamin Grant didn't spill my secrets to her. It's obvious he didn't. But if they separated—if he'd already lost her—what else did he have to lose?

It doesn't make sense.

Nothing makes sense.

My chair legs squeak against the hard floor as I shove it under the table. "I need a smoke. I'll be back." I don't look at her. I *can't* afford to look at her. My heart can't take breaking one more time.

So, I walk out.

She finds me a few minutes later, leaning against the distressed brick wall in the adjacent alleyway. I take a deep drag on my cigarette and pretend not to notice her until I can't pretend anymore.

"Evan."

My name escapes her lips like a kiss, or a poem, or the prelude to a song. The catch in her voice is enough to force my gaze in her direction, and I trail my eyes over her, drinking her in beneath the streetlight. I can't pretend to be unaffected by her. I can't pretend that I'm not melting, not sinking, not falling, falling, *falling*...

I blow smoke out through my nose and relish in the way it burns. "How's Olivia holding up?"

Josie approaches me with timid steps, tucking her arms around herself for warmth. She looks slightly surprised—probably because I asked about Olivia before anything else. "She's doing really good. Better than me," Josie replies with a bemused sigh. She looks down at her heels crunching against the gravel—sex heels that she didn't wear for me. "How's Summer?" she asks, meeting my eyes. "We miss her."

"She's good. She misses you guys, too." That's an understatement. There hasn't been a day that's gone by where my daughter hasn't asked about a play date with Olivia. I blink, then fix my stare on Josie as she comes to a stop a few feet away from me. Under these lights, I can see that her hair is different... a little shorter, a little lighter.

But the way her eyes fill with a familiar mix of desire and vulnerability when she looks at me hasn't changed one bit.

Why didn't you fucking tell me? I bite back the words, but my resentment leaks out anyway.

"So, you were here to pick up some stranger tonight? Please, go ahead. I didn't mean to interfere." The bitter undertones are dripping from every word that spills out of my mouth.

Josie clenches her hands in front of her, pursing her lips. "Delilah was exaggerating. *She* might be here for a rebound, but I'm not looking for that. I was just… getting out. Learning how to be single again, I guess."

"Hey, I'm not one to judge. You're a free woman now. You can fuck whoever you want." I know I sound petulant, but I can't help but feel that way, damnit.

She shakes her head, her gaze settling to the left of me. "Please don't do that, Evan. I know I haven't contacted you, but… what we have is *messy*, and I can't do messy right now."

Messy—because she fell for me while she was married.

Messy—because of what we did in their bedroom at her Christmas party.

I'm tainted now.

I'm *messy*.

I take a drag off my cigarette, letting it out slowly. "You don't need to explain. You don't owe me anything, Josie. I said my piece at the gym on Christmas Eve, and it's done." I don't look at her as I flick my cigarette to the ground and stomp it out. Taking a deep breath, I move around her, but she reaches out and clasps her hand around my arm to stop me. I close my eyes, trying not to succumb to all the ways my body is reacting to her touch. "Josie…"

"Please don't think that I'm underplaying this," she whispers softly. "I've thought about you every single day for the last three months."

My eyes open, my head turning to find her gaze. We hold there, our breath hitting the cold air, our bodies warming from the currents that permeate our skin. There's a question on my tongue, and I debate asking it, but I kind of need to know. "Am I the reason why you left him?" I don't know what I want her answer to be. It *had* been the ultimate goal—to be the reason Benjamin Grant's marriage dissolved—but now… I don't know if I want that kind of responsibility. It doesn't feel as good as I thought it would.

It feels hollow.

Josie's eyes flicker across my face, wide and expressive. I can see her answer before she speaks it into the night. "Yes," she breathes out. "But… I didn't leave him *for* you. I left him *because* of you."

I face her fully, stepping closer, forcing my hands into fists so they remain by my sides. "There's a difference?"

She dips her chin and swallows. "The real reasons I left were for *me*. I needed to find myself again—rediscover the person I'm meant to be…" Her eyes flick away momentarily. "I – I've not always been confident I can do that on my own, but I need to try—I *have* to try."

Her hand is still on my arm. I'm not sure if she even realizes this, but I don't pull away. In fact, I move in closer.

"The way you and I started, Evan… it was unhealthy. If I'd left him and gone straight to you, we—"

"It's okay," I cut her off, covering her hand with my own.

Shit, she has no idea how unhealthy it was. Even though I'm disappointed, I know this.

I fucking get it.

Josie sucks in a poignant breath, maintaining eye contact. "You make me question *everything*, but not in a bad way—in a necessary way. I had no idea all the things I was sacrificing because I was afraid of chasing my dreams. I was afraid to want *more* out of life than what I was settling for." She takes a step closer. "When I met you, I started remembering who I used to be. I started to feel… brave."

Her eyes are becoming glossy, and she bites her lip as she blinks back the tears, regaining her composure. "My world was flipped upside down when Adam died. I wasn't doing well on my own; I was afraid of failing Olivia, and I finally just… settled. When I married Ben, I thought that because I had a successful husband and a big house and a hefty bank account, that it was selfish of me to want more." Josie raises her hand and gently rests it against my cheek. "But I don't really care about any of those things. I just want to feel alive. I want to play my guitar, and travel the world, and sleep under the stars. I want *real* love. The kind that makes you want to wake up every morning and be a better person than you were the day before." She inhales, swallowing hard. "You opened my eyes, Evan. I found the real me again, the girl I buried away years ago… the girl I thought I'd lost."

I lean down and press my forehead to hers, wrapping my arms around her waist and holding her tight. Her words have my head reeling, my heart racing, my blood pumping.

Josie smiles through her tears. "You make me want to go skinny dipping at midnight, and dance in the rain, and wish on falling stars, and believe in a life so exhilarating, so *liberating*, that it feels almost tangible." She melts against me and finishes, "And while it's the greatest feeling in the world, it's also the most terrifying, and I have no idea what I'm doing."

I nod against her. "I know exactly how you feel." Her tears are falling fast, so I wipe them away with my thumbs, cradling her face between my palms. I kiss her forehead, then the tip of her nose, then her cheek, and before I can find a new place to kiss, her mouth finds mine, and I am lost.

Josie whimpers when our tongues meet, and she clings to my arms, gasping and making those little sounds that drive me fucking crazy. I walk her backwards until she's pressed against the brick wall, and I kiss her, I kiss her deep and unwavering, and I *never want to stop kissing her*. I only drag my lips away to trail them down her jaw, to the arch of her neck, and I pull the tender flesh between my teeth until she makes that sound again. Josie wraps her arms around my neck, arching into the wall, tilting her head to give me permission to taste her further. My hands find their way beneath her camisole, and she squeaks in surprise when I cup her breasts encased in lace.

"Evan," she moans, grinding against me like she needs more than I can give her in a dingy alleyway. "Is Summer at home?"

I continue to kiss her neck, then graze my lips up to her ear and nibble the lobe. "No."

"Forget what I said before," she sighs, her fingers digging into my scalp and tugging at my hair. "Take me back to your place."

TWENTY-SEVEN

The Uber driver hates us.

We decided not to drive because we'd both been drinking, and even though I only live a mile from the bar, walking would take longer than we were willing to wait. So, in the three minutes it took for the Uber to pull up, Josie and I re-entered the bar with messy hair, flushed skin, and shirts tucked into strange places. We gave an incredibly awkward story on why we needed to leave—*together*—that literally no one believed.

"My Uncle is dying… actually, he died," I said, stuffing my hands into my denim pockets and shaking my head with intense sorrow.

"I'm going to help with the arrangements and everything," Josie added.

Logan raised a quizzical brow. "Your uncle, Amos? I thought he died, like, seven years ago."

"The other one… Uncle, um…" I waved my hand around in front of me, my brain suddenly blanking on one goddamn male name out of the five million that probably exist. I was staring at Logan, and it was the only name that came to mind. "Uncle Logan."

"You have an uncle with the same name as me?" Logan inquired, his eyes narrowing. "How did I not know that?"

"He lives in Venezuela."

Josie lowered her head, her voice excessively sad. "*Lived*," she corrected, and she was so convincing that I'd almost started grieving for fictional Uncle Logan.

Everyone stared at us, utterly silent.

We booked it.

We were both drunk on lust and rum, and it all sounded so much better in the twelve seconds we talked it through as we skipped up the bar steps.

Now Josie is straddling my lap in the backseat of this poor guy's Uber, and he keeps clearing his throat, hoping maybe we can control ourselves in the ridiculously short drive over to my house. But I can't seem to keep my hands off her, and my tongue hasn't left her mouth since she shut the door and crawled into my lap. She grinds into me, and I try my best to suppress a groan, so I don't make this guy hate his life even more than he probably already does.

"God, the things I'm going to do to you..." I moan into Josie's ear, a quiet promise, and I feel her response in the way she trembles in my arms, pressing herself harder against my groin. I bury my face into her neck, muffling the sound that leaves my lips.

A few more seconds tick by and we're finally pulling into my driveway.

Thank God.

We climb out of the vehicle, muttering apologies to the driver, and I yank Josie's hand, dragging her all the way up to my front door. My hands are actually shaking as I sift through my keys and drop them onto the stoop, and we both start laughing because we feel like horny teenagers about to lose their virginity.

The door pushes open, and we practically fall through the threshold, our hands all over each other, our mouths fusing together once more. I kick the door closed, walking backwards until we find the first piece of furniture available, which is my couch. I collapse onto it, taking Josie with me.

It's dark, but I can still make out her face from the moonlight shining in through my bay window, bathing her in a milky glow. *Fuck*, she's beautiful. I go still for a moment, running my hands down her body, memorizing the curve of her waist, the bow of her hips, the way my fingertips feel gliding along her outer thighs. She leans forward until our foreheads are pressed together, and my breath hitches, overcome with so much more than desire. Josie is perfect in every way. Benjamin did not deserve her.

I swallow, my eyes squeezing shut.

I don't deserve her.

My alcohol buzz is fading. But Josie doesn't seem to notice my split second of reservation, and her hand trails between my legs as her eyes lift to mine, twinkling with implication. She begins stroking me through my jeans, and it feels so damn good, even just like this, I can't help the audible groan that escapes my mouth. A coy smile blooms on her lips in response to my reaction. Dropping to her knees in front of me, she fumbles with my belt buckle, moving on to my zipper, and *holy shit*... I think she's about to go down on me.

Fuck, fuck, fuck... I want her mouth so badly. But there's a shard of guilt digging at me.

"Wait, Josie..."

She stares up at me, her eyes glazed over with lust.

Fuck it. She wants me as much as I want her, and she's single now, damnit. I pull her from the floor and trade places with her on the couch in one swift move. "I need to taste you first," I nearly growl. The sound she makes in return is like a helpless cry as I unbutton her jeans and begin to tug them down her hips. When it takes forever, she arches off the couch, trying to help me push them down her thighs, giggling.

"Sorry, these jeans seemed like a good idea when I wasn't planning to take them off so quickly."

I laugh along with her, eyeing her exposed panties as I give up on freeing her legs entirely. Her giggles turn into a shaky sigh when I lean down and place my open mouth over the thin material, exhaling a hot breath over her sensitive area. She shudders as I probe at the lace with my tongue.

When she wiggles her hips in my face with a whimper that asks for more, I have to resist the temptation to rip them off... but I'm *dying* to hear her beg.

Beg for me, Josie.

"Oh, my God, Evan... please... *please*. Stop teasing me," she obliges with desperation, and I can no longer resist.

I pull the lace to the side and drink her in. She's as fucking perfect as I knew she would be, with hair trimmed short and neat at the top, becoming bare down lower—where my fingers once were. I touch her there, sliding a finger through the wetness between those lips, and she squeaks and squirms. She's helpless beneath me, her knees trapped by the skinny jeans, so she can't even spread her legs. But that's all right... I have access to everything I need.

My hands push beneath her camisole and under the cups of her bra, groping at the softness of her breasts until I feel the peaks of her nipples tighten, my mouth descending on her. Her moan is a mix of relief and anticipation, and *fuck*, my dick is so painfully hard, I can't help but take one hand off of her to push it down the front of my pants. I press the heel of my hand against myself, telling my dick to wait, while stoking the fire even more. It jumps and pulses back, but I'm too busy between Josie's thighs to give it the attention it's looking for.

She arches into me as my tongue follows the path of my finger—up, then down, until I'm stopped at the apex of her thighs. I consider pausing long enough to free her legs so she can wrap them around my shoulders, but when I follow the path back up to her clit, feeling her jerk and moan, the appeal of knowing she is at my mercy takes over, and I dive in fully.

I take my hand off my cock and spread her with my fingers, my other hand still massaging her breast. She gasps when I flatten my tongue, swiping from bottom to top once again, and when I swirl it in circles where I know she needs me most, she digs her fingernails into my shoulders. I moan into her body, and she jumps at the vibrations, arcing into me as much as she's able.

She's moving her hips along with my mouth, helping me find the rhythm she needs, clawing at my neck and scalp. Her little gasps are peppered with tiny cries as her legs stiffen beneath me, and she pulls my head tightly into her, so my mouth is fused to her body while my tongue works her furiously. She lets out an exhaled moan that contains my name, then inhales loudly, throwing her head back against the couch cushion.

Her hips are thrusting wildly as she holds my head to her. My tongue stays still as she rides it the way she needs. I drink in the taste of her, longing to thrust my fingers inside and feel her tighten around me—but that's for another time. I'm as much at her mercy as she is at mine, the buzz of alcohol replaced by a different kind of high. As she pushes up into me, I lose all control. My own hips are thrusting against her legs, trapping them even more, and with my mouth open against her, I lift my eyes and watch her as she pulls in a sharp gasp, her skin turning pink all over.

Josie's fingernails are digging into my scalp to the point of pain, and I revel in it. I'm drunk on her arousal, lapping at her to keep momentum as she stiffens and stills. Then she reaches that pinnacle, coming against my open mouth with tiny jerks of her hips and cries of ecstasy on her lips. I reach down and press firmly against my aching cock until I'm ready to explode, and then I pull back, looking down on her.

She's so fucking beautiful with her skin flushed, chest heaving, eyes squeezed shut. When she opens them, they're glimmering with endorphins and desire, her pupils nearly swallowing the amber irises. A smile curves her lips as her breathing calms, and I can't help but mirror it, hoping she can't see the sadness creeping into my eyes.

Because that guilt has returned, and I know…

It has to stop here.

Fuck... *it has to stop here.*

Josie curls her upper body into a sitting position, still trapped in her jeans. The way she bites her lip could be confused for shyness, but the flirtatious smile gives her away. "I want you inside me," she says breathily, placing a kiss against my mouth, tasting herself.

She reaches for my pants, but I move back.

A furrow of confusion crosses her brow. "I'm on the pill now, in case you're worried about—"

"It's not..." My words trail off. I had justified continuing this when I was giving something to her, but I've been selfish enough, and the thought of taking anything else while she's still unaware of my deceit is more than my conscience will allow.

Her frown deepens when I move beyond her reach, but for this moment, she is still blissfully unaware, and my heart is breaking beneath the weight of the truth I'm about to reveal.

Fuck, I'm so sorry to do this to you, Josie. I'm so goddamn sorry.

"Shit..." I murmur, my muscles locking. I rise, taking two steps back and sucking in a hard breath. "I can't do this, Josie... I can't..." My eyes close when my voice breaks, and I shake my head. I can't seem to make myself say the words out loud, but it's too late to back down now. I've already started, and she needs to know—I fucking *have* to tell her...

I have to.

"Evan, what... ?" Some kind of realization crosses her mind, and her eyes widen. "Oh, God," she says in a soft, strangled voice. "Are you involved with someone else?"

Hell... I wish it were that simple. Josie has no fucking clue what I'm about to dump on her right now. "I assure you, I've thought of no one but you since..." I say softly, gesturing vaguely behind me.

"Then, what?" She struggles to her feet, situating her underwear into place, but not bothering to pull her pants up or down.

I close my eyes, linking my fingers behind my neck. My tense exhale is born of months of inner turmoil. *Say it,* I keep telling myself over and over. *Just fucking—*

"Say it," she whispers.

My eyes open, meeting hers. They are somber and unsure. Nervous. She knows something is coming, it's just nothing she could ever guess.

"I hit your car on purpose."

She stares at me for a moment, her expression unreadable.

And then... she laughs.

I think maybe she didn't hear me, or didn't *want* to hear me.

"You're joking."

Or she thinks I'm joking.

There is no relief in this truth, and for a split second, I want to take it back—to tell her she's right, I was just kidding, and I almost... I *almost* do. Because this is a fucking terrible idea. I *know* how this ends. And my rapidly deflating dick says we should be fucking right now. She *wants* me.

She won't want me in another minute.

And that's because she doesn't know me. She doesn't know the ugly side of me. She doesn't understand what I'm capable of. She doesn't know what I've done.

A flash of worry crosses her face. "Evan..."

"I'm not joking, Josie. I hit your car on purpose."

Gravity settles in her expression. The worry is mixed with a tiny bit of fear and a whole lot of confusion. She hesitates. "What are you talking about?"

I move forward and reach for her hands, compelled to touch her one last time. She lets me, but it won't be for long. I lace our fingers together, hoping she can forgive me, praying she can understand, but knowing, *knowing*, that she won't. She can't.

Honestly... she shouldn't.

I can't even forgive myself.

"Jesus, Josie, I had no idea what I was getting myself into. I never thought this would happen. I never expected *you*."

I never expected her.

Josie pulls her hands from mine sooner than I'm ready for—because it will always be too soon. She takes a hesitant step back. "What's going on, Evan? You're scaring me."

I lower my eyes to the floor. It might make me a coward, but I don't think I can look at her while I say this. "I knew who you were when I went to the gym that day. I purposely hit your car in the parking lot, so I had an excuse to talk to you. So I had a way into your life."

"What?" She makes that laughing sound again, but it sounds less like a laugh this time and more like a sharp huff of inconceivability. I open my eyes, hating myself for the look I've put on her face. "Why... why would you... ?" She pauses as my words sink in, trying to take a step away but finding herself stopped by her pants. She brings her hands in front to cover herself, pinning her suddenly distrustful eyes on me with accusation. She swallows. "Were you stalking me?"

"*God,* Jos—" I want to say no, but I can't, really. Not truthfully... it's just not exactly what she thinks. "It's not what you're thinking." I press my fist to my mouth and take a breath in through my nose. When I take a step forward, she shakes her head, bending without looking away from me and grabbing her pants, yanking them back up over her hips.

"Don't come near me," she says in a strained voice. Panic fills her eyes as she fights with her jeans, and I realize with horror that she thinks I'm going to take what she was freely offering just a moment ago.

"Christ, Josie, I'm not going to hurt you." Instinct tells me to move forward, to reassure her, but I'm stopped. I'm stopped by her fear... I'm stopped by the truth.

Goddammit—I am such a motherfucking liar.

I told her I wasn't going to hurt her... but it's all I've done.

She's finally won the battle with her jeans, and as she buttons them, I see her glance with trepidation at mine, so I fasten them before I continue. Now, I do take a step forward, needing her to hear me, to listen.

She takes two steps back, eyeing the door.

I stop.

"I was never *intending* to hurt you..." There's a weight in my chest, and I struggle to breathe through it. "It wasn't about you," I say softly.

Frustration mixes with her anxiety as she plants her feet, clenching her jaw and fists. Her voice is shaky. "Evan, you need to tell me what the *hell* you're talking about right now." Tears fill her eyes, even though she has no idea what I'm about to say.

I think through my next words as regret descends over me. So much regret. Regret for buying into this ridiculous revenge plot in the first place. Regret for not being able to see a better way. Regret for involving an innocent in the hurricane of my grief.

Regret.

Regret.

Regret.

I should regret ever having met Josie, too.

But I can't.

Sucking in a shuddering breath, I tell myself this is for the best. I can't have sex with her under false pretenses. We can't build any kind of relationship on lies.

There's a stabbing lump in my throat as I swallow the bitter truth—as I spew it back out like poison. "The man my wife had an affair with was your husband, Josie… it was Ben."

Her jaw drops.

I watch her chest rise as her lungs fill with a choking breath. Then, she shakes her head.

She shakes her head, but she doesn't speak.

She shakes her head while her eyes glaze over.

She shakes her head, blinking through the tears that begin to spill silently down her cheeks. And then, as her face scrunches up in anguish, she finds her voice.

"No," she whispers.

But she believes me… I can see it.

I close my eyes, nodding. "He was having sex with my wife for six months before I figured it out." My words are a groan of pain in my ears when I finally voice it aloud.

I'd spent so long holding onto those words—I held them tight until they became thorns in my soul, bleeding like the wounds from the rose the day of my breakdown in my kitchen. But unlike the thorny stem boasting a beautiful blossom at its end… here, there is only more pain.

Pain that I now inflict on her as I inform her she has not only been betrayed by one man… but two. Not only her husband, but the man she's been falling for. The man who intentionally deceived her.

Me.

I open my eyes, seeing that she's covered her mouth with one hand while the other is pressed over her heart. Her eyes are full of tears and horror, and it breaks my heart, but I have to keep going. She has to understand that this was never about hurting her.

"Benjamin turned my world upside down, Josie. He ruined my life. I *hated* him."

Her hands move to her flushed cheeks, sliding over her ears, like she's trying to block out the truth as it keeps spilling from me. "Stop it, Evan. I can't listen to this. I can't… I need to—I need to go." She bolts for the door.

I step in front of her, blocking her exit. I can't let her leave like this.

Not yet.

I'm not finished.

"Wait," I plead, and it sounds strangled. "Please let me finish. You can hate me all you want, but just let me finish."

Tears slip down her cheeks, and she swipes them away, still eyeing the door; but she waits.

"Josie… this is going to sound absolutely horrible, and I know there's no excuse for what I've done—but I swear to God, everything that's happened between us has been *real*. I need you to believe that."

I weave words together in my head, trying to figure out how to explain, but nothing sounds right, nothing sounds even remotely right…

Because it's not.

It's all wrong, and I can't believe I couldn't see it before. It's so fucked-up—just thinking about it makes me feel like a monster. And maybe I am…

Maybe I am.

There is no way to make it sound less horrible, so I plow forward. "I made it my mission to get revenge on your husband. I wanted to take from him what he took from me. My need for vengeance consumed me, it swallowed me whole, it overpowered all of my logical reasoning." I run my hands over my face, pausing to breathe.

Pausing… because the rest is even harder to say.

Lowering my hands, I force myself to look at her. Silent tears are pouring down her face, and her breaths hitch. It's almost more than I can take, but I look at her—I look at her because she deserves that much. "My revenge plan was you," I tell her, choking on the last word. "I intended to sleep with you in order to get back at your husband."

I finally reach for that sledgehammer, and it pulverizes us both.

Josie is struck silent for a moment before a wretched sob escapes her and she spins away from me, her hand over her mouth, her shoulders heaving with disbelief.

I approach her gently. Cautiously. I dare reach out to touch her arm, to offer some semblance of comfort. "Josie, I'm so—"

She whirls around and slaps me hard across the face.

"You bastard."

Tears stream down her pink cheeks as she shakes her head with shock and incredulity. Her eyes hurt me more than her words. More than the sting of her slap. I deserve every razor sharp insult that spills from her mouth, every slap across the face.

I'm the lowest of the low. There is nothing she could do to me that could ever come close to what I deserve.

She shoves at my chest. Once, twice. I stumble a step but remain still, letting her slap me again. I accept every bit of her justified rage, and it doesn't matter what she does to me—my body is numb. All I can feel is the pain in her eyes. The betrayal. The wounds that I put there.

"Fuck you. *Fuck you*, Evan. How *dare* you," she cries. "How dare you play me like that!" She spits out the words through gritted teeth, and with her hands balled up, she starts beating on my chest like I'm her human punching bag.

I let her do that, too.

"How could you *do* that to me?" she screeches. "I *trusted* you. I *cared* about you. I—" She stops to take a breath, hardly in control of her erratic breathing. "All that time… you…" She's close to hyperventilating as she wheezes, "You were… *grooming* me?"

I cringe at the word. "God, no. It's not like that. I never expected this. I thought you would be… *different*. I thought you were this stuck-up trophy wife, and it would be easy and painless, and…" The horror in her eyes lets me know that I'm not making a good case for myself.

Her fingers rest over her lips as she swallows between heaving breaths. "I feel sick," she mutters.

I try to backpedal, but it's no use. "Shit. What I'm trying to say is… I had no fucking clue it would go this far. It stopped being about revenge a long time ago, but I couldn't tell you then. I couldn't tell you the truth because I knew it would gut you. So, I walked away. I walked away, and I thought it was over, but then I saw you tonight, and…"

Josie crosses her arms over her chest, rage overtaking the horror. "Yes, Evan, please tell me what your rationalization was about tonight, after you so chivalrously walked away a few months ago."

I swallow. My thoughts are addled and confused, and I don't have a good excuse for myself, but I keep going. *I have to keep going.* "I don't know. I thought it would be okay if you didn't know how it started because the *real* truth is in everything that's happened between us. The way I feel about you. The way you've changed me from the inside out. I thought that maybe where we ended up was more important than how we began, but it's not… it's not. *Fuck.*" Crumpling back against the wall, I tent my hands over my face, pull them down to my chin, then blow out a shaky breath. "I just wanted to hurt him, Josie. Nothing else mattered until *you* mattered. And when you saw me in my kitchen that day breaking down, it was because of you. *You* were my trigger. I realized what was happening, I knew I was in too deep, and I knew there was no way out without hurting you."

Josie is staring at me with eyes so wounded, I feel like I'm looking at a version of myself from almost two years ago. I wouldn't wish that kind of heartache on anyone I cared about. And here I am, the very *cause* of it.

I'm no better than Katrina.

I'm no better than Benjamin.

I'm no better than my hate and grudge and shallow lies.

"I should have walked away the moment I knew I could fall in love with you. And I'm not sure when that moment was—maybe it was when I watched you singing into your hairbrush with the girls, or maybe it was at the Farmer's Market, or when I saw you play your guitar for the first time and felt my stone walls breaking down and crumbling at my feet. Hell, maybe it was the first goddamn second I laid eyes on you."

I push off the wall, watching as she averts her gaze. Her anger seems to waver a little, and I'm encouraged to go on. "When you go so long feeling numb and broken, detached from everything, and that spark comes back... it's really hard to walk away. I spent so much time wallowing in the darkness, and when I saw that light—I *craved* it, Josie. I craved *you*... being around you, how you made me laugh and smile, how you made me feel alive..."

Josie rubs her arms, then drops them at her sides, standing up straight and lifting her chin, her eyes dark and narrow, pinned on mine.

I want to reach for her, but I know I can't. So, I take a deep breath and settle for the only thing I have left. My last confession. "I need you to know that I've... fallen in love with you. And that I'm so sorry, Josie. I'm so fucking sorry."

She's still staring at me, silent, her shoulders moving up and down from the weight of her breaths.

I dip my head and close my eyes. "I love you."

She continues to stare at me, wordless.

"But I don't deserve you," I finish.

"Ding, ding, ding." Josie raises her finger in the air and waits for me to look up at her. Her voice is low and raw, teetering on dangerous. "That right there has been the only ounce of truth that has come out of your mouth since you hunted me down, fed me bullshit, and *used* me for your own twisted vendetta."

A breath rushes out of me at the sting of her words.

My heart clenches. It shatters. It fucking decimates.

Josie closes her eyes and opens them slowly, a deadly calm reflecting in her amber irises. "Stay away from me, *Evan*. If that's even your name."

She turns around and walks away, picking up her purse, her heels clicking against my hardwood floors with each even step.

"Do you love me?"

I don't know why I ask her that. It doesn't matter. Any chance for us is long gone.

Nothing fucking matters.

Josie pauses mid-step, her head twisting slightly over her shoulder, but she doesn't look at me. She inhales. She exhales. "I loved a lie."

And then… she's gone.

When the door slams shut, I fall to the floor.

Falling, falling, *falling…*

It's over.

It's fucking over.

She is the sacrifice I made when I chose to be selfish.

TWENTY-EIGHT

"Jesus Christ."

Logan is sitting across the table from me, slack-jawed and slightly ashen. He's a relatively blasé person, so getting this type of reaction out of him means I *royally* fucked up. I push a French fry around my plate, rolling it through the splatter of barbecue sauce, then drop it. I lean back into my chair, unable to even look at the shock and disappointment on his face.

It's been three weeks since Josie walked out my front door, blocked me on Facebook, and issued a restraining order against me.

I thought I knew pain, but I had no fucking clue.

Logan whistles a sound of dire amazement and scratches his head, running a hand down the center of his face. "Jesus Christ," he repeats.

I purse my lips. "Yeah."

"What else did you do?" he asks, chomping on a fry. "I mean, don't get me wrong, that was fucked-up—but Amber had to deal with getting a restraining order on an ex-boyfriend, and I know they don't give them out just for deceiving someone."

"She had it classified as stalking," I cringe, staring at the plate I'm not going to touch. "I guess having been married to an attorney comes with connections that make that shit easier. Pretty sure there was a judge at her holiday party."

"Wow... yeah. I get why you didn't want Amber to know. She would have cut your balls off, man."

I wince at the thought, knowing how accurate that statement is. "You won't tell her?"

"I won't tell her," Logan says. "But give me a heads up if you think she might find out, so I can remove all sharp objects from her reach."

Blowing out a tense breath, I tap my foot against the sandwich shop floor. My best friend likely thinks I'm a psychopath, and I don't know what more I can say. "I can't believe I'm even talking about... *me*. It feels like I'm recounting a story—something I'd write about in one of my books."

Fiction. Not something I would actually do.

Not something I actually did.

Logan takes a bite of his sandwich, then tosses it onto his plate. He stares at me as he chews. "Anger is a powerful beast, and you had every right to carry it around. I don't envy what happened to you, man. But you unleashed it in all the wrong ways."

"It felt like a drug," I sigh, trying to explain the complicated feelings. The elixir that spiked my blood for so long. "I don't know what else to compare it to. It literally controlled me. I was a different person."

He shrugs his shoulders as he swallows down his food. "I mean, there *is* a bright side to all of this," he tells me.

I lift my eyes to him. "I honestly can't think of what that could be, but enlighten me."

"Things can't possibly get any worse. It's all up from here, buddy. Congratulations."

I release a breathy chuckle, finding a small amount of humor in his words, "So, how awful of a human being do you think I am now?" I'm kind of afraid of what his answer might be.

Logan studies me, prolonged and careful—long enough that I know he's trying to make me sweat. He leans forward, elbows to table, and cocks his head slightly through a smile. "I'm trying to think of something hilarious and sarcastic, but I'm going to go the more noble route instead. That sad puppy dog look in your eyes is breaking my heart."

If he were closer to me I'd smack him, but I grumble instead.

"Look, Campbell. I've known you for over a decade now. I know you're a good guy. I know you're an awesome fucking dad, and Summer is the luckiest kid on the planet to have you." Logan takes a sip of his soda, looking contemplative. "Amber and I both saw a positive change in you the moment that chick entered your life, and while it was under shitty circumstances, there's no denying she made you better. Take it and run with it, Evan. If you slip back into your old patterns and harbor new anger and bitterness, it was truly all for nothing. Let this be the catalyst for change. Get your shit together and start the hell over." He slumps back against his chair and pops a potato chip into his mouth. "Don't focus on the bullshit—you can't change what you did. Just focus on the little bit of good that came out of it. You're capable of finding love again. You're capable of wanting more than what you've settled for. Keep writing. Keep being an awesome fucking dad. Keep your head up."

The tension drains as my nerves abate. *Damn, he's good.* "Shit, Logan. I think you're in the wrong line of work."

"Bartender? Nah. It's perfect. I've basically mastered the pep talk."

My smile wanes a bit as my thoughts drift back to Josie and that forsaken look in her eyes. I run my hand along the back of my neck. "Think you can pep talk Josie into possibly forgiving me someday?"

Logan shakes his head, his gaze apologetic. "I think that *if* you have any chance in hell of smoothing things over with her, the only thing you can do is wait it out. There's no amount of begging, or apologies, or grand gestures that can fix this right now. Only time."

Only time.

I exhale a solemn sigh, knowing he's right. And to be honest, I know I don't deserve that woman—a future with her was extinguished the moment I tapped her bumper in that gym parking lot. I'm not looking to rekindle our flame. I'm not dreaming about the day she falls into my arms and confesses her undying love for me.

All I want is for her to forgive me.

Not even for *me*... for her. For her own heart. All she ever wanted was to be free, and I gave her the heaviest burden imaginable. It *kills* me.

But I'll wait. I'll wait for the day when she lets go of all the pain I filled her with, and maybe we can meet up and have coffee, or raspberry wine, and she can tell me about how happy she is. Maybe she'll be in love. Maybe she'll have more children. Maybe she'll be traveling the world with her guitar.

I'll be waiting for that moment, and when it happens, then maybe, just *maybe*, I can finally forgive myself.

I'll wait forever, Josie Bennett.

Summer has been begging me to fill the air in our bicycle tires and take a trip to the park. It's a mild April morning—the last day of spring break before Summer goes back to school. Before I know it, summertime will be here and I'll lose my daughter for two whole months... and God, I'm *dreading* it. She's my anchor. My silver lining. My best friend. So, until that day comes, we will go on all the bike rides, eat all the ice cream for breakfast, and stay up way past her bedtime until she passes out on my shoulder, drooling and snoring, and I can tease her mercilessly about it the next day.

"Almost done, Dad? We have to hurry," Summer says, tapping her foot beside me in the garage.

I glance at her as I finish filling the rear tire of her bike with air. "Why do we need to hurry? It's only nine A.M."

"Rain. Don't you grown-ups check the weather?"

I look up to the sky, noting that it's crystal clear. Not a cloud in sight. "I don't think it's going to rain, bunny."

"Yes, it is. There's a storm moving in from the east."

Shooting her a curious side-eye, I situate myself on the bicycle seat and back out of the garage. "I'm not sure where you get your weather reports, but someone lied to you."

Summer hops onto her bike and speeds off in front of me, in a hurry to beat this imaginary storm. We ride up to the playground and park our bikes against our usual sycamore tree. Before I have a chance to even catch my breath, Summer is pulling me by the arm, dragging me down the hill and through the woodchips. "What is going on, Summer?"

"Come on, Dad," is all she says.

When we round the corner by the slide, I realize exactly what my daughter has just done.

Shit.

The wind is knocked out of me, and I halt in my tracks.

She doesn't see me yet—her head is bowed as her thumbs tap away at the buttons on her phone. She tucks a strand of honey-colored hair behind her ear, her tan double-breasted coat hanging open and billowing behind her. I'm about to make a break for it and ground my daughter until she leaves for Tennessee, but I'm too late.

"Olivia!" Summer shouts, waving madly, jumping up and down on both feet.

Josie's head jerks up, and she freezes just as Olivia plows ahead and the two girls run into each other's arms, hugging, swaying back and forth, and laughing with pure joy.

If I weren't so shaken by the sight of Josie standing in front of me, and also a little bit terrified I might be going to jail *because* Josie is standing in front of me, I'd be near tears from the sweetness of this reunion.

My eyes trail from the girls up to Josie, and I swallow back the hard lump in my throat. I shake my head and back up a few steps. There's a split second of familiar longing in her eyes—that striking vulnerability I can't seem to get out of my head. But her walls go up just as fast as she stalks over to the girls.

"What is going on?" she demands, slipping her cell phone into her coat pocket. Her gaze is stone cold as it travels between me and Olivia. "This is not okay."

"Don't be mad, Mom. We haven't seen each other in *months* and it's not fair," Olivia insists, shifting her begging eyes to her mother.

Summer nods in agreement. "We missed each other. It's the only way we could get you guys to hang out again."

I tense my jaw, my eyes closing as a cool breeze skims my face. "You don't even have a phone, bunny. How did you contact each other?"

They both say in unison, "Roblox."

Josie and I look at each other, our eyes holding for a beat longer than she seems comfortable with. Flustered, she sweeps her hair to one side, clearing her throat. "Let's go, Olivia."

"What? No, please, Mom," Olivia insists.

"We'll be good, I swear!" Summer adds.

My heart swells with a distinct kind of sadness. The sadness of knowing that my daughter's best friend has been stolen from her due to my piss poor decisions and she thinks *they* are responsible. I cross the short distance to my daughter, despite the risk of getting closer, and crouch down on my knees, spinning Summer around to face me. "Summer. Bun. You need to listen to me, okay?"

She nods, knowing I mean business.

"This has nothing to do with you or Olivia. There are some things going on that you're too young to understand. I'll explain it all one day, but right now you just need to know that you did *nothing* wrong."

I can feel Josie's eyes on me, but she says nothing.

Olivia pipes up. "Can we still play?"

I rise to my feet, scratching my head. I dare glance in Josie's direction and direct my response to her. "I can go sit over there." I point my thumb over to the tree where our bikes are resting. "I'll stay out of your way."

Josie crosses her arms over her chest, her eyes drifting to the grass beneath her brown boots. She bites her lip before replying. "That's fine."

"Yay!" the girls shout, then race over to the monkey bars.

I want to ask her how she is, if she's gotten back on her feet, if her heart is any closer to healing. I want to talk about the girls and joke about how sneaky they were to set this up behind our backs. I want to give her a hug and tell her that I'm sorry I can't say any of those things.

I choose not to wear out my welcome or do anything to jeopardize this play date, so I take several steps backward, then turn and head over to the tree. Sitting down, I drape my arms around my knees, holding my wrist with my opposite hand. I watch as Josie takes her place on the nearby bench—the same bench we sat on all those months ago when she plugged her number into my phone and a blossoming friendship began.

I try not to think too hard. I try not to dwell on the things I lost, but just knowing she's there sends my mind reeling through the memories... the *what ifs*. There's an ache in my chest that feels like longing.

It feels like regret.

Josie's eyes graze over to me multiple times, and I always duck my head or turn away. I noticed that her wedding ring is still absent—it seems our situation hasn't affected her decision to separate from her husband. Of course, knowing he cheated on her probably didn't help those matters. My mind strays, and I wonder if she's gone on any dates. I wonder if she's had her *rebound*. I wonder if she's thought about me.

I wonder if she's forgiven me.

No... I already know the answer to that. I could see it in the hardness of her eyes.

The air begins to warm as the sun rises higher and the morning ticks on. It's a little after ten A.M. when I feel like we should probably get going. I wish the girls could play forever—I know this is likely the last time they will ever see each other. I stand slowly, breathing out through my nose, and approach them on the swings. I see Josie tense out of the corner of my eye as I near her, and she folds her arms. She is guarded. I'm not sure if she's afraid of me, angry, or just uncomfortable.

God, I hope she isn't afraid of me.

"Time to go, Summer," I say, watching as the girls swing higher and higher.

"Aw, man!" Summer exclaims, while Olivia mimics a similar declaration of disappointment.

Josie stands from the bench and takes a few steps closer, still hanging back, keeping her distance. The girls jump down from the swings and hug goodbye, waving to each other as they run over to their respective parent. I tousle Summer's hair and she elbows me in the side with a giggle. I glance up at Josie before I retreat, and there is the faintest smile on her lips as she watches us interact. There is nostalgia in that smile.

Regret.

What could have been.

Then her eyes drift up to mine and the smile promptly fades. We hold each other's gaze this time, and my skin heats up, my heart pumps faster, and there are so many things both said and unsaid spilling between us as we stare blatantly at each other.

Josie is the first to break away, and she wraps her arm around Olivia's shoulders, guiding her from the playground. I do the same with Summer, but in the opposite direction.

I walk away.

TWENTY-NINE

SPAGHETTI NIGHT ISN'T THE SAME ANYMORE.

I'm in even more of a stupor than I usually am as I chop onions and sauté garlic in the sauce pan. I'm still reeling from our park adventure this morning, replaying scenes, wondering if I should have said something more, or wondering if I should have taken Summer and bolted the moment I saw her.

I suppose it could have been worse. I wasn't stabbed, punched, or maimed, *and* she didn't call the cops on me.

Bright side.

I'm particularly focused on that look in her eyes before we went our separate ways. She hasn't forgiven me yet—but maybe someday, she will. I'll grasp every shred of hope I can.

It's enough for now. It's all I have.

Summer strolls into the kitchen with her earbuds secured into her ears and a baggy anime t-shirt hanging off her petite frame. I can hear Melanie Martinez blaring from the speakers, and when multiple eff-bombs are fired, I yank on the earbuds and give her a stern look. "Language," I say.

She scoffs at me. "You say *way* worse things."

I blink at her, then fold. "Good point."

I hand her back the earbuds.

We spend supper chatting about Olivia and how much fun Summer had today, and at one point, I'm forced to change the subject because it's just too much. So, we talk about school, summer break, and all the things she wants to do when she visits Tennessee again, as well as all the things she wishes she could do *here*. She helps me rinse the plates and loads the dishwasher as I seal and put away leftovers, and it's after seven o'clock when she reminds me that it's garbage night.

The sun is low behind the clouds as dusk sets in. A light spring breeze skims my face while I traipse out the back door and down the steps, heading across the wide patio that connects the house to the garage.

I stop dead in my tracks when I see him.

There's a man sitting on my patio swing—it catches me so off guard, it takes a moment to process who it is. Then, the last time I saw him comes rushing back in a flood of memories I'd rather leave behind for good.

Benjamin Grant.

He sways languidly on the swing, back and forth, as though he belongs there. His eyes stare straight ahead, not acknowledging me at all.

What in the fuck?

I don't speak right away, mostly because I'm entirely perplexed by his visit, but also because I have zero things to say to him. He's not a part of Josie's life anymore. *I'm* not a part of Josie's life anymore. There's no reason for us to see each other.

Why the hell is he here?

Okay, I guess I *do* have something to say to him.

"What the fuck are you doing here?" I demand.

Benjamin turns his head towards me, a fake smile beaming on his face. "Evan," he greets, as if he just noticed my presence. He looks back out at the street, his feet glued to the cement, pushing the swing forward and back. Forward and back.

That doesn't at all answer my question. In fact, now I'm more confused than ever.

I approach with a semblance of caution and a lot of annoyance. "Leave."

He chuckles, and as I move a few steps closer, I can smell the alcohol radiating from his pores.

He's drunk. Shocking.

"I just wanted to talk, old friend," Benjamin says with mock cheerfulness. There's an unmistakable slur to every syllable. Unease plucks at my nerves—the last thing I want is for my daughter to come out here and see her best friend's father confronting me in this state.

"I'm not your friend. We've never been friends. Please, just go."

"Oh, *right*," he answers, nodding slowly. "You only pretended to be my friend so you could fuck my wife."

This is literally the last thing I want to be doing right now.

I'd rather drink a bottle of ketchup.

I'd rather let boxelder bugs crawl up my boxers.

I'd rather do both of those things at once, than stand here exchanging volatile quips with a drunk and bitter Benjamin Grant.

"Get the hell off my property," I repeat, stepping closer, my hands clenching into fists at my sides. "We have nothing to say to each other."

Rising off the swing on unsteady feet, he teeters from side to side as he tries to find his balance. He threads his fingers through his wavy hair, which has grown out quite a bit from the last time I saw him. He also has a substantial amount of scruff along his jaw, but not in the deliberate kind of way—it's more in the "I let myself go" kind of way. He looks like a mess. "Evan, Evan, Evan…" he sing-songs, taking wobbly steps toward me, throwing his hand out in an offered handshake that I don't return. "I came here to congratulate you. She left me. You *won*."

I sigh. It's a sigh that registers as both exasperation and irritation. "I didn't win anything. Josie hates me."

His chuckle is dry. "I'd much rather have her hate me than see the utter indifference in her eyes when she looks at me."

A poignant silence sweeps between us, and I almost feel sorry for this man.

Almost.

"You took her from me, Evan. Your plan worked. You fucking succeeded." Benjamin begins to slow-clap as he moves in closer. He smacks his hand against my shoulder, giving it a tight squeeze. "Well done."

Liquor laces his breath, his proximity making my skin crawl. I push his arm away, taking a swift step backwards while he teeters for balance.

Benjamin continues on, pacing my patio with his hands in his hair, pulling at the strands as he skulks back and forth. "I mean, I guess I shouldn't put *all* the blame on you, Evan. It's only fair to take some responsibility, you know? My marriage was great until Josie wanted more babies and discovered I couldn't have children. That's when it started… yeah—we grew distant after that. And then I let it fester with long hours at work and…" He glances at me, shrugs, then looks back at the pavement. "Katrina."

I stiffen at her name.

Benjamin is half laughing, half crying, gesturing with wild motions as he rambles on. "My wife needed me, and I pushed her away. But I loved her, Evan—I really *loved* her. I still do. And I should have fought harder, I should have supported her, but I had this notion that she would always be there. She was like that... she was *loyal*. And then you came along." He looks up at me with a heavy sigh. "I never expected *you*."

I'm trying to think of something to say, torn between playing therapist so he gets the fuck out of here, and kind of wanting to just knock him out and let him sleep it off. But before I speak, I falter—I rewind. I backtrack to something he said that I almost didn't catch. I inhale a sharp breath as realization settles in my gut. "Wait, you... you can't have children?"

It sinks in deeper when I hear myself say it out loud.

He squints at me, his alcohol-laced brain slow to follow. "Sterile as a surgeon's needle."

"How long?" I find myself moving forward as if getting closer to him will pull out more answers. I'm unable to hide the trace of desperation in my tone. "Recent? Your whole life?"

He shrugs again. "As far as I know, I was born that way."

And then my heart breaks all over again.

Benjamin puckers his lips. It takes him a few moments to catch on, but then a smile creeps onto his face. "Ahh... *you're* talking about Katrina's baby." He nods. "Yep. All yours."

Oh, God.

Oh, *God*.

Katrina aborted *my* baby?

I always said that I didn't know which would be worse... but this is worse. This is *so much worse*.

Bile climbs up my throat and I swallow it down. "Jesus," I breathe out, interlocking my fingers over my head and spinning around. "I can't believe she got rid of our baby."

I'm stewing in my revelation, my back to Benjamin, when he utters the words that make my lungs fill with ice.

"What? Ooh, you never figured that one out?" Then, he actually... *laughs*. "Katrina never got an abortion."

My heart stops.

Maybe the whole world stops.

Something stops because I'm unable to breathe or speak or move.

I'm completely still for what feels like an eternity before I turn around, slowly, carefully, and face Benjamin. "What are you talking about?"

He sniffs as if this is the most nonchalant conversation he's ever had.

"She was planning to. Hell, I even drove her to the appointment myself, but she couldn't go through with it. She was going to tell you she miscarried until she worked up the courage. I don't think she could bear to see you so fucking excited about a baby she wasn't planning to keep. She never did work up the courage, though, of course…" he shrugs. "Guess she never told you the truth either. Huh."

It doesn't make sense.

It doesn't make sense.

My mind races, going back as far as it can, and I start to weave together pieces of the puzzle. She stopped drinking alcohol—Katrina *always* had a glass of wine before bed. I thought it was strange, but I'd chalked it up to her depression.

She put on weight.

She only wore baggy sweaters and sweatshirts up until she left for Tennessee. Even on warm days. My brain finally puts two and two together and comes up with…

Mason.

Mason?

I think of his blue eyes and how they looked identical to Summer's. How he looks a lot like her in general. And he'd be the right age.

Mason is… *mine?*

Holy shit.

Holy fucking shit.

Summer has a brother.

I have a son.

Benjamin is pacing again, seemingly bored with this discussion. "I always suspected Katrina hoped she'd raise the kid with me… after I left Josie. But I couldn't leave Josie… I didn't *want* to leave Josie." He spins on his heel, nearly tipping over, his finger in the air. "You know, maybe I can still get her back. Maybe I can fix this. We used to have something special… I *know* we did. We can get that spark back, right? We can start over."

His words barely penetrate my enormous shock. My chest is tight, my stomach clenching. "I have a son." It's a whisper, it's a wonder—it's fucking metamorphic. I exhale and repeat on an incredulous laugh, "I have a son."

Benjamin's eyes narrow as he studies the way I double over, hands on my knees, sweat on my skin. "Congratu-fucking-lations." He stomps toward me across the patio, going from sulking to wrathful with each angry step. "Maybe *you* should hit up Josie and patch things up. She always wanted more kids. You can be a happy fucking family built on lies and betrayal. Sounds fair."

My sudden bout of elation ebbs as I straighten. "Fair? Let's not forget who started all of this in the first place. You put your dick in my wife. You broke up our family."

"I don't put my dick where it doesn't belong," he snarls back. "She *begged* for it."

Normally, I'd be three quick steps away from popping my fist between his eyes, but his words fall flat. Don't get me wrong… I'm pissed. But I'm not pissed for *me*—I'm pissed for Josie. Benjamin is trying to get under my skin, but all he's doing is showing me that if *any* good came out of my disgraceful revenge scheme, it's that Josie left this piece of shit behind, and she'll someday find a man who actually deserves her.

Bright side.

I stare at him, unflinching. "And while Katrina was supposedly begging for you, your wife—who you claim to *love*—was at home begging for her husband to actually *see* her."

His eyes flash with something almost frightening.

"I didn't take your wife, Benjamin," I finish. "You lost her. And you lost her long before I came into the picture."

Benjamin stares at me, his gaze cold and hard, his jaw twitching while his nostrils flare with simmering rage. The only thing making him appear less hostile is the fact that he's practically toppling sideways as he sways from his alcohol stupor. "You son-of-a-bitch. You still think you're better than me; still telling yourself I'm the villain in your sad story." A laugh escapes through gritted teeth. "And here I actually felt sorry for you. I didn't tell Josie about your dirty little secret because I felt *bad*. I felt bad for *you*, you pathetic motherfucker." He jabs his finger into my chest as he punctuates each word. "I. Felt. Bad. For. You."

I take a step back, chewing on my inner cheek. "I don't think I'm better than you. I came to terms with that a while ago, and let me tell you, it hurt. But I know what I've done. Betrayal isn't subjective… it all hurts the same."

"No, you *do* think you're better than me. I see it on your smug fucking face." Benjamin pokes his finger at me again, nearly stumbling. "Say it. You think you're better than me."

I'm silent—rigid and unwavering as I stare back at him.

"Say. It." He's practically spitting, only inches away from me. *"Fucking say it."*

I don't blink or wince, and I don't back down. "I'm not better than you,

Benjamin. But Josie seemed to think I was, and that's what really pisses you off."

With wild eyes, he pats at his pocket again, his hands shaking, then he opens his coat and reaches inside. I'm not sure what I'm expecting to see—a flask, maybe. Or one of those miniature shot bottles. Benjamin Grant is so hot and cold, so back and forth, I never know if he's about to deck me or ask me out for a drink.

I sure as *fuck* never expected him to pull out a gun.

My

blood

runs

cold.

I stumble back several steps, then freeze as the pistol pointing at me wavers in his unstable grip. My heart thrums in my ears, and I raise my hands into the air, palms facing him, like I'm trying to calm a wild animal. His skin is clammy as I study him, sweat pooling along his hairline.

A look of pure desperation crumples his face. "Maybe you're right," he says. "Maybe you *are* better than me." And then he turns the gun around, resting the barrel against his own forehead. "Maybe I should do everyone in this world a favor and take myself out of it."

"Ben… stop. Just put it down, put it away. It doesn't need to be like this." I try to sound calmer than I feel, but I recognize the look on his face—I see it like a mirror of my past. It may have taken on a different shape for me, but I've been there… and I know rock bottom when I see it.

Benjamin and I just handled it differently.

"She doesn't want me anymore," he nearly sobs. "She doesn't want me… and now I've been *encouraged* to stay away from the office until I *get my shit together.*" I flinch when he gestures in the air with the gun, aiming nowhere in particular. "But how am I supposed to do that? Tell me, Evan, how do you *get your shit together* when your world is falling apart?"

I think about my own rock bottom and the choices I made. "I can't tell you that," I say honestly. "I didn't do a very good job of it myself."

"You know, you have a point," he huffs a dry laugh, and in a blink, the gun is turned back on me. "This *is* your fault."

"Jesus, put the gun away." I'm not sure how to reason with an erratic drunk person, and I've never been held at gunpoint before, so I'm clueless as to how I'm getting myself out of this. "You're drunk, Ben. You're not thinking clearly."

He shifts from one foot to the other with a sniff. "Oh… I think I'm pretty clear. My life is falling apart. It's your fault." He shrugs his shoulders. "So, here we are."

I back up a step, trying to get closer to the house. I only realize how badly I'm shaking when my knees nearly buckle. "So, you came here to shoot me?"

"You... me... what's the difference?" The gun waves from me to him, then back to me again.

"Am I really worth the risk of you going to jail for the rest of your life?"

"There you go, making this all about you again. Don't flatter yourself, Evan. You don't get to be a defense attorney without knowing a few tricks."

I swallow. He may have a point there. Out of desperation, I grasp at a new angle. "Olivia," I say, my nerves shredded and my heart beating itself into a crescendo. "Think of Olivia—you're her *father*. This will destroy her."

Benjamin rolls his jaw, contemplating my words. "I was only her father by marriage. My marriage is over. Josie took her, too."

"You're still her father. You're the only father she's ever known."

He inhales a weighted breath, then scratches his head with the butt of the pistol. His eyes close, his features tight.

"You're not a killer, Benjamin. You're drunk and upset—don't jeopardize your entire future because of a temporary moment of weakness."

Benjamin's eyes pop open and he pins them on me. "You think I'm weak, Evan?"

I shake my head frantically. "That's not what I meant."

He stares at me for a few startling, uncertain moments before spinning around and screaming out loud into the dusky sky. "Fuck!" he shouts, waving the gun while punching the air with his other fist.

I'm debating my next course of action.

Do I run? Do I continue to talk him down? Do I try to call 9-1-1 from inside my pocket? Do I tackle him?

Benjamin whirls around, pointing the gun back at me, and the questions and scenarios run rampant through my head. That's when something rips me from my panicked haze.

A familiar presence. A small voice.

"Dad?"

Summer.

I don't even have time to turn and face her before a shot rings out, a deafening, piercing crack—a sickening explosion that will haunt me until the very day I die.

My ears are buzzing, my body tingling. Everything is murky, and I blink through the fog. My feet are frozen to the ground. I hear Benjamin yelling. He's running towards me in slow motion, his mouth moving, spouting gibberish. His eyes are frantic. *Wild.*

He runs past me.

Did he shoot me?

I suck in a gulp of air so sharp, it cuts me on the way in.

Then reality hits me like the bullet that never did.

Summer.

Sound returns. Movement returns. Everything returns.

I spin around.

My daughter is lying on the patio.

My daughter is lying on the patio with a hole in her chest.

Benjamin is kneeling beside her, frantically pressing numbers on his cell phone. "Holy fuck. Oh, shit. I didn't mean it. It was an accident. It just went off. Fucking *shit.*"

I thought I knew pain.

I had no fucking clue.

I race over to her. My knees crack against concrete as they hit, and in the next heartbeat, I have her in my lap. Her eyes are open, straying to mine, terrified and dazed.

"Dad?" she squeaks out.

I stare at my daughter, speechless, cradling her face, unable to process the horror in front of me. It's my worst nightmare come true.

My little girl.

"Bunny... bunny, listen to me, okay?"

Her eyes gloss over. A single tear rolls down her temple. Her lips move, but no sound comes out.

I can feel wet heat saturating my jeans, and I know it's her blood. The stain on her shirt is growing bigger and brighter—redder and redder and *redder.*

My vision is blurry, my face wet. I must be crying... but I need to stay calm. *I need to stay fucking calm.* "Look at me, Summer. Look at me."

Her eyes flutter, but she forces them open, locking them with mine.

"Truth bomb?" I say, stroking her hair and her cheeks. Her warm tears. I press one of my hands to her chest to try and slow the blood.

There's so much blood.

Her answer is ragged, barely audible. "Always." She does her best to focus on me, but she's drifting... drifting.

Oh, *fuck*, my heart.

My voice hitches as I speak. "You're the strongest person I know. The bravest person I know. You're my funny bunny," I tell her, caressing my fingers through her hair. "Do you remember what I told you when you fell off the monkey bars and broke your arm?" Her eyes roll back, and I gently tap her cheek. "Look at me, bun. Stay with me. What did I tell you?"

"It only... hurts... for a little while," she whispers on shaky breaths.

I nod through my tears, suffocating on anguish, choking on every word. "Think about how good it's going to feel when you're all better. I'll make you spaghetti every day if you want. We'll eat cookie dough ice cream for breakfast, and I'll play my awesome, terrible music so we can dance together in the living room."

The corner of her lip twitches as she tries to smile, but it doesn't stick. Her head lolls to the side, and I catch it in the crook of my arm, cradling her closer.

"I love you, Dad." There's a raw plea in her little voice, but she's trying. *God,* she's trying.

Please... please don't let this be happening.

I shake her gently, trying to keep her awake without hurting her further. I need her to stay conscious, but she's bleeding out so fast. There's nothing I can do but watch as her life pools into my faded blue jeans.

I rock her back and forth, burying my face against her neck. There are sirens in the distance. Benjamin is still here beside us; I can hear his hysterical apologies. But it's all background noise...

All I really hear is the sound of my heart cracking in two.

"I love you, bunny."

And then I break.

I break at the sound of my own voice saying those words.

I break because I'm fucking terrified that it will be the last time I get to say those words to her again.

Fight for me, baby girl.

I crumble to pieces around my daughter's limp body, whispering fighting words into her ear as my fingers press against the weak pulse in her neck. It's thready and struggling beneath her pale skin—but it means she's still here, trying to hold on... trying to stay with me.

It means there's hope.

Stay with me, bunny. Stay with me.

The world spins as a wave of dizziness claims me, and I notice that I've forgotten to breathe. I have to keep it together, I have to be strong for Summer, but oh, my God, *this can't be real...*

Nothing feels real.

Please don't take my little girl away. Please... please.

My palm is still pressed against her chest. I look down through my tears at the pool of crimson staining both of us as the gruesome realization hits me... her blood is on my hands.

This is what I created.

This is what I set in motion.

This is the price of vengeance.

30

THIRTY

THEN
MAY

*K*ATRINA IS STANDING IN THE DRIVEWAY.
Her oversized hoodie hangs down over her shorts as she grips the handles of two suitcases, glancing up at me. "I'll be back for our court date next month," she says, her tone stoic and unemotional.

I'm standing a few feet away in the grass, my arms folded over my chest, my heart beating faster than I would ever let on. "Okay." I keep it simple. I keep it impersonal. I refuse to show her how much I'm breaking inside.

Katrina is headed to Tennessee to stay with her mother—maybe temporarily until she gets back on her feet. Maybe permanently. There's not much keeping her here in Illinois. My birthday bombshell hit hard. She was ostracized from her social circle, who were all invited guests, and there was so much contention and animosity from her co-workers, she was finally asked to leave her job, too.

Even Benjamin dumped her. He got cold feet and didn't have the balls to leave his wife.

Part of me envies his wife—she probably has no idea what he did. She doesn't know the pain, the all-consuming heartache, the gut-wrenching feeling of betrayal that seeps into your bones and sucks you dry. She doesn't know the stifling darkness that clouds your mind and infiltrates everything good. I feel different now. I have a stain on me. A scar. A bloody wound that will never fully heal.

It changed me.

I inhale a shaky breath and tighten my stance as I watch Katrina pull her hair up into a messy bun. She looks like how rock bottom *feels*—like she's a woman who's had everything taken away.

But *she* set this all in motion. Her choices created this.

She hauls her suitcases into the trunk, then turns to face me before getting into the car. "Have Summer keep in touch. Maybe get her a phone or something."

I have no intention of getting her a phone.

Summer is staying with me until we figure out our parental agreement. I feel like it's in our daughter's best interest to stay here, in her home, in her school, with her friends. She doesn't deserve to be ripped away from everything she knows because of her mother's careless, hurtful choices. She doesn't deserve to be ripped away from *me*.

Katrina only agreed to this for now because Summer *begged* to stay.

I saw how much it destroyed Katrina, listening to our daughter beg and plead to live here with me. Watching as Summer's eyes teared up at the very prospect of leaving me behind and driving off into a frightening unknown.

I can see how much it's eating away at her right now, and I can't help but find a shred of satisfaction in it. *These were your fucking choices, Katrina. This is the result. You're getting what you deserve.*

I set my jaw and nod slowly. "Yeah. Okay."

Katrina stares at me with vacant eyes for a heartbeat longer, then reaches for the door handle.

"Why did you do it?"

The words tumble out of me before I can even hold them back, spilling into the tepid breeze and falling at our feet. Katrina wavers with her fingers curled around the handle, going still and silent. I've never asked her this question before, but it's plagued me every minute of every day from the moment I discovered her awful truth.

Why, why, *why?*

We had a good life. *She* had a good life. Sure, money was tight, and we both had to work hard to pay the bills, but we loved each other. I thought we truly *loved* each other.

Why wasn't that enough for her?

Katrina cautiously spins to face me, her eyes still level with her sneakers. She tucks a loose strand of hair behind her ear, and I wonder if she's been waiting for me to ask her this. I wonder if she's had her answer all laid out in her mind, stored away, waiting to be released. Katrina shuffles her feet and swallows. "We had a good thing for a while, Evan." She glances up, just for a second, and then back down. "I just wanted more."

I bristle at her answer. I let it invade me, consume me—light a fire under my skin.

More. More money, more time, more vacations, more frilly things.

More, more, *more*.

She'll never realize that I gave her everything. I gave her all I had to give.

But I wasn't *enough.*

I don't respond, so Katrina tugs at the handle and hops inside the vehicle. I wince when the door slams shut. I flinch when the engine rumbles to life. I grimace when the tires squeal as the car rolls back.

I watch my entire life pull out of the driveway and disappear down our neighborhood street.

Then I shake my head at that thought. *No...* not my entire life.

I still have Summer.

I'll always have Summer.

NOW

I am alone.

My hand is caked with dried blood as my cell phone trembles in my palm. I try to make sense of the numbers and buttons, but everything is fuzzy, bleary, mixed up and out of sorts. I blink away the haze and go back to my task, but I can't remember how phones work.

There are a few people in the corner, watching me. I almost walk over with my bloody hands and bloodier clothes and ask them to explain to me how this damn phone works.

I need to call Katrina.

I need to tell my ex-wife that our daughter is dying.

She's dying.

Summer is dying.

I pace the hospital waiting room, finally managing to complete the call after several flustered minutes and even more curious stares from onlookers. The phone rings.

And rings.

And rings.

Katrina picks up. "Hey, Summer."

I nearly burst into fresh sobs at the sound of my daughter's name.

She thinks it's Summer. She has no reason to believe otherwise because I never call her. I swallow back the tears, find my breath and my courage, and reply, "It's me."

She's silent for a beat. She's not expecting to hear my voice. But when she does and it registers, she knows… she *knows* something is wrong. "Evan, what happened?"

I don't think. I just blurt it out. "Summer was shot. She was shot in the chest and she's in surgery now. They… they don't know if she's going to make it."

There's a strangled sob on the other end of the line.

I need to stay calm. I need to stay fucking calm.

I try to keep my tone even, afraid that if I let the fear take over, I will break apart so hard, so irreparably, I'll never be able to get through this. "You need to get here fast. She might—" My voice breaks, so I clamp my mouth shut.

"Oh, my God. Oh, my *God*," Katrina wails.

My eyes close as I breathe in deep. "Make sure to bring my son with you."

I end the call.

I force myself to stop pacing and lean back against the waiting room wall, staring down at my blood-stained jeans. The last half-hour has been a complete blur, and I know that I'm in shock at this point. I'm shutting down. I'm protecting myself from the grief and the darkness and the devastation that is waiting for me on the sidelines, ready to pounce, ready to sink its teeth into my guilty heart.

Benjamin was taken into custody. He confessed to everything, claiming Summer startled him and the gun went off by mistake. It was an accident. A horrific accident.

I know that if I'm ever alone in the same room with Benjamin Grant someday, there will be another *accident*.

I hold up my phone again, glancing at the screen. There are traces of blood spattered on the face, and I run my fingertip over the dried droplets, closing my eyes.

"If you ever feel like that again, if you ever need to break apart, you don't need to break alone. I'm here, and I understand. I'll help you."

I wonder if Josie knows yet. I wonder if she's aware of what her husband did.

Before I even realize what I'm doing, my phone is pressed to my ear, and it rings.

And rings.

And rings.

Josie picks up, and there's a pause at first—a hesitation. "I really hope this is a pocket dial, Evan," she sighs, and there's a warning in her tone.

But it doesn't matter. None of it matters.

Her voice manages to bust through the protective shield I've spent the last half-hour building around me, and I almost choke into the speaker, "It's Summer."

I slide down to the floor, hitting the ground hard, and that's where Josie finds me ten minutes later. I see her breeze in through the revolving doors, frantic, her eyes searching before finally landing on me at the opposite end of the room. She raises a hand to her mouth, frozen for just a moment as she stares at me, tears brimming in her eyes. I try to stand. I *want* to stand. But my legs aren't working, *nothing* is working, so I just stay crumpled on the floor with my head against the wall and wait for Josie to approach.

She runs.

She runs all the way to me, collapsing beside me and pulling my head to her chest. I feel her tears in my hair, her warm breath on my skin, her heart beating quickly beneath my ear.

That's when I break.

I finally break apart, break down, break in half, as I release all the anguish I've been holding inside. I expel it all, sobbing against Josie as her arms tighten around me.

"God, I can't believe it…" Her voice hitches, cracks. "I can't believe Ben…"

I clutch at her wrist with my bloody hands, squeezing tight, clinging to the only light I have left. She presses her cheek to my head. She is trembling, too, crying softly and whispering words of comfort. Her fingers stroke my hair, gentle and soothing.

"Evan, I'm so, so sorry," she murmurs, her wet tears sluicing me in her own remorse. "I'm here. I'm here…"

I continue to break.

I break hard and messy, ridden with guilt and impossible remorse.

But I don't break alone.

I'm not alone.

Medically induced coma.
 Chest tube.
 Blood transfusion.

These terms are thrown at me, all ominous, but the only thing I hear is… *she survived.*

Summer survived surgery.

It lasted too many nerve-wracking, touch-and-go hours, but the doctors worked a miracle. *Summer* is a miracle, and somehow, she managed to stay here.

She didn't leave me.

It's a few minutes after six A.M. I've been at the hospital over ten hours now, and I'm currently lying beside my daughter on her recovery bed, listening to the steady beeps, buzzing machines, and the sound of her precious heartbeats thudding against my eardrum. I've never heard a sweeter sound.

Josie is in the waiting room, along with Amber and Logan, and Katrina should be arriving any minute. I've been keeping her updated through text messages as she makes the drive up with Mason and her mother.

Mason.

Whenever the weight of the last ten hours becomes too heavy to bear, I think of Mason. I think of holding him in my arms for the first time and looking into his blue eyes, watching his little face light up. Knowing he's *mine.*

On the single worst night of my life, I have something positive to cling to. I have a bright side.

He's mine. My baby didn't die.

Everything in me wants to lash out at Katrina the moment she steps foot into this room. How could she keep him from me? How could she hide my *son* from me? How could she deprive me of the first year-and-a-half of his life? For all of my flaws, I'm a good father. I'm a damn good dad.

But I can't lash out. Anger only breeds more anger.

I see that anger for what it is, now. Hollow. A dirty, meaningless trick. A cousin of vengeance.

Anger leads to me lying beside my unconscious daughter in a hospital cot while she fights for her life.

This little girl next to me… *she's* what matters. Not anger, not self-righteousness.

Not revenge.

"How is she? Oh, my God, how is she?"

Katrina barrels into the room, and it's the first time I've seen her since our final court date almost two years ago. She races toward the bed, and I scoot away, moving into a sitting position, then standing to my feet. Katrina's eyes are red and swollen, her ashy blonde hair a matted mess, and she's wearing pajama pants and a tank top. She looks up at me as she kneels down beside our daughter, clasping Summer's hand between her own.

"She's stable," I say quietly. My throat is still raw from spilling my grief into Josie's arms earlier. "Prognosis is undetermined, but she's stable for now. She's healing. These first twenty-four hours will be the most critical."

Katrina presses her forehead to Summer's shoulder, murmuring consolation into her ear in between sniffles. "I can't believe this. What happened?"

I sit down in the chair on the opposite side of the room and tent my hands together, tapping the tips of my fingers against my chin. I haven't told Katrina the details yet. She kept asking, but I refused—I didn't want to disclose the harrowing truth via text message while she was driving into dire uncertainty. I swallow a breath that sticks in my throat, not even prepping her for the bombshell I'm about to drop on her. "Benjamin Grant shot her."

Katrina makes a gasping sound as her head jerks up and her face goes white. "What?" she croaks out.

She shakes her head, staring at me in horror and disbelief. I can see her start to quiver while she gawks at me, her face draining of more color with each passing second. "That's n-not…" she stammers, then swallows. "He wouldn't… I mean, how? *Why?*"

She must think she's to blame. Only… Benjamin Grant didn't even know who I was—who Summer was—until I inserted myself into his life, all just to satisfy my need for revenge.

I did this. The thought settles into me once again as I glance at my little girl.

I did this.

"It's my fault," I murmur, ducking my head and staring at the sterile floor. I clink my teeth together, avoiding her gaze. "I fell in love with his wife and broke up their marriage. He came over to shoot *me*... or himself. Maybe he was trying to scare me... I don't know. Summer startled him. He was drunk. It all happened so fast..." I inhale a jagged breath and cover my face with my hands.

"Jesus, Evan," Katrina whispers, her voice cracked and dry. She's quiet for a minute. "You fell in love with Josie Grant?"

I look up at her, surprised. "You know her name?"

"Of course. I Facebook-stalked her for months." She covers her mouth as she takes another shaky breath, averting her eyes. Then she squeezes Summer's hand as fresh tears flow down her cheeks. "What a nightmare," she says through her fingers.

"It's my fault," I repeat, watching as Katrina shakes her head, squeezing her eyes shut.

"Not just yours."

Her eyes slowly open.

I see remorse there for the very first time, and I wonder if she's spent any time over the last two years regretting what she did to us. Did it only hit home now... after *this?* Or does she *regret?*

Then I remember that she's kept my son a secret from me, so she can't be too broken up about it. My anger flares. "Why didn't you tell me you kept the baby? How could you do that to me?"

Mixed emotions glide across her face. "This isn't the time to talk about that," she says stiffly.

I stand from the chair, my temper charged. "When is the time? When he's all grown up and off to college? What the hell, Katrina?" I stomp towards her, noting the way she crouches away, guiltily. "I wanted that baby more than anything."

Her tears continue to flow as she turns her ahead away. "*I know*. That's why I did it." She glances back at me, and I can't read her expression—there's too much there. "I wanted to hurt you, Evan. I wanted to hurt you like you hurt me."

"Like I hurt *you?* Are you listening to yourself right now?"

Katrina stands, facing me fully, her cheeks pink with fury. "I lost my job, my friends, everything, because of you! Because of that stunt you pulled," she exclaims. "You could have just *told* me you'd found out the truth—we would have dealt with it. But you chose to humiliate me in front of *everyone.* I know I screwed up, I know I made a mistake, but I fell in love with him." Her voice hitches and she stops to take a breath before unleashing more. "You ruined my life and took my daughter away from me. I see her ten weeks out of the entire goddamn year! So, I took your son away from *you.*" Her chest heaves as she finishes, "You didn't deserve to have Mason, too."

I let out a disbelieving laugh. "I can't believe you're pinning this all on me. I reacted out of complete and utter *heartbreak.* You destroyed me, Katrina. I loved you so much. I was blindsided by your betrayal." I'm shaking my head, astounded by her words. "I thought he was *gone.* You kept my son, my *child*, a secret from me for two fucking years. That's insane."

Katrina lowers her eyes, biting her lip and scuffing her shoe against the floor. "Yeah, well, I was going to tell you eventually," she mutters quietly. "I hated you for a long time. I was running on pure anger, and I never really got over it. All I could think about was revenge."

I open my mouth to speak, to counter, to throw her bullshit explanation in her face. But then, I waver. Her words sound all too familiar. All too… *relatable.* My stomach sours when I realize her lust for revenge was no worse than mine.

Betrayal isn't subjective. It all hurts the same.

My own words haunt me as I stare at the woman I once loved with every ounce of my heart. That love is long gone, severed by lies and anger and deception.

But I don't hate her either.

I don't know when I stopped hating her—hell, it could be right at this exact moment, but all I see when I look at her is a different life. The old me. Something I want to leave behind. Katrina will always be a part of my life, as we share two children together, but my emotional attachment, my bitterness, my obsession over her affair… I'm letting it go.

I'm letting *her* go.

Katrina sits back down, defeated and brimming with sorrow. "I'm so sorry, baby," she says to Summer, nuzzling her face against her cheek. "What a mess I've made."

I stand behind her and watch, concentrating on the slow rise and fall of my daughter's chest. I release a healing sigh and close my eyes. "What a mess *we've* made."

We spend the next few minutes in silence, reflecting on what was and what is, taking in the sounds of the room, pacing around Summer's bed. I finally breathe in deep and make my way to the exit. "I'm going to go meet my son," I say, catching Katrina's remorseful eyes before I walk out.

When I enter the waiting room, Josie, Logan, and Amber are sound asleep in their respective chairs. They've all been here just as long as me, waiting, caring, supporting. Olivia is with Delilah—I'm hoping she can come by soon to see Summer.

I'm hoping Summer will be awake to see Olivia.

My gaze settles on Josie and the way she's curled up in the chair, her feet pulled up beside her with her cheek propped up on her hand. A few strands of honey hair have separated from the others and are draped across her mouth, billowing and fluttering with each breath she takes. *Josie is here.* She helped me when I fell apart, just like she promised she would—despite everything that's happened, despite everything I've put her through; she is here. I don't know what it means. I'm not sure if we will go our separate ways again, or if she's any closer to forgiving me, but I'll take this moment for what it's worth. Even after all I've done, Josie is *here*, sleeping in a stiff hospital chair. She's been here for almost eleven hours.

For me. For Summer. For *us*.

It's a powerful moment, and it makes my breath catch, my skin tingle, and my heart stutter with ridiculous possibilities I have no business even considering.

I force my feet to move away, focusing on the possibilities that I know to be true.

My son is on the opposite side of this waiting room, and I'm going to hold him for the very first time. Katrina's mother, Sandra, is facing away from me, but I know it's her by her telltale white bob and the tiny head popping up over her shoulder. Mason is hoarding goldfish crackers in his mouth as he struggles to break free from his grandmother's hold. He's wearing baby blue overalls and rubbing his eyes, tired and antsy. I gather my wits and begin to approach. Sandra goes still when she sees me, her body stiffening, her walls going up.

That's fair. The last time I saw the woman, I brandished her daughter a shameful adulteress in front of over thirty people.

"Sandra," I greet, tipping my head. I don't want to make small talk. I don't want to apologize or justify my actions. I just want my son. "Can I hold him?"

Mason squirms free, and this time, Sandra lets him. He scurries over to the center of the waiting room, his balance much steadier than when I saw him on Summer's video Christmas Day. He begins sifting through a pile of magazines, flinging them off the coffee table, tearing pages with his clumsy hands. I step forward, crouching down beside him and taking in his chubby cheeks, noticing how his nose mirrors my own. "Hey, buddy."

Mason looks at me, then away. He's far too focused on Family Circle.

"I'm your Dad," I whisper, and the words almost make me melt into the sticky maroon carpet beneath my feet.

He lets out a sound that mimics a giggle, then points to something in the magazine. "Ca!" he announces with enthusiasm, pointing to the image on the advertisement.

It's a car.

A fast car—a Stingray, to be precise.

Mason looks mightily pleased by his discovery, and I know now, without a doubt, he is my son.

I grin, scooping him up into my arms and squeezing him to my chest. I kiss his blonde curls, my eyes closing as I savor his scent, the way his tiny body feels in my embrace, and the indescribable sensation of holding my child for the first time.

I kiss him again with a purposeful sigh, and when I open my eyes, I lock my gaze with Josie from across the room. She's awake now, standing and looking right at us. I haven't told her about Mason, so there's a question in her eyes, mingling with softness. I bounce Mason on my hip, relishing in his squeals, my eyes still pinned on Josie and the way her hair is sticking up from static on one side. It makes me smile.

I'm not expecting it, and I'm certainly not prepared for it, but she smiles back at me, and I'm flooded head to toe with a feeling I can't put into words. Hope? Optimism? Nothing quite fits. It's all that and more. It's the feeling, the tickle, the *knowing*, that I'm on the other side of the darkness. I'm over the hump.

Summer will be okay.

I will be okay.

Mason reaches up and grabs ahold of my lips, giggling as I look down at him.

Everything that truly matters will be okay.

THIRTY-ONE

KATRINA AND I ARE TAKING TURNS IN THE RECOVERY ROOM WITH SUMMER.

Two days have passed, and Summer is still healing, still breathing, still warm and alive. Her vitals have been good and there have been no complications. I'm huddled beside her on the bed, my arm loosely draped across her stomach, when Katrina enters through the door with two cups of coffee in her hands.

"You should go home and get some sleep tonight. I can stay here," Katrina says.

I don't sit up, so Katrina sets the coffee down on a nearby side table. I haven't been home in forty-eight hours. I've been surviving on shitty coffee, sandwiches from the gift shop, and about seven minutes of sleep.

"I'm fine," I tell her.

I dozed off once while I was lying next to Summer and had a vivid nightmare that she didn't make it, that she died in my arms, and I haven't allowed myself to close my eyes since. I'm not sure when I'll be brave enough to sleep again.

Katrina pulls a chair to the opposite side of the bed, and the legs squeak against the floor as they drag. She sighs. "I took a nap at the hotel this afternoon. My mom's there now with Mason. I'll stay through the night with her." She can see the reluctance on my face and shakes her head. "Go home, Evan. Come back in the morning… I'll call you if there's any change."

My eyes lift to the wall clock—it's after six P.M. The last time I looked at the time it was noon. I've been lying here for six hours, wide awake, listening to my daughter breathe.

I feel another presence enter the room, so I pop my head up, spotting Josie standing in the doorway with her hands folded in front of her. Her eyes cut between me and Katrina, then settle on me.

"Sorry, I didn't mean to interrupt. I can come back later," Josie says, turning away to leave.

I sit up straight. "No, you're good." Swinging my legs over the side of the bed, a shot of dizziness sweeps through me. It takes a moment for me to find my strength before I rise to my feet and pace over to Josie who is lingering with her hand on the door. "I think I'm heading home for a bit to shower and sleep. Katrina's going to stay with Summer tonight."

Josie and Katrina glance at each other, and I watch as something unspoken passes between them. Katrina flusters, then hardens, clearing her throat as she focuses on Summer. When Josie turns back to me, I nod my head at the door, a silent request to talk outside. We step into the hallway as Josie folds her arms, spinning around to face me with her gaze fixed to the floor.

"I just wanted to see how she was doing," Josie says, pointing the toe of her ballet flat into a crack in the tile. She lifts her eyes to me and adds, "How you both were doing."

She's wearing a long, flowing dress dappled in pink and purple wildflowers that falls at her ankles, and I wonder if the weather is warming up based on her apparel. I blink, finally registering her statement. "Oh… yeah, we're hanging in there. I really appreciate you being here. I, uh…" I scratch my head, desperate for a shower, and bite my lip. "I'm not sure I would have made it through that first night without you."

Josie crosses her arms tighter, her eyes flickering away from me, then returning. She nods, a faint smile curling her mouth. "Of course."

We're quiet for a bit, facing each other with questions and uncertainty, and when we go to speak, we speak at the same time.

"Josie, I—"

"Evan—"

We laugh lightly, ducking our heads. My hands slip into my pockets, and I try again. "Do you want to grab dinner? I haven't eaten much, and I could use the distraction."

It's a bold request. Possibly too bold, judging by the startled look on

Josie's face. She withdraws a bit, fiddling with a dangling bracelet on her wrist as she flips her hair over her shoulder.

Here I am, interpreting Josie being here for me during a personal tragedy as a sign that I've been forgiven. It's a fairly shitty card to play after all I've done, but it's not intentional—and fuck, it's not like I would have chosen this card for anything in the world.

She clears her throat. "I don't think that's a good idea. I'm sorry, Evan."

I can tell that she's sorry. Her eyes stray to me, searching for my reaction, gleaming with confliction and apology.

But Josie has nothing to be sorry for.

Nothing.

I smile again, letting her know I understand. *I get it.* "I really do appreciate you coming," I say softly, reaching out to squeeze her hand—but only for a brief moment. Only to show her how much I mean those words. When I let go and dip my head, I purse my lips together, nodding with acceptance.

Then I step around her and make my way down the long corridor. I feel her eyes on me as I round the corner and disappear out of sight.

It smells like impending rain.

I tried to sleep; I really did. I showered and changed, ate some leftover spaghetti while trying not to break down as I reminisced over the last time I ate that exact batch of spaghetti with Summer two nights ago—and then I laid down for approximately eleven minutes. But my mind was racing, my heart was too heavy, and I just needed to go for a run and lose myself for a little while.

So, I'm running.

My breaths escape me hard and fast, heaving in time with the slap of each sneaker against the pavement. The clouds are rolling in, concealing the small trace of light that still lingered from the setting sun. I'm about a half-a-mile from my house when I feel the telltale drops of rain, trickling lightly from the gray sky and cooling my heated skin. I realized as I was running that today marks the two-year anniversary of my discovery of Katrina's affair. It rained that day, too. I've hated the smell of rain ever since, but today… it's different.

Today it's not so bad.

It's refreshing and calming, almost *cathartic*, and I'm releasing every last bit of hostility I've been clinging to. I kind of want to laugh and cry at the same time, but I just run faster, breathing in the earthy musk as the rain falls harder, pelting me while I turn onto my neighborhood street. It's downpouring now, and I'm tempted to keep running, to run straight past my house and go another mile… but when my house comes into view, I do a double-take.

My feet slow. My heart quickens.

There's a brief moment where I wonder if sleep deprivation has caught up to me and maybe I'm hallucinating, so I blink rapidly as my pace continues to decelerate.

But she's not a hallucination. She's real.

And she's sitting on my front stoop beneath the awning, her arms wrapped around her knees.

Josie rises to her feet when she spots me. She smooths out the fabric of her wildflower dress, which is slightly damp from humidity and mist from the rain. I come to a complete stop on the sidewalk, standing in front of the steps leading up to my front door.

Leading up to *her*.

The rain continues to pummel me, *drench* me, and I run my hand through the soaked hair stuck to my forehead. We don't speak. All I can hear is the sound of my heart pounding against my ribs, much like the raindrops showering the metal awning above Josie's head.

Th-thunk, th-thunk, th-thunk.

She's here, she's here, she's here.

My feet move towards her, squeaking inside my wet shoes, my eyes never leaving her face. Her hair is wild, slightly frizzy from the rain, and I can't read her expression well, but her stare is wide-eyed—like maybe she's just as surprised as I am.

I want to know what she's thinking, why she's *here*, standing on my doorstep in a downpour. But as I climb the steps and move in closer, I somehow think I know. And when I'm standing right in front of her, face-to-face, and she inches back to allow me space under the awning… *I wait.*

We stare at each other, our gazes never breaking—never wavering—

and

I

just

wait.

But not for long.

In a blink, she reaches out and grasps my face between her hands, pulling my lips to hers. Our mouths collide with a collective gasp of desperation and relief. Josie arches into me, her hands sliding back to twine her fingers through my wet hair. We ignite in an instant, and I push her against the front door, angling our mouths so I can kiss her deeper. Our tongues wind together until our teeth clash, and when our moans of longing rise in a crescendo that can only end one way, I reach over her shoulder and grab the door handle.

With our mouths still fused, I whirl her around, stumbling into the house backwards, tugging her along with me. I blindly push at the door and connect, hearing it slam. One by one, our shoes are kicked off, landing somewhere across the room as she clutches at my shoulders, plastering her body to mine, our balance wavering. We fall back against my entertainment center, sending picture frames toppling to the floor. My hands tangle her in her hair.

I can't stop kissing her.

I don't ever want to stop kissing her.

When I feel her hands lifting the shirt stuck to my skin, I pull myself away so she can yank it over my head. Her hands glide over my chest, almost in wonder—like she can't believe she's finally touching me like this —then they move downward, and I groan when I feel her fingernails trailing along my abdomen. My fist wraps around her hair, and I yank her head back, grazing my lips down the side of her neck. A sharp gasp escapes her, then she's panting, whimpering, trembling in my arms as her hands find the waistband of my running shorts, her fingers curling inside the fabric. She jerks the wet shorts and boxers down together, letting them fall at my feet, leaving me exposed to the air... to her roving hands.

God, she makes me so fucking hard.

Josie's hand wraps around me in an instant.

Christ.

I hiss, my hips jerking forward. My lips slide along the side of her jaw, and the breath I exhale near her ear sounds more like a moan. Her hand pumps me a few times, and fucking hell, I need more... but I can't decide what I need more of first.

Everything.

God, I've missed everything about her...

"Fuck, Josie..." I scoop her up, spinning us around until we crash against the opposite wall, my arms wrapped around her back to take the brunt of the collision. I lower her slowly until her feet touch the floor, planting my hands on either side of her head to hold myself steady as I lean down to kiss her. Her hips thrust against me, seeking the friction of my erection, while her hands skim up and down my naked body. When they land on my ass, her fingers dig in, pulling me flush against her.

"Evan... *more*. I need more," she breathes out, and *fuck*, that word echoes in my head.

More, more, *more*.

I grasp at her hips in a blind frenzy to obtain *more,* frustrated by the barrier of her dress. I'm desperate to touch her, to feel her bare skin. Reaching down, I clutch the material until I've inched it up enough to find the hem, then I pull it up over her head in one motion, flinging it over my shoulder. Our mouths find each other again, locking together as my hands run down her exposed breasts, over the curve of her waist, and this time when I pull her hips into me, there is only one thin layer between us.

Josie's head rolls back against the wall, a whimper leaving her when I press in, rubbing my cock along the thin cloth between her legs. She rises to her tiptoes as I bend my knees enough to yank down her underwear. They fall at her feet, and she steps free, her warm, bare skin finally pressed to mine as she pulls one leg up to my hip.

The heat between her legs is driving me fucking crazy, and I am lost...

Lost to the need.

Lost to her.

There are so many things I want to do to her, so many ways I want to have her—but for now, I *have* to be inside her. She is with me, pliant and willing, so I lift her up the wall, spreading her legs wider until I'm positioned perfectly between them, feeling her fingernails digging into my shoulder blades.

Our mouths part and we lock eyes, savoring the sizzling potency of this moment as I lower her onto me. When the head of my cock enters her tight heat, I thrust upward, watching her mouth open wider on a gasp. Her eyelids flutter, and my forehead dips down, pressing to hers, while I move inside her with one hand planted on the wall and the other arm tucked beneath her.

A sense of urgency rises up from within me, but I push it down, forcing myself to move slowly. I revel in the feel of her around me, the way her internal muscles squeeze my cock as I slide her inch by inch down the wall, then push her back up again.

Holy shit.

It's a tight fucking fit—so hot, so goddamn wet—and I can feel the way her legs tremble as she wraps them tightly around me. She's trying to meet my movements now, her body urging me to go faster, begging me with the small, desperate noises in her throat.

"Ah… please, *please,*" she moans, and the frustration in her voice breaks my restraint.

I take her mouth in a quick, hard kiss, biting her lip, showing her what she's about to be in for. "Hold on fucking tight," I say, in a voice so low and hungry, it's nearly a growl. Josie wraps her arms around my neck as I brace us against the wall…

And then I fucking *let loose.*

She cries out with every thrust as we slam into the wall, and when she pants, *"Oh, fuck"* and *"Yes… oh, Jesus… yes,"* I have no choice…

I plow into her relentlessly.

I'm breathing like I've been running for miles, sweating like it, too, but I'm driven by the instinct to *take,* and to *give,* and to *fuck*—and when her teeth latch onto my shoulder, the sound that comes out of me is like a roar.

"Ooh, fuck, Josie… I'm… *fuck.*"

She's so tight around me, tight everywhere—from her arms around my neck, to her legs around my waist, to the pulsing vise grip around my cock. The pressure builds to a dizzying level, right on the edge of release, and I have to brace us against the wall just to keep us upright.

But *goddamn*, I need more, I need to be deeper, go harder, so I swing her around and pull her down onto the rug without pulling out. I pound her into my living room floor. Like a fucking animal. Josie matches every thrust, every grunt and moan, every bite, nick, and scratch.

This is months of wanting, craving, *needing.*

This

is

everything.

I'm drowning in her. I'm desperate to feel and fill every goddamn inch of her. My hands are cupping her cheeks and I glide my fingers into her hair, curling them into fists and tugging, burying my face into the curve of her neck. Our bodies are slick from sweat and rain as they tangle together, and Josie begins to tense beneath me, squeezing her legs tighter, gripping the nape of my neck. I try to keep my eyes open, because fuck, she's so beautiful when she comes, but my own orgasm overtakes me with such ferocity, all I can do is slam my eyes shut, press my forehead to hers, and let it wash over me.

This is the effect of our unparalleled chemistry, our repressed desire, months and months of *holding fucking back*... culminating in an explosion like nothing I've ever felt.

Josie's with me, she's right here with me, and our cries are like harmony, softening to moans, then to heaving, panting breaths... and as our muscles loosen and the intensity recedes, I collapse on top of her, both of us lying in a naked, sweaty heap of satisfaction on the floor.

"Holy fuck," I practically wheeze.

Josie is so winded, all she can do is nod in agreement as her head falls backwards, her fingers sliding through my hair, then down my back.

A heady silence envelops us as we come down and the aftershocks begin to dissipate. I slide out of her and move the bulk of my weight off of her, but keep our legs entwined with my arm wrapped securely around her waist. I have no idea what's supposed to happen next, and I want to ask her; I want to know if this was *just* sex—if it was only the inevitable pinnacle of our unresolved sexual tension.

But words become elusive, and I find myself nodding off as I lay beside her on the rug, feeling her body rise and fall in my embrace.

The last thing I remember is Josie's fingers in my hair, her lips pressed against my temple, her warmth melting me and allowing me to drift away...

I finally sleep.

A fragment of light poking in through my parted curtains is enough to stir me from sleep. I'm in my bedroom... but I can't remember how I made it to the bed.

Still wrapped in a groggy haze, I snuggle closer to the warm body cocooned against my bare chest. Then I blink away the sleep and go still.

Josie.

I lift my head off the pillow and am met with a halo of honey hair fanned out beside me as the bedsheet dips low off her hip. For a moment, my breath is stolen from me. I feel weightless and mesmerized as I drink in the sweep of her shoulders, the curve of her waist, and the flowery fragrance of her skin.

Fuck... she's beautiful.

And *double fuck...* we had sex last night.

Finally.

Vague memories of staggering to the bedroom, half asleep, with Josie on my arm, flash through my mind as I exhale and roll onto my back, carefully untangling myself from the angel next to me. Inching my way to the opposite side of the bed to where my cell phone is charging on my nightstand, I check my notifications with a tight knot in my belly. I slept way too long, and I need to know that Summer is okay. Thumbing through my texts, I make a mental note to reply to my parents who have been waiting by the phone for a new update, and land on a recent message from Katrina.

KATRINA: *Baby girl is still doing good. Hope you got some sleep – K*
It's followed up with a picture of Summer resting comfortably.
Thank God.

With my nerves quelled for the time being, I fall back onto the bed, scooting over to Josie. Slinking my arm around her, I splay my fingers out across her abdomen, then lean in to nuzzle my face against the arc where her neck meets her shoulder, breathing deep and kissing her gently. When I feel her rouse awake, I trail my hand upwards and cup her breast, relishing in the breathy gasp she makes as she arches into me.

"Good morning," I whisper into her ear, then I nibble on the lobe, pulling another squeaky moan out of her. I feel the coil of lust swelling low in my gut, prompting my hips to push forward against her ass as my dick hardens.

Josie rolls onto her back, staring up at me with glossy eyes and parted lips. "Morning," she replies, and her voice is raw and ridden with sleep. It's one of the sexiest sounds I've ever heard. "What time is it?"

"Six-thirty," I say, leaning down to kiss the tip of her nose. "I need to get to the hospital."

Josie nods, the ghost of a smile touching her lips. "I woke up in panic at midnight and frantically texted Delilah that I fell asleep at the hospital." She pulls the sheet up over her face, as if to hide her guilt. "Am I the worst mom ever?"

I tug it back down, smiling wide. "Definitely not."

"She needs to be at work by nine, so I should probably get going."

There is disappointment in her tone, maybe a little sadness—and I feel it, too, even though I also have somewhere to be. I press two fingertips to her mouth, then glide them along her chin, her neck, her chest, taking the sheet with me. My fingers descend down her body, relishing the silky feel of her skin… but I pause when I come in contact with a patch of skin that feels soft and puckered. I look down at her, my memory jogged by the jagged scar along her ribcage.

The scar from her accident.

Josie tries to pull my hand away, turning suddenly shy, but I shift my weight over her, situating myself between her legs as I inch downward. I stop when my face is flush with her abdomen and press my lips to the scar, grazing my tongue along its raised edges.

Josie lets out a sigh as she squirms beneath me, her hands making their way to my head and sifting through my mess of hair. "It's not attractive," she says softly.

I lift my eyes to her, frowning at the statement. "Everything about you is attractive... especially your scars." Crawling up the length of her, I pause when we're face-to-face, propping myself up with my arms to hold her gaze. "It means you survived something terrible. It means you're stronger than whatever tried to break you."

Her breath hitches in her throat as she links her wrists around my neck, bringing my mouth to hers. I kiss her slow and soft, feeling her legs entwine around my waist. Her tongue explores my mouth as she writhes beneath me.

She whimpers when I pull away to catch my breath, her features still masked with melancholy. There's a trace of desperation glimmering in her eyes as they skate across my face, her eyebrows dipping.

"Josie, what are we—" I'm about to ask her what this is, what we're doing, but she yanks my face back to hers and plunges her tongue inside my mouth.

Fuck.

But something still nags at me, so I gather the strength to pull away, garnering another needy, desperate look. I blow out a slow breath. "Josie, wait."

She swallows.

"You filed a restraining order against me," I say softly but firmly. There is no animosity in my words. No accusatory undertones. Only fact.

But the words hang between us, a heavy reminder of what we're trying to ignore. What we're pretending didn't happen for the sake of this moment —for a glimpse into a happily ever after that I don't even fucking deserve.

Josie shrinks back like the thought alone makes her physically ill. Her eyes dance away, pained and sorry, then float back to me. "I know."

"You did that for a reason, and it wasn't that long ago."

"I know," she echoes gently.

I lean forward, kissing the tip of her nose and inhaling deep. I'm trying to read her. Trying to understand what she wants—what she needs from me. "A lot is happening. Emotions are high, feelings are still there, and now that we have a taste for what this could be… it's going to be hard to stop. But I *will* stop if you think—"

She cuts in, gripping the base of my neck, her head shaking side to side. "The restraining order is over. I already filed a motion to terminate."

My heart flutters with relief. "You did?"

She nods. "Yeah."

I reach for her hand that is latched around my neck and lace our fingers together, splaying them beside her head on the pillow. I study our clasped palms, entirely aware of how perfect they fit together, how perfect *we* fit together. *Does this mean…?*

I blink down at her, my eyes likely filled with shimmering hope. "Are you saying—"

Josie shuts me up with her mouth again. Her hand squeezes mine as her tongue sweeps inside, her body arching up against me. Her legs part on instinct while she kisses me with feverish need.

My cock swells to full-mast as it grazes the warm juncture between her thighs, our bodies still bare. Still aching and wanting. A groan escapes me when she grips my hair in a tight fist, then pushes me onto my back, rolling us both over until she's on top. Josie's hair hangs down like a radiant cloak, tickling my cheeks, and I cling to her hips as she gazes down at me with an unreadable expression.

But her body is far from unreadable. I know exactly what it wants as she grinds herself against my erection, her eyes fluttering closed, her cheeks flushed pink.

"Josie…" I grunt, maneuvering so I can thrust inside her.

Her eyes slowly open, her lip caught between her teeth, and she leans over until those lips are whispering into my ear. "Tell me a secret."

I squeeze her hips, my fingertips digging into her soft flesh. My mind tries to conjure up something funny and random, something light, but there's only one thing filtering through my brain, and it spills out of my mouth before I can stop it. "I'm in love with you."

Josie falters, the tiniest breathy sound releasing into my ear, and then she lifts up until she's staring down at me, searching my face. I'm not sure if I should backpedal or take it back, or maybe I should just start fucking her, but she inhales a shaky breath, grips my shoulders, and bends down to brush our lips together. She swallows, whispering against my parted mouth, "That's not a secret."

Before I have a chance to reply, she raises her hips and sheaths herself onto me.

"Fuck..." I groan, my eyes closing, my grip on her tightening.

We spiral into a greater unknown, a daunting uncertainty, with tangled limbs and pounding hearts. I don't know what this is; I don't know where we go from here. All I know is that I'm drowning in her...

I'm fucking drowning.

But as she rides me, her nails clawing at my chest, her back arched and her hair moving with the bounce of her hips, everything else just fades away.

Only time will tell where our story leads...

And I can wait.

I'll wait forever, Josie Bennett.

THIRTY-TWO

"SHE'S AWAKE!"

Olivia is curled up beside Summer on the hospital bed when she makes the announcement.

I look up from my crossword puzzle, my heart skipping at least a dozen beats, and I'm pretty sure I should be dead right now because of it. My chair nearly tips over when I shoot straight up and race to Summer's bedside. The doctors saw improvement in her condition and felt it was safe to bring her out of the medically induced coma, so we've been waiting with bated breath ever since they withdrew the drugs. Katrina joins us from the other side of the room, and we both huddle over our daughter, reaching for one of her hands.

Olivia hops off the bed and stands beside Katrina, watching as her best friend blinks herself back to reality.

Summer sees Katrina first, her eyes widening, confused and dazed. "Mom?" Her voice is cracked and raw, barely audible—but to me, it's the most beautiful sound in the world.

"Yes, baby. I'm here." Katrina is sobbing, tears spilling onto the fuzzy bed covers. "We're both here."

Summer slowly turns her head until she finds my eyes. My lungs collapse, and my chest explodes, and I nearly flatline. My heart can't even take it. "Bunny," I whisper, and *fuck*... now I'm crying, too.

She smiles as she squeezes my hand, her own eyes watering. "What happened?"

Katrina and I glance at each other, unsure of what to say, or how much to say, or if we should say anything at all. I kind of just want to stare at Summer until my heart skips too many beats and I keel over.

"You got hurt, bun." I reach down and run my fingers through her hair, deciding to keep it simple. We can always explain more later. "But the doctors are taking really good care of you, and you'll be able to come home soon."

"You are so strong," Katrina adds, offering a misty-eyed smile.

Summer looks at each of us, her brows furrowing in contemplation. "Does this mean I can stay home from school for the rest of the year?"

We all laugh, and that's when Summer notices Olivia standing off to the side. Her face lights up, and I think she's more excited to see her friend than she was to see her parents. "Olivia!"

Katrina moves aside and Olivia bolts forward. "Summer, I was so worried about you! What did you dream about?"

Summer ponders this, her face twisting with deep thoughts. "I had a dream we were on a rollercoaster, and it got stuck upside down on one of those loop-di-loops. You would think that would have been the worst part, but then Dad's loud, growly music started playing and it wouldn't stop, and then Shigaraki showed up and brought Nomu, and it tried to eat us."

"No way!" Olivia exclaims.

Katrina and I look at each other again in confusion.

Summer catches our curious reactions and grins. "Anime. You wouldn't understand."

My little girl is back.

The next few minutes are a blur of nurses, doctors, tears, and profound gratitude. I can't stop touching Summer, holding her hand, and gazing into her open eyes.

She's alive.

When you look tragedy in the face, *real* tragedy—the kind of tragedy you likely won't recover from—every other wrongdoing and heartbreak you've experienced feels like a day at the fucking beach. So much perspective comes into play. I almost lost everything, my whole damn heart. It's eye-opening and soul cleansing, and it's that feeling of not wanting to take a single thing for granted ever again.

It's a push; it's a nudge. It's an excuse to be *better*.

I will be better.

I make my way into the waiting room, eager to share the good news. Amber and Logan are here again, along with Josie, Sandra, and Mason. My parents are even flying in tomorrow for their first visit in over nine years.

Apparently, the elation is evident on my face because Amber tackles me instantly.

"Goddammit, Campbell," she says, slinging her arms around my neck as we teeter on unsteady feet. "Don't scare me like that again."

I smile broad, a breathy chuckle of relief passing between my lips, and I give Logan a fist bump over Amber's shoulder. I catch Josie's gaze when she stands, her eyes bright with solace as she wrings her hands together. We make our way towards each other after Amber releases me, and Josie wraps me up in her own warm hug, cradling the back of my head with one hand.

"Thank God," she whispers into my neck, holding me tight.

I pull back, still smiling, and say, "I want you to meet someone."

I pace over to Sandra and pluck Mason off her lap, giving her a small nod as I pull him onto my hip. Josie, Amber, and Logan are all watching curiously as I join them.

Josie tightens her purse strap over her shoulder, her gaze fixed on the toddler in my arms. She's blank for a minute, perplexed. Then she looks from his face to mine, then back again. A sudden recognition sweeps across her features, and I swear I can hear her gasp. "Oh, my God…" She looks back up at me, wide-eyed. "Is that…?"

"What?" Amber says, crossing her arms with an arched brow. But it doesn't take long for Amber to find that same recognition, to take in the strikingly similar features on Mason's little face, and she lurches forward with a lot more than a gasp. "Holy fuck-balls, are you fucking kidding me?"

I glance around the room, clearing my throat when we garner unwanted attention. "This is Mason. My son," I announce, pride lacing each word. *My son.* The words are weighty and exhilarating, and when Mason rests his head on my shoulder, as if he's shy about the sudden attention, I can't even express what the gesture does to me.

Logan steps closer, slapping me on the shoulder and letting his hand linger as he looks between me and the bashful toddler. "Hell, man. You know I'm not one for sappy shit, but I'm feeling pretty damn warm and fuzzy right now." He winces at his own proclamation. "No one heard that. I literally never said it."

"Erased," I joke, swatting his arm and returning the smile he can't seem to hide.

I step over to Josie who looks confused and joyful and taken aback by the revelation. I bounce Mason up and down, my eyes flickering to her. "I'll explain everything later," I say softly. She nods in acceptance, and my hand tingles at the feel of hers reaching for me, offering a light squeeze.

As much as I want to tell Josie everything, I have a more pressing issue to attend to.

Summer needs to be formally introduced to her little *brother*.

Olivia skips past me towards the waiting area when I enter Summer's recovery room. My feet are swift and eager as I approach her bedside, watching the giddiness sprinkle over Summer's features when she spots Mason in my arms.

"Mason!" she squeals, carefully moving her body into a sitting position.

Katrina stiffens a bit as if she's nervous to reveal the truth to our daughter. She scratches at her wrist and fiddles with a straggly strand of hair dipping over her shoulder.

I sit down on Summer's bed as Mason wriggles from my grasp and catapults himself into Summer's arms. I pull him back before his clunky foot meets her fragile chest.

Summer laughs, unscathed by the toddler attack. "You're a silly baby, Mason," she says, scrunching up her nose.

My eyes skate across Summer's face, which is a little pale, a little ashen. Her dirty blonde hair is sticking to her pillow as she leans back and gives Mason a hug. "Bunny, there's something we need to tell you," I say gently. I notice the way Summer's mouth parts open, her gaze gleaming with curiosity.

I duck my head, then return my attention to my daughter. I open my mouth... and suddenly have no idea what to say.

"Um... Summer, uh..." Katrina is even less helpful.

Summer's eyes flick to her mother, then back to me, as I glance between my two children, getting ready to try again.

Summer kisses the little head in front of her, looking back up at both of us. "Are you trying to tell me that Mason is my brother?" she asks. "Because I already figured it out."

I can hear Katrina exhale a sharp breath beside us as we stare at our daughter and our son, together.

Summer raises both eyebrows, then glances down at Mason who is trying to manhandle her IV line. She pulls him in for another giant squeeze, grinning as wide as the knot of joy in my belly.

I look at Katrina, and she looks at me, then we both look back to Summer. "You knew?"

Summer nods. "It was obvious. He has my eyes, and he *hates* meatloaf, just like me."

Laughter spills into the room as I run my palm along Summer's arm, clutching it gently. "I think he only hates meatloaf because it was your mother who made the meatloaf."

Katrina's eyes float over to me, startled by the joke; stunned by the chip in my armor. I meet her gaze and truly *see* her for the first time in years. I see the apology all over her face—the softening and clemency that surely matches my own. We don't speak the words aloud, but they are there, crackling between us, louder than ever.

Forgiveness.

Hating is easy. Vengeance is easy. Destruction is easy.

There is no growth there.

I know now that I am done with easy. I'm done with settling for a mediocre existence when I am capable of so much more. I'm capable of giving my daughter so much more, *teaching* her so much more. And now I have a son who deserves a father who will fight and bleed and defend what is right, no matter how difficult or painful it may be. I'm done with my lazy, careless response to life's hardships.

Growth is uncomfortable… but getting uncomfortable is the only way to grow.

I'm exhausted when I pull into my driveway that evening. I lean back against the leather seat, closing my eyes and taking in the sounds of the peaceful night through my open window. Before I step out, my phone vibrates, and I see a text from Josie come through.

JOSIE: *Delilah agreed to watch Olivia for a bit. I thought of a few things I have at the house for Summer. Can I bring them by? We can talk. :)*

I gnaw on my lip as I read over the message multiple times. I've been wondering all day if our rendezvous the night before was just a one-time thing, but there hadn't been a good time to discuss. Our relationship is complex—fragile, delicate, hanging by a blind thread.

But fuck if I'm going to say no to Josie being in my bed tonight. At least, I'm hoping that's the subtext behind "we can talk"—with a smiley face at the end.

ME: *You read my mind. Let me shower first. Come by in an hour?*

JOSIE: *Sounds good. See you soon.*

I blow out a breath of thrill and confusion. I'm on edge, filled with conflicting emotions and too many unknowns. There is just *so much* happening right now. My daughter is recovering from a life threatening injury. I have a son—*I have a fucking son*—and I have no idea how or when I'm going to see him again. Katrina is in town and it's strange and unsettling, but we're healing and forgiving, which is also strange and unsettling.

And then there's Josie.

The woman I betrayed. The woman I thought I'd ruined.

She doesn't seem to hate me, and I don't know how to process that.

Part of me is overjoyed by this development, but part of me doesn't think I should get off this easy.

I open my car door and press my shoes to the pavement, noting the dull ache in my legs and the sway of my feet. I'm tired, *so tired*, and I can't wait to step inside the shower and let the hot jets pelt me, washing away the residue of the last few days.

As I make my way across the patio, a sense of déjà vu sails through me when I see a shadowy figure sitting on my back steps. My heart skips, my stomach drops.

Oh, *hell no*.

I can tell it's a man, and my mind starts to swim with thoughts of Benjamin Grant and how I've been too wrapped up in everything else that I haven't had time to look into his case.

Is he out on bail? Did he talk his way out of charges? As he said, a defense attorney would know a few tricks. After being held at gunpoint, it's impossible not to harbor the smallest tinge of fear that he's come back to finish the job.

Fuck.

I'm working on this forgiveness thing, but he nearly killed my daughter, and it's going to take a lot fucking longer than a few days to let it go. If there's one thing I know for absolute certain, it's that I *cannot* deal with Benjamin Grant right now, even if he's just coming to grovel.

Maybe one day... but at least not yet.

But I can't let the anger fester. Not again. I just can't.

I shuffle to the right, not moving any closer. From this vantage point, I can get a better view of the trespasser. He sits casually on the step, dangling his hands between his knees. When my vision focuses and my eyes adjust to the patio light reflecting off the figure, my stomach curdles as recognition glides through me.

Emmett.

Fucking Emmett.

What reason could that asshole possibly have to be here?

He stands from the steps, and I can vaguely see the self-righteous smile curling on his lips. An altercation with Emmett sounds like a worthy finish to top off the utter mind-fuck of the last few days. If I were writing a book, this is exactly what I would write into this scene. A little intrigue, a little angst, maybe even a few throat punches.

Riveting shit.

I throw my walls up as I approach with equal parts caution and immense aggravation. "What the hell are you doing here?" I demand, crossing over to him with narrowed eyes.

Emmett claps his hands together, rubbing his palms up and down like he's up to no good. "Evan," he greets, far more eager to chat than I am. "I heard about what happened to your kid, so I wanted to send my condolences."

"Most people just send flowers."

"Yeah, well…" He shows me his empty hands with a shrug.

I blow smoke out my nostrils. Well, it's actually just regular oxygen, but it feels like smoke due to the fiery blaze spreading underneath my skin. He's using my daughter's life and death ordeal as a tool to fuck with me.

I fear those throat punches might occur a little sooner than I expected.

"Get the fuck out," I seethe, my fingers balling into fists.

Emmett throws his hands up, palms forward. "Whoa, I'm not here to fight, okay? I seriously just wanted to issue my sympathies. It's got to be hard coming to terms with the fact that you're responsible for your daughter almost dying."

I fly.

I fly across the patio so fast, I don't think Emmett even realizes what hit him. My hands are twisted around his shirt collar as I throw him against the side of my house with a sickening *"thwack."* Emmett lets out a groan when his head collides with the siding, trying to scramble free. My grip is unrelenting.

Emmett is breathing heavily, half laughing to mask the fear flashing in his eyes. "Anger is what got you into this mess, Campbell. Watch yourself."

My fingers loosen, only because his words strike a chord with me, and I take a reluctant step back. He relaxes on his feet, letting out a relieved breath he can't disguise.

"I told you I'm not here to fight," he insists, massaging the back of his neck with his palm. "But if what I'm saying pisses you off this much, maybe it's because it's true, and it's easier to take your anger out on me than to take responsibility."

I glare at him. "Don't fucking "Guilt Trip 101" me. Get the hell off my property."

Emmett straightens, smoothing out the fabric of his pretentious polo. "You really think you deserve Josie? You think you can give her a good life after everything you've put her through? I can't imagine a relationship built on lies and deception lasting the test of time." He laughs with forced amusement. "Honestly."

I close my eyes tight, grinding my molars together. I have to shove down the instinct to blame him for telling Benjamin in the first place. Because if he'd never known, Summer wouldn't—

I take one more step back, steepling my hands in front of my mouth while I try to breathe. The fucking eight count is long gone, but I've got to stay calm. I can't go for the blame. If I hadn't made the choices I did, we never would have been on that rollercoaster in the first place.

I know this now.

I know this.

There's just one thing that's really been bothering me…

"How did you even know who I was?" It's probably not a question I should be asking—all I'm doing is engaging him. Egging him on.

But it's been nagging at me since the night he said my real name in Josie's driveway. Of all people to figure me out, why the random asshole who works with Benjamin Grant?

Emmett tilts his cocky head to the side and studies me, his gray eyes sizing me up from my unruly hair all the way down to my worn out sneakers. "When you started showing up at their house, I knew you looked familiar. I couldn't put my finger on it, though, and it was driving me crazy." He goes silent as if that's the big reveal.

Cool. That answers my question perfectly.

I blink at him, waiting for more explanation to trickle through his thin lips.

Emmett leans back against the vinyl siding, planting his hands on his hips and curling his fingers. "Firkin."

I'm not entirely sure if this is supposed to be a riddle, or if he thinks I'm a mind reader, but the puzzle pieces aren't connecting yet. I squint at him. Firkin was the restaurant Katrina used to work at... but what does that have to do with anything?

He just fucking stands there, smirking at me.

"You're not a sphinx, Emmett. Explain."

"Your ex-wife was a waitress there."

No shit.

"She and Josie had something in common," he continues. "Besides you and Ben."

My mouth parts, but no sound comes out. I'm sure I look completely confused and also a little pissed to hear how much I have in common with Benjamin Grant, for fuck's sake.

The smirk on this smug bastard just keeps growing. "I've been a regular customer at Firkin for eight years. Used to go there for a drink after work every Thursday. Then it was Tuesday and Thursday. Then Tuesday, Thursday, and Fri—"

"Holy shit, I get it... *fuck.*"

"Anyway," he continues. "There was this hot blonde waitress that kept me coming back; I couldn't get her out of my head. Even took her on a few dates. Then one day I had the brilliant fucking idea to take my friend Ben with me. Unfortunately, he liked my little blonde waitress, too."

My mind is spinning, trying to make sense of what he's saying. Katrina worked at Firkin for less than a year before she left town. She wasn't there eight y—

Wait, is Emmett saying *he* had a thing with Katrina, too? What is he telling me right now?

I rub my forehead. "Fucking hell, just say what you mean and get out of here, already."

"Wow," he deadpans. "You're no fun. *Josie* worked at Firkin after her first husband's accident."

Josie? I lift my head and stare at him, my jaw slack. The last thing I want to do is give him the satisfaction of surprise, but... *"What?"*

"Oh, yeah... a long time ago. Way before Katrina ever set foot there. She was a sad little thing, poor girl. Trying to support a newborn on her own. No family. No money. Just as pretty as she is now, too. I could never resist the type." His tone is so fucking condescending despite his claim of being irresistibly attracted to her. I have to clench my hands at my sides to keep from knocking him out right here on my patio. "She was all hung up on the dead guy, you know. I had to pursue her for ages before she finally went out with me. And then I brought Ben with me one day, and he swooped right in and stole her out from under me."

"Which you never got over because you saw her first," I say dryly.

"Exactly." He swings a finger through the air. "See, you get it."

Wow, this guy is a piece of work.

"I made sure to stay present in her life, though. Couldn't let her forget about me, just in case things didn't work out with Ben, you know. And then, a few years ago, luck found me in the form of Katrina." He winks at me, and I tighten my fists even more. "I saw the way Ben started looking at her when she served us. Turns out my old friend has a thing for pretty blonde waitresses who are dissatisfied with their lives." He notices my glare, then chuckles. "Then she started flirting right back. It was obvious she had a little crush on Ben, and I knew that she was going to be my ticket to getting Josie back."

Holy shit, this guy is a fucking sociopath.

"You used *my wife* to try and break up another man's marriage... because you liked *his* wife?" I exclaim, incredulously.

"Hey, you can't blame a guy for using what's in front of him."

"You are unbelievable." I'm still gaping at him; I can't even process the audacity.

"I don't give up easily," he says, as though it's a virtue.

"She *married* him, Emmett. It was over. She was off the table."

He lowers his chin and glares back at me, putting his hand up to his ear to mimic a phone. "Hello, pot, this is kettle."

Anger roils my blood as I shake my head. I should know better than to even be having this conversation with him, but for some reason, I keep going.

"To be fair," he continues, "I didn't really *do* anything except find out when Katrina was working and make sure we were sitting in her section during her shifts. Then I just had to sit back and be patient. They took care of the rest of it themselves."

I force back the swelling lump in my throat—it burns more than I wish it would. I need this asshole to get to the point and get out of here before he eggs me on even further. "That's a pretty fucked-up story, Emmett. But what the hell does any of this have to do with how you knew me?"

"You used to visit Katrina at the restaurant quite a bit," he shrugs. "I noticed at the time because I had my eye on Ben and Katrina. Now, I'm a pretty fucking observant guy, especially when I'm looking for an advantage —makes me a damn good lawyer, too—and I saw the way you looked at her, so in love. There were practically little animated hearts in your eyes..." Emmett sighs, trying to sound fucking dreamy, but only coming across like a giant tool. "And I saw what you *failed* to notice—that she was blowing you off, moving away when you would touch her, keeping her focus on Ben."

My eyes close as the acid rises up my throat.

I'm over this. I'm past this. It's done.

"Anyway," Emmett quips, tapping his hands against his thighs. "Ben never noticed you because he's the most oblivious idiot on the planet." He chuckles pathetically, then finishes, "But the flirting between he and Katrina kept getting heavier, and pretty soon I noticed Ben was going there every day she worked, whether I went with him or not. Then I knew it was only a matter of time."

My mouth twitches, but I say nothing.

"Before too long, my patience paid off, and it was obvious there was more going on than flirting." He lifts one shoulder with a self-satisfied smirk. "So, I waited for Ben's marriage to fall apart, figuring Josie would need a shoulder to cry on when she found out her husband was having an affair, and I happen to have two very sturdy shoulders available."

"But that didn't happen," I finish for him. "He never left her."

"You can imagine my disappointment..." Emmett sighs dramatically. "I was so close I could almost taste it. But I figured it would happen eventually. She would either find out about Katrina, or he would find some other cute blonde waitress to screw. He's that type."

"I'm surprised you didn't just tell her yourself."

"I thought about it," he says, cocking his head. "But nobody likes a tattletale. Besides, Ben would have known I'd told on him, and I really didn't want him to make my life a living hell. I have to work with the guy, you know."

Wow. My head is swinging back and forth with disbelief. "So... are you telling me you orchestrated my wife's affair? Just to try and get in Josie's pants?" My blood is pumping fast—*too* fast. I wonder if I should be concerned.

"That's really your takeaway from this?" he wonders, rolling his eyes at me like a teenager. "No, Campbell, I didn't *orchestrate* anything. I saw my advantage, made sure everything was lined up properly, then sat back and watched."

"That's pretty much exactly what I mean by— *fuck,* never mind." I've got to stop encouraging this guy.

"I'll be honest, I couldn't figure out why you looked familiar at first," he says, scratching the back of his head. "Then I saw you with your kid at Thanksgiving, and it clicked. You used to bring her into the restaurant with you sometimes. So, I did some research like the good attorney that I am." He shoots me a beaming grin, like I should be impressed.

Totally.

"That is some twisted shit, you know that? You're one sick motherfucker."

Emmett sniffs loudly as he shrugs his shoulders. "Takes one to know one."

I flinch. The correlation does not go over my head, and I think that's what stings most of all. Am I really any better than this guy? Was *my* sick, twisted shit any better than his? Swallowing, I let out a choppy breath. "I reacted out of pain. Heartbreak. You just did it because you wanted something someone else had."

It's a lame excuse, and I know it, and he calls me on it immediately.

Emmett's finger is back in the air, wagging in my face. "Don't try to pretend you're any better than me, Campbell. And don't try to hide the fact that you had fun doing it. Pursuing Josie, seducing her, dreaming about the day you'd exact your revenge on Benjamin Grant." He snickers with indignation. "I bet you got off on it."

"It wasn't like that at all," I shake my head.

He mellows a bit, the hollows of his cheeks puffing with air before he blows it out. "Listen, pal. I didn't come here to shoot the shit, as much as I love bonding over all the things we have in common." Emmett winks before his features turn stony. "I'm just here to tell you that you need to stay away from Josie. You're obviously no good for her."

I'm still and silent, my feet stuck to the cement like there's adhesive on the soles of my shoes. I'm trying so hard not to let his words in, to not give them any life. He's just trying to get under my skin, and I can't let him win —and yet I feel the words seeping into my dips and cracks, soiling the slow-healing wounds. I feel them burrowing… because I don't really believe he's wrong.

"Oh, come on," he says. "Don't be selfish. You've already put her through so much—she doesn't deserve it."

My jaw clenches. "And what does she deserve exactly? You?"

"Ha." Emmett runs his hand along the side of his cheek, scratching the short bristles of his five o'clock shadow. "Someone better than you, at least." Then he pauses, hands slipping into his pockets as he hunches forward with a light chuckle. "Probably better than me, too. But you had your chance… and somehow, I think you're the type to take the high road, huh? Walk away before you hurt her even more."

I'm left speechless on my patio, torn between punching him and agreeing with him, when Emmett spins away on his heel, putting his back to me. "Do the right thing, Evan." Then he adds, whistling as he walks, "For once."

THIRTY-THREE

I'M IN THE KITCHEN WHEN JOSIE KNOCKS.

I hear her call my name before jogging to the front of the house to open the door. I'd left it unlocked, sending her a text to let herself in and come find me in the shower if she was interested—but I turned the water to cold again, this time to try and cool my temper from Emmett's visit, and was out in two minutes.

Because, fuck cold showers.

She's barely stepped into the kitchen when I'm on her. Her lips are parted to speak, but I don't want to talk right now. I want to show her exactly how I'm feeling. My hands trail up her body, and before my mouth meets hers, I whisper, "Can it wait?"

She answers by closing the distance in a breathless kiss.

Thank fuck.

Soon, her hands are beneath my shirt, running over the muscles of my chest, but when I make a move to unbutton her jeans, she lays a hand on top of mine. "Evan, I…" Her lips are swollen from my kisses, her cheeks flushed; I'm certain she wants me, but there's a look of hesitancy in her eyes. It reminds me of the text she sent saying we should talk.

I can't lie, I was really hoping that was code.

I lean into her, nibbling on her earlobe just to hear her sigh. "I want you," I say, low and quiet. "Can I have you? Then we can talk."

A sound leaves her—hard to decipher—but there's something desperate about it, and when her eyes flare and she pushes at my shoulders, I follow her lead. Josie walks me backward, kissing me with each step, and as I see the kitchen table out of my peripheral vision, I take control. She gasps in surprise when I spin her around. Before she can blink, I have her facing the table, hips pressed against the edge with my pelvis pushing into her ass.

If I hadn't already told her I planned to have her, there would be no question.

I wrap my hand around her hair, tugging her head back until it rests against my shoulder. "Yes?" I whisper, grazing my lips along her neck.

Her chest is heaving as she whimpers, "Yes."

I don't even give her time to take a breath before I react.

I flick the button of her jeans open with one hand while I flatten the other between her shoulder blades, pressing her breasts to the tabletop. She lets out a strangled huff and grips the edge of the table with her fingers, like she knows exactly what's coming… like she's preparing to be ridden hard.

Smart girl.

I bend over enough to shove her pants and underwear down, grateful she removed her shoes on the way inside so I'm able to pull them completely free and spread her legs wide for me. "Damn, you're fucking gorgeous from behind," I groan as I unzip my pants to free myself.

"Only from behind?" Josie lifts just enough to give me a sly grin over her shoulder, and I take that opportunity to smack her ass hard. I revel in her squeal and the way her skin instantly turns pink with the print of my hand. *Fuck,* I could get used to this.

I could get *addicted* to this.

"Uh-uh," I reprimand her, already doing a mental tally of how many pieces of furniture I own that I should bend her over. "Did I say you could move?"

She wiggles her bottom at me like an invitation. I'm already hard and ready, so when I run my fingers between her legs and find her soaking wet, I waste no more time. Lining myself up with one hand, I drag the other down her spine until it rests on the arch of her back, and then I thrust inside her.

"*Ahh,*" we moan simultaneously, and when Josie adds the plea, "Fuck… *Fuck me, Evan,*" I fucking come undone and do as she commands.

I unleash.

With my hands on her shoulders, and hers still clutching the table's edge, I lean over and pound into her, hard and fast, as though we are racing to a finish line…

And I suppose we are.

She pushes back against me, matching my rhythm, our grunts and groans and panting breaths filling my kitchen until all the memories in this room pale in comparison to the woman crying out her orgasm into my kitchen table.

Her muscles squeeze my cock in a vice grip as the broken syllables of my name fall from her lips in time with my thrusts. I feel the pressure build, the aching need to *get there,* and I increase my speed until I feel like I'm sprinting, heading for the edge of the cliff, and I fall over after her. Our fingers entwine as we hold onto each other, and then we are falling, falling…

… *falling.*

Every muscle in my body seems to contract as I pulse my hips into her with small jerks, while my cock does the same inside her as it empties.

And then I'm limp, collapsed on top of her.

Relieved.

After a moment, she stirs beneath me, her cheek resting against the wood table. Even though my body is aching to just *stay* there and savor her forever, the part of my brain that can still make sense of basic needs knows that I should let her breathe—so after I lean over for a quick kiss, I push up from the table and away from her. My dick mourns a little as it slips from her heat, but I remind myself this is just the beginning… that I'll have her at every opportunity.

The miracle of her even *being here* hits me all over again. She rises after me, breathless, and I envelop her in my arms, my lips pressed to her forehead as we take a second to recover.

As the initial high begins to dissipate, I'm overcome with gratitude. "Thank you," I tell her. She lifts her chin, looking into my eyes, silent for a moment as she searches them. I'm confident all she sees is truth because I have nothing else left to give.

She stiffens briefly, then quirks a smile. "You're thanking me for sex?"

I *know* she knows it's more than that, but I reply anyway. "I'm thanking you for… everything."

It's such a simple way to explain all the things I'm feeling, but for now, it's all I have.

The amusement in her smile softens, wanes, and we just stare at each other for another minute. She looks reflective, possibly conflicted. There are so many thoughts swimming in those bourbon eyes, so many words, so many things unsaid. I make a vow to myself that one day I'll uncover all of them.

One day I will understand all the wonders and mysteries of this woman.

One day I will find a better way to express how much gratitude I have for everything she is... other than a flimsy "thank you."

Finally, she inhales a choppy breath and rises on her toes to touch our lips together, sighing against me. It's not a relieved sigh, or a happy sigh—it's kind of strained. Almost painful.

She pulls away and bends down to retrieve her jeans and underwear before I can analyze it more, then nods toward the bathroom, excusing herself. I take the opportunity to grab us snacks out of the fridge and two bottles of water, then saunter into the living room.

I smile to myself, hearing her bustle around my bathroom.

Grateful. It's all I can think about, over and over. I'm so damn grateful.

When she returns a few minutes later, I'm waiting for her on the couch, having spread a few meager offerings out on the coffee table. She sits down, but doesn't slide right up to me like I anticipate, instead maintaining a gap between us and angling her body towards mine. Only our knees touch.

She must be ready to get down to business.

The mood shifts away from the hunger and desperation of the kitchen, replaced by an innate gravity now filling the room—it's heavy. Palpable. "I guess there's a lot I need to say," I tell her, pulling in a deep breath and wondering how I'll ever put all of this into words.

My feelings, my regrets, my hopes... my love.

Shit... *love.*

I almost choke on that breath.

"There's a lot I need to say, too." There's a poignant depth in her eyes that I can't completely place, but it makes my heart drop just a notch. Josie fiddles with the hem of her blouse, forcing a small smile. "But first, I want to know all about your son."

The mention of the child I thought I'd lost stirs my own smile, and I take another breath as I tell her about the things she's missed—skirting around exactly *how* I found out, since Benjamin's name is still a bit of an elephant in the room. The bottom line is, I not only have a miracle for a daughter, but now I have *two* miracles... one I never even knew existed. And although Katrina and I haven't worked out all the details yet, I'm finally going to have the opportunity to get to know my son.

My son.

Wrapped up in my growing excitement, my joy, the words rush out before I can think them through. "I can't wait for you to get to know him, too."

When her smile falls, I go still.

My chest tightens with awareness. My heart drops another notch.

Josie shakes her head with glistening eyes, and I'm suddenly struck with how presumptuous I've been.

She's quiet, her hands folded in her lap, her knees still pressing into mine as though her body needs to be touching me, but that's as far as she can allow.

"Josie..." I whisper.

Don't say it. Don't say it.

But she doesn't need to say it... I already know.

I know what's coming.

I know it's over.

Please, no, my mind pleads. But even as I think it, wish it, beg for it... I know that I have no right to ask her to stay.

I don't deserve her.

I've always known that much. Through all of my lies, deceit, and false pretenses, that has always been the one glaring truth.

Josie finally clears her throat, holding back the tears misting her eyes. "I'm glad we did this, Evan, I am... yesterday, and today. I'm really glad." She clenches her hands in her lap as I try not to crumble into desperate pieces in front of her, anticipating the "but" I know is coming.

I don't deserve her, I repeat to myself. *I don't deserve her, I don't deserve her*—and before she even has a chance to say anything else, I blurt it into the quiet living room. "I don't deserve you."

Her tongue pokes out to wet her lips as she collects her thoughts. "It's not about that," she says softly, and I can't help but argue.

"It is, Josie..." I lean over enough to take her clasped hands in mine, and she loosens her fingers to grip onto me, shaking her head. But I need her to hear me. "I am so, so grateful for everything you've given me, in spite of all the shit I've done. And if you hadn't been there when Summer—" I choke on the words, unable to bring myself to think too hard about the events of the last few days. "I know I jumped to conclusions... I know—"

"Evan, just let me finish," she interrupts, which is a good thing, because I could be here groveling until next week and never even begin to cover it. "We could go on forever about people getting what they deserve, but I really don't think life works that way. I'm not without fault either—I got involved with you while I was married to Ben. I made my own choices that I'm not proud of."

I open my mouth to tell her that I tricked her, that she's not at fault for anything, that I won't let her blame herself…

But she leans in to stop me with one hand on my cheek, the other still held between mine. "It's pointless, though, and I won't sit here and try to divvy up fault or blame. I just wanted to tell you that I *wanted* this—what we did here—finally getting to be together. It was something I took for myself, even knowing how complicated we are. Even knowing…" She inhales a sharp breath, faltering.

"That it can't go on."

A devastating silence infiltrates us when I say the words for her.

Josie nearly breaks down, her decision hurting her just as much as it hurts me.

I glance down at my hands in her lap, biting the inside of my cheek. "I know you don't trust me right now. I know I haven't earned it."

I know. I get it. I understand.

But I fucking hate it, too.

My heart pounds as I swallow down the emotion. As disappointment washes over me. As I try not to let the self-loathing creep back in.

Her hand moves to my jaw, shaky and unsteady, forcing me to look at her. "I *wanted* to be with you like this, Evan. I needed to know what it was like, so I let myself have it, I let myself have *you*… and maybe it was selfish of me, but I don't regret it," she says. "I can't."

"But that's where it ends," I whisper back. It's all I can manage through the heartbreak that clogs my throat. I don't have the right to talk her into more than she's willing to give.

I gave up that right the moment I gave into vengeance.

"If it was just about forgiveness, I'd say that's something we could work on," Josie continues, tracing my jawline with the tip of her finger. "But it's not just about what you've done, or even about how this all started. I've thought hard over the last few weeks…" She grips my hand. "And I realized, through all of this, that maybe I wasn't being entirely honest with myself."

Pulling her palm away from my face, I entwine her fingers with mine, waiting while she pieces her thoughts together.

She chews her lip, takes a deep breath, then exhales. "This isn't just about you, Evan. It's about me… I lost myself a long time ago, and I thought maybe you were the answer, my way back to the girl I used to be, but that's not fair to you," she says.

I swallow back a disbelieving laugh before it's able to escape. In what world is *she* the one who hasn't been fair? I don't say it, though… I don't say it because she's staring at our hands, lost in her thoughts, and when she lifts her eyes to mine, they are swimming with tears.

"I need to get my power back."

I nod, frowning, unsure of where this is going.

"It's part of why I didn't contact you when I left Ben in the first place," Josie continues. "After Adam died, I was so broken, so lost… then Ben came around, full of sweet promises and hope for a better future. For my daughter… for Olivia. I thought I could love him. And maybe I did at one point, I don't know, but…" A tear slips down her flushed cheek. "He was never Adam. He never made me feel the way Adam made me feel."

I swallow. I wait.

"Then there was you."

My heart squeezes, like there's a fist wrapped around it.

Then there was me.

The liar. The puppeteer.

The fucking sledgehammer.

Josie blinks away more tears. "You made me feel something, Evan. You made me feel… *everything*. Just like I felt when I was with Adam. And when the truth came out, when you confessed your plan—your deception—I just…"

"I broke you. I broke you, Josie. I'm so fucking sorry…" I pull her forehead to mine, my throat stinging with remorse. I nearly choke on it.

"That's just it." Her head swings back and forth through a new wave of tears. "You didn't break me. I never got put back together."

I move back an inch, searching her eyes. Reading her emotions. Trying to understand.

She pulls her lips between her teeth, hesitating. "I visited my sister after everything happened. After you…" Her gaze lifts to mine. "I was a mess. Lost, confused… unsure of anything. Carrie told me I had two things to think about. One—did I believe you? Were you being sincere when you said everything changed, that you genuinely fell for me along the way?"

"Josie, I swear to God I—"

"The answer was yes."

Relief seizes me. Our eyes hold tight.

What's the second thing?

"Two…" she breathes out, her voice catching. "Was it enough?"

We both go quiet as the question sinks in; as we stare at each other, our heartbeats thrumming with a thousand different feelings as I lift one hand to grip her waist. The moment is striking, and I don't think I'll ever forget it. It will stick to my memory the way Josie Bennett sticks to every single piece of me. I can hear the refrigerator running in the kitchen behind us, humming and vibrating. A sharp draft blows through outside, rattling the shutters. My hand is resting atop her hip, just beneath her shirt, and I'm hyper aware of the way her skin feels beneath the calloused pads of my fingertips—the way my thumb is tracing languid patterns along the softness.

It's not enough.

She scoots closer to me, and I can't stop myself from pulling her in even more. But she stops short of letting me hold her, and now our heads are bent together, our foreheads just shy of touching as she looks up at me through eyelashes laced with teardrops. "*I'm* not enough, Evan." Her voice breaks, but she doesn't let it stop her; she struggles through the cracks as tears begin to flow freely down her cheeks. "I'm not enough—not yet. I'm not sturdy; I'm not built for this, for what we have. It's too powerful," she says, untangling one hand from mine and laying it on my chest. "I need to fix myself, find myself, become the strongest person I can be for my daughter… and I need to do it alone. I need to heal—otherwise, I'll never be able to fully trust you. We'll never make it. We'll never…"

"Be free," I whisper. The willpower she had seems to drain away, and as her shoulders sag, she leans into me, our foreheads resting against one another for a few seconds. And then her next breath comes out as a sob, and I *do* pull her to me. "It's all right," I murmur into her hair. "I understand."

And this time, I really do.

Josie pulls back eventually, and as we gaze into each other's eyes, I memorize the curve of her nose and the delicate set of her jaw. "I'm happy when I'm with you," she sniffs, her smile still holding more sadness than I'd like to see. "Please know that. You really have made me happy."

But it's not enough.

My insides pitch as I process her words. There's truth in them—I can hear it. Feel it. There's happiness there, mixed with a million other things. Happiness, affection, and maybe even love. I have to believe some of that is for me.

But it's the other things lacing her words—remorse, sorrow, self-loathing—that causes my heart to sink. I know exactly how that feels.

I was prepared for this, I remind myself. *I was prepared to walk away.*

My forehead drops to hers once again, my hand curving around her neck and squeezing the nape. There is a deep, resounding ache in the center of my chest, spiraling to the surface as I try to force down my tears. The back of my throat prickles and burns. A sound breaks free as I close my eyes, and it might be a cry, or a gasp, or a stifled sob... but I think it's actually a goodbye.

It's all beyond words now; those are paltry little things that could never do us justice, so I don't bother searching for them.

She leans forward and presses her lips to mine, like a swan song. My mouth parts, letting her in, letting her in one last time, and we are both drowning in our heartache and pain and final farewell. The kiss is slow, so slow, like maybe we can stop time—maybe we can go *back* in time—maybe we can reverse all the damage done and start the hell over. We are so good together.

We could have been so good together.

But it's too late.

So, instead, I just kiss her...

And I kiss her...

And I kiss her.

And when we finally pull apart, out of breath and out of tears, I hold her in my arms for even longer.

Before Josie stands to leave, she reaches over and plucks a long-stemmed rose from an oblong vase, her fingers careful to avoid the thorns. It was one of the many floral arrangements delivered for Summer over the last few days. Josie studies the flower, her eyes caressing the narrow stem, the prickly barbs, and the blood red petals. Her cheeks are still coated with tears, with sad goodbyes, as she glances up at me.

I inhale a frayed breath and ask, "Do the thorns make the rose any less beautiful?"

My previous words echo all around us, seeping in like harrowing grief. I take Josie's hand in mine, kissing it, telling myself, *"This is right, this is right, this is right."* It needs to be this way.

I squeeze my eyes shut and let go of her hand before the reply even leaves her mouth.

I let go of *her.*

"No," she whispers, placing the rose back inside the vase. "But it makes it harder to hold."

"I will never, ever believe in the words "too late" because it is never too late to be exactly who you wish, do exactly what you should, say exactly what needs to be heard, and live the exact life you should be living."

— **Tyler Knott Gregson** —

THIRTY-FOUR

ONE
YEAR
LATER

"MASON!"

My toddler charges ahead of me, breaking free from my hand and dodging my attempts to reel him back in as I chase him down the sidewalks of downtown Libertyville. I swear to God this kid planned his escape from the moment he batted his ridiculously long eyelashes at me, asking for his sippy cup—it was all a ploy. A way to distract me while I fumbled through the diaper bag for his apple juice like a chump.

He knew exactly what he was doing.

The little con man.

I'm forced to pick up my pace. I start out with a brisk walk, hardly breaking a sweat. My demeanor screams, *"Ha! I've got this. I'm totally about to catch my child. Any minute now. I have complete control over this situation."* I even nod and smile at a woman passing me with a baby stroller, oozing an exorbitant amount of Single Dad Confidence.

No rush... everything is under control.

I move a little faster when he starts gaining speed. How the hell is he gaining speed? My legs are a thousand times longer than his.

I start to sweat, just a little, as my pace quickens.

Yep, I'm running now. The fear is visible. Anyone who passes me will know the truth: my two-year-old has defeated me.

Everything is not under control.

"Mason, stop!" I shout as he heads toward the busy intersection. It seems that yelling is only making him run faster.

And holy shit, he's fast. I thought I was in pretty good shape—I exercise daily, take my vitamins, and eat my green vegetables only when Summer is watching. I'm an active, healthy man who should absolutely be able to catch up to a tiny, wobbly person wearing a Mickey Mouse t-shirt with macaroni and cheese stains and mismatched socks.

Just before I reach for his arm, Mason faceplants on the sidewalk.

I grimace internally. And then, I wait for it.

One. Two. Th—

"Waaahhh!"

Ah, hell. I scoop up the hysterical toddler, inspecting both knees for damage. His kneecaps are scuffed with mild scrapes, so I offer him soothing words of consolation and pepper squeaky kisses in between his neck and shoulder, prompting the cries to transform into giggles.

Works every time.

I continue to bounce him up and down in my arms, waiting for the color in his cheeks to return to its normal, peachy hue. Then I bribe him with sugar.

Dad of the year.

"Want a muffin, buddy? Will that help?"

I can smell the coffee shop from here, as we're only a few paces away from Birdy's Coffee House around the corner.

Mason's tears seem to disintegrate at the mention of the treat. "Muffin!" He tries to squirm out of my grip, fixing those baby blue eyes on me with a silent plea, but I hold firm—I'm not falling for his manipulation tactics again. Fool me once, as they say.

But then my phone rings in my back pocket and I *have* to put him down. Mason tries to make a break for it, but I snatch the back of his t-shirt between my fingers before he gets too far, reaching into my pocket with my other hand. I glance at the caller before swiping to answer.

It's Katrina.

It's the end of May, and Summer is almost finished with school—which means I'm in a perpetual state of anxiety as I count down the days until I need to drive the kids down to Tennessee. Katrina has been calling me every other day, making sure I don't forget anything. She's reminded me to pack Mason's favorite teddy bear named "Mr. Bear" at least twenty-eight times.

"Hey," I answer, curling my fist around Mason's chubby arm as he pulls me forward towards the street.

"You packed Mr. Bear, right? Did I ask that yet?"

Twenty-nine times.

"I haven't packed it yet. He sleeps with it every night," I reply into the speaker.

"Oh, God, maybe pack it now. Just in case."

"I won't forget, Katrina."

Her worried sigh is evident on the other line. "Okay, well... I have news."

Mason and I round the corner, almost colliding into a double jogging stroller. I tug his arm back before there are more injuries to heal with more muffins. "News?" My mind is divided as I try to keep Mason by my side, which is much harder than it seems like it should be, while listening to Katrina.

"I'm moving back in August."

She's earned my full attention.

I stop in my tracks, scooping my child up under one arm as I lean back against the storefront building to process this. "You're moving back to Illinois?"

"I am," Katrina says, her tone a little frayed with nerves, but mostly rich with excitement. "I finally finished school and applied for a few teaching positions out that way. I'm sick of the distance, Evan. I don't want to be so far from my babies for these large chunks of time." She lets out a rush of breath as if those words had been stuck inside her for far too long. "What happened with Summer last year really put things in perspective. You and I are in a better place now, and it doesn't have to be like this anymore. I need to come home."

I scratch the back of my neck. Knowing that this is the last time I'll be away from my kids for eight long weeks feels like a tremendous weight has been lifted. "Shit, Katrina. That's awesome. Congratulations."

"Thanks. I got a position at one of the elementary schools in Mundelein, so once I tie up a few loose ends here, I'll be moving and starting a new life as a teacher. It feels pretty surreal."

I dig my shoe into a sidewalk crack as I stare down at a swarming anthill.

Surreal. Yes, the last year has certainly felt pretty surreal. As Summer worked toward a full recovery, Katrina agreed to put Mason on the same visitation schedule as our daughter for this year. It made the most sense. It seemed like the fairest arrangement in terms of keeping the siblings together and allowing me to make up for lost time with my son. Katrina stayed in town until August, only going back to Tennessee to finish her last year of college and leaving Mason with me. I was now the single father of two children. *Two.* My daughter and my son. It's been a whirlwind of a year as I get to know my little guy and soak up all the sweet moments between Summer and Mason. They are obsessed with each other—*obsessed*. Mason follows his sister around attached at her hip, and Summer eats it right up. She always insists on changing him, getting his snacks, picking up his blocks, reading him bedtime stories. She's taken on the older sister role as I always expected she would, and then some.

I smile, letting my son back down on the sidewalk, keeping a grip on his wrist. He crouches over, enthralled by the hundreds of tiny ants dispersing throughout the sandy hole. I tug him upright and continue our walk to the coffee shop a few doors down, whistling into the receiver, still absorbing the news. "Well, that will sure make our lives a hell of a lot easier. Should I tell Summer?"

"Do you mind if I tell her?" Katrina asks as background noise crackles in the distance.

"Yeah, of course."

She pauses, then finishes, "Thanks, Evan."

We say our goodbyes and end the call as I step into the café, my mind reeling. Mason finally pulls free, giving a victorious squeal as he darts over to the main ordering counter. *Rascal.* I order a coffee and two muffins, then stand off to the side and wait, my eyes trained on my toddler who looks like he's up to no good. He's eyeing a nearby highchair with a baby who has a very attractive Mickey Mouse sippy cup in his hands. I know that look. I know it all too well. My little thief is already planning his grand heist. Luckily, I'm on top of it and grab Mason by the arm before he can snatch the treasure out of the baby's grip. I nod a quick apology to the parents, then spin back around towards the counter.

As I turn, I accidentally bump into someone, prompting them to spill their napkins at my feet. *Shit.* I bend over on instinct, scooping up the loose napkins and standing up straight to hand them over. "Sorry about th—"

I freeze when my eyes meet with those of Benjamin Grant.

The napkins float back down to the ground.

My breath seems to escape me for a staggering moment as an entirely different life sweeps through me like a typhoon.

Benjamin's jaw tics briefly, his eyes reflecting the same off-balanced alarm I am feeling, and a chillingly distinct picture of Summer lying on the patio flashes before me.

It's the first time I've seen the man face-to-face since that night.

I take two steps back. My fingers twitch as my hand drops to my side, but once the initial shock settles, I take a deep breath in through my nose…

And then I exhale, remembering the months after. The tension in my muscles begins to dissipate.

With the combination of his law knowledge and connections in high places, Benjamin escaped more serious charges, receiving only probation for the drunken, accidental shooting of Summer.

After that, there was the question of what *my* reaction would be—should *I* file charges? Should I sue?

And fuck, that was a hard decision to make. It was so fucking hard. This time, it wasn't about me and my feelings of betrayal… it was about my daughter. He shot my nine-year-old daughter. She could have died, and it's a miracle she didn't.

Vengeance came knocking on my door, doing its best to worm its way back inside, whispering sweet temptations into my ear—but I was still living the consequences of learning the hard way, and I wasn't easily swayed. This time, my eyes were open. I had a choice to make: I could react in a way that would seem like justice to most, or I could take a different route…

Forgiveness.

I couldn't live with anger and darkness in my life again; it was a slow poison that had rotted me from the inside out. At that point, I was still in the process of purging it from my system, and I could not—*could not*—allow it to fester again.

Not even under the label of justice.

And then, as I was being inundated with advice from everyone I knew, Benjamin Grant stepped up to the plate and made the decision just a little easier.

He owned it.

He paid for all of Summer's medical bills and a generous amount on top of that, in case there were any complications or anything else she needed.

Of course, there was that devious little thing that gets away with living in the grey area—cynicism.

Cynicism also tried to pay a visit, suggesting that it was easy for a wealthy person to offer cash if it would get them out of bigger trouble.

But I banished that away, too. Those thoughts aren't helpful in the end. And it doesn't even fucking matter… the end result is the same, so I chose to let it go.

I let it go.

Truthfully, it was the most freeing choice I've ever made.

So, I allowed Benjamin Grant to fade into the past, hardly thinking about him since. Part of me expected him to leave town and start over in a place where the stain of shooting a little girl wouldn't follow him—but then again, a defense attorney is probably one of the only people in the world who doesn't have to disappear after an incident like that.

And now he's here—standing in front of me, unsure of what to say, wondering if he should say *anything*, while fidgeting with the Americano in his right hand. He glances down at Mason who is clutching my pant leg and hopping back and forth from one foot to the other. A peculiar look washes over Benjamin, and his face seems to relax somewhat, his eyes morphing from unease to something softer. He shifts his gaze back up to me.

"Evan!"

The sound of my name jolts me out of my trance. I blink, pivot, then notice my order sitting on the counter.

Glancing down, I see that Mason has begun a mission to retrieve the napkins from the floor, and I bend to take his wrist, guiding him over to pick up my coffee and muffins. When I turn back around, Benjamin is still there, several steps away, his arm around the waist of an exotic looking woman with long black hair. She's speaking to him, but he seems lost in his own world, his eyes still fixed on me.

Mason plows ahead, garnering an affectionate glance from the woman pressed into Benjamin's side. Her gaze shifts between the three of us, noting the peculiar tension, and she smiles fondly. Directing her attention at me, she wonders, "You two know each other?"

My chest tightens.

So many memories flash through my mind.

So many feelings. So many emotions.

Betrayal, rage, vengeance, violence, hate…

I look at Benjamin. Benjamin looks at me.

I'm not sure where the words come from, but I respond with, "Just an old friend."

Benjamin's eyes glaze over, his breath hitching as he inhales sharply. His Adam's apple bobs in his throat, and he just stares at me, silent and still.

And then, a trace of a smile tugs at his lips and I'm struck with a profound sense that could never be summed up in conversation.

It's... an apology.

A resolution.

I tip my chin, accepting the gesture for what it is and offering one of my own in return.

I head to the exit and push through the glass doors with my son toddling next to me. My smile widens as a feeling I didn't know I was missing settles in my chest...

Closure.

"Hana's here!"

It's Thursday night. Summer abandons her plate of scrambled eggs, waffles, and *not* burnt bacon as she bounds toward the front door, her loose hair swinging behind her. She shoves her anime-decorated cell phone into her back pocket—the one she begged me for, so she could still talk to Olivia whenever she wanted. I debated the decision, but hell, it's better than Roblox, I guess.

Fuck Roblox. I still don't get it.

She has limited internet access, so she literally only uses it to chat with her mother and Olivia. And I can't say I regret the decision. Even though the girls haven't seen each other in person for over a year, their bond is just as strong as ever. They are constantly texting and video chatting, having virtual dance parties, and talking about terrible pop bands that are infinitely worse than my metal music.

I take a rag and wipe Mason's face as he climbs off the booster seat and scampers away to join his sister at the front of the house.

"Hey, Summer. Hey, Mason," Hana says, offering a cheerful greeting to both children.

I make my way into the living room, waving to Hana as she closes the door and steps out of her shoes. "Thanks again for coming. You're a lifesaver."

She beams over at me and tugs her kimono around her waist. "You know it's my pleasure. I can't get enough of these two."

Summer grins, sliding forward and back against the hardwood floor on her socks. "You're definitely our favorite babysitter. Well, *my* favorite babysitter. Mason just goes along with whatever I decide," she teases. "Plus, you let me stay up way past my bedtime and bring Reese's Peanut Butter Cups that I can store in my secret hiding place, so Dad doesn't steal them."

Hana ducks her head shamefully, a smile spreading.

I reach for my leather jacket lying across the back of the couch and slip my arms through the sleeves, chuckling. "All I heard was *bedtime* and *I have the best Dad ever*." I wink at Summer, then offer Hana a grateful smile. "I'll be home in a few hours. Make yourself a plate of food. It's in the fridge."

Hana nods. "Sounds great. Thank you."

"Congratulations on your engagement, by the way. I saw your announcement on Facebook."

She glances down at the diamond on her left hand, lighting up at the sight of it. "Gosh, it all happened so fast. I hit such a rough patch in my life, then John came out of nowhere and lifted me back up. It's funny how that happens, huh?"

I drift away for a quick second, a nostalgic moment, then glance back at Hana with an earnest expression, nodding slowly. "At the end of hardship comes happiness."

It's a big crowd tonight.

I feel the energy in the air as I weave through the masses, bumping shoulders with more people than I can count. Finding a secluded spot at the back of the room with an available section of wall to lean on, I look around the venue at the people sipping on cocktails while they wait for the show to begin. I'm at a local bar and music hub called Austin's. It's dimly lit, full of buzz and chatter. I'd been here once before with Logan when we came to see an obnoxious metal band. It was a solid five years ago, and I don't recall much of the evening because it was the same night I swore off Jägerbombs for life.

But I intend on remembering all of tonight.

I bring the plastic cup of soda to my lips as I stuff my opposite hand into the pocket of my leather coat. I can't seem to stop fidgeting, shifting from one leg to the other, tapping my fingers against my hip inside my pocket. I'm not sure why I'm addled with nerves—it's not the first time I've been to one of her shows. But there's something in the air tonight; something feels different. There's more people, more lights, more conversations, more photographers.

More.

It feels like a breakthrough… a new level.

Honestly, I think I'm nervous for *her*. This is a damn good turnout, and I wonder if she's expecting it.

Josie walks across the stage a few moments later, and that same feeling sweeps through me like it always does. The tingling. The familiar heat that prickles my skin. The memories…

The sound of her laugh, the scent of her hair, the warmth of her fingers threading through mine. All of it hits me in the chest, knocking the wind out of me for one crushing heartbeat. I chug down a few sips of my beverage as I press myself tighter to the wall, as if maybe it will swallow me up and help me stay camouflaged and out of sight. I'm wearing a baseball cap, but it's too dark in here to wear sunglasses. I wore those one time at a smaller café performance and garnered several "looks" implying that I was a pretentious douchebag.

Fair enough.

But Josie has never spotted me. I think it's because when she sings, when she performs, she goes to another place. Her eyes close, her body relaxes, and I imagine her mind traveling far away until she is lost. Lost in her own voice, her own untouchable magic. She *becomes* the music.

I try hard to stay out of sight because my intention is not to catch her eye. My goal isn't to make contact. I'm here because her music *means* something to me, and I can't *not* be here.

I'm here because I'm really fucking proud of her.

Josie played at a small festival last month, and I ran into Delilah in the crowd. It was a little tense at first, slightly awkward, but she sucked down her Margarita so fast the tension eased up pretty quick. She promised she wouldn't tell Josie she saw me, and as far as I know, she kept her word. Delilah was there with a new guy who seemed to treat her well. She looked happy, which was nice to see. We chatted a bit about life over the past year, about my new books, about Summer and Mason. She avoided the topic of Josie, which I understood, but I couldn't stop myself from asking one thing that had nagged at me for the last twelve months: "Is she dating Emmett?"

Luckily, Delilah snorted and spit out her drink, successfully squashing all of my concerns.

I realize it shouldn't really *be* my concern, but I don't remotely trust that guy, and damnit, I was feeling petty as hell.

"Lord, no," Delilah said, reining in her laughter. "I mean, he tried. He *really* tried. One time he tried so hard he stormed out of Josie's apartment with a broken nose. Haven't heard from the guy since."

That's my girl.

I smiled wide, because hey, I'm not perfect—I may or may not have found immense satisfaction in that slimy weasel Emmett being clubbed in the face by Josie's lead fist.

The fucker deserved it.

The sound of Josie's guitar strings reverberating throughout the room brings me back to the present. I adjust my cap so it's down over my forehead, disguising me as much as possible. Josie sits on a stool in front of the microphone, her feet propped up, her cheeks flushed pink. Her hair has grown out long and thick, pooling over her shoulders and glowing with highlights and honey. She's wearing a white, breezy dress with spaghetti straps and a magenta floral print.

I think they're roses.

I can't help but let a somber smile slip.

She leans into the microphone, giving a little introductory spiel while strumming her pick along the strings. Even from here I can tell that she's slightly jittery, presumably from the tremendous number of attendees crammed onto the dance floor giving her their full attention. She plays it off well, exuding as much confidence as she possibly can, but I know her well enough to see her nerves. I feel them mingling with mine.

But then she opens her mouth to sing, and she is transported, her nerves seemingly turned to dust. She is lost, and I am lost. I'm lost in her slightly raspy vibrato and the way her whole body expels the words as if she's pushing them straight out of her soul. I'm lost to the way she doesn't just play the music; she doesn't just sing the music. She *is* the music.

She leaves a piece of her soul with me with each and every note, and I know I'll carry every one of those pieces with me until the day I die.

The crowd erupts in whistles and cheers as she finishes her first song. I toss my plastic cup into a nearby trash can and join in the applause, clapping slow and purposeful from my place in the back. I adjust my hat as Josie introduces her next song, giving a vague meaning behind it and sharing small details. The details catch my ear, as well as the title: *"Say It."*

Holy shit. I think Josie wrote a song about me.

About… *us*.

When the lyrics come to life, I'm launched back in time a year-and-a-half, and my feet feel flimsy as I straighten my stance. My heart beats fast, my palms clammy as I swipe them along the front of my jeans. It feels like Josie is singing directly to me… and that's because she is.

That's because she *is*.

I'll sneak a cigarette with you
Beneath the autumn moon
We can talk about our broken hearts
Our scars
And our tattoos…

The song goes on, and I absorb it in a way I've never felt music before.

I *am* the music.

When the final note has been sung, I'm breathless, like I was part of an intimate conversation I had no business being a part of; like she engraved her words right into my bones. I swallow back my grief and sorrow and "what might have beens" as I teeter on unsteady legs. I can see the emotion on Josie's face while she strums the final chord, ducking her head and keeping her eyes closed shut. Everyone claps, but I can't seem to force my hands to move.

Then she looks up, scanning the crowd.

She's searching, and searching…

Her eyes land on me.

She freezes.

If I had any breath left, it's undoubtedly been sucked out of me now.

As the applause fades out, Josie doesn't seem to notice. She's still staring at me, her lips parted slightly, her brows creased with striking realization.

I don't know if anyone else is looking or wondering what has the singer so distracted. There could be a spotlight on me for all I know, but my awareness is consumed solely by the mesmerizing gaze of Josie Bennett.

I take my hat off and run my fingers through my hair, my chest heaving and tight. I'm not sure how to handle this fusion, or how to break this hold, but the only thing that feels right is to leave.

I should leave.

With her eyes still pinned on me, I step away from the wall, that wondrous, startled expression on her face never wavering. I ease back towards the doors, maintaining eye contact for one more moment, *just one more moment...* and then I turn around.

I walk away.

THIRTY-FIVE

I WROTE A BOOK.

Okay, I've written a number of books—nine, to be exact. With every new book I gain more followers, more devoted readers. With every new book I feel more financially secure. With every new book I feel more excited, more determined to write the next one.

Then I wrote this book... and it changed my world.

All of my stories mean something to me—all of them take me back to the time I wrote them, to the days I spent in the minds of those characters, to the way life felt as I split my headspace between reality and fiction. But none of my books hit me like this one.

When you write something that truly resonates with you, that digs deep into your soul and rips the words right out of you... well, that's when the magic happens. That's when you know you have something special.

And that's exactly what happened. Once this book was finished, it felt... *big*. I decided to just go all in, and after years of being completely happy self-publishing, I finally pursued an agent and got myself a book deal. I'm officially a traditionally-published author.

I was right, too... the book *was* big.

All of a sudden, it was at the top of the bestseller lists and all over the bookshelves in Barnes and Noble.

It's been pretty fucking crazy.

And today I'm at my first major book signing at a popular bookstore in

Milwaukee, and there are readers lining up outside the doors to have the privilege of my crummy signature.

Whew.

Fucking crazy, indeed.

I'm not even completely sure this is really happening. Maybe I'm having an extremely vivid dream—except…

"*Finally*. You're famous enough to sign my boobs."

Amber is here, asking me to sign her boobs.

I guess I wouldn't be dreaming about that. Probably.

She and Logan came to help me set up my table as we wait for the doors to open and for the hundreds of diehard fans to storm through and shove their books, and possibly their boobs, in my face. I don't usually get nervous—I love interacting with my readers, but every time I glance out the window and see that line grow longer and longer, I kind of want to hurl.

I turn to Amber who is flipping through the pages of one of my extra copies. "Can't I just sign your arm?" I question, pulling more books out of boxes.

"The boobs are sacred. The boobs *mean* something." She swings her head back and forth, popping her bubblegum while fingering the pages with her comically long black talons.

"They mean I'll lose a hand and you'll be in charge of the signing today."

Amber raises one perfect eyebrow at me. "Logan won't cut off your hand. You're his best man in our wedding next weekend. It wouldn't look good for pictures."

Logan is sitting on the floor with his legs spread out, dividing the books into piles. He shrugs, not looking up from his task. "It's true. The photographer wasn't cheap, and Amber's mom will cut off *my* hand if I do anything to jeopardize the photos."

I exhale, tossing a stack of books onto the table. "I don't even know how this is a legitimate conversation right now."

Amber throws me a wink. "I'm just trying to distract you from the line outside that's currently wrapping around the building and weaving into the Walmart parking lot." She twists her head around, staggering backwards to view the crowd on the other side of the window. "Just kidding. It's past Walmart and starting to stretch over to Home Depot now."

"Jesus." I feel my stomach tie in knots as I scrub a palm over my face, forehead to chin. "I think I need alcohol. Please tell me one of you brought alcohol."

Logan pulls a bottle of whiskey out from behind his back and holds it up, still focused on his piles. I sigh with relief, snatching it up and twisting off the cap.

"Wait, we should do a cheers," Amber interrupts, yanking the bottle from my hand.

"I'm good. We don't need to cheers to oil diffusers or hairless cats or Nickelodeon."

"All worthy, but I was actually going to cheers to you and your incredible success," she says. Amber grins bright, waving the whiskey in front of my face.

Logan stands up, shoving his fist against my shoulder until I wobble back, prompting me to return the gesture with double the force.

"Asshole," Logan half laughs as he catches his balance. "Cheers to this guy. Cooler than me, but certainly not better looking."

I try to punch him again, but he anticipates the blow and hides behind his fiancé.

Coward.

"Cheers to Evan, author extraordinaire," Amber announces, holding the bottle high above her head. "Also a damn good friend and an even better dad."

I try to hold back the smile, but it's not working. "Thanks, but you two getting sappy on me is going to make me blush. So, you can knock it the fuck off now." They're laughing at me as I steal the liquor bottle and take the first swig, then pass it to Amber, grimacing at the burn. "Keep that under the table."

A few moments later, the coordinator pops over to my booth and gives me the ten-minute warning. I probably pale instantly, but I don't keel over, so I'm calling it a win. Logan and Amber finish decorating my table with books as I collapse into a chair and pull out my phone. I exhale long and slow, then start up a video chat with Summer. I promised her I'd call before things got started.

She accepts the call right away. "Dad! Are you doing famous people stuff right now?"

A laugh slips as I lean back in my seat with a sigh. It's mid-July, so I'm four weeks out from traveling down to Tennessee for the very last time and holding my kiddos in my arms again. I can't fucking wait. "Almost, bunny. Here, check it out—all these people are here to get my autograph." I spin the camera around until it's facing the window, and Summer audibly gasps on the other end.

"Whoa, cool! Are you nervous?"

I turn the camera back on selfie mode and make a "pfff" sound, dismissing the very notion. "Me? Your father? *Nervous?*"

She stares at me, smiling, awaiting my response.

"Absolutely terrified. I almost threw up on Logan."

Summer giggles, blowing me a kiss into the phone. "You've got this. I wish I could be there with you."

"Next time, bun. I'll make sure you're my assistant," I tell her.

She hops up and down, pleased with such a prospect, twirling a strand of hair around her finger. Her hair has lightened quite a bit from the Tennessee sun, and it makes her eyes look even bluer than they usually do. Then Summer carries me down a hallway to a quieter location and says, "Truth bomb?"

I smile and give her my full attention. "Always."

"I'm really proud of you."

My nerves evaporate, replaced with simmering emotion—*well, shit.*

I think my biggest regret over the last few years has been the realization that I let my daughter down. I always prided myself on being a good father; no matter how black my heart festered, no matter how far my rage took me, I was a *good dad.*

But was I? Now, I'm not so sure. Good dads lead by example, and the example I set was reprehensible. Summer is still a happy kid, seemingly unscathed by the events that unfolded over a year ago, but that doesn't mean she is. All I can do now is continue to move forward, continue to learn from my mistakes and show my children that no one is perfect. Own your shit and do better. It's never too late to make a change.

But I don't want to dwell on that right now because *right now*, only one thing matters.

My baby girl is proud of me, and that is everything.

The truth is... I'm kind of fucking proud of me, too.

"WHAT WE DESERVE" *by Evan Hart.*

My eyes have skimmed over my own book cover seven-hundred-and-fifty-two times today, and I'm not done yet. The line is starting to dwindle, though—I'm on my fourth bottle of water and third shot of whiskey. Carpal

Tunnel set in about an hour ago, turning my super spiffy autograph that I spent an embarrassing amount of time practicing, into illegible chicken scratch. At one point, my hand even gave out and my signature looked like I had a stroke mid-sign. The reader seemed elated by this, claiming it was adorable, which didn't make much sense to me, but I went with it. Turns out, when people admire you, even the most awkward or ridiculous stuff becomes cute.

I don't get it.

I spent most of the day answering questions while I signed, as this story connected my readers to me in a way my other books have not. And that's because it's the most vulnerable story I've ever written.

It's my story.

It's *our* story.

It's no secret this book is about my life—I made that very clear in the final pages, as well as in my blog features, podcasts, and online interviews. The most common question I get is if it was difficult opening myself up in this way, painting myself in such an unflattering light to the entire world.

As much as I would love to say no, the truest answer is... it's complicated.

My story has been... polarizing. While it's been overwhelmingly popular and resonated with more people than I could ever imagine, it's also received controversy and backlash. Many people admire it for its bravery and honesty, while some call it morally reprehensible and believe its popularity sends the wrong message. I had to grow really thick skin practically overnight because I've gotten maimed and skewered, and that's never easy.

But here's the secret those people don't realize: reviews like that only pique curiosity. In short, the controversy made my book more popular.

Go, me... I guess.

I get it, though—some people find it hard to stomach the things I did and the dark paths I took. Hell, I can't blame them. *I* find it hard to stomach.

As far as I'm concerned, writing this book was the most eye-opening, cathartic experience I've ever had. It helped me heal. It's the truth, and it's *my* truth, and there's no growth without recognition or awareness.

I think back to the proverb Josie had on her wall. I thought I understood it back then. Katrina was my rose, and I put our love up on a pedestal... and when it fell, all I was left with were the thorns. The deep cuts.

But now? Now, I'd like to amend that sentiment; I respectfully disagree.

It doesn't have to be about roses falling and leaving pain behind because there will always be hardships. There will always be thorns.

Roses grow *in spite of* the thorns. There's beauty at the end of that painful stem.

But only if it's allowed to bloom.

I've grown, finally, and that's the least I can do after the pain my choices caused. All I can do now is make choices that create something beautiful out of the pain.

Those first few months after Josie walked out my front door for the last time were some of the most soul-crushing days I've ever weathered. That's saying a lot, considering the heartbreak I've been through, but that shit stemmed from anger, rage, and bitter resentment. There was emotion there. *Feeling.*

The loss of Josie felt like something else entirely. It was an emptiness. A hollow missing piece. A goddamn void. The only way to counteract the black cloud lingering overhead was to tap into my creative mindset and manifest that dissolution into something beautiful.

Once, Josie told me that I made her feel brave, so when I started writing this book, I let her do the same for me. Getting honest and putting that vulnerability into my craft… that part wasn't difficult. It was *freeing*. I was able to harness my mistakes, my regrets, my shameful actions into art. It ended up being the best way to push through the fog of depression that swirled around me, bringing me down, sucking me dry.

It allowed me to take that ugliness and let a new phase of life grow at the end of it.

I dove into my new manuscript with a purpose I'd never had in previous books. I changed names to protect identities, of course, but everything else that spilled out of me was regrettably true.

Benjamin Grant told me it would make a good book one day, and it turns out he was right.

It was a risk, though, a big one, and I had no idea it would touch people the way that it has. I am essentially the villain in every sense of the word—I'm the antagonist in my own story. But I think, in a way, we are all flawed to a degree. I know I'm not a "bad" guy, but I did some bad fucking shit, and the number of fans and readers who have messaged me and said, *"I can relate with you"*… is mind-blowing.

And a little frightening, maybe, but who am I to judge?

A reader steps up to me as I chug down my fifth bottle of water, holding out my book, which is opened to the last page. He pushes his wire-rimmed glasses up his nose, fidgeting nervously in front of me. "Why didn't you write *The End?*" he wonders, stuttering a bit as he speaks.

I smile at him. Most people don't notice its absence. But it wasn't an oversight.

Picking up my pen, I sign my name at the top of the page. At least, I think it's my name. I may have stroked out again, so the legibility is questionable. "I couldn't bring myself to write it," I tell him. "It didn't feel like an end."

The guy quirks a smile, but only half of his mouth turns up and his left eye twitches as he taps his foot.

I nod, closing the book and handing it back. "Thanks for reading. I appreciate it."

There's a noticeable blush in the young man's cheeks as he takes the book from my grip with sweaty hands. He begins to turn away, then glances back. "F-For the record, I-I don't think you deserved everything that happened to you," he says, awkward and shaky, but there is conviction behind his words. "M-maybe you can write a sequel with a happy ending."

"I'm still waiting to see what happens," I tell him. "But this is a good start." I gesture all around me, at the table, the books, the line of loyal readers. I will never take any of it for granted.

He quirks one more half smile at me and turns away. I'm left alone for a sparse second, blinking slowly as I look down at the plastic table cover marked with numerous pen malfunctions. I let out a sigh as another book is placed in front of me. I don't glance up right away, still digesting the last encounter, but I smile as I flip open the book to sign. "How are you today?" I ask, keeping my tone friendly and personable. I'm about to sign my name when my eyes stray to the top of the page, and I falter. There's already a message written in the place I'd normally scribble my autograph:

"Life isn't about what we deserve. It's about what we choose."

I look up.

Josie is staring back at me, every bit of her honey-colored hair pulled up beneath a hat.

I'm not prepared for the moment, just like I wasn't prepared two months ago when she spotted me in the crowd at her show. I don't think I'll ever be prepared for the way she looks at me with her bourbon eyes, brimming with passion and vulnerability. I swear this time there is a new light in them—a brighter light. It flickers and burns, telling me she is well, telling me she is thriving.

Telling me she is free.

I swallow. It appears I've lost the ability of speech, so I just sit there, gazing up at her. Josie's eyes trail my face, searching for something I can't pinpoint. Whatever she's looking for, I think she finds it, because a smile tips her lips and she seems to relax as she exhales. It's a breath of resolution.

She says nothing… and I say nothing, but the words she scrawled onto the front page of my book say enough for the both of us.

I think.

Wait. What the fuck does it mean?

I should ask her. I should just ask her.

But I don't.

Her hands pull away from the book, leaving it with me, and as I stare down at the words, trying to make sense of them, I feel her drifting away.

She leaves, and I don't move.

It's about what we choose.

We *choose* how we react to what life puts in front of us.

I think back to a little girl I saw on television once—she was Summer's age, and she had the sunniest disposition I'd ever seen. She also had cancer, and I'll never forget her words: "You can't choose what life throws at you," she said. "You can only choose how you react to it."

It's about what we choose.

I would never admit this to Logan, but I sat in my living room and cried.

My daughter's reaction to her ordeal has been much the same, and I'm struck by how resilient these kids are, how brave… how much we have to learn from them. It's no secret the choices I made weren't good ones, but I'm trying to do better.

Maybe that's what she means… maybe she sees that I'm doing better.

Wait, is she telling me… ?

Fuck, I don't know.

Something hits me in the back of the head, putting an abrupt stop to my spinning thoughts. "Jesus, Campbell, are you dumb?"

Amber and Logan are sitting shoulder to shoulder behind me against the wall, and something hits me in the back of the head a second time. I notice a gum wrapper fall beside my chair. "What?"

Amber shakes her head with pity, her lips pursed tightly together. "You're still sitting. Why are you still sitting?"

Visions of every romantic comedy I've ever been forced to sit through race through my mind.

I look up at the next person in line, a college-aged girl, and she's pointing toward the door Josie just left through, gaping. "Is that… is that the girl from your book?"

I blink at her astuteness, then turn my eyes to the glass doors... but it's too late. Josie is gone.

I feel another gum wrapper hit me in the head.

"I've got a whole pack. I can do this all day," Amber shrugs, nodding her head to the front of the building. I'm still in a trance when she adds, "Stop her, you idiot! Get the damn girl."

I push myself out of the chair as though I'm in a dream, looking helplessly at the remaining people in line. "I..." I aim my thumb over my shoulder, pointing at the door. "I might be a minute... I need to..."

"Go... *go!*" everyone in line starts yelling.

So, I do. I dash through the store, weaving through fans and shoppers as the daze finally falls away. I push through the doors, seeing Josie's back just beginning to disappear around the side of the building. "Wait!" I yell, relieved when she pivots toward me. She's holding a red rose.

I wave the book I don't remember bringing with me. "Does this mean..." I begin hopefully. "Does this mean you choose me?"

Tears fill her eyes as she opens her mouth, but I can't hear her response...

I can't hear her because everyone from the store is crowded around us, applauding. The sound crescendos as she sprints forward, dashing into my arms, and—

Thwack.

I blink, shaking off the dull ache from whatever just hit me in the head. When I look down, my book is lying on the stained carpeting at my feet.

"Did you just throw my own book at me?" I rub the crown of my head, peering back at the source of the assault.

Logan and Amber are gawking at me, incredulously. "The gum wrapper wasn't getting through your thick skull," Logan shrugs.

"Don't be such a pussy. I didn't even throw it hard." Amber frowns at me. "But I can." She holds up another book like a threat. "What the hell is wrong with you, anyway? She was *right there*, and you just sat there with your ass glued to the chair like an... ass."

I glance around, and there I am, sitting with my ass glued to the chair like an ass.

Damn writer's brain.

Wait, did any of that even happen?

I look down at the book still beneath my hands, the neat cursive staring back at me: *"Life isn't about what we deserve. It's about what we choose."*

I exhale, feeling oddly relieved, despite the fact that I just let Josie walk out the door. A college-aged girl is waiting patiently in front of me, clutching my book in one hand while she waves shyly with the other. "Hi…" she says, holding the book out. "Is everything okay?"

She's apparently not as astute as I'd imagined.

Signing her book with a smile, I give her the cursory, "Thanks for reading," and turn to Logan, who has pulled a chair up next to me.

I gratefully take the water bottle he offers, just as he whispers, "That might not actually be water," in my ear.

I down it, swallowing hard, trying to hide the fact that my insides are on fire. "That is definitely not water," I choke back at Logan.

He shrugs. "No shit, I warned you. Now, are we going to talk about the fact that you just let Josie walk out the door without saying a word?"

"I know this is weird, but I don't feel like her being here was about that." When his brow furrows, I glance down at the book I never closed. "I mean, it's a message, obviously, but I don't think she meant for me to go chasing after her."

He shakes his head in amazement and disbelief as another book is set in front of me.

I lean towards him, speaking out of the side of my mouth as my hand moves the pen blindly across the page. "By the way, *please* don't ever let me write a rom-com."

THIRTY-SIX

I SIGNED OVER EIGHT-HUNDRED BOOKS.

Logan and Amber stayed to help me pack up, and between their car and mine, everything has been loaded. They had the brilliant idea to celebrate at the bar, but I'm fucking exhausted—so, like the true friends they are, they're going to go celebrate *for* me while I drive home, then collapse.

I'd always considered myself an extrovert, but I'm officially peopled out.

Possibly forever.

As they pull out of the parking lot, I make one last trip inside to thank the staff and make sure I didn't leave anything behind. Tossing my keys back and forth between my hands, I stride across the lot to my car. The sense of overwhelm from the entire day is receding into a dull haze, and while I still sometimes wonder if it's all real, mostly I'm just…

Grateful. I'm so fucking grateful.

"Excuse me, Mr. Hart?" calls a voice from a good distance behind me. I turn to see a redheaded girl in her late teens that I recognize from the bookstore coffee shop—the crooked nametag on her blouse tells me she is "Zoe." My table was set up in the far corner, so the line ran right past her counter, allowing people to order without having to step away. After watching her struggle to keep up with orders all day, I sent Amber over to give her a generous tip on my behalf. There's no way minimum wage makes up for all she went through.

She's out of breath when she reaches me, having walked briskly while carrying a large coffee in one hand and my book in the other. "I'm so sorry to bother you on the way out," she mutters, completely winded. "But I couldn't get a break, and I'd really like to give my mom a signed copy."

"Oh, of course," I reach in my pocket, exchanging my keys for a pen, and with the book balanced awkwardly on my knee, I scribble out something that looks nothing like my signature. Hopefully, it'll do.

"Thank you so much," she says, watching as I flex the numbness out of my fingers. "I think your book might be what she needs. She just had an experience like yours, kind of… being cheated on, that is." I glance up, noting that color has bloomed on her ivory cheeks, her eyes fixed toward the ground. "Anyway, she's in the angry stage. I'm hoping that reading someone else's story—someone who's been there—might help her find a way of dealing that's less… vengeful, I guess."

My smile is genuine as I regard her. One of my favorite things that has come out of this, is knowing that I can tell people I understand. *I've been there. I handled it wrong. There's a better way.* And hopefully, that will encourage other people to find healthier ways of navigating their pain before the consequences come back to haunt them.

I'm just about to hand her the book back when it hits me. "Wait, let me add one more thing."

And then I write the words: *"Life isn't about what we deserve. It's about what we choose."*

I stare at those words for a moment with a feeling of poignancy. They're like a mantra for the broken, for those on the cusp of a decision—whether to wilt under hardship, or to march forward. It's the difference between growing past the thorns, or letting them cut you until you bleed out. And even though it's the first time I've written those two sentences, I know there are many more ahead. It makes me smile to think Josie has left me with something that could be a light to so many others in the future.

Zoe thanks me as I return the book. "Oh, I brought you this," she adds, trading the book for the coffee in her opposite hand.

Grinning, I wave it underneath my nose, inhaling the distinct aroma of autumn spices. "Is this… ?"

"Pumpkin Spice Latte. We have some stock stored away in the back for fall, and since you mention it in your book, I thought maybe…"

She made me a Pumpkin Spice Latte. In the middle of summer. Because the character in my book—who is obviously me—had the balls to admit to liking them.

I kinda feel like I've reached a whole new level.

"It's amazing… thank you," I tell her, sweeping it under my nose again. "PSL in July. I feel special now." I don't even care that the temperature is in the upper eighties and Zoe just handed me a scalding drink.

She shrugs, biting her lip and giving me a shy smile as she takes several steps backward. Her eyes stray briefly over my shoulder, then return to mine. "I just wanted to thank you for the extra tip, even though it wasn't necessary."

I duck my head, my smile widening. This whole "being a good person" shit feels pretty fantastic—I must say, Kindness is a far better companion than Vengeance.

Rachel shakes her pompoms in celebratory agreement.

"Tell your mom there's a blossom at the end of the thorns," I tell Zoe, lifting my coffee cup in cheers. "She just has to let it bloom."

Dipping her chin, she tucks a strand of autumn-colored hair behind her ear, gives me a quick wave, then spins on her heel. I watch her hug the book to her chest as she crosses through the parking lot.

Then I turn—

And I freeze.

My heart stops. My muscles lock. My breath stalls in my back of my throat.

And when that breath finally escapes me, her name comes with it.

"Josie."

Hair like honey. Eyes like bourbon.

Josie Bennett.

There's a long, drawn-out pause, and then I say on the exhale, "You're still here." I drink her in from head to toe—Josie is dressed in one of the summer sundresses she loves, her hair no longer stuffed up under a hat. She is the epitome of life and light, a modern day Aphrodite, and I'm stunned by her presence. Drunk on her proximity.

She's still here.

The words pound to the beat of my heart—*she's still here, she's still here…*

She's

still

here.

Josie gazes up at me, wide-eyed, irises shimmering with what's left of the swiftly setting sun. "Hi," is all she says.

So soft, so simple, and yet the sound of her voice reverberates through me—

a white wave, a crescendo, an equally perfect and painful memory. Buried feelings rush forth, sluicing me with emotion so powerful, I nearly choke. Fumbling for my next words, I have no idea how to read her, or what she's doing here, or what I'm supposed to say, so I just mutter, "Did you forget something inside?" I can't be presumptuous—I won't. Not again. I swallow hard and pop my thumb over my shoulder. "The doors are probably still unlocked, we can—"

"Evan..." Her head swings back and forth as she takes another step towards me, our eyes locked. Mine are flooded with confusion, and hers...

No.

She's not here for me. She can't possibly be here for me... *like that.*

My brows pinch together, my chest tight. I stare at her, watching every micro-expression that flickers across her face. Then I realize that I'm squeezing my cup of coffee so hard, the cap pops off and the burning hot liquid spills over the rim, splashing my fancy pants. "Shit..."

Josie rushes forward and takes the coffee cup from my hand, setting it down on the hood of Francis. "Here, let me..." She reaches into her giant bag, that I think must be a purse, and pulls out a small pack of tissues, swiping a few and dabbing them against the coffee stain.

My breath hitches, my muscles going completely still at her nearness. I clench my jaw as her eyes lift up to me, so wide and vulnerable. She looks back down, her hand moving over my thigh with the tissue, her body still impossibly fucking close. The scent of her hair has my blood pumping hard and fast, and the warmth of her skin radiates into me, scalding me hotter than the coffee.

Memories burn me, too.

Memories I've kept stored away, like the feel of her skin against mine, her kisses, her laughter, the way she said my name, the way we danced and sang and made beautiful music together...

Josie, Josie, Josie... she's here.

My eyes close tight, and I just feel. I feel her everywhere, and I savor it... I savor *her...*

Because it might be the last time she—

"I'll be honest... I expected you to come after me."

Her words puncture through my haze.

Wait... *what?*

My eyes ping open and I blink down at her. She nibbles her lip before taking a small step backwards and meeting my stunned stare. "You what?"

"Uh, yeah... I guess I've been reading too many of those romance books," she shrugs, cringing a little, with what looks like embarrassment. "But then when you didn't—"

"Josie, I didn't think…" I try to explain, but she keeps going.

"I realized I was being a little presumptuous, coming over here like I just assumed you'd still be single… and interested." Her chin tips down as she looks up through her lashes, like she's not sure she wants to know the answer.

My heart pounds with hope, picking up speed with every word. "I'm single and interested," I rush out on a single breath.

Visible relief washes over her, and she stands up straighter, a glow sparking in her eyes that spreads heat through my body.

"Wait, did you say you've been reading *romance* novels?" I can't keep the grin from stretching, and I lay my hand over my chest like she's wounded me. "And here I thought you preferred the darker stuff like I write."

"Your last story is my favorite," she says, pushing her purse strap higher on her shoulder.

"You mean *our* story." I watch her lips curve into a gentle smile at my words while her face lights with so much warmth, I have to put my hands in my pockets, so I don't grab her and kiss her right here.

"Our story," she repeats thoughtfully. "It has a little bit of everything—darkness, humor, passion, revenge, betrayal. I love it… thorns and all."

It doesn't have a happy ending, I think to myself—but when a look of melancholy dims the light in her eyes, I realize I said it out loud.

I close my eyes and inhale, an apology on my lips. But a soft touch on my arm interrupts me.

"Evan."

"*Josie*," I whisper the name my heart has whispered since maybe the first time I saw her, and I open my eyes.

She pulls a rose from her purse.

Josie steps forward with purpose and takes my hand in hers. Turning it over so she's cradling my open palm, she very gently lays the flower on it. Feeling the lightest prickle of thorns, my mind turns to the day I trashed my house, the day I closed my hand around a stem just like this one, the day Josie was there to put me back together…

The day I fell so hard for her, there was no turning back.

"I know I was the one who walked away," she tells me, and her voice wavers a little as her eyes brighten with moisture. "I needed to at the time—

I needed to find my own power before I could take on another person's pain…"

I'm nodding while she speaks, because as hard as it's been, I understand.

I understand a lot of things now—and here, in this darkening parking lot, I take my free hand and wipe away the freshly falling tears of the woman that has been on my mind every minute we have been apart.

"But even though it was my choice," she continues, "I want you to understand how hard it's been without you in my life. How much I've missed you. How much it's hurt."

"Truly beautiful things are like that sometimes, though, aren't they?" I remind her, watching the recognition flash across her face as I echo the words she spoke in her kitchen. It was the day she told me the meaning behind the roses. "They can cut you, they can make you bleed…"

"But that's how you know you're alive," she whispers.

I skim my hand from her face, down to her neck, continuing along her arm and watching the faint ripple of goosebumps break out beneath my touch. When I reach her hand, I pull it gently to my chest, flattening it over my heart so she can feel it there, hammering against my ribs.

Beating for her.

I lean in closer; a few inches more and our foreheads would be touching. I can feel her breath stir around my face as she does the same. "Tell me what it means," I say softly, and when her eyebrows raise in question, I dip my head, so my lips are near her ear, my voice dropping even lower. "What you wrote in my book, Josie. What does it mean?" And even as I ask, I know… I think I know…

I hope I know.

"It means I choose you, Evan," she declares, her eyes fixed on mine. "I choose you for the father you are to Summer, and for the way you treat Olivia as though she is just as special. I choose your creative brain, your sense of humor, and your Fleetwood Mac covers. I choose dancing amid bubbles at Farmers Markets and drinking raspberry wine until we can't keep our hands off each other. I choose you for the honesty you found on the other side of the lies, and for your bravery in sharing it with the world. And I choose you because you're taking those bad choices and you're making something beautiful out of them."

Fuck.

"Josie…"

"I choose you, and I forgive you," she continues, moving closer, then closer, until she's almost flush against my chest. "I forgave you a long time ago… and I appreciate you giving me the space to grow and heal. But I'm ready to grow *with* you."

Her words steal my breath, and I couldn't hold back another second if my life depended on it.

I reach out and take her face between my hands, leaning forward to pull her lips to mine, and then I kiss her…

And I kiss her…

And I kiss her.

Her message filters through my mind.

Life isn't about what we deserve. It's about what we choose. And sometimes life makes choices for us, choices that hurt, and that's terrible and heart-rending, but we have the choice to let it break us or to persevere. To become stronger.

Better.

You can't choose what life throws at you, but you can choose how you react to it.

The truth is, we deserve nothing. We need to fight for what we want. We need to fight for the things that make us want to go skinny dipping at midnight, and dance in the rain, and wish on falling stars. We pave our own way. We create our own destiny. We choose the life we fucking *want*.

Eventually, we are forced to pull back from the kiss long enough to catch our breath, and I lean over to her ear. "Say it," I tell her in a low voice.

Josie takes my chin in her hand and tugs me back until our foreheads touch, looking up through long eyelashes. Her bourbon eyes are full of starlight and infinite possibilities as she whispers, "I'm in love with you, Evan Campbell."

Wrapping my arms around her, I cradle her to my chest and release a contented sigh into her honey hair. I say it right back. "I'm in love with you, too."

We choose this.

We choose each other.

She smiles through her tears. "How's this for a happy ending?"

I reach out and cup her face between my hands, soaking up the way she melts right into me. Her eyes flutter, her smile still glowing bright as I drop my forehead against hers. I breathe in deep, assuredly, without question. I don't hold back. "Feels like a beginning to me."

We choose to be the blossom that grows at the end of the thorns.

EPILOGUE

Josie

FORGIVENESS.

It hides in all of us. Breathing. Hoping. Waiting for the day we tear down our walls, let go of the pain that ruled us for so long, and finally *release*.

Sometimes it's subtle, merely a tickle, buried beneath the layers of a carefully assembled rage. Veiled by a ruthless thirst for punishment—for *vengeance*. It will poke us gently and whisper in our ear, but we ignore it. We dismiss it. We carry on with our reprisal, with our hate, with our bitter grudges.

It's easier that way.

Sometimes it lies dormant for months, years, decades, until we are triggered by something good—something worth fighting for. Something better than our hollow lust for revenge.

Then, we implode. We fall to our knees.

We question everything.

For some, it comes out of nowhere.

People we never expect come out of nowhere, and we are blindsided.

Those people drive us like love drives the dreamers and hope drives the broken. They carry us through the bleak, empty moments, pushing us forward, promising better days ahead. They make us want to do better, *be* better. They burn us from the inside out.

But isn't that the point?

In a way, we need them to. We need them to reach deep inside, burn away the ugliness, and help us forget the pain that created the innate hunger to avenge.

No… not forget.

Accept. Accept the pain, acknowledge it, and let it go.

In the end, they say forgiveness is earned. And maybe that's easier for some to believe, but truthfully, I think forgiveness is chosen. We choose what weights to carry and which burdens to release. We are responsible for our own happiness. We need to fight for the things that bring us peace.

And that's exactly what we did.

I never expected to be sitting here on this secluded beach at midnight with all the pieces of my heart scattered around me like dandelion wishes in the wind. I never expected him to be sitting by my side, his hazel irises catching the light of the moon, our hands perfectly entwined. I never expected any of it.

I never expected *us*.

Evan lets go of my hand and reaches for his guitar, pulling the strap over his shoulder and cracking a smile. He nods his head at me, encouraging me to do the same. I oblige, picking up my instrument and facing him in the sand as the moonlight bathes us both in a subtle spotlight.

Summer and Olivia perk up when they hear the strings of the guitars echo across the beach.

"Ooh, dance party?" Olivia inquires, rising to her feet and twirling in a clumsy circle, her strawberry blonde hair following close behind.

My daughter. My little girl.

So happy.

Summer hops up, abandoning her cotton candy on a beach towel, and starts busting out some pretty impressive dance moves. She then reaches for her little brother, Mason, who is drawing designs into the pebbled sand with his finger, and swings his arms back and forth.

I admire the girls from afar—a little older, a little wiser, but their friendship just as precious as it was the day they first met on a sunny playground.

Evan has always regretted the fact that his revenge plan was the catalyst for our love story; he hated how something so ugly was the trigger for something so beautiful.

However... I disagree.

It was *them*.

Our sweet girls.

They were the catalyst. If they'd never met that day at the park, we never would have set up that first play date. I never would have gotten to know Evan—the *real* Evan—the softer, vulnerable side to him he so desperately tried to hide from me all those years ago.

His plan would have failed.

Our story would have never been written.

Giggles erupt from all three children, and I wonder if we even need to play anything because their laughter is music to my ears. I turn to Evan and see a light reflecting in his eyes as he watches our babies skip along the empty beach, a tepid breeze sweeping through. I curl my coral-tipped toes in the sand, strumming the guitar chords with my pick, gazing at the man I love with my whole heart.

We've started a tradition. Every September, right before the prospect of autumn kisses away the summer sun, we don't hold back. We will venture out late at night, then sit on the beach and sing to the stars while the children dance and laugh and gorge on sweets. I sing to him, and he sings to me, and everything else melts away.

We sit there for almost an hour playing aimless tunes, unable to wipe the smiles off our faces. When the last note is swept away by a mighty draft, we set down our guitars and Evan tackles me backwards, until my back is to the sandy shoreline and he is draped over me, chest to chest, heart to heart. My hair splays out in brilliant waves, framing my face, beckoning him to thread his fingers through the golden strands. He leans down to kiss me, softly at first, something exquisitely tender, then he glides his tongue along my lips until I allow him entry. Within the heat of our kiss, I know exactly what he has in store for me later. My thighs clench with anticipation.

"Gross!" Summer shouts from a few feet away, prompting Evan to roll off me with an embarrassed chuckle and take his place beside me in the sand.

Laughing at the intrusion, I sit up, dragging him with me and reaching my opposite hand over to my backpack. "I brought something," I say, and there's an air of playfulness in my tone.

Evan pulls his knees upright, looking over at the bag as I begin to unzip, his curiosity piqued.

"To celebrate." I pluck out a bottle of raspberry wine and two glasses, my eyes gleaming as I wave the treasures in front of his face. "Have a drink with me?"

"I'd love to," Evan tells me, but instead of accepting the glass, he snatches my wrist and yanks me to my feet. "After a dance."

"Oh, jeez…" I know where this is going.

Sure enough, he reaches into his pocket and pulls out his cell phone while I discard the wine and glasses in the sand, my amusement evident.

Within moments, the peaceful night is assaulted with terrifying, screechy vocals and a cacophony of earsplitting instrumentals that could only have been produced in some category of Hell. My head swings back and forth as all three children try to shout their disapproval from the other side of the beach with their hands over their ears.

Evan pays them no mind. Instead, he smiles brightly, whisking me into his arms.

"Evan, this isn't music," I tease, rich laughter escaping me. "You can't dance to this."

"Sure, you can." He spins me into a circle, snuffing out my claims, while my giggles intermingle with the sounds of death metal serenading us. "There is rhythm." He spins me again. "There is soul." He dips me. "There is magic."

Our eyes meet on the dip as they always do, and that familiar magic courses through my blood. Evan pulls me to his chest, kissing the top of my head, and I melt into him, our bodies lightly swaying in perfect time. I close my eyes.

I'm happy.

I'm in love.

I'm finally free.

When the song ends, we collapse back into the sand, and I reach for the wine and glasses once again. Evan scoots closer to me until our shoulders are touching and tucks a rebel wisp of hair behind my ear. He watches as I pour the berry liquid into the respective glasses, then takes the one I hand him, tipping his glass to mine. "Cheers?"

My head bobs, my mouth puckering as I rack my brain for a worthy cheers. "To flying squirrels."

"To the word "mellifluous"—it's a damn good word."

I giggle. "To Richard Marx, circa the late eighties."

"To holding onto the nights."

"Okay, piggy-backer," I tease, narrowing my eyes at him. Then I clink my glass with his and add, "To not holding back."

"To not holding back," Evan echoes, his eyes glimmering with wild perfection. "I'll drink to that."

We gaze at each other over the rim, smiling as we sip our raspberry wine, eager to head home and get to all the things our eyes are promising.

But first, we drink.

Then we pour another glass, and then one more, because, hell—

We deserve it.

THE END

AUTHORS' NOTES & ACKNOWLEDGEMENTS

Where do we begin?

Once upon a time, I (Jennifer) wrote a book called *What We Deserve*. I really loved this book. I loved it so much, I spent six months querying it to agents until it got picked up by a small publisher. Sadly, that publisher closed its doors over the summer, putting the book back in my hands. I re-read through the manuscript, truly feeling I had the bones of a GREAT story. Evan has never been far from my mind since I wrote "The End" fifteen months ago...

Only, there was one small problem. The book needed a massive rewrite in order to bring it up to my current writing standards.

So, back to the shelf it went.

Until there was Chelley.

You know when you meet someone during your lifetime, and you're just like, "Oh, there you are! My person!"

Chelley is my person. Our writing styles, sense of humor, and storytelling methods are eerily similar. So, when I told my husband I was probably never going to publish this book, he had a brilliant idea... why don't I bring Chelley on board, and we can rewrite it together?

Y'all. I can't even.

This story was brought to life in a way I never anticipated, and it's finally the story I always dreamed it could be—renamed, revised, and remastered. Chelley embraced Evan so perfectly, there are times when I don't even know who wrote what. It's been such a whirlwind, emotional, and profoundly satisfying experience, it's hard to find the words to do this journey justice.

Also... some may also recognize the release date of December 30th as being the same day I published *Still Beating*—the book that truly changed the course of my journey—one year ago to the date. I met Chelley through that book, so the full circle of it all is truly special to both of us.

It was simply meant to be.

Thank you, Chelley.

I would also like to personally thank my husband, Jake, who not only had the genius idea of bringing Chelley into this project, but came up with bones of this story from the get-go. I'll never forget sitting on our front porch as a summer storm rolled in, feeling inspired by the smell of impending rain. Jake turned to me and said, "Your next book should be a revenge story. Everyone loves a revenge story." One of his favorite movies is *The Count of Monte Cristo*, so we spent the next few hours trying to come up with a plot that would work for a romance. This was in June of 2020, and finally... December of 2021, this story will finally see the light of day. Thank you, Jake, for being my idea man, my sounding board, my lifeline, my behind-the-scenes hero, and my one true love. I couldn't do any of this without you.

I choose you. Every day.

All the thanks in the world to my amazing children, Willow, Liam, and Violet, and to my family for always pushing me, believing in me, and keeping me inspired. You are my greatest gift.

Chelley's Thoughts:

It's amazing how life can bloom into something you'd never have predicted. Less than a year ago, I was struggling to put words on the page, knowing there was a writer hiding somewhere within me, not really believing this dream could happen.

Not for me.

I lacked the experience... the focus... the support. I had no idea what I was doing.

Until there was Jennifer.

Our meeting started with a casual message, but there are times when you just *know,* and I will never forget looking at my husband that night and saying: "I feel like this is big. Lifechanging kind of big."

Really, I had no idea.

It's less than ten months later, and we've written a book together. My first book. A book we are both so, so proud of.

Together, we found a blend and a balance that has felt no less than magical. But Jennifer is more than a writing partner—she is a kindred soul who has taught me so much, walking alongside every step of my first solo project and inviting me into her own. She is a friend whose kind heart and selfless spirit astounds me every day.

Thank you, Jennifer.

Thank you for trusting this new writer on the block with a story that had so much potential, and for not only being willing, but *eager* to share it with me.

Thank you for being my biggest supporter and my loudest cheerleader (sorry Rachel, you're gonna have to pass the pom poms).

Thank you for making me believe in myself as a writer.

There are no words for how grateful I am.

Thanks also goes to Jennifer's husband Jake, whose brilliant idea set this whole thing in motion. It's hard to believe that spark was lit just two short months before publication. I doubt anyone realizes just how important your presence is behind the scenes, and I am in awe of your ideas and your beautiful covers. It probably comes as no surprise that *The Count of Monte Cristo* is one of my favorite films, too.

To my husband Iggy: Thank you for your belief in me through all the years we've been together, and for your support as I pursue this dream. I could not have done this without your enduring patience during the long hours I sat behind a laptop creating complex lives for fictional people. I promise I will never forget the ones who are truly important. And I swear one day I really will write that vampire novel you helped me brainstorm.

To our son Greyson, my reason for always trying to be better: I am astounded by your brain and your creativity, and I hope that I can inspire you to pursue your passions in life. You have been so patient with your introverted mama through this process. I am so proud of the person you are.

And to all of you reading this: Live bravely; your potential is infinite. Don't let fear keep you from pursuing your dreams, because when you reach for them, you are letting a piece of your soul run free, and that is when the most beautiful things can happen.

We would both like to thank our incredible beta readers: Serena McDonald, Paramita Patra, Kelly Green, E. R. Whyte, and Amy Gordon Waayers, as well as my original team of beta readers who received the first draft way back when (special thanks to Emily Gutzmann who truly believed in this story and contacted me regularly for updates on its release—you helped keep it fresh in my mind and hopeful it would one day get its time to shine.)

Serena, we are especially thankful for your contagious enthusiasm, all-cappy screaming, your aggressive love for Evan, and for spreading the word. Thank you for all your help; you're the best.

Thank you to our amazing promo team and early readers for cheering us on, showing such incredible support and excitement for this story, and for sharing your love with beautiful graphics and reviews. This community means so much to us both. Thank you for the messages, the tags, the comments, and the kind, encouraging words (okay, sometimes angry and outraged, but we love those, too).

We are so grateful and blessed.

If you enjoyed this story, we have a new collaboration project in the works which may or may not center around the characters from this book. If you thought this one put you through the wringer, hold on tight—we've got a hurricane coming your way.

Do you want an exclusive bonus scene, featuring a sneak peek of Evan and Josie's wedding from Summer's point of view?
Be sure to sign up for our newsletter!

THE EVAN PLAYLIST

Listen to the Playlist **here**
"Someone Else" — Rezz, Grabbitz
"Little Lies" — Ari Hest
"Policy of Truth" — Eric Tessmer, Nancy Wilson
"Ride" — Cary Brothers
"Careless Whisper" — Seether
"Carnival of Rust" — Poets of the Fall
"Your Love" — The Outfield
"Runaway Train" — Soul Asylum
"One Thing" — One Direction
"Come and Get Me" — Sleeping Wolf
"A Different Kind of Pain" — Cold
"Song #3" — Stone Sour
"Hollow" — Submersed
"Madness" — Muse
"Broken" — Seether, Amy Lee
"This Night" — Black Lab
"Not Strong Enough" — Apocalyptica, Brent Smith
"Found My Place" — Pete Murray
"Light On" — David Cook
"Waste My Time" — Saint Asonia

MORE FROM JENNIFER

If you enjoyed this story and would like to chat more about it, check out *The Thorns Remain Discussion Group* on Facebook!

And feel free to join my reader's group:
Queen of Harts: Jennifer Hartmann's Reader Group

Follow me on social media:
Instagram: @author.jenniferhartmann
Facebook: @jenhartmannauthor
Twitter: @authorjhartmann
TikTok: @jenniferhartmannauthor

www.jenniferhartmannauthor.com

LOTUS
Remember Oliver and Sydney, Evan's quirky neighbors? Their story is written, and you can read their dramatic friends-to-lovers romance in Lotus (I beat Evan to it!)

To the rest of the world, he was the little boy who went missing on the Fourth of July.
To Sydney, he was everything.
Twenty-two years later, he's back.
This is Oliver Lynch's story…
This is their story.

STILL BEATING
#1 Amazon Bestseller in three categories!

When Cora leaves her sister's birthday party, she doesn't expect to wake up in shackles in a madman's basement.
To make matters worse, her arch nemesis and ultimate thorn in her side, Dean, shares the space in his own set of chains. The two people who always thought they'd end up killing each other must now work together if they want to survive.

THE WRONG HEART
When my husband died, he left my broken heart behind.
He left another heart behind, too—his.
I know it's wrong. I shouldn't be contacting the recipient of my husband's heart. I don't even expect him to reply…
But there's a desperate, twisted part of me that hopes he will.
No names.
No personal details.
Just a conversation.

The only thing I have left of my husband is inside him.

THE DUET SERIES — ARIA & CODA
When the lead singer of his rock band starts falling for a pretty waitress, Noah will do whatever it takes to make sure she doesn't get in the way of their dreams.
But it would be easier if that waitress didn't accidentally spill her darkest

secrets to him one night, triggering a profound connection neither of them saw coming.

CLAWS AND FEATHERS

Small town cop, Cooper, is intrigued by the mysterious new girl who walks into his father's bar, but the last thing he expects is for her to go missing that same night.

Finding Abby is just the beginning. The only way to truly save her is to unravel her secrets—a task that proves to be more challenging than he could ever anticipate.

DESIRE AFTER DARK ANTHOLOGY
Releasing January 11th, 2022!

Over twenty of your favorite authors have come together to bring you your next book boyfriend… the hot bad boys you can't resist, the swoon-worthy heroes that will sweep you off your feet, and all the sexy studs you'll meet between the pages. This and more awaits you in the Desire After Dark anthology, a collection that proves boys are better in books and desire really is better after dark.

Jennifer has a new angsty standalone in the works, hopefully releasing Spring of 2022. It's a contemporary romance with a slight paranormal spin! Stay tuned!

MORE FROM CHELLEY

Join my reader group to chat more!
Chelley St Clair's Saints and Sinners

Follow me on social media:
Facebook: @chelleystclairauthor
Instagram: @authorchelleystclair
TikTok: @chelleystclairauthor

COMING SOON

While **The Thorns Remain** *is Chelley's first published work, she has a new book in progress, planned for release in early 2022! Follow her on social media for release updates and teasers.*

The Bayou Never Tells *is an angsty, slow burn, steamy romance about Silas Montgomery and Ivy Summer, two people from very different worlds who try to resist their unexpected commonalities and sizzling chemistry while thrown together on an awkward road trip set in the deep Southern U.S.*

Readers that love badass heroes who are tortured, steamy, and foul mouthed with a marshmallow center will love Silas.

ABOUT JENNIFER HARTMANN

Jennifer Hartmann resides in northern Illinois with her devoted husband, Jake, and three children, Willow, Liam, and Violet. When she is not writing angsty love stories, she is likely thinking about writing them. She enjoys sunsets (because mornings are hard), bike riding, traveling anywhere out of Illinois, binging Buffy the Vampire Slayer reruns, and that time of day when coffee gets replaced by wine. Jennifer is a wedding photographer with her husband and a self-love enthusiast. She is excellent at making puns and finding inappropriate humor in mundane situations. She loves tacos. She also really, really wants to pet your dog. *Xoxo.*

ABOUT CHELLEY ST CLAIR

Chelley St Clair enjoys writing gritty, emotional love stories often featuring broken, morally questionable heroes. She's had a dozen crazy careers, providing loads of fascinating tidbits to round out her imaginary worlds.

In real life, she is a chronic daydreamer living in Tennessee with her husband and son, who patiently make sure she isn't lost or falling over anything while her head is in the clouds.

Printed in Great Britain
by Amazon